Night Tide

A SEAL COVE ROMANCE

ANNA BURKE

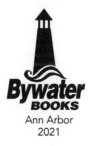

Bywater
BOOKS

Ann Arbor
2021

Books by Anna Burke

Novels

Compass Rose
Thorn
Nottingham

The Seal Cove Romance Series

Spindrift
Night Tide

Night Tide

Bywater Books

Print ISBN: 978-1-61294-181-3

Bywater Books First Edition: January 2021

Printed in the United States of America on acid-free paper.
Cover designer: Ann McMan, TreeHouse Studio

Bywater Books
PO Box 3671
Ann Arbor MI 48106-3671
www.bywaterbooks.com

For Tiffany.
And for those of us living with chronic pain, I see you.

Prologue

Lillian Lee didn't believe in love at first sight, but she did believe in the inevitability of hate. The data backed it. She'd felt it, hot and liquid, coiling in her stomach the first time she'd locked eyes with Ivy Holden.

This is it, she'd thought, trying not to bounce on her toes or show any other outward signs of excitement—or fear. Walking onto the Cornell University College of Veterinary Medicine campus for orientation marked the culmination of years of hard work and the beginning of many more. There were only thirty vet schools in the States. Getting into one required top grades, dedication, a flawless interview, and, in her case, a student loan larger than most mortgages. Lillian pushed that last thought aside. This was her dream. Like all dreams, it required sacrifice.

At the moment, that sacrifice seemed to be of the human variety.

Everyone knew team-building activities were par for the course for orientations. She grimaced at her accidental pun as she surveyed the Hoffman Challenge Course looming out of the grass ahead. Her palms left damp stains on her jeans. Impossibly tall wooden struts supported equally improbable platforms, all connected by networks of ropes she had a horrible premonition she'd be expected to climb. Her peers milled around her. Some looked as daunted as she felt. Others laughed and chattered in groups, already finding friends in their cohort. Her heart lurched. *I belong here*, she reminded herself. These were her future colleagues. She repressed the lingering insecurity their bright, confident laughter inspired, and adjusted her glasses. Maybe the lenses were magnifying the course. Nobody in their right mind would climb that high.

"This looks like as much fun as a lobotomy," said a tall girl with short dark hair to her left. Lillian caught her eye and noted the nametag: Morgan Donovan.

"You afraid of heights, too?" she asked.

"I have a healthy respect for the division between humans and other primates. We chose the ground."

"Seriously." Lillian eyed the ropes. Even looking at the upper levels made her feel sick. A warm breeze stirred the leaves of the trees in the distance. Trees that looked just as tall as the ropes above her. A bumblebee hummed across the clover at her feet. *She's got the right idea.* Ground level was the level she was most comfortable navigating. The insect zigzagged from flower to flower, and she wished she, too, could fly away like the bumblebee, floating just a few inches off the ground.

"Are you allergic to bees?"

She looked up to find Morgan studying her. "No, why?"

"An allergic reaction would get you out of this."

She laughed just as the leader began giving instructions. The sound caught the attention of a slender girl with immaculate waves of blond hair, who turned around with her glossed lips twisted in a moue of disapproval. Heat rushed to Lillian's cheeks. The girl's green eyes flicked over her as if she could catalog everything she needed to know about Lillian in the time it took for her eyes to travel from Lillian's braided hair and glasses down to her scuffed sneakers. The result of her assessment, her smugly superior face said, didn't even merit pity.

God, I hate blondes. The sense of entitlement that came with their lack of proper pigmentation baffled her, and this one, with her lululemon yoga pants and perfect eyebrows, symbolized everything about the breed Lillian despised. She dug her toes into her sneakers as she entertained a fantasy of Blondie shrieking as she fell from the ropes.

"If they make us partner off," she said as she turned back to

Morgan, "want to be my partner?"

"Sure. Nice to meet you, Lillian." Morgan's easy smile alleviated the shame still prickling the back of her neck from the blond girl's dismissal, and she allowed herself to relax. Maybe things would be okay.

Partners, however, were chosen randomly. Lillian knew what would happen long before the orientation leader paired them off. Dread soured her mouth. Luck didn't favor the Lees.

"Lillian, you're with Ivy," the leader said in a peppy voice.

"Next time," said Morgan as she drifted away.

She turned to face Ivy, preparing to paste a smile to her face for the sake of politeness. The smile curdled when she met the other girl's sneer.

"Nice shirt."

Lillian glanced down at her T-shirt, which she'd bought at the Cornell store—the first off-the-rack item of clothing she'd purchased in years. Across the front, the words *Treating Magical Creatures Since 1894* circled the Cornell veterinary school crest. The shirt had made her happy when she put it on this morning. Arriving at Cornell, pursuing her dream—these things really had felt magical. Now she felt stupid and childish, even though several other students were wearing the exact same thing, and regretted spending twenty dollars on cheap cotton. The shirt had probably been manufactured by child labor overseas, anyway. Nothing magical about *that*.

"Thanks," she said, knowing she'd think of the perfect comeback later that night when it was of absolutely no help to her.

"Didn't I see you in the kennels earlier?"

She shrugged, aware of the blush creeping up from the collar of her shirt. Yes, Ivy probably had seen her in the kennels, not that Lillian would have noticed, as her first shift that morning had involved more diarrhea than should have been biologically possible given the size of the dogs. She could still smell it lingering on her skin despite her shower. "Do you have a problem with that?"

"I didn't realize you were a student."

"Most of the kennel staff are students."

"How provincial." Disdain dripped from the word and from Ivy's perfectly arched brows. She stared around the field as if even the grass was more interesting than Lillian.

Anger built as they waited for more instructions. All the other pairings were making friendly conversation. Morgan and a pretty girl Lillian thought was named Tysha were chatting about something that, apparently, required Tysha to lean into Morgan's every word. Morgan's grin suggested she enjoyed the proximity.

"Friend of yours?"

She jerked around. Ivy had startlingly green eyes. They gave her face a predatory, almost feline, cast.

"Yes." She decided Morgan would, in fact, be her friend, because if the alternative was girls like Ivy then she was going to have a very long and very lonely next four years. Ivy made a noncommittal noise that managed to sound both bored and also judgmental as hell. Lillian's nails carved half-moons in her clenched palms.

Don't let her see she's riled you. Girls like Ivy had teased her all through middle school, mocking her poorly fitting secondhand clothes and thick glasses. The thrift stores near Bath, Maine, rarely carried anything name brand, and her family hadn't been able to afford fashionable frames until her mom's most recent promotion at Bath Iron Works. Besides, she had better uses for her money than clothes that would just get covered in dog hair and dirt. Jeans were jeans. The brand didn't matter, as long as it covered her ass—or so she told herself each time she rummaged through her drawers.

She did not need someone like Ivy reminding her of those childhood torments. Thus resolved, she folded her arms over her chest and clenched her jaw.

The first activity consisted of a low ropes course that hardly merited a harness, according to the muscular guy in front of them. He proclaimed loudly to his partner about how "into bouldering" he was back home. His partner, a girl with long legs and an increasingly frustrated expression, edged away from him.

Lillian thought he was probably Ivy's type: blustering, generically attractive, and brimming with the confidence of an average white male. He'd go on to make twice as much money as his female counterparts for doing half the work.

Nerves were making her bitter.

A low ropes course was still far too high. Worse, the activity required teamwork to traverse. She tried to pay attention to the rules, but the ringing in her ears made it difficult, and by the end of the explanation she still had no idea what was expected of her.

"We did this for undergraduate, too." Ivy sounded bored.

"You went to Cornell?" She congratulated herself on managing to sound civil.

"Yeah. You?"

"University of Southern Maine."

"A state school?"

"They have a good pre-vet program." *And an even better scholarship.*

"Sure."

Heat exploded in her chest as Ivy drew out the word. "At least my parents didn't have to buy my way into college."

Ivy's lips thinned, and the glare she fixed on Lillian was diamond edged. The arrival of a staff member with a pair of harnesses, however, prevented her from replying.

Point goes to the scholarship kid. She couldn't help the smug smile that twisted her own lips.

"You ladies excited?" asked the staff member. Either she was immune to the frostbite radiating from Ivy, or she chose to ignore it. "I'm going to show you how to put these on. You'll be perfectly safe if you follow instructions."

That "if" had to be a joke.

Ivy fastened her harness without help, a hint of angry color in her pale cheeks. Reality slammed back into Lillian as the staff member placed the bundle of straps and buckles in her arms.

"You doing okay?"

"It's no higher than the ski lifts at Telluride," Ivy said. "She'll be fine."

"Excuse me?" Lillian rounded on her, aware sweat was dripping down her back and likely staining her new shirt. How dare this girl speak for her?

"What? It's not a big deal. Unless you're scared of heights?"

There probably were activities for people petrified of heights. There was no shame in that. All she had to do was ask, and she'd be left safely on the ground. But Ivy was watching her with a hand on one hip, and so she raised her chin and let the woman tighten the harness around her body.

"I'm fine." The harness cinched across her hips. She plucked at the thick nylon and pulled her shirt free of the buckle. When she looked up, she caught Ivy staring at her again through half-lidded eyes. Her stomach swooped. "What is your problem?"

Their helper inhaled in surprise at her tone.

Ivy gestured at the harness. "Didn't realize you had a waistline."

"Ladies—"

"I'll go first," Lillian said. *Fuck Ivy.* Fuck her entitlement and her judgment and the way her skin itched beneath Ivy's gaze.

"Good." The woman steered her toward the base of one of the massive posts with perhaps a touch more force than was merited. "You'll wait at the landing for your partner, and then . . ."

She tuned out the rest. Once the ropes were clipped to her waist, she set her hands on the spikes that served as a ladder and hauled herself skyward. What did that even mean, Ivy hadn't realized she had a waistline? Just because she liked shirts that fit comfortably didn't mean she lacked a figure. Not everyone needed to strut around in skin-tight athleisure. In fact—

". . . worst that can happen is your hand gets tangled when you fall," Mr. Into Bouldering was saying loudly from below. "A friend of mine broke his wrist that way."

Her feet froze on the rung. She'd broken her arm when she was thirteen. It had taken her moms six years to pay off the hospital bill. A broken wrist could end her veterinary career before it even began. All her savings had gone into rent and paying for the Cornell student insurance package, which she knew wouldn't cover nearly enough in an emergency. Maybe someone like Ivy could afford to live carelessly, secure in the knowledge their safety net would catch them, just like the nets that dangled below the ropes course, but Lillian knew better. If she fell, she'd land on grass, shattered, and there would be no second chances.

"You'd have to be an idiot for that to happen." The irritation lacing Ivy's voice distracted Lillian, and she glanced down.

The earth spun dizzyingly, and a roaring sound pulsed in her ears. Her hands felt glued to the rungs. Someone was saying her name, but their words seemed to come from far away, and they echoed in her skull.

Ivy's emerald eyes were the last thing she saw before she passed out.

Chapter One

The couch, the book, and the wine should have felt glorious after a long day spent reasoning with anxious owners and dealing with a particularly feisty African Gray parrot. However, as a cold September wind blew leaves against the window of the farmhouse, she found it hard to buy into the opening of the historical romance in her hands. The improbably endowed duke and his rival's equally improbably proportioned wife had just met for the first time, and both were instantly infatuated. She took a sip of wine. Normally she loved the comfortable formula of romance novels.

And yet.

She shut the book. Two weeks had passed since Brian had called things off. The fact that it hadn't come as a surprise didn't help. She'd known their long-distance relationship, sustained with intermittent visits between his graduate work in South America and her schedule at the clinic, wasn't enough for him, but she'd hoped he could hold on long enough to finish his dissertation—which he'd been dragging out for three years.

She took a measured breath and counted to three. *Breathe in, breathe out.* At least she didn't need to have *that* fight anymore. Her Italian greyhound, Hermione, opened one eye from her position curled up on Lillian's chest and glared her displeasure at the disturbance. Muffin, the larger of her two dogs, was no doubt digging holes out in the yard.

"Sorry, princess."

Dogs were better than people anyway. Brian could postpone finishing his dissertation as long as he liked. It was no longer her problem, and it freed up time for more pleasurable activities, like reading.

Not that she was having much success. Maybe she needed a mystery novel. A few dead bodies might make all the difference. Of course, that would require she move, and Hermione's visible slit of pupil suggested only monsters would commit such crimes.

The farmhouse door opened from the other room. She listened for the sound of footsteps, trying to gauge which of her roommates had just returned home. The clack of dog nails on the hardwood, followed by the hot breath of a sable German shepherd in her face, indicated the new arrival was Morgan Donovan.

"Morgan, I need your help."

She heard Morgan kicking off her boots in the mudroom, followed by the sound of dirty clothes joining their brethren in the washer. A button clanged against the metal side. Morgan appeared a moment later in clean garments, but a sprig of hay clung to her short mop of dark curls and an aroma of horse followed her.

"Can you grab me another book? I'm trapped."

Silence. She tilted her head to get a better look at her friend.

Morgan stood in front of her with her hands buried in her pockets and her knees locked, as if she wanted nothing more than to flee. The freckles scattered across her cheekbones stood out against her flushed cheeks, and her slate blue eyes avoided Lillian's.

"Are you okay?"

"I need to talk to you."

Lillian scooped up Hermione and resettled her in her lap as she sat up. "Did something happen with Emilia?"

"What? No. She's fine." Morgan seemed fascinated by the patterns on the carpet. "Danielle hired a new large animal vet."

Danielle owned the veterinary practice where both Lillian and Morgan worked, and they'd been sorely in need of a new large animal veterinarian. Morgan had covered more than her fair share of work for months.

"That's good news."

"Yeah. Um, listen. There's something you need to know."

Dread coiled up from the springs of the couch and into her stomach. Something about the way Morgan still refused to meet her eyes warned her change was coming—change she wasn't going to enjoy.

"Just tell me."

"The new vet is Ivy Holden."

That couldn't be right. She blinked, her forehead wrinkling. It sounded like Morgan had just said Ivy Holden. Obviously she'd misheard, as that would be cruel even by the standards of the cold and unfeeling universe, and her earlier reminiscence had simply conjured the woman's name like a bad smell.

"Who?"

"Ivy Holden. From Cornell."

Air hissed out of her lungs. Her diaphragm filled, instead, with shrapnel. She shook her head and willed Morgan to take back her words. Ivy couldn't be coming to Seal Cove. This was Lillian's place. Ivy was in Colorado, safely far away, and their story had ended six years ago when they had graduated and gone their separate ways.

"I'm sorry. She's the best candidate we've had. You know how long we've been searching for a new vet."

"Right." Her voice sounded like it belonged to someone else. "Of course. You have to do what's right for the practice."

"It wasn't up to me. Trust me. I tried convincing Danielle she wasn't a good fit."

"But there were no other applicants?"

"None I'd trust with my cases."

Deserts contained more moisture than her mouth. "When does she start?"

"End of September."

The shrapnel pierced her diaphragm and burrowed toward her heart. "That's next week."

Morgan examined the ceiling. Lillian followed her gaze. The exposed beams did not collapse, however, sparing her this conversation, and contrary late afternoon sunlight illuminated dust motes and a few floating dog hairs.

"Lil, I—"

"I've got to go check on some plants."

She didn't wait to hear Morgan's protest, and made a beeline for her greenhouse, which opened off the back of the house. A disgruntled Hermione trotted close behind. Warm, humid air filled her lungs as she shut the door. Morgan didn't follow.

This was her space. None of her roommates enjoyed gardening, and they could generally be relied on to leave her alone in here. Living with three other people made such arrangements necessary and she'd never been more grateful for their unspoken rules than today.

What. The. Fuck.

The scream she'd stifled in the living room pulsed in her blood. To give her hands something to do, she grabbed the hose and watered the nearest tray of plants. Thoughts danced and died in the mist. She hung the hose on its hook when she'd soaked the last of her hanging pots and seedlings and surveyed her domain. Hibiscus grew in her tortoise Circe's enclosure, and hanging plants provided shade over the sandy floor. Growing tables and tortoise-friendly potted cultivars occupied the rest of the greenhouse. Fuchsia dangled its purple flowers over a dwarf lemon tree. Trellised tomatoes rebelled against their restraints near the door.

She wished she could join them.

Ivy was going to work at the clinic. At *her* clinic. She sank to the ground, not caring that her pants would get covered in dirt, and buried her face in her hands. Sunlight pooled around her, tinted green by her jungle. Hermione gave her knee a cautious sniff.

"No," she said into her fingers, and shuddered as memories she'd suppressed for years tore through her.

Ivy Holden closed her eyes and leaned her head back against the seat as the plane taxied toward the runway. She didn't want to see Colorado fading to a patchwork of fields and mountains beneath her. It was bad enough she'd gotten stuck next to a toddler, who already had taken an interest in her that bordered on demonic. He'd even run his toy train along her leg, something his mother had definitely seen and chosen to ignore. Judging by the purple circles underneath her eyes, the woman had lost the battle for control of her progeny some time ago.

The red light of her own eyelids, however, provided little relief. She heard Kara's voice: confused, heartbroken, demanding to know the real reason Ivy had decided to leave. Kara would survive. One day, she might even see this for the favor it was. That didn't make Ivy's current pain any less sharp. She'd planned on staying in Colorado indefinitely. She loved the mountains and the way the aspen trees turned yellow in the fall, nothing like the riot of reds and oranges back east, but perfect in its own way. She loved, too, the equine practice she'd left, where she'd worked since graduating from Cornell and had envisioned as her professional future. Then there was her house with its view of the Rockies and the creek that tumbled over the stones at the foot of the sloping hill of her backyard, which her Jack Russell Terrier, Darwin, loved plunging into during the summer. As if on cue he growled from his carrier beneath her seat. The toddler shrieked and immediately leaned down to peer at him.

"Can I pet?" the boy asked.

Darwin growled again.

"He's a little scared right now," she said, though in truth Darwin hadn't been scared of anything in his life. He'd defied Darwin's law since she'd adopted him, hence his name, and right now she suspected he would like nothing more than to snack on this child's greasy fingers.

"Can I pet?" the boy asked again.

"The lady said no," said his mother in a voice suggesting she needed a stiff drink, a vacation, and perhaps a time machine that would allow her to rethink the wisdom of reproducing.

Ivy didn't like children. Specifically, she didn't like children who were not related to her or her friends, and she really, really didn't like being stuck in situations like this where she could not escape from the nasty neonates. That was part of the reason she'd ended up in veterinary medicine. Animals made sense.

They could also be confined to pet carriers.

A spasm of pain contracted around her ribs and she held her breath, waiting for the muscles to release their grip. The pain diminished after a few minutes but did not dissipate entirely. She let it melt into the thrum of the plane's engines as the pilot prepared for takeoff.

She couldn't help opening her eyes to look out the window as the ground dropped away. Home. The pain in her chest came from her heart now, and she wondered for the thousandth time what her life might have been like had things turned out differently.

Instead she was headed east to a new job in a new town. Seal Cove was close to the island where her family spent the summers, and moving closer to family, while not something she had considered a priority before, was now a necessity.

Don't go there. Not yet.

Seal Cove. A friend had told her about a practice hiring in Maine, and the position was exactly what she needed: ambulatory in a mixed practice. Once again, she blocked the doubts that kept her up at night. If worse came to worst, she could transition to small animal medicine, and Seal Cove would provide that opportunity.

Lillian Lee's face rose before her as clouds obscured her view of the landscape below. *Lillian.* If Ivy had ever needed proof the universe had a twisted sense of humor, this was it.

"Wait, isn't that the chick you hated?" her sister, Madison, had asked when she'd told her about her connections to the Seal Cove staff.

Hate, however, didn't quite encompass the nature of their relationship. It was more than hate. It had been enmity; the kind of fierce awareness of another person that bordered on obsession and that had shadowed her entire veterinary school experience. But as she had explained to Madison, who was the only person in the world who knew the real reason she had decided to move, the job had been too perfect in every other way to turn down. Besides. She liked Morgan Donovan, despite her association with Lillian.

Several layovers and an upgrade to first class later—why had she booked economy on that first leg?—she landed in Portland, Darwin in tow. Her things should have arrived already via moving truck, and Freddie, the horse she'd had since age 13, was on his way across the country via the VIP trailering service she'd booked for him. The Portland airport was small and clean and thankfully easy to navigate. She waited for her luggage with Darwin vibrating in his carrier, eager to leap out and investigate—or terrorize—her fellow travelers.

"There you are."

She grinned as her sister pulled her into a hug. Her hair smelled like Briogeo shampoo, and Ivy breathed in the familiar scent as she returned the embrace.

"I missed you. How long have you been waiting?"

"Not long. I hit traffic coming from Boston. Is that your bag?" Madison pointed at the duffel headed toward them and snatched it up at Ivy's nod.

She followed her sister to the parking garage. Darwin, who had tried to mark everything he passed on his way, sniffed at the door of Madison's BMW enthusiastically. She scooped him up before he could scratch the paint.

"How are you feeling?" Madison asked as she slipped sunglasses on over eyes the exact same shade of green as her own.

"Like I could sleep for a week."

"Not an option. We have things to do. Mom is thrilled you're back on this coast and is having a party on the island tomorrow."

"She couldn't have waited another, I don't know, day or two? I have to get unpacked."

"Pay someone else to do it."

"Things go in a—"

"Yes, I remember how anal retentive you are. Okay. What's the address?"

Ivy directed the GPS to her rental house and restrained Darwin from leaping out of the window at a squirrel. Her sister chattered on about the latest island gossip. Madison came up on the weekends with the rest of the crowd they'd grown up spending the summers with. Like Madison and Ivy, most had gone on to law school or med school, with the rest washing up in business school or living off trust funds. She hadn't been a part of that world for a while, and the thought of reentering those circles gave her a headache. What she really wanted, more than anything, was to curl up beneath her down duvet and go to sleep. The movers should have at least set up her bed; she was certainly paying them enough. She'd cancel on her mother, she decided as Madison pushed the upper boundaries of the speed limit. Her eyes wanted to drift shut instead of taking in the passing pines and autumn foliage, and she pulled her sunglasses out of her purse. At least Madison wouldn't be able to see how tired she looked with shades on.

"This is so cute," Madison said when they pulled into the driveway of Ivy's new home. The cottage was set back from the road, and she could see the Damariscotta River through the trees. Brilliant fall foliage surrounded the lot, and fallen leaves piled up against the shingled siding. "You're like a little elf, living all alone in the forest."

"Please never call me a 'little elf' again."

Madison's heels clicked on the paved driveway as she practically skipped up to the door. Ivy released Darwin. He took off on a tour of his new kingdom, scattering squirrels and leaves as he went while she dug the keys her agent had mailed her out of her purse. After a brief struggle, the lock turned.

"Oh. My. God." Madison pivoted in a circle as she took in the hardwood floors, picture windows, and the sweeping views of the river beyond. "It's so gorgeous! And rustic! Look! You have a woodstove!"

Ivy looked. There was indeed a woodstove, as well as a fireplace on the opposite side of the wall, and there was another woodstove in the master bedroom. That had been part of the appeal of the house: warmth. She let Madison explore and counted the exclamation points at the end of her sister's sentences.

Boxes filled the rooms. Her furniture, at least, was set up, though she would definitely be rearranging things, and she collapsed onto her couch and groaned. Her entire body hurt. Travel, stress, and lack of sleep tacked their grievances onto the list of complaints her body had already issued. She fumbled in her purse for her medication and swallowed it dry, grimacing as the pill stuck on its way down.

Lillian Lee.

She stroked Darwin, who had curled up on her chest, and wondered if Lillian still chewed on her pens or if she'd outgrown the oral fixation that had been the cause of four years of torment for Ivy. Maybe she'd upgraded to syringes. The thought amused her even as she discarded it. The violation of safety protocol would no doubt drive Lillian

15

crazy. She'd always been too good at following the rules.

Don't think about Lillian. Madison clicked back into the room, still wearing her heels, and immediately began talking about interior design before plopping down on the couch and kicking off her shoes. She couldn't help one last thought from slipping in.

Darkness. Loud music. Too much alcohol in her system and the smell of snow as she pushed her way out of Natalie's apartment and into the quiet Ithaca night, the scent of Lillian's perfume still clinging to her shirt.

Lillian checked her appearance in the clinic bathroom one last time. Her maroon blouse complimented her white coat and also, unfortunately, magnified the flush of angry color on her cheeks.

Today was not going to be a good day.

Morgan met her outside the bathroom, trailed, as always, by Stevie, her technician and their third roommate. Stevie yawned widely. Her blond hair in its perpetual ponytail bore a rumpled look, suggesting she'd napped in the truck on her ride to work with Morgan. Lillian envied her. Sleep had evaded her almost completely.

"Coffee?" Morgan held a mug out, and Lillian took a robotic sip.

"What time is she getting here?"

"Danielle told her to be here at 7:30."

Lillian glanced at the clock on the wall. 7:20. Ten minutes, assuming Ivy arrived exactly on time, until her least favorite person in the entire world showed up to ruin her life. Again.

"You okay?" asked Morgan.

"Totally. Like you said, I'm not the one who has to deal with her. I'll hardly see her. You'll have Poison Ivy all to yourself."

"Poison Ivy?" asked Stevie.

"That's what we called her in school," said Morgan.

Danielle Watson walked into the break room before they could elaborate. Her curly gray hair and weathered skin always made Lillian think of how Morgan would look in another few decades. Today, however, she had no warm feelings for her boss.

"Please come welcome our new staff member."

"More like staph infection," Lillian said to Morgan under her breath as they left the sanctuary of the break room. In the lobby, over the sound of a barking dog getting dropped off for surgery, she heard a familiar voice.

Venom pulsed through her.

"Hi, I'm Dr. Holden," Ivy announced to the receptionist.

Danielle vanished through the lobby door.

"You're going to strangle yourself with your stethoscope," Morgan said.

Lillian hadn't realized she'd been twisting it around her neck. She let it fall back around her shoulders and sank her fists into the pockets of her white coat as the door swung back open.

Ivy Holden reentered Lillian's life without fanfare. She wore a gray oxford shirt over dark-washed utility pants that probably cost more than Lillian's rent. They hugged her athletic frame, and her blond hair hung loose around her shoulders in the kind of casual wave only expensive hair products could achieve. Lillian instantly felt underdressed. Ivy shook Morgan's hand and flashed her a smile filled with perfect teeth. As she did so, Lillian noticed the first difference from the Ivy she'd known previously.

In vet school, Ivy's makeup had been flawless but a touch ostentatious. Now, she wore only the faintest suggestion of product—another thing that was easier to pull off with money—and the natural tones accentuated the contours of her cheeks, her flawless jawline, and the full curve of her lips. She avoided looking into Ivy's eyes until the last possible second. When she did, the force of that gaze made inventorying trace amounts of mascara and eyeshadow impossible.

"Good to see you again, Dr. Lee," said Ivy.

There was something about Ivy's eyes that reminded Lillian of a cat. The slight slant. The perpetually sardonic arch of her brow, as if she knew something the rest of the world didn't. And, of course, the shocking green of her irises. That green had always seen right through her.

"Dr. Holden, so good to see you, too." She mimicked Ivy's formal address. Ivy's grip on her hand was warm and firm, and she returned it, exerting a touch more pressure than was perhaps necessary. Ivy's lips curled up in a faint smirk. She proceeded down the line of technicians and assistants, leaving Lillian to grit her teeth.

"Dr. Holden will mostly be working on ambulatory, but she'll take cases here as needed," Danielle explained to the assembled staff.

Lillian locked eyes with Morgan, who gave her a minuscule shrug, as if to say, "I didn't know she was mixed practice either."

Ivy in the barn was one thing; Ivy on her turf was quite another. Her very presence violated the sanctuary of stability she'd built around her over the past few years.

"I didn't realize you practiced small animal medicine."

Morgan stiffened at the snarl in Lillian's voice, but she ignored the warning in her friend's eyes. She couldn't afford to appear weak. Like her namesake, Ivy could put a root into the smallest crack and, given enough time, crumble even the thickest walls. She would not let that happen again.

"I'm interested in getting back into it," said Ivy, her voice smooth. Her hair flowed over her shoulders, and Lillian, who had sat near her for four years in lecture halls, entertained her old fantasy of hacking it off with a rusty knife. "My last practice was equine, but I wanted a change."

"And our practice has expanded," said Danielle. "This is the perfect opportunity for us."

"Of course." Lillian smiled through her teeth.

"Don't worry. Exotics are all yours," said Ivy.

Was she imagining the taunt in her words?

Danielle led Ivy away to fill out paperwork, and Morgan pulled Lillian into an empty exam room. Stevie followed.

"Did you hear her? 'Exotics are all yours,'" Lillian said in a low voice that approximated Ivy's pretentious mannerisms fairly well, in her opinion.

"Deep breaths, Lil."

She tugged her arm out of Morgan's grasp and paced the room. Her breath came too quickly, but she didn't care. All the old emotions had come crashing back around her, as if she'd shoved them on a precariously high shelf and foolishly bumped against it. She hated how inferior Ivy made her feel by just existing. Her poise. Her expensive wardrobe. Her stupid fucking eyes.

Stevie hopped onto the exam table and dangled her legs. "We

18

could key her car."

"Her sister is a lawyer."

"Then I'm out of ideas."

"She's just so arrogant." Lillian stopped pacing and turned to her friends. Morgan wore a carefully neutral expression on her face. "What?"

"Nothing," Morgan said a little too quickly to be convincing.

"You think I'm overreacting?"

"I didn't say that."

"Your face does."

Stevie snorted.

"I just think you didn't exactly give her a chance before jumping down her throat."

Lillian stared at Morgan in disbelief. "Give her a chance? Do you remember who this is?"

"I remember Ivy."

She hated when Morgan got like this. The only time Lillian had really seen Morgan lose her cool was over women. Now that she and Emilia were together, however, Morgan's implacable attitude had resettled.

"Then you know giving her a chance is like—" She cast around for an analogy. "Turning your back on a tiger."

"Rawr," added Stevie, rather unhelpfully.

Morgan glanced at the door. "Just remember you're the board-certified specialist, and she and I are just lowly general practitioners."

"True." She paused. Petty victories were better than none, but Morgan didn't get it. This went beyond one-upmanship. "Not the lowly part. Just . . . is it wrong if that does make me feel better?"

"You?" said Stevie. "Competitive? Not at all."

"I'm going to drug your food one of these days."

"Malpractice. I'm sure Ivy's sister would love to represent me."

A smile twitched one corner of her mouth. Perhaps she was overreacting a tiny bit. All Ivy had done was walk into the room. Things were different. She'd grown, freed from the shade of Ivy's influence, and this time she wouldn't let Ivy turn her into someone she didn't recognize.

Not that I've gotten off to a great start.

"Fine. I'm not promising to give her a chance, but I will be polite."

"Good, because I do not want to get in the middle of you two ever again. Do you remember when we were stuck in the same lab group?"

The rogue smile twisted into a grimace. "Yes."

"What was that like?" asked Stevie.

"Literal hell."

"It was her, not me," said Lillian. "She questioned everything I said."

"And you never questioned her?"

"She was wrong."

"She's hot, though."

"Thank you, Stevie, for that edifying bit of knowledge."

"I don't remember her being that gay," said Morgan with a thoughtful expression.

"She's not." Lillian did not want to have this conversation. Not now, not ever.

"Oh, she definitely is. Did you see her swagger? And that hand-shake?" Stevie fanned herself.

"Well her personality sucks. And I hate blondes."

"What did we ever do to you?" Stevie stroked her fair head in wounded solidarity.

"Lil," said Morgan. "You're freaking out."

She ran her hands through her hair and let out a long breath. "I know. I just feel like I'm twenty-five again, and I hate it."

"Yeah, well," said Stevie as she slid off the counter and clapped a hand on Lillian's shoulder, "with great age comes great wisdom."

"Fuck off, Stevie."

"Ouch." Stevie shot Morgan a wounded look. "It's not my fault I'm aging better than both of you."

Ivy trailed Morgan through the Seal Cove large animal facility and tried not to compare it to the state-of-the-art equine practice she'd just left. The barn was clean and well lit, even if it didn't have an equine surgery suite, and the technician, Stevie, seemed pleasant enough.

"Who are the other large animal technicians?" she asked Morgan.

"You'll get Shawna for now. She had a doctor's appointment this morning, but she'll be in soon. She knows the ropes."

Having a technician she trusted was essential, especially now. Already she missed Max, her preferred tech in Colorado, and she shot Stevie a covetous glance. "Any chance you can spare this one?"

Morgan laughed. She had a nice laugh: warm and rich, and Ivy allowed herself to relax fractionally. She might have been friendlier at school with Morgan if it hadn't been for Lillian.

"If you think you can handle her, sure."

Ivy tried to focus on the rest of the tour, but as Morgan pointed out the supplies in the treatment area, her thoughts drifted back to Lillian. Some things didn't change. She'd seen the flash of anger in Lillian's eyes when Danielle Watson explained Ivy would be working both large and small animal shifts. She suppressed a smile. Goading Lillian was too easy. It always had been, and she recalled the angry flush on her cheekbones with satisfaction. She'd been so worried about how she'd react to seeing her again that she'd forgotten how much she enjoyed provoking her.

Other things did change. Gone were the washed-out jeans and baggy T-shirts Lillian had worn in school. The blouse she'd worn today, while partially hidden by her starched coat, fit her properly, and the material looked like it was of decent quality. Her slacks, too, fit—which presented more of a problem. Lillian Lee had been cute at best in her baggy secondhand wardrobe with her glasses and her tousled hair.

She wasn't cute now. Her hair seemed sleeker, her glasses trimmer, her style cleaner, and her face . . . Her face hadn't changed. Those large brown eyes, so soft until they met her own—when they hardened into cassiterite—still gutted her. Eyes like that could break a person open. She dropped her gaze. That proved to be a mistake. Lillian's full lips, quick to smile for everyone but her, made her want to bite something.

"Lillian specialized?" she asked Morgan as they left the barn to tour the clinic truck.

"She always liked exotics."

In school, both she and Lillian had been interested in surgery.

She wondered what had happened to change Lillian's mind. "I didn't know."

"I'm surprised you didn't end up in a specialty."

Ivy remembered her parents' horrified expressions when she told them she had decided to go into equine general practice. "I fell in love with ambulatory during my internship."

Morgan leaned against the truck and met her eyes. "Really?"

"Does that surprise you?"

"Honestly? Yeah."

"Was it the lip gloss?" She crossed her arms over her chest and met Morgan stare for stare. *Better we get this out of the way now.* Stevie, she noticed, looked like she needed a bucket of popcorn to match her enthralled expression.

"Maybe."

"It's dangerous to underestimate a horse girl. I can do terrible things with baling twine."

"Truer words were never spoken," said Stevie.

"You just seemed so set on surgery."

"I was." She patted the hood of the truck. "And then I wasn't."

Morgan nodded, and Ivy saw a glimmer of respect in her eyes.

Surgery had been her parents' dream. They'd wanted her to go into human medicine. When she expressed an interest in veterinary medicine, they'd adjusted, but only on the grounds she achieved a similar level of prestige. Equine surgery had seemed like the best alternative for Ivy to get what she wanted, and she enjoyed surgery—just not as much as she'd found she enjoyed being on the road, visiting farms and talking to clients, and getting away from the pressures that had shaped her entire life. That, however, was not something she was about to confess to Morgan.

"You mostly did horses in Colorado, right?"

"Yes. Livestock will be a switch for me, but I'm looking forward to it."

She'd spent the past month reading over her notes from school and scouring veterinary journals, trying to catch up on the last few years of research. While she didn't feel entirely prepared, she also knew that was part of the game. The only way to really learn any profession was to do it, and she did, at least, know how to handle clients.

"Most of our clients are good people. Small farms. They won't give you a hard time."

Ivy bristled at the implication. "Trust me, I can handle assholes."

"I bet you can," said Morgan, and Stevie covered a "that's what she said" with a cough. Morgan gave her technician a quelling glare.

"What?" Stevie glared right back. "That's your job description. 'I stick my hands up animal butts for money.'"

"On second thought," Morgan said to Ivy, "if you want Stevie, she's yours."

Ivy braced herself for Darwin's explosive greeting as she opened the front door. His routine consisted of a series of impossibly high jumps, interrupted by pauses to spin in tight circles at her feet, before he shot past her to pee on the nearest bit of shrubbery.

Opening the door to her rental felt strange. She missed Colorado and her friends, most of whom were her coworkers, and the easy familiarity of their banter cast the awkwardness of her first day into sharper relief. Kicking off her boots, she watched Darwin zoom around the yard, scattering leaves as he went until he remembered her arrival signified his dinnertime and shot back into the house.

Ten minutes and a change of clothes later found her sitting on her couch with a cup of tea, wearing sweatpants and a cashmere fisherman's sweater and staring out at the water. Darwin curled on the couch's back with his nose pressed to her ear. Red and orange leaves drifted down in the evening light, and a few boats made their way up and down the river. Maybe she'd get a kayak this summer, if she hadn't rethought this whole thing and slunk back to Colorado by then. At least she could spend the winter skiing. The thought of skiing alone, though, only worsened her mood. She also wasn't sure she could trust her body on the slopes.

I could join a yoga studio, she thought as a wave of nerve pain skittered across her ribs. Yoga wasn't really her thing, but she'd be around people who didn't hate her for the person she'd been in her early twenties, which was a plus, and it was also gentler on her joints than running.

Steam from her tea wreathed her face. She breathed in the mint fragrance. She couldn't blame Lillian for the way she felt. Neither, however, could she seem to stop herself from falling back into old patterns. Something about Lillian Lee had always made her want to push and keep pushing until one of them snapped. Part of her welcomed it. At least Lillian was something tangible she could fight, unlike her body, and it wasn't like they could hurt each other any more than they already had.

It was many and many a year ago,
In a kingdom by the sea,
That a maiden there lived whom you may know
By the name of Lillian Lee.

The high school English teacher who'd made her memorize that Edgar Allan Poe poem couldn't possibly have imagined the depths of torture it would bring her. Annabel and Lillian were too easily interchanged.

Her phone buzzed. She glanced at the caller ID, then ignored it and waited for the voicemail to come through. Only then did she pick up. Kara's voice sounded against a windy background. "Hi. Just calling to see how your first day went. I know . . . I know we're not talking, right now, but I wanted . . . I just . . . Anyway. Hope you're doing okay."

She deleted the message. Kara was better off without her.

24

Chapter Two

"I am so angry at myself for sending you to Briar Hill," Lillian said to Emilia as they set out on their jogging date.

"Second week is going well, then?"

Emilia Russo, who was dating Morgan after a summer of tension that Lillian and the rest of their friends had watched unfold like a beautiful train wreck, had taken a job at a nearby veterinary hospital instead of the opening at Seal Cove, thanks to Lillian's recommendation. Her reward for her good deed? Ivy Holden.

"She is just as arrogant as she used to be. She waltzes in like she owns the place and starts ordering my techs around—"

"Technically aren't they hers now, too?"

"And then has the gall to tell me I prescribed the wrong dose for one of my patients—*my* patients—when all the literature says a lower dose is actually more effective long term. As if she would even know. She hasn't done small animal in years."

"That is some bullshit. But you won't overlap in exotics, at least."

"I wish we would. *That* would teach her."

The feel of her feet pounding the pavement usually helped her burn off steam. Tonight, however, it only seemed to fuel her anger. One full week of working with Ivy had proven that absolutely nothing about their relationship had changed, and the second was not getting off to a good start.

"I swear she's out to get me."

"It is a little weird she ended up here," said Emilia.

"Just wait till you meet her. It will happen eventually."

They turned down a quiet road paralleling the river. Another jogger appeared ahead of them with a little dog.

"Not food," Emilia told her greyhound.

"I'm going to need to start taking blood pressure medication. I can't be in the same hospital as her. She's like a dog fart. She permeates."

Ahead, the jogger paused to retie a shoe. She didn't pay any attention. All she could think about was the smug smile on Ivy's face when she'd suggested Lillian catch up on the latest issue of *Clinician's Brief.*

"Should we cross to the other side of the road?"

"Why?" Lillian asked.

Emilia pointed at the figure drawing rapidly near.

"You have to be fucking kidding me." She came to a dead halt, surprising Emilia, as the other jogger looked up from tying her shoe.

Ivy's ponytail swayed as she recoiled in surprise. Her running pants clung to her muscular thighs—she must still be riding—and her shirt was the sort of athletic racer-back crop top Lillian hated on principle. Growing up in the early 2000s had forever embittered her against clothing that bared her midriff. It didn't help that Ivy pulled it off, just like she pulled off everything else.

"Um," said Emilia.

Lillian broke eye contact with Ivy and glanced at her friend, who was staring at both of them with a quizzical tilt to her eyebrows. Ivy's dog, meanwhile, had taken advantage of his owner's distraction to size up Emilia's. The greyhound pretended not to see him. It occurred to Lillian after a moment that there had been a very long and very awkward pause, and that as the point of commonality, it was up to her to break it.

"Emilia," she said, snarling in an approximation of a smile, "this is my new coworker, Ivy Holden."

As if her name was a charm, Ivy stood in a graceful motion that made Lillian want to hamstring her and called her dog back to her side, where he sat and wagged his stub tail. "Nice to meet you. Sorry about Darwin."

"Darwin?"

"Proof of Darwin's law," said Ivy.

Emilia laughed, which made Lillian hate her just a little bit. Ivy wasn't funny. Her charm so often had teeth.

"This is Nell. She likes to pretend she's the only dog in the room."

"A perfect combination then. And, once he flushes things from their burrows, Nell can chase them."

"If only we were on a foxhunt," said Lillian in her coldest voice. Ivy had told her a story once about going foxhunting, and the image had haunted her: Ivy in a red coat astride her horse, hounds baying. In her nightmares, Lillian was always the fox. "Sorry to interrupt your workout."

"Not at all. Were you jogging this way?" Ivy pointed down the road they were following.

"No," said Lillian, at the same time Emilia said "yes."

Ivy's smile grew. "Mind if I jog with you for a bit?" While Lillian gawked at her, Ivy turned to Emilia. "Lil and I went to school together. We used to work out at the same time. I always found her dedication . . . inspiring."

"If by dedication you mean my ability to lift more than you, then yes, I agree."

Although judging by Ivy's shoulders, those days were over. She'd added muscle in the intervening years, whereas Lillian had stopped lifting regularly and mostly focused on running. *There's a metaphor I should never examine too closely.*

"We'll see about that. How far are you going?"

They'd already done a mile, and usually averaged three or four. "Five," she said. Emilia shot her a sideways glance.

"Nice. I've been doing six, but I probably should take it easy today."

Lillian didn't scream, for which she was very proud of herself.

"Let's get to it, then." She took off at a faster clip than normal. She'd regret it soon, but not as much as she'd regret appearing weak in front of Ivy.

Emilia and Ivy caught up shortly. She hoped Ivy would jog on Emilia's other side, but instead she flanked Lillian "for the sake of the dogs."

What about my sake, she thought about saying, but settled for staring at the shoulder of the road as it unspooled before her.

"Can your dog handle a jog this long?" Emilia asked.

"This little guy?" She saw Ivy smile at her dog out of the corner of her eye. "He can go longer than I can."

"Something he and I have in common."

This time, Ivy's smile was solely for Lillian. The smirk—she refused to grant it grin status on principle—was as familiar as her favorite sweater. The challenge in Ivy's eyes hardened her resolve even as her heart rate accelerated. This was how it had always been between them. No truce, no mercy, no ground ceded—only war.

"Colorado must be beautiful this time of year," said Emilia. Lillian got the impression she was trying to steer them into less volatile territory. She'd learn quickly there was no such thing, but she let Emilia draw Ivy into conversation while she waited for her next opportunity to pounce. Ivy had her charm on full force. She laughed when appropriate and asked leading questions to keep Emilia talking. Was she imagining that Ivy seemed to be having a hard time catching her breath? She picked up her pace fractionally. Ivy, mid-question, matched her with a grim set to her lips.

Lillian's legs, lungs, and abdominals were on fire by the time Emilia called for a cooldown. She tried not to stagger as she broke into a walk. They were all breathing hard. Ivy's face glowed, a reminder she never turned the beet red shade Lillian did, and she laughed in between deep breaths.

"Damn, Lil. I forgot how fast you are."

It was the closest thing to a compliment she'd ever received from Ivy Holden.

Ivy collapsed against her front door and rested her face against the cool wood. She hurt. The nerve pain started in her shoulder blades and spiked down her arms and into her hands, electric jolts that made her fumble her keys as her vision blurred.

She'd lied to Lillian. These days, she was lucky to make it three miles before her body gave out. In periods of relative calm, when her symptoms were at bay, she could work out harder and longer, but the stress of the move had triggered her neuropathy. Kicking off her shoes with half-numb feet, she checked that Darwin had water and made for the bathroom. The sound of the tub filling with hot water soothed her as she stretched. When the deep tub was close to overflowing and a Lush bath bomb foamed across its surface, she slowly lowered herself beneath the water.

Heat sometimes helped. Other times it made things worse, but at least it provided a different sensation. Besides, baths were her happy place. The hot water slowly worked some of the knots from her muscles. She rubbed her thighs with the heels of her hands. Darwin leapt onto the tile rim of the tub, trotted around it, and curled up on the towel she'd laid out for herself.

Well, she thought as the perfume from the bath salts suffused her senses, if nothing else, today had proven she was still an idiot over Lillian Lee.

It had also been a reminder of how much Lillian still hated her.

She let her hands float on the surface, holding the fizzing bath bomb between them and letting the chemical reaction buzz against her skin. It soothed her angry nerves. She wished it could soothe the turmoil running beneath.

She'd given Lillian many reasons to dislike her over the years, from taunts to deeper acts of cruelty and humiliation, favors Lillian had returned in kind, but she knew she was responsible for tipping the scales from dislike to deepest loathing. The memory still scalded. Too late, she realized the jasmine-scented steam from her bath smelled like the perfume Lillian had worn the night their second year when Ivy had broken everything. There had been snow and music and then—

"Get the fuck out of my house, Lee."

She had hoped time would erase those words and the person she'd been when she said them. Today, when she'd seen Lillian jogging toward her, she'd realized how foolish that hope had been.

I have to apologize. But what could she even say? She'd promised herself she would play nice, but that had devolved almost instantly into their old rivalry. All her Colorado vows to put the past behind her seemed impossibly distant. The past had played too much of a role in shaping the person she was now. The *doctor* she was now.

Her body flared with a new burst of pain. She would pay for today, but even as she whimpered, causing Darwin to lick her face in worry, she remembered the total concentration on Lillian's face as they flew down the road beneath the October sky, and the sharp, crystalline edge Lillian's presence brought to her world.

"Well, that was intense," said Emilia as they stretched in the kitchen of the big white farmhouse where Morgan, Lillian, Stevie, and Angie lived.

"What was intense?" asked Morgan, who leaned against the counter and watched Emilia with reverent eyes.

"We just had a good workout." Lillian had hoped to forestall Emilia from mentioning their encounter with Ivy, but luck, as ever, was against her.

"You'll never guess who we ran into. Literally," said Emilia.

Morgan tore her eyes away from Emilia and glanced at Lillian. "Ivy Holden."

"How did you know?"

"Lil's face. She looks like she swallowed a lemon."

"Love you too."

"What, exactly, is the deal with you?" asked Emilia. "I know you hated her in vet school, but she seems nice—just a bit competitive."

"She's not nice."

"You two definitely have some weird energy."

"And that," said Morgan as she wrapped an arm around Emilia's waist, "is the understatement of the new century."

Lillian focused on releasing tension from her calves. Morgan knew almost every detail of her enmity with Ivy, save for the ones that mattered most. The shame of those—*Ivy, smiling; Ivy, mercurial and cruel and gorgeous in the morning light*—still burned.

"At least we got a good workout. I've never seen you move so fast, Lil."

"Remind me it was my fault tomorrow when I'm sore and grumpy." She tried to keep her tone light. They didn't need to know her heart rate still raced despite her cooldown, or that a part of her wished she was still running, her feet hitting the pavement in time with Ivy's, and all the world a road.

She excused herself after a few minutes of idle chatter and headed for her greenhouse. She needed peace and quiet and the sharp sap-infused scent of growing things to clear her head. Once she was safely ensconced in her glass castle, she settled onto the folded mat she kept tucked in a corner amid her potted citrus trees, closed her eyes, and attempted to clear her mind. Hermione promptly hopped into her lap. Muffin sprawled on the floor and gathered dirt in her shaggy coat.

Breathe sunlight in, darkness out.

Breathe clean air in, toxic out.

She tried several of her usual mantras. Ivy's smirk disturbed them all. Circe bumped against her leg and she stroked her shell without opening her eyes. The animal comfort of Circe's sun-warmed carapace and the weight of Hermione in her lap grounded her. She knew she needed to find a healthier way of dealing with Ivy's presence in her life. Challenging her to footraces wasn't the worst approach, but she'd run the soles off her shoes within the month without intervention. Surely, at thirty-one, she was above Ivy's games. Her breathing slowed at last, and she concentrated on her inhales and exhales.

I can be the bigger person.

Maybe there was an upside somewhere in this mess. She tilted her face to the sunlight. Ivy pushed her. There had been times during her residency where she had almost missed the intensity of their competition, as it had been an extra spur to stay up that much later to study that much harder. Perhaps she could benefit from that again.

Or not.

She was a board-certified exotics specialist. She had nothing to prove to Ivy. Tomorrow was her day off. She would spend it gardening and reading and cuddling with her dogs, and she wouldn't think about

31

Ivy at all.

"Lil?"

Morgan. So much for the sanctity of her greenhouse. Morgan let herself in and settled onto her heels.

"Want to meditate with me?"

"No thanks," said Morgan.

"She's not getting to me."

Morgan raised both her eyebrows. "You're *letting* her get to you."

"I'm not, I'm— She's such a bitch."

"She's actually been quite pleasant."

"To *you*, maybe."

"Emilia said you were the one who was rude today."

"She's the one who moved here! This is my home. What am I supposed to do, bring her cookies and say, 'Welcome to the neighborhood?'" She hated how her voice quavered.

"Nah. You can make me cookies, though."

She swatted Morgan's arm.

"Try giving her a chance. For your sake—anger isn't good for you."

"I'm not—"

"Your cortisol levels are through the roof." Worry creased Morgan's brow, and Lillian softened.

"I'll try. I'm not making any promises, though."

Morgan tousled her hair. She pushed the mussed strands out of her eyes and glared, then tossed a leaf in Morgan's direction. Too light, it fluttered back to earth. Morgan caught it before it hit the ground. Late evening sunlight caught the sere leaf. Three points. Clearly delineated veins. A pale border. Her breath caught as her mind cataloged the species.

"Fitting," Morgan said as she examined the leaf. "It's ivy."

Chapter Three

Ivy stepped off the ferry and into her mother's arms. Prudence Holden was a classic example of New England gentility. Blond, blue-eyed, athletic, and gracious, she kissed Ivy's cheek, wafting perfume with every motion, and then frowned.

"You look tired." She brushed her thumb across the tender skin beneath Ivy's eyes.

"I just moved across the country."

Prudence accepted the reply and launched into a lengthy update about the residents of Rabbit Island while Darwin made threatening eyes at a nearby golden retriever.

Autumn was Ivy's favorite time of year on the island. Birch trees shed yellow leaves while the grass turned golden and the hardwoods glowed red and orange against the fierce blue of the October sky. The wind blew cold, briny air off the water. She breathed it in gratefully as she navigated the sidewalks and listened to her mother rattle off all the things that still needed to be done before they closed the house up for the season.

Summer cottages with large porches and shuttered windows lined the paths. She ran her hand carefully over the Rosa rugosa, touching the rosehips and plucking a ripe one. The tart flesh cleared the bitterness from her mouth as she contemplated the reason for her visit. She couldn't put it off any longer.

Their cottage sat on a granite hill overlooking the Atlantic. Smaller islands broke the expanse of horizon in soft brushstrokes of green, and whitecaps dotted the sea. The porch wrapped around the house for a 180-degree view of the water. Wicker furniture stood sentinel before window boxes full of dying flowers, and as she passed through the creaking wooden door, she pictured the porch in winter, snow mounting on its railings, the wind from the ocean driving ice against the windowpanes.

Her mother settled into an armchair in the living room and faced her, framed by a driftwood sculpture and the large stone fireplace. Silence stretched between them. Her mother wasn't dumb. Ivy's refusal to discuss why she was moving had set off alarm bells Ivy could practically hear in her mother's voice every time they spoke. At one point she'd even asked if Ivy was pregnant, which had made for a good joke with Madison. She settled onto the sofa and pulled a wool blanket around her shoulders.

"Talk to me, Ives," her mother said. "I still don't understand why you broke up with Kara. She was perfect!"

"Mom."

"I just don't get it. The move, the breakup—it's not like you."

She'd imagined this conversation a hundred times over the past year. It never went well. She considered beating around the bush, but that would mean talking about Kara, which she had no desire to do.

I'll tell her.

Her mouth opened. Words queued behind her teeth. It was such a short sentence. Three words. Four, if she spelled out her condition instead of using the abbreviation. A few words, and her mother would never look at her the same way again.

"Things with Kara didn't work out."

Her mother's eyes softened as the lie trickled from Ivy's lips. "Oh, sweetie. But why?"

"I—" *I lied to her about everything? I left without giving her a chance? She deserved better?* She couldn't say any of those things, and so she reached for something—anything—that would convince her mother

34

to drop the subject. "She cheated on me."

Prudence sucked in a breath and pursed her lips in outrage. "She *what?*"

"Yeah. It sucked. Can we not talk about it?"

"Of course." Anger lined her mother's face, but she saw relief, too, that there wasn't a more sinister reason for her departure. "Something to drink? Your father should be back soon. He took the boat out with John Fisher."

"Sure. I'll get it, though."

She fled to the kitchen, where the lights assaulted her with knowing brightness, and she leaned her head against the sleek black fridge, letting its hum dull the ache of the lie. Kara hadn't cheated on her. Kara was blameless, perfect, and this was proof she was better off with someone else. Someone who, unlike Ivy, was whole.

I'm such a coward.

The promise she'd made to herself, that she'd tell Prudence everything once she was in Maine, pressed in on her from all sides. She wanted to call Madison, but her sister would be working, and what would she say? *I can't do it. I'm scared she'll look at me with pity. I'm scared she'll think I'm weak. I'm scared, so fucking scared, this will change everything.*

Soon. She'd tell her mother soon. Opening the fridge, she pulled out a bottle of Latour Chardonnay and poured two glasses. The amber-tinted liquid sparkled in the sunlight filtering through the window, and she looked out over the ocean to the low, treeless islands that were all that separated sea from sky. Wind whipped whitecaps up over the rocks. She imagined the spray of the waves on her face instead of tears and returned to the living room and her mother and the lies she'd spun to cover up a truth she knew she needed to face soon.

Lillian finished explaining to Jacqueline O'Malley that excessive handling was the reason for her bird's condition. It was always an uncomfortable conversation for the client. Loving owners, unaware that too much physical contact created a state of near-constant arousal in birds, lavished affection on their pets. She didn't fault them. Animals were easy to love. *Much easier than people.* But the hormones stimulated by those innocent touches took its toll on avian bodies—and inevitably on the client's psyche once they realized what was happening. No one wanted to think about their animals that way. Sure enough, the woman's face flushed, and she stared at her bird in horror.

"I had no idea," she kept repeating.

"It's a common problem. I see it all the time," Lillian said with as much gentleness as she could. "You can still interact with him."

She demonstrated the proper way to handle the parakeet and suggested the woman get a second parakeet for the bird to bond with. Birds were social creatures. Who could blame them for responding to touch. Didn't the same thing happen to humans?

Don't go there.

She hadn't seen Brian for several months before they split. Shame coiled in her belly. She didn't want to think about Brian, but her body had recently started reminding her of its needs. As she excused herself from the room, she wondered if she should consider dating—not that there were many options in Seal Cove, and not that she particularly wanted to deal with the complications associated with meeting new people. And what was the point? Eventually they would realize she wasn't good enough, and they would discard her, just like everyone else.

"Good morning," said the last person she wanted to see in her current state of mind. *Or ever.* Ivy stood before her, impeccably dressed in a pale pink button-down, white coat, and navy chinos.

"Good morning," she said cautiously. Ivy was supposed to be on large animal today, monitoring inpatients and taking appointments for people who preferred trailering their animals to the clinic to paying the farm visit fee.

"I have one of your clients. Their horse is here with a melting ulcer, but they had some questions about your treatment plan for Mabel."

"The bearded dragon?"

"Yes. Would you mind taking a look at her chart? I can also tell them to leave a message."

"What were their questions?"

As Ivy talked, Lillian studied her. Ivy's face had thinned slightly in

36

the intervening years, but other than that she looked almost the same as the girl she'd traded barbs with across a lab table. Her tone today, however, was coolly professional instead of needling, and for several brief moments she managed to pretend this was like any other conversation with a colleague.

"Thank you." Ivy held her eyes. The pause stretched, and with it Lillian's held breath. Vines curled in the corner of her vision. She thought of the bird from earlier; like him, she'd once mistaken attention for something else.

"No problem," she said, and tore her eyes away. It was harder than it should have been.

Still, Ivy had been almost pleasant. That in itself was remarkable enough for comment.

She told Angie about the interaction later that evening as they sat around the fireplace.

"Maybe she's matured," said Angie. It was easy to forget Angie owned the house. With her hair piled messily on top of her head and one leg flung over the back of her chair, she looked more like the manager of a kombucha stand than the owner and operator of 16 Bay Road, the house where they lived, and the site of the doggy day care and boarding facility associated with Seal Cove Veterinary Clinic.

"I doubt it. People like her are too entitled to change."

"When do I get to meet her? For research purposes. I mean I've obviously stalked her online, but that's not the same thing."

"I don't know. The holidays probably."

"I think you're letting her get to you too much." Angie's cat, James, purred on her lap. Angie stroked his large, blocky head.

"She's not getting to me."

"She's all you've talked about since she started."

"That isn't true." Lillian paused. "Is it?"

Angie's silence was answer enough.

"She made my life hell for four years. I can't just let that go."

"She can't make your life hell anymore, though."

"Yes, she can." Her very presence was enough to undermine every-thing she valued: logic, sanity, and self-preservation.

"How? She can't take your job. You said yourself you only see her a few times during the week, and she doesn't hang out with us. If she starts something at work, Danielle will sort her out."

"Haven't you ever met someone who just angers you by existing?"

"Yes. My exes."

The comparison between Ivy and Angie's exes, who had all taken more from Angie than Ivy had ever taken from Lillian, unsettled her. Ivy could be a bitch; she wasn't a sadist. She also wasn't an ex, because to be someone's ex meant meaning something to them in the first place. Ivy didn't deserve that much from her.

"Okay, she's not quite that bad."

"Forget Ivy." Angie's eyes brightened. "We should go out."

"What?"

"We should go to Portland. Find a club or something. Get your mind in a different place."

"Angie, I haven't been to a club in years."

"Okay, then we should go to Stormy's."

That sounded like a decent suggestion. She hadn't seen their friend in a few weeks. "Right now?"

"Why not?" Angie gently dislodged a displeased James and stood, stretching as luxuriously as her cat.

"I'll get changed."

"Just wear your sweatpants."

"I'm a doctor. I have to have standards."

The memory of cutting green eyes and the Cornell ropes course still chafed. She could picture Ivy's smirk if she bumped into her around town in her lounge clothes. *Didn't realize you had a waistline.*

Angie, whose favorite attire was yoga pants and a sports bra, shrugged. "Suit yourself. I'm wearing this."

Currently, "this" consisted of leggings and a slouchy sweater, which looked suspiciously like Morgan's. Where Morgan was known to steal cheese from her housemates, Angie had light fingers in the laundry room. Lillian shook her head and went in search of a pair of jeans.

Stormy's pub and coffee shop, Storm's-a-Brewin', was quiet compared to the summer months. Only a few end-of-the-season leaf peepers occupied the tables beside Stormy's regulars. Lillian and Angie sat at the bar where they could talk to Stormy as she served drinks and lattes indiscriminately. Stormy's wild, curly hair hung loose today, and tight ringlets sprang from her head in all directions. Red lipstick highlighted her generous mouth, and she wore a sweater dress beneath her apron that accented her curvy figure. Lillian smiled as she watched her work. Stormy's vibrancy filled any room she entered. The energy in her café sparkled with potential.

"Hey angels," she said when she saw them.

"You look gorgeous as always," said Angie. "What's new?"

"It's slowing down." Stormy leaned against the bar and glanced around the room. "And honestly, I'm glad. I've got a line on some coffee beans I want to try small batches of this winter, and my brewer's been experimenting with some new IPAs I'll have to test on you."

"Poor us," said Angie as she straddled a bar stool. Lillian sat beside her with a little more dignity.

"What's up with my favorite animal saviors?"

"Lillian's arch-nemesis has returned to torment her."

"She's not my arch—"

"She is totally your arch-nemesis. Actually, she'd make a great villain."

"Why's that?" asked Stormy.

"She's got that blond ice princess thing going on," said Angie.

"Add her to one of your comics."

Angie brightened at Stormy's suggestion.

Lillian considered the way Ivy would look rendered in ink: the sharp line of her jaw and the juxtaposition of her narrowed eyes and soft mouth. She suppressed a shiver. "You have to call her Poison Ivy."

"That is perfect. Stormy, get me a pencil and a napkin."

Stormy obliged, and Angie pulled up Ivy's photo from the clinic website on her phone and began to sketch.

"Anyway," said Lillian, "everything's fine."

"Heard from Brian?"

Her stomach clenched. "No. And I don't think I will."

"Asshat." Stormy brought her dark brows together in a fearsome scowl.

"It's okay. Really."

"So okay that you're feeling single and ready to mingle?"

For all that she'd briefly entertained the idea, hearing it from Stormy's lips poured ice into her daydreams. The chill spread through her body, and the thought of another disappointment sobered her. For Stormy's sake, however, she decided to shrug her reluctance off with a joke. "Dating seems like a lot of work."

"But you'll get to experience the thrill of getting ghosted."

"Oh no. Did it happen again?" She searched Stormy's face for signs of pain. Her friend had terrible luck when it came to romance—even worse than her.

"I'm getting used to it. I didn't even like the last one that much. They were too into themselves."

"Go to Portland," Angie said without looking up from her drawing.

"So that I can get ghosted by hipsters and run into people I used to know? Nah. Portland's good for clubs and food, but I'm not touching the dating scene."

"I don't think I even remember how to flirt," said Lillian.

"Sure you do." Stormy pushed a drink toward her. "Try this first. Then hit on me."

Lillian took a sip of the drink. The pale IPA exploded with bitter citrus, and her eyes widened. "This is amazing."

"I thought you would like that one. Drink up."

"I want to savor it."

"You can savor the next one." She poured a dark, frothy beer for Angie. "And this is the coffee stout I was telling you about."

"You are a goddess," Angie said in between sips. "I could live off this."

"That's what I like to hear. Okay, Lil. Turn that charm on."

"How about . . . no."

"Get it, girl," said Angie.

"Please? Do you know how often I have scumbags trying to pick me up? Show me that classy Lee magic."

"Classy Lee magic?" Lillian raised an eyebrow.

"I know you like classical music and shit."

"Why?" Lillian lowered her voice and gave Stormy her best approximation of a seductive smile. "Does that turn you on?"

Stormy stared at her, then turned to Angie.

"Zero out of ten, no points for effort," said Angie.

"Hey, I was trying!" She laughed despite her protest as Angie's comically skeptical expression eclipsed the earlier mention of Brian.

"Whatever you need to tell yourself. Check this out."

She held the napkin up. Lillian took it and felt the buzz of the alcohol dull the noise around her. Angie's drawing captured Ivy's hauteur, but it also captured the strength of her jaw and the feline tilt of her eyelids. Vines coiled around her, tipped with the familiar leaves of three that signified poison ivy. Her hand tightened on the napkin and her fingers left indentations when she forced herself to relax. Ivy looked different rendered in pencil. Not softer, exactly, but dangerous in a way that promised rather than threatened.

"This is really good."

"Keep it."

She stared at the sketch in her hand and wished she had the strength of will to look away from Ivy's graphite eyes.

"Ooh, draw Lillian next." Stormy provided another napkin. "What's her superhero name?"

"That's easy. Tiger Lily."

"You need to do a series. Poison Ivy and Tiger Lily."

"Alternatively, you could not," said Lillian.

"On a planet far, far away, where plants are sentient, Poison Ivy seeks to take over the peaceful nation of . . . uh . . ."

"Trillium."

"Trillium?"

"It's that pretty white flower that grows in the woods. Here." Stormy pulled it up on her phone. "We're naming that IPA Lil just tried after it, actually."

"Perfect." Angie sketched a few lines on the napkin. "The nation of Trillium, which is protected by a squadron of elite warriors, led by, of course, Tiger Lily. Or maybe she's the princess." She squinted at the napkin. "I'll have to think on it."

"Look what you've done," Lillian said to Stormy.

"Inspired art?"

"Get me another Trillium, please." She pushed her empty mug back for Stormy to refill. The drawing remained clutched in her hand.

Ivy ran the curry comb over Freddie's withers. His blood bay summer coat was darkening as his winter hair grew in, and she stroked the soft brown fuzz with her empty hand.

The stable where she had decided to board him was decent. It wasn't one of the high-end eventing stables where he'd spent most of his life, but he didn't seem to mind. The pasture turnout was large, his stall was roomy, and, most importantly, the indoor arena was heated. She paused her grooming when she noticed the chunk missing from his shoulder.

"You getting along with the other ponies?"

He continued munching the leftover wisps of hay in the rack. He'd been middle of the hierarchy in his turnout group at his old stable. She hoped the horses here let him into their ranks without too much abuse. The bite would scar.

Several more wounds revealed themselves as she removed the protective layer of mud from his coat. She'd talk to the barn manager about turning him out with a quieter group. At eighteen, Freddie was still in great shape, but he wasn't six anymore. He deserved peace and quiet.

After she'd dabbed his wounds with the ointment she kept in his tack box, she saddled him up and led him to the outdoor arena. Wind blew leaves across the packed sand. Freddie pricked his ears at the blustery weather, and Ivy felt a thrumming excitement pass through his body into hers. He hadn't been hacked in a few days and she was looking forward to burning off his energy—as well as her own. Fields bordered the arena, flanked by woods. The barn grew some of their own hay, and green still clung to the shorn fields despite the recent frosts. She mounted and gathered her reins in stiff fingers, eyeing the woods for signs of deer. Freddie arched his neck and waited for her command.

She moved him out at a brisk walk. He covered ground easily, and she loved his smooth gaits. They'd been together for sixteen years. He'd been her first high-quality horse, and she'd promised him he'd die in her care, instead of getting shuffled around and sold as happened to so many horses. So far, she'd kept her word. She was grateful for that sentimentality now that her body was betraying her. When her hands refused to react with the dexterity she'd depended on, he responded to her legs and seat. She hardly used the reins at all these days.

He broke into an eager trot when she asked. They wove serpentines and circles around the ring, alternating between a working trot and a canter until he'd warmed up, and then she put him through his dressage paces. Her mind wandered as their bodies loosened and melded through the leather of the saddle. The crisp, cool air reminded her of Colorado. Homesickness, however, was preferable to the emotions lingering beneath it: guilt, shame, relief. She let the wind strip them from her cheeks as Freddie cantered in a tightening circle. He gathered beneath her, his energy contained, and the brown of his coat beneath her fingers reminded her of Lillian's eyes.

A figure leaned on the rail when she finished. Ivy looked down, startled to see Morgan.

"Hi," she said as she dismounted. "What are you doing here?"

"Checking on a horse. Is this your boy?" Morgan had eyes only for Freddie, who pricked his ears. He knew an admirer when he saw one.

"This is Freddie."

"German warmblood?"

"Yeah."

"He's gorgeous."

"He knows it." She led Freddie over to where Morgan waited. Morgan held out her hand and he whuffled it with his lips. "Do you ride?"

"Nope."

"Really?" Most of the large animal vets she knew rode, even the ones more passionate about cows than horses.

"I love horses," said Morgan, speaking more to Freddie than Ivy, "and I can ride, but I prefer hanging out with them on the ground. Stevie's the horse girl."

"Stevie? Your tech?"

"Yep. She's doing mounted archery, now. Crazy shit."

Ivy had a vivid image of Stevie thundering toward a target with a bow in her hands and laughed. "I'd like to see that."

"Ask her. I'm sure she'd show you."

Ivy's laughter faded. "Lil would just love that."

Morgan fixed her blue-gray eyes on Ivy. "Why did you take the job?"

The bluntness of the question took her breath away. Did Morgan know the extent of everything that had happened between her and Lillian?

"I wanted to be closer to family. My parents have property on an island off the coast."

"There are other hospitals."

She couldn't gauge the tone of Morgan's voice. She didn't seem aggressive, but the quiet interrogation had its own heat. The muscles in Morgan's arms and shoulders strained against the fabric of her shirt as she stroked Freddie's neck. Not that Morgan's physicality was a threat. She'd never seen Morgan Donovan lose her cool, and there was no violence in the lines of her body. Still, she was acutely conscious of how unpredictable her own musculature had become, and the comparison irritated her. Her decisions were not Morgan's business.

"Seal Cove was hiring."

"But you knew Lillian worked here."

Ivy stayed silent.

"Look." Morgan rubbed the back of her neck. "To be honest, I never understood your and Lil's thing. Just . . . don't fuck with her, okay?"

Ivy flushed. "I have no intention of fucking with her."

Cool eyes held hers. "Good."

"Morgan," she said as Morgan turned to leave. The urge to explain, to justify, surprised her. *That was a long time ago*, she wanted to say. *I'm a different person, now.* She opened her mouth to defend herself, then thought better of it. Morgan seemed the type who preferred evidence over words. Instead, she asked, "How . . . how upset is she I'm here?"

Morgan tapped her fingers on the fence rail. "Lil's fine," she said, but they both knew she was lying.

"I'm glad to hear that. Please let her know my decision had nothing to do with her."

"I'll let you tell her. The last time I tried to arbitrate between you two I nearly got a scalpel in my eye." Morgan grinned, and Ivy's stomach muscles relaxed fractionally at the friendly overture.

"Spay lab?"

"Spay lab," Morgan confirmed.

"Well, Lil did threaten to stab me with a dirty needle."

"Good times," said Morgan with a shake of her head. "Sorry to interrupt your ride. For what it's worth, I'm glad to have you at the practice."

Unspoken were the words: as long as you don't hurt Lillian.

And what if Lillian hurts me?

Chapter Four

October blew itself into November with a nor'easter that knocked power out from the region for a day and required both Ivy and Morgan be on call. A month had passed since she'd arrived, she reflected as she navigated the debris-strewn roads. At least Shawna, her technician, had turned out to be a good fit. The shorter woman was a few years older than Ivy and had muscles that rivaled those of the stallion they were examining. The stud, a handsome thoroughbred, did not enjoy being tied. Ivy hated horse owners who let their animals get away with this kind of flighty behavior, but Shawna kept him under control while Ivy performed her examination.

She pulled out a vacutainer needle and several vials to draw blood for routine lab tests. As she placed the needle, her fingers twitched, and the vacutainer tumbled to the barn floor. The owner picked it up and handed it back. She thanked him and opened a new needle to hide her panic. If she couldn't keep a grip on a syringe, how was she supposed to draw blood?

Pain sparked along her hands. Ignoring it, she wiped the stallion's neck with alcohol and placed the needle. It took her longer than it should have. Shawna held the horse still as she placed the vacutainer and filled the sample tubes, and she allowed herself a small exhale of relief.

"I've got some hand warmers if your hands get stiff in the cold," Shawna said as they packed up. Rain still spit out of the pewter sky, though the wind had died down, and Ivy knew the rawness of the weather probably wasn't helping her condition. Had Maine really been the best choice?

"It's nothing."

Shawna side-eyed her as she shut the back of the truck. Her short black hair peeked out from beneath her red beanie, and the damp chill had reddened her cheeks, making her look like one of the ubiquitous garden gnomes Ivy passed on her rounds—though no garden gnome had ever mastered the "I smell bullshit" face quite the way Shawna had.

Ivy averted her gaze.

"Hell of a day, anyway." Shawna stretched before hopping into the cab. Ivy cringed at the sound of her spine cracking.

"Yeah."

She climbed into the passenger seat in silence, feeling queasy. The stiffness in her hands remained, and shocks traveled up her arms into her shoulders as she began the paperwork. *Thank god this is the last appointment of the day*, she thought as Shawna swerved to avoid a large tree limb in the road.

"Got plans for the weekend?" Shawna asked.

"We're on call on Sunday."

"But not Saturday. My kid's got a hockey game."

Ivy listened to Shawna talk about her son while trying not to think about what she might have been doing on a Saturday back in Colorado. Skiing, if the slopes had snow, or having a drink with Kara and a few of their other friends. She hadn't fully realized how completely immersed she'd been in her old clinic. Here, where she knew nobody during the winter season, she was alone—a feeling she couldn't remember ever experiencing before. It wasn't that making friends was difficult for her, but Lillian complicated things. She couldn't exactly suggest grabbing a drink with her coworkers.

So, apologize.

But that was out of the question. She doubted her lips could even form the words, assuming, of course, she could think of any words to encompass their tangled history.

Back at the clinic Shawna checked the supplies in the truck while Ivy headed to the computer. Darwin trotted at her heels. Georgia, the head tech, greeted him with a cookie and Ivy with a pitying grimace.

"You look soaked through."

Ivy glanced down at her clothes. She did feel damp, and the short walk from the truck had plastered her hair to the back of her neck.

"It's gross out there."

"Georgia, when you get a minute—" Lillian broke off as she rounded the corner and saw Ivy. "Sorry to interrupt."

She didn't look sorry. She looked pissed. Ivy slid into a computer chair and turned her attention to the screen. "You weren't interrupting. Just talking about the weather."

"Oh. Well. Georgia, can you get a blood pressure on Benji for me?"

"Sure thing."

Lillian stood for an awkward minute before settling into the computer farthest from Ivy. The clicking of the keyboard beneath her fingers reminded her of the way Lillian used to chew the end of her pen when Ivy really pissed her off. The urge to probe the old wound rose like an itch.

"Surprised to see you here still."

"Why?" said Lillian.

"It's seven o'clock on a Friday night. So much for that specialty nine to five."

"Jealous?" Lillian still hadn't looked over at her.

"Of exotics? Hardly."

Lillian swiveled in her chair. A strand of hair had come loose from her bun, and her eyes flashed. Ivy felt the familiar flare of satisfaction that came with getting under Lillian's skin.

"I'm surprised you have so few letters behind your name," said Lillian.

"I wanted to be able to fit it on a vanity license plate."

"Does it go nicely with your Porsche?"

"A Porsche? On these roads?"

"BMW, then. You like those three letter acronyms."

"Still driving stick?" Ivy asked.

Lillian flushed. She'd struggled with the old stick shift Volvo she'd driven at school, twice stalling out in front of Ivy.

"Some of us had to buy our own cars."

Ivy laughed, which she knew would infuriate Lillian further. "You're not still driving that thing, are you?"

"No." Lillian turned back to her computer. Her perfect posture radiated fury. Pushing her further was a bad idea; she didn't need an assistant overhearing her mocking a colleague. If she stopped, however, she'd be left to finish up her paperwork and go home to her couch, which, while cozy beside the woodstove, suddenly seemed unbearably lonely.

"Let me guess. You drive a Prius now."

"A Prius? On these roads?" Lillian mimicked Ivy's earlier statement, and she couldn't help grinning.

"Jeep then." She'd seen one parked in the lot.

"She drives a Subaru normally," said Georgia. Ivy registered her return with a sideways glance.

"Normally?"

"Her car's in the shop."

"Georgia—" said Lillian.

"She didn't hit another pedestrian, did she?" said Ivy, unable to suppress her smirk.

Lillian made a choked sound that might have been a curse.

"Dr. Lee hit a pedestrian?"

"She claims it was an accident," said Ivy. "But I was pretty badly bruised."

Georgia blinked.

"Dr. Holden cut me off." Lillian's voice rose the way it did when she was frustrated. Ivy's stomach tightened at the color peaking in her cheeks. Getting hit had been worth it for the brief moment of concern in Lillian's eyes before she'd realized Ivy was mostly fine.

"I believe pedestrians always have the right of way."

"In *crosswalks*."

"Dr. Lee," said Georgia, looking back and forth between them with a mixture of amusement and concern, "I got that blood pressure."

"Right. Thank you." Lillian pushed back from the counter and stalked away, leaving her alone with her fading smile. *That devolved quickly.* Was it possible for them to fight about absolutely every topic under the sun? And why did she have to be such a goddamn snob whenever Lillian was around? What did it matter what kind of car Lillian drove?

"At least my parents didn't have to buy my way into college." Old words. Old wounds. She input her treatments with her mind still half on the conversation and was only vaguely aware of what was going on around her. Georgia emerged from the room and carried on a hushed conversation on her cell phone.

"... in the hospital? Ah, mami ... Dios Santo."

Hospital?

Georgia stood in the corner with her perfectly pressed curls wrapped around her hand as she visibly tried to keep herself together.

"Is everything all right?" she asked the technician.

Georgia slipped her phone back in her pocket and took a shaky breath. "My mother's in the hospital."

"Go," said Ivy, getting to her feet. "I can cover for you."

"Dr. Holden—"

"It's no trouble at all."

"Thank you." Georgia wiped her eyes and fumbled in her scrub pockets for a vial of medication, which she reshelved, and then took off. Shawna and the receptionist had already left for the night, which meant, Ivy realized too late, she was alone in the clinic with Lillian. The muffled sound of Lillian's voice penetrated the otherwise silent hospital. She returned to her work with a new tension in her shoulders.

"Where's Georgia?" Lillian asked fifteen minutes later.

"I sent her home."

"You what?"

"Her mother's in the hospital. It seemed like the decent thing to do. I'll help you with whatever you need."

"You'll—" Lillian broke off and ran her hands through her hair, further upsetting her bun. "Is her mother all right?"

"I didn't ask. She seemed too upset."

"Right." Lillian looked around. "Well, I'm done here. Who's up front?"

"Nobody."

"Right," Lillian said again. "Okay."

"Do you know how to check clients out?"

"I've been here three years. Yes. I know how to check a patient out, Ivy."

Ivy bit back a retort. "Is there anything I can do?"

"No."

"What was wrong with Benji?"

"What, are you a specialist now?" Lillian ripped off her white coat and flung it over the back of her computer chair.

"I just—"

"It's bad enough you're here. Don't poach my clients. Don't tell me how to do my job. Just—" She exhaled sharply.

"How am I poaching your clients?"

"You're seeing small animal cases. *My* cases."

"I was hired to see some of your cases."

"You were hired for large animal. Nobody said anything to me about an additional small animal veterinarian."

That's because it was part of my contract negotiation, despite the listing. She'd been firm on that point. She needed a position with flexibility, in case the progression of her disease sped up. Shame boiled in her gut.

"Perhaps Dr. Watson thought you needed case relief," she said, for owning up to the truth was never going to be an option. Not with Lillian.

"I don't need case relief." Lillian was breathing hard. "What I need is for you—"

"Lillian." Ivy said her name sharply, hoping to cut her off before she finished that sentence. "Walls are thin."

Lillian glanced at the wall dividing them from Benji and his owners, and the expression on her face should have struck Ivy down with avenging lightning. It didn't.

"I swear to god, Ivy."

"Do you need a ride home?"

"What?" Lillian's glare faltered in confusion.

"Your car's in the shop. I asked if you needed a ride home," Ivy repeated.

"Georgia offered—" She paused. "I'll call Morgan."

"Don't be an idiot. You're on my way. I'll drop you off."

The glare returned full-force. "I would honestly rather walk."

"Lil—"

"Please shut up so I can do my job."

Ivy shut up. Lillian's fingers jabbed the keyboard violently as she typed up her discharge letter, and Ivy watched her, hating herself for antagonizing her and unable to resist admiring the way Lillian's nostrils flared with anger and the tight, upright set of her shoulders, as if her anger was a solid thing Ivy could reach out and touch. Back in Colorado, she'd thought overcoming this dynamic would be easy. They were older, presumably wiser, and if nothing else, professionals; squabbling like children should have been beneath them.

"Let me give you a ride home," she said quietly when Lillian's fingers slowed. "It's ridiculous for you to call Morgan when you're on my way."

"Fine." Lillian didn't look at her, which gave her another opportunity to stare at her profile. Light from the computer screen lit the planes of her cheeks and the stray pieces of hair that brushed the curve of her neck.

I wouldn't want anyone else as my enemy.

In truth, she hadn't thought of Lillian as her enemy in years. She understood now what that hatred had always been: part jealousy, part resentment, and part desire.

Ivy liked people who professed not to care. She went for those who, like her, had grown up aware of the advantages their privilege gave them and were neither ashamed nor afraid to use it. Yachts, trust funds, summer homes and apartments abroad. What fun could be had in constantly being reminded she'd done nothing to deserve her social status, that her grandparents and then her parents had invested in oil, that her money was stained with the blood and corruption and the corpulent weight of the fossil fuel industry? Lillian, with her righteous poverty, her scholarships, her secondhand clothes—Ivy had hated wanting her, because the judgment in Lillian's gaze raised too many questions.

Lillian managed to check out her patient, cursing both the computer system and Georgia for sending home the receptionist as she struggled to remember how to put in the charges. Why did medical software have to be so damn complicated? She didn't need another reminder of how little she actually controlled. When Benji and his owners had at last departed, she braced herself on the desk with her hands splayed against the slightly greasy surface.

I am not this person, she told herself. She was calm. She was a woman who grew plants and loved dogs and running in the evenings, not someone who raged at her coworker and fantasized about slashed tires and revenge. Then again, Ivy had to have an ulterior motive for her generosity. She always did. Being alone in a car with her was like walking straight into her jaws. When *was* the last time she'd been alone with Ivy? Years, at least. There had been that night—no. She refused to think of it, especially right now.

"All set?"

Ivy was watching her. Lillian felt her eyes and gathered her resolve before turning to face her. Ivy rested her shoulder against the wall. Her face looked washed out and tired beneath the clinic's harsh fluorescence, and her high cheekbones cast dark shadows. That somehow angered her still further. How dare Ivy look tired. How dare she look human, when she was so much easier to hate in her golden, flawless, vengeful state.

"Yeah," she said, aware of the distance between their bodies in the same way she'd always been. It was the awareness she felt around fractious animals, conscious they might bite at any moment, and it was the awareness she imagined a predator might feel around a particularly dangerous prey; the wolf, circling the elk, waiting for a sign of weakness with one eye on the deadly antlers and the other on its hamstrings. She half wanted to growl.

This is not you.

Isn't it, though? Another thought she would deal with later. Or never. She stalked past Ivy, noting the scent of her perfume beneath the smells of horse and hay, something out of her price range, to be sure, with undertones of rose, and she shrugged into her jacket.

Rain still fell. She heard it battering the roof, though the winds had died down since yesterday, and the temperature hovered just above freezing. Ivy pulled on her own coat, grabbed her shoulder bag, and led the way out of the clinic.

She paused to shut off the lights and lock up. When she turned around in the dark evening, Ivy's blond hair had been whipped out of its braid by a lingering gust, and she was standing by a dark pickup truck.

She balked. "I thought you said you drove a BMW."

"You said I drove a BMW," said Ivy. "This is my baby."

The Dodge Ram—diesel, with those extra wheels in the back she found ridiculous—hulked in the lot. She'd seen it before, now that she thought about it, but had assumed it belonged to a client or one of the techs. She couldn't tell what color it was in the dark. Maybe blue or gray. Regardless, it was a behemoth.

"Compensating for something?" she said as Ivy opened the passenger door for her. The considerate gesture triggered alarm bells.

"Yeah. The weight of a horse trailer. I used it on the job in Colorado, and for Freddie."

"You still have Freddie?" Lillian hauled herself into the cab and breathed in a mixture of barn and pine air freshener. Not the cheap kind, but something that legitimately smelled like walking into an evergreen forest.

"Of course. Don't sound so shocked."

"I just figured he'd be too old to compete," she said as she sank into the leather seat. Her own car was an appropriate distance from the ground, not the level of a small skyscraper. Ivy fumbled 'with her keys. She seemed to be having difficulty getting them into the ignition.

"I don't toss my animals out when they get old." The heat in Ivy's voice warmed Lillian.

Back in familiar territory.

"Just clothes?"

"I like variety."

"And waste."

Ivy finally managed to fit the key and turn the engine over. It rumbled to life with a roar, followed by music.

"Bruce Springsteen?" Lillian said. "That's so basic, Ivy."

To her surprise, Ivy laughed. "He's sexy."

"He is not."

"Listen to this one." Ivy skipped a few tracks and began to sing along to 'Thunder Road.' Her voice was low and slightly raspy, different from her speaking voice, and Lillian stilled in her seat. Bruce Springsteen's voice faded as she concentrated on Ivy's. *Hot damn*, she imagined Stormy saying. *Girl can sing.*

"See?" Ivy said.

"Still basic," said Lillian, but her throat felt dry and heat coiled in her stomach.

"I am basic. Do you still listen to classical?"

"Yes," said Lillian, surprised Ivy remembered. "Among other things."

"Like what? I'll put it on."

"Brandi Carlile."

"So gay," Ivy said without malice. She switched the music and turned it down, and Lillian pushed aside an unexpected twinge of regret.

"I didn't know you could sing."

"Me? I can't sing. Didn't you just hear me?"

"You—" Lillian cut herself off before she complimented Ivy Holden. It didn't matter that Ivy's voice was slightly off-key. There was something about its huskiness that sent chills down her spine, and that was not a place she was willing to go. "You're not terrible."

"My mother put me in voice lessons for years. She'd be thrilled to hear that. You still play piano?"

"Not very often." *How do you know I play piano?*

Ivy put the truck in gear. "Where do you live?"

She explained how to get to 16 Bay Road and marveled at how little she felt the potholes as Ivy pulled out of the lot.

"Lil," Ivy said as the stark outlines of leafless trees flickered past, "I didn't come here to fuck with you."

"I'm not that egotistical."

55

"No, I just—" Ivy broke off. Lillian watched her profile. Ivy's classical looks summed up everything about her: privilege. Women like Ivy got what they wanted, always. "Can we—" Ivy faltered again, and Lillian saw her knuckles whiten on the steering wheel.

"Can we what?" She thought she knew where Ivy was going, but she'd be damned if she helped her get there. She'd fallen for this charade once before.

"Can we call a truce?"

"I don't know, Ivy, can we?" She heard the bitterness in her voice and wished she could be less transparent.

This time, Ivy's laugh was humorless. "Could we try?"

She didn't answer her immediately. Instead, she thought about what a truce might look like. She couldn't picture it. They'd only ever fought, in one way or another.

"I guess. What do you want to do, come up with a safe word for when you piss me off?"

"A safe word?" Ivy took her eyes off the road to meet Lillian's, and she hated the thrill that look sent through her.

"A joke, Ivy."

"You sure?"

Damnit. The coy undertone slid into her bloodstream like a needle, promising the kind of high that would take part of her with it when it faded. One of the many things she hated about Ivy was how much control Ivy seemed to have over Lillian's composure. She wielded it like a weapon, and Lillian was not about to let herself get cut again.

"Fine. Why not?" she said, deciding that playing along would show Ivy how little she cared.

"Okay. Pick one."

"You pick."

"It was your idea."

The name of Stormy's beer and Angie's imaginary nation slipped from her lips. "Trillium."

"Trillium? What is that?"

"A flower."

"Trillium." Ivy repeated the word. "I like it."

"Ivy," she asked, still thinking of Angie's comic, which she hadn't been able to throw away, "why *are* you here?"

Ivy took her time answering. "I wanted to be closer to my family. Our summer home is off the coast."

Summer home. Obviously Ivy had a summer home. Her family probably had several, as well as memberships to ski lodges in the Alps and country clubs and all the other trappings that came with wealth. It occurred to her for the thousandth time, as they sat in silence listening to the sound of the tires crunching dead leaves and music wafting from the speakers, that Ivy Holden didn't have to work. She certainly didn't need to be in a backwater town like Seal Cove getting her hands dirty in a barn. People like Ivy belonged in boardrooms and behind closed doors, making the decisions that excluded people like Lillian from the table.

And killing the planet. There was always that.

"It's winter," she said, pushing her resentment down. "Is your family still here?"

"No. My sister is in Boston, though."

She wondered if Ivy had any friends in the area, and then decided she didn't care. "This is me," she said as the lights of the farmhouse came into view. Ivy turned into the drive and put the truck in park but did not kill the engine. Lillian put her hand on the door handle, then paused. "Thanks for the lift."

"No problem."

She wanted to say something else, but she didn't know what, and so she stared at Ivy in silence. Ivy gave her a small smile. It was unlike her usual mocking one, and Lillian wasn't sure what to do with it.

"Bye, Ivy."

"See you around."

She shut the truck door and retreated to the safety of her house.

The dogs greeted her with their customary exuberance. She plucked Hermione off her scrabbling paws and tucked her under her arm, accepting the Italian greyhound's kisses with the side of her face. Muffin, her monstrous mutt, nudged her nose under her hand and wiggled her entire body with joy.

"I missed you too," she told the tripod dogs. Muffin flattened her already flat ears and beamed.

Morgan wasn't home, which didn't surprise her. Her friend spent much of her spare time with Emilia these days, and the remaining housemates had a betting pool going about when the two would move in together permanently. Lillian had her money on January.

Stevie and Angie lounged in the living room. Lillian thought about cooking something to eat and then settled for pouring herself a glass of wine, still holding Hermione, and collapsed into her favorite armchair. Muffin flopped at her feet with a floor-shaking thud.

"Rough day, babe?" Angie asked from behind a tattered paperback. Stevie napped on the couch beside her. Stevie's dog, a pit bull named Marvin, curled himself into an implausibly small shape on top of her sleeping body. Angie periodically took a strand of Stevie's blond hair out of her mouth and tucked it behind her ear.

"Something like that," Lillian said.

"You're home late. Did She Who Must Not Be Named give you a hard time?"

Lillian considered telling Angie about Ivy, but she didn't know what she'd say. The conversation they'd had in the truck had been— what, exactly? Not friendly, but not hostile. Somewhere in between. Truce, she reflected, was a good word; it implied future conflict. Ivy calling for a truce wasn't something she'd seen coming, nor did she trust it. Letting her guard down around Ivy never yielded positive results.

"Emergency came in at five," she said to Angie. "Just a long day. Besides—don't we reserve She Who Must Not Be Named for the queen of TERFs?"

"Truth. Or, as I like to call her, the Destroyer of Childhood Joy."

"I thought we decided we weren't going to let her take that away from us?"

"You're using my love of wizarding fandom to distract me from your sad face."

"I am not—"

"Mhmm."

"Okay, maybe I am, but I'm fine, I promise. How's the kennel?"

"Slow." Angie's doggy day care and boarding facility made most of its money in the summer, when tourists and locals went on vacation.

She had regulars, however, who kept her in business year-round, and at least the holiday season was coming up.

"Stevie looks like she's down for the count."

Angie glanced at Stevie's sleeping face. Her lips were parted, and a stubborn strand of hair kept sliding over them despite Angie's intervention.

"This girl can nap anywhere. Have you thought more about going to Portland? Stormy and I might head up there on her next night off."

"I don't think I can keep up with you."

"We'll dance, grab some drinks, and come right home. I promise." Angie gave her a beseeching look that Lillian didn't buy. When Stormy and Angie got together, they partied hard.

"It's not my scene, Ange."

"It could be. I'll loan you a dress."

"I have a dress."

"I'll loan you a *sexy* dress."

Lillian gave Hermione a kiss on the top of her narrow snout. "If you can get Morgan and Emilia to come, I'll go."

Morgan would never agree to go to a club, which basically guaranteed her safety.

"Deal."

Ivy scrolled through her Instagram, wrapped in a thick wool blanket with Darwin tucked against her chest and the woodstove door open to reveal the merry blaze within. Her Colorado friends were already skiing, and while the majority of her feed was filled with horses, dogs, weird cats, and photos of everything and anything cozy, which usually calmed her, she found herself growing irritable.

Leaving her social circle had been hard, of course, but a large part of her was relieved. Turning down invitations to go out because she felt like shit was easy when there were no invitations. The last month had been a reprieve from guilt and dodging questions, and she was grateful for it.

She was also lonely. The people she might have made friends with were Lillian's friends, and that wasn't a viable option. Reaching out to her mother or sister would generate contacts, but they'd be well connected and, while probably pleasant, more than she felt she could deal with. She didn't want to perform anymore.

Her fingers searched out Lillian's account of their own accord. Lillian's feed was so *her* it made Ivy smile. Plants, animals, and her friends. She recognized Morgan, Emilia, and Stevie, but didn't know the other two women who appeared regularly. One was a curvy woman with incredible hair, and the other was a sultry brunette with a penchant for yoga pants Ivy respected. She paused on a shot taken outside an ice cream parlor. The curvy woman, wearing a Captain Marvel shirt and a peeling, fake Ruth Bader Ginsburg tattoo with the word 'Notorious' circling her bicep, held her cone out for Lillian while a horrified Stevie looked on—clearly upset that she was not the one getting to sample the cone. Lillian looked happy. Scrolling further, she paused. A handsome white man with his arms or hands or eyes always on Lillian populated the older photos. Here he was, carrying a three-legged Italian greyhound or eating a tomato in a greenhouse. Here he was again, holding Lillian in his arms in the snow. She clicked on his tag and found his feed, which was thankfully not private. *Geologist. Avid outdoorsman. Brown PhD candidate.* His bio told her all she needed to know. Lillian could do better.

His disappearance from Lillian's photos, combined with her negligible presence on his account, suggested the relationship had ended. She did not analyze the smug satisfaction this brought her.

Further stalking revealed that the woman with the intensely curly hair was Stormy, and she owned a coffee shop and microbrewery in town called Storm's-a-Brewin'. Ivy considered her woodstove, Darwin, her blanket, and her sweatpants, then looked out the window to where the branches lashed the sky against the moon.

For the moon never beams, without bringing me dreams
Of the beautiful Lillian Lee;
And the stars never rise, but I feel the bright eyes
Of the beautiful Lillian Lee

Damn Ms. Parker and her obsession with poetry. She twisted the fringe of the blanket between her fingers. Leaving the house sounded like a terrible idea. Her body ached and burned in turns, and drinking beer always made her symptoms worse. Besides, chatting up one of Lillian's friends, even if she was a bartender, felt a little bit like stalking. Spending the rest of the weekend alone, however, or calling up her sister, felt even worse. Driving with Lillian had awakened a restlessness she wanted to shed.

"Want to get a drink?" she asked Darwin. He twitched an ear at her and grumbled as he buried his nose deeper into her stomach. "Come on, munchkin."

She threw on her favorite pair of jeans, an Everlane silk shell, her AllSaints leather jacket, and a pair of Hunter rain boots; fastened Darwin's plaid coat around his wiry neck; and forced herself to walk out the door.

Parking in town was easy in November. She found a spot near the brewery for her truck and, Darwin under her arm, walked into Storm's-a-Brewin' with as much confidence as she could muster—which, she knew from experience, was a significant amount.

The interior of the coffee shop-slash-bar was warm and cozy. The walls were a tasteful shade of red, bordered by brick and hung with local art. Small square tables filled most of the floor space, but the bar had a line of stools, and there were couches in one corner and a raised platform that looked like it served as a stage when it wasn't home to a collection of children's toys.

Heads turned toward her as she entered. She was used to this, and ignored them, careful not to make eye contact with the group of young men at the table nearest her. She strode toward the bar and slid onto a—thankfully cushioned—stool, keeping Darwin on her lap where he couldn't cause trouble. An older couple sat two stools over, and several kids who might have been anywhere from eighteen to twenty-five chatted just past them. Low music played over the speakers. She didn't recognize the singer, but the woman's voice soothed her as she settled into her seat.

"What can I get you?"

She tore her eyes away from the menu and came face to face with Stormy. The woman's corkscrew curls were pulled back by a polka dot bandana, and her long-sleeved maroon sweater dipped to reveal a generous amount of cleavage. Despite the sensuality she radiated, her smile was warm and open behind her red lipstick.

"Could you do a soy Earl Grey latte?"

"Of course." She turned to the frother on the other side of the bar. Ivy listened to the familiar sound of steaming milk and wondered what she was doing here.

"Anything for the dapper gentleman?" Stormy asked as she handed a red cup to Ivy. "Puppuccino?"

Darwin, whose ears had perked up as the drink drew closer, wriggled in her arms.

"Sure, why not?"

"What's his name?"

"Darwin."

"And what a charming little man you are. May I?" Stormy held her hand out, and when Ivy nodded, let Darwin sniff it. She filled a small cup with whipped cream and presented it to him with ceremony.

Darwin inhaled it in a series of gulping slurps that spattered the bar.

"It amazes me," said Stormy as she leaned on the bar to gaze adoringly at Darwin, "how the big dogs are so delicate, and the little ones are such monsters."

"You've got him pegged. Is this your bar?"

"It sure is. Stormy." Stormy held out her hand and Ivy shook it. "Let me guess. Your name is Ivy."

"How did you—"

"Call it a hunch. How do you like Seal Cove?"

"Honestly, I haven't seen much of it."

"Sure you have." Stormy swept her hand around the bar. "This is it. Not that I'm complaining. There are a few other bars, but they serve cheap beer and conservatives."

"And what do you serve?"

"At the moment, coffee, tea, and my own brews. Are you a beer drinker?"

"I used to be."

"Sober?"

"Not . . . exactly. It just doesn't agree with me the way it used to."

Stormy nodded, as if this made all the sense in the world. "You know Lil then."

"I did mention I don't drink beer, right?"

"Do you need a drink to talk about Lil?" Stormy raised a penciled eyebrow. She wasn't Ivy's usual type by a long stretch, but she had "sexy bartender" pegged. The urge to lean in and confide everything to her was surprisingly strong.

"You could say that." She wondered how much Stormy knew. The fact that she was being friendly suggested either Lillian hadn't told her much, or she was just being professional.

"I'm from Portland originally. I left because the market was saturated. All the markets." She gave Ivy a meaningful look. "I wanted to get away from my exes."

"Lil and I never dated." Her hold on Darwin tightened, and he wriggled uncomfortably.

"Exes, enemies—is there a difference?"

"Did she say we were enemies?"

"Not in those words." Stormy settled her chin in her hands and gazed up at Ivy through long lashes. Her eyes were dark, but Ivy couldn't tell if they were brown or green or a nearly black shade of violet. She fought to keep her own eyes away from the woman's cleavage. Stormy might not be her type, exactly, but there were limits to anyone's willpower.

"What did she say?"

"Nothing I can tell you. Where are you from, Ivy?"

"Colorado, most recently. My family has property on Rabbit Island."

"You're a Bunny?"

"Born and raised," Ivy said. "This is the longest I've ever spent on the Maine mainland."

"Well, we're not fancy, but we have fun." Stormy slid away to tend to another customer, then returned. "How's your tea?"

"Quite good."

"You should come by in the morning and try the dark roast. Or light, if you like. We roast it ourselves."

"Maybe I will."

"Lillian drinks the medium roast, which I respect but don't understand."

"Which do you prefer?" Ivy asked.

"Dark. I like to feel my coffee."

"Same."

Stormy tickled Darwin under his chin. "And bring this one."

"It's great you allow dogs."

"My best friends are veterinarians. I couldn't let them bring theirs in and deny the public. Besides. I love the little snoot boopers."

"Do you have a dog?"

"Not right now." Stormy stroked Darwin's ear, then straightened. "Have you ever lived in a small town before?"

"Not one this small."

"Portland isn't far. I head in when I start getting claustrophobic."

"I thought you said you avoided it." Ivy threw her a smile to show she was joking. Stormy tapped her finger against her chin to indicate she ceded the point.

"I go with friends when I feel like dancing. Actually, we're going tomorrow. You should come."

"I think that depends on who 'we' is."

"Me, my friend Angie, Morgan and Stevie, Emilia, and Lillian if we can convince her."

"I don't think—"

"You work together, right?"

"Yes, which is why—"

"Come out with us. Burn it off."

The invitation floored her. She clutched Darwin to her chest and stared at Stormy, whose eyes brimmed with a mischievous blend of sympathy and understanding. Had Lillian put her up to this? Had she told her friends about what Ivy had done to her—to them both—years and diagnoses ago?

Stormy's face betrayed nothing.

"I'll think about it."

"You should. Here, give me your number. I'll text you when we're heading down that way, and if you're up for it, we'll see you there. There's a queer pop-up dance party at Johnny's."

Queer. She narrowed her eyes at Stormy. The statement wasn't necessarily an assumption, as straight people attended queer events all the time, but combined with the invitation itself and her history with Lillian, her suspicions were aroused.

Unless, of course, Stormy was flirting with *her*. She blinked and Stormy laughed, which told Ivy she had not hidden her expression well enough. Not flirting, then, but definitely toying with her. She relaxed. Let Stormy toy. This was a game she'd played all her life.

"What is the deal with you and Lillian, anyway?" Stormy asked before Ivy could pursue that line of thought further.

"We got off to a rough start in vet school. It . . . stayed rough."

Stormy made a noncommittal noise in the back of her throat. "Rough isn't always a bad thing."

Loud music. Too much tequila. Lillian's hips beneath her hands as she shoved her against the wall.

The memory should have dulled over the years. It should not have hit her in Stormy's pub with the force it did, cleaving her down the middle and revealing the molten secret at the core. Nor should Stormy have looked quite so knowing as she analyzed the effect her words had on Ivy.

"It's none of my business," Stormy said with poorly suppressed satisfaction.

Ivy needed to backpedal, and fast. "Me and Lil are . . . complicated."

"Also not always a bad thing."

"It is with Lil."

"Who started it?"

"I did." This, at least, was safe enough territory.

"What did you do?"

"I laughed at her."

Stormy winced. "I bet Lil just loved that."

"She did not. Haven't you ever met someone you've just hated on sight for absolutely no reason?"

"Several of my customers," said Stormy. "And do not tell them that."

"That's basically it. Nothing special." She finished her tea and congratulated herself on getting out of hot water. Coming here had been a mistake.

Stormy's dark eyes met hers and held them. "Don't get me wrong, I love it here, but I sometimes miss running into my rivals. It kept life interesting."

"That's one word for it."

"I can think of a few more." And with that, Stormy bustled off to deal with a sudden influx of clientele, leaving Ivy alone to contemplate the things she'd left unsaid—and Stormy's offer.

Going into Portland was idiotic. She'd pay for it with her health for days, perhaps weeks, but, as she watched Stormy turn a flirtatious smile on her next customers, she knew she'd go. If nothing else, it would piss Lillian off.

Trillium, she thought, and a vivid image of Lillian saying their safe word drowned out her caution.

"I cannot believe you agreed to come out," Lillian said to Morgan. The six of them were all crammed in Stormy's Jeep, and she had to nearly shout to be heard over the music. Angie rode shotgun, and Stevie, Morgan, Emilia, and Lillian were all crammed into the back seat. Stevie, as the smallest, lay across their laps, which made Lillian deeply uncomfortable. Seatbelts were often the difference between life and death.

"I haven't seen her dance," said Morgan, looking at Emilia.

"Traitor."

"You look nice." Morgan gestured at the ensemble Angie had insisted on squeezing Lillian into. Her top swooped lower than anything she owned, and the jeans—her own, at least, not Angie's—were her tightest-fitting pair. She felt exposed and out of her element and was already missing her greenhouse. She hadn't gone clubbing since undergraduate, and she hadn't liked it much then, either.

"I feel naked."

"That's kind of the point," said Stevie.

"Keep your eyes up front," Morgan said to Stevie.

"I wouldn't check out Lil's tits. It would be like checking out my sister."

"It's more coverage than anything going on up front," Morgan added, shooting a look toward Stormy and Angie, who were dancing in their seats.

"You look hot. Relax," said Emilia.

"You know what else is hot?" Lillian asked. Perhaps sensing a rhetorical question, none of them answered. "Sweatpants, a fire, and a cup of tea."

Stevie jabbed her elbow into her ribs. "Okay, grandma."

It took them only forty-five minutes to get to the city and find parking. Lillian wrapped her jacket closer around herself to fend off the November chill as Stormy and Angie bounced ahead of them on the sidewalk. Stevie looked torn between Morgan and Angie but opted to stay with the larger herd, bumping her shoulder into Lillian's and grinning. "Chilly, Lilly?"

"God, you're like a child sometimes."

"That's why you love me." Stevie looped her arm through Lillian's and, though she didn't want to admit it, her added body heat did fend off some of the cold. Morgan, Lillian noted, had not been wrestled into revealing items of clothing, and had been allowed to wear her usual jeans and button-down, complete with comfortable-looking leather boots. Even Emilia, who looked stunning in a slinky dress, had opted for a low-slung pair of heels instead of the pair Angie had insisted Lillian cram her toes into. Her feet were already screaming at her.

Stevie had femmed up her look for the night. Her skin-tight black pants and black boots were paired with a soft V-neck T-shirt, which would shimmer beneath a blacklight, showing off her collarbones, arms, and even a hint of cleavage. Those attributes were currently all hidden beneath her thick Carhartt jacket.

"And we're here," said Stormy.

"What is this place?" Morgan asked, balking.

The brick building in front of them was old, ugly, and crumbling in a way that screamed derelict. Bass music pounded from within as they moved up the line at the door. She checked her coat twice—once herself for valuables, and once to the man in the booth. Inside, darkness, strobe lights, and dancing bodies lit with glow sticks assaulted her vision. Lillian clung to Morgan, who was busy watching her girlfriend, and squinted against the barrage.

"This is hell, isn't it?" Stevie asked from her left.

"Pretty much."

Angie and Stormy were already on the dance floor, turning heads as they moved in time to the music. Morgan was no better—she looked like she was in a deep trance as Emilia led her out to join their friends, leaving Stevie and Lillian standing awkwardly near the door. Stevie's face fell as several dancers zeroed in on Angie. Lillian put a hand on Stevie's elbow and gave her a reassuring squeeze. She didn't want to see Stevie hurt any more than she wanted to see Angie hurt. At least none of the strangers were Alanna, Angie's off-and-on fuck buddy and all-around asshole.

"Drink?" Stevie asked.

"Several."

The bar wasn't any quieter, but at least alcohol would make her feel slightly less uncomfortable. She avoided making eye contact with the people gathered around it, acutely aware of the sensation of air on her chest. When was the last time she'd dressed up to go out?

"Hey," Stevie said to the bartender, a cute transman in a vest.

"What are you drinking?" he asked.

"Whatever she wants, and whatever you have that will get this over with quickly." Stevie smiled at him in a way that took Lillian aback. She'd only ever seen Stevie flirt with Angie, and this was an entirely different version of her friend. The bartender grinned and served up a shot of something golden, not taking his eyes off Stevie as he asked for Lillian's order.

"I guess whatever that is."

She never found out what they'd been served. All she knew was it burned, and she drank more of them than was wise while Stevie flirted her way to a lower bar tab. A woman in a tight dress and impeccable eyebrows slid into the space beside Lillian to place her order. She turned to Lillian while she waited and looked her up and down. The open admiration, combined with the effect of the liquor, made her shiver. It had been a while since a woman had looked at her like that.

"Want to dance?" Stevie said in Lillian's ear.

"Yes," she said, looking away from the stranger. Stevie took her hand and hauled her toward the source of the ungodly noise. It was like someone had put pop music through a blender, which was probably trendy, but just gave her a headache. Stevie delivered her to the circle of bodies containing Morgan, Emilia, Angie, and Stormy, and some of her anxiety faded—though that could also have been the drinks.

"There you are!" Angie threw herself into Lillian's arms and proceeded to move her hips against Lillian's with so much command Lillian was forced to move with her or be knocked off balance.

"Get it, girl," said Stormy.

"I hate you all," Lillian said as Angie tossed her loose hair back and laughed.

The song changed to one she recognized, and she allowed herself to dance despite the heels, grateful for her daily workouts as the burn in her thighs intensified. Emilia pulled away from Morgan, who looked so pathetically devastated that the rest of them burst into hysterics, and took Lillian's hand. She let Emilia twirl her around.

"Look at you, turning heads," Emilia said as she reeled her in.

"Shut up."

"No, really."

"I thought you were on my side." She had to shout to be heard over the music.

"Fine, you look hideous and everyone hates you."

"Thank you."

The song changed several more times as the crowd grew, and eventually she broke away to find the restroom. Once she'd managed to locate the facilities, navigate the line, and perch above the seat—there was no way in hell she would ever sit on a public toilet seat—and then force her way back out again, she realized she'd lost her friends. The crowd of bodies pulsed in time with the music, and she leaned against the brick wall to take some of her weight off her heels.

"Crazy, right?"

She glanced up to see the woman from the bar wipe a manicured hand across her forehead. Lillian dreaded small talk. She could do it with clients, but not in situations like this.

"Yeah. Crazy."

"Better than the last one," said the woman.

"I wouldn't know."

"First time?"

"Yeah."

"Then you should be dancing." The woman held out a hand to Lillian. Hesitating only a moment, she took it. This was why she'd come, wasn't it? Or why her friends had wanted her to come—to dance with strangers and forget about Brian and Ivy. Her new dance partner was very pretty, with full lips, liquid brown eyes, and glossy dark hair that cascaded down her back in waves. The dress was a little tighter than what Lillian considered tasteful, but that wasn't necessarily a bad thing she decided as the woman pulled her closer. She could smell the alcohol on her breath, along with her perfume and the underlying musk of her sweat.

"I'm Sara."

"Lillian."

"Nice to meet you, Lillian."

Sara moved well, gliding against Lillian and pulling away, aware of her body and what it could do. Lillian tried to relax. This was what people did. It was normal.

Sara's hands moved, too. Her sides shivered as Sara's palms passed over them, but when hands moved to her ass, she stiffened.

"No?" Sara asked.

"Not yet."

"Whatever you want."

"I think I need something to drink."

"Of course." Sara let her go with a smile that managed to hold regret and understanding. She didn't follow.

Lillian stumbled as the floor changed from wood to brick. A slim man with cheerful yellow suspenders steadied her. "Look at you in those heels, girl," he said with admiration. She thanked him and wove her way to the bar, cursing Angie under her breath.

The bartender from earlier had been replaced with a butch woman younger than Lillian who smiled at her respectfully and who reminded her of Morgan.

"Water," she said. The bartender nodded and filled her a plastic cup.

"Anything for your friend?" asked a voice to her left.

She whirled, spilling ice water down her front, and glared at Ivy Holden.

"What are you doing here?"

"Hello to you, too."

Ivy's black dress bared her shoulders but covered her arms to the wrist, and her blond hair looked artfully windblown as it fell down her chest. Her makeup, too, was a study in the subtle art of casual glamour—a touch of lipstick, lush mascara, and a contour job that would have made the man who'd admired her heels swoon with envy. Ivy looking gorgeous wasn't anything new. Ivy crashing Lillian's night off, however, was.

"What are you doing here?" she repeated.

Ivy opened her mouth, then shut it, as if she'd thought better about whatever she'd been about to say. "You look nice, Lil."

"Fuck you."

"I'm serious."

"I don't care if you're serious or not." She turned back to the bartender, who had just finished serving the couple next to them. "Can I get—"

"A vodka martini. Ciroc, if you have it."

The bartender's eyebrows shot up into her hairline. "We do. Shaken?"

Lillian was too furious to speak.

"Yes. And I'll have one of the same."

"You can't do that," Lillian said as the bartender moved to mix the drinks.

"We called a truce, remember?" Ivy jerked her head at the dance floor. "But don't let me interrupt. You looked like you were having fun."

"You're not interrupting anything," Lillian said as curtly as she could, then realized she might have been better served returning to Sara and her wandering hands. "A truce doesn't mean you buy me drinks."

"Pretty sure it does, actually. Don't enemies toast or something?"

"Here you are," said the bartender.

"Put it on my tab," said Ivy.

"Hold on—"

"Please," Ivy said to the bartender, who nodded and backed away, probably sensing an impending bloodbath and going to find the bouncer.

"Anyway, isn't this a little too pedestrian for you?" Lillian said. "Don't you prefer yachts?"

"When I can get them, sure. This is fun, though." Ivy leaned back against the bar and presented Lillian with her profile as she sipped her drink. "Try the martini, Lil."

Lil. Ivy hadn't earned the right to use her nickname. Because tossing her drink in Ivy's face might get her thrown out, and because if she didn't put something in her mouth she might scream, Lillian drank. The vodka, predictably, was excellent, and she suspected the bartender had upped the quality of the vermouth from wherever they stored the spirits they served the wealthy people who kept places like this in business. She would not give Ivy the satisfaction of acknowledging its quality.

"I don't see your usual clique," she said. "Don't blondes just find you, like, magnetically?"

"Give it time. I'm new in town, remember?"

"Call up your country club."

"I didn't take you for a mean drunk."

"Just for you, Poison Ivy."

"See," said Ivy as she took another sip, "this is what I missed about you. You know exactly how to make a girl feel special."

The martini was sinfully good. Part of her wanted to shove it away to prove a point, but the part of her that had downed three shots earlier protested that if Ivy wanted to blow her money on women who hated her, that was her prerogative, and who was Lillian to waste a good drink?

"She didn't strike me as your type, anyway," Ivy continued.

"What would you know about my type?"

Ivy's green eyes avoided hers, and the barest suggestion of a blush colored her cheeks. Lillian wanted to slap her. She didn't get to play vulnerable after what she'd done. Ivy swirled her drink and watched her olive tumble around its depths.

"I'm right though, aren't I?" Ivy said at last as she looked up. "Or else you'd still be out there, and she wouldn't be all up on that chick."

Lillian didn't spare Sara a glance. "Were you watching me?"

Ivy shrugged.

"Ivy."

"What?"

"What the hell is this?"

"I told you. I want a truce."

"This isn't a truce." Lillian gestured at the space between them.

"I bought you a drink, didn't I?"

"So now I owe you?"

"That's not—"

"Save it." She turned on her heel, which was a mistake. Her ankle gave on her and she tilted sideways, spilling her drink and careening toward the bar.

Ivy caught her.

"Easy," Ivy said, and her voice was low and soothing, the way she might have spoken to a spooked horse. Lillian pulled away like she'd been scalded. An Ivy who sang off-key and who caught her instead of giving her an extra shove was dangerous. It made her unpredictable. She should never have let Angie talk her into these shoes or this outing. She belonged at home with her dogs and a glass of merlot, not in Portland, and Ivy—why *was* Ivy here? Ivy had dodged the question, but it wasn't like she'd come with a group of friends, unless they, like Lillian's friends, were somewhere on the dance floor. It was ludicrous to think Ivy had followed her here. That was beyond her usual brand of evil.

Ivy watched her with an uncharacteristically guarded expression while she turned over these ideas. Lillian met her eyes and held them, searching for a sign of whatever logic was driving her actions from within their swampy green depths.

Not swampy. Try as she might, faulting Ivy on her looks was a losing battle. Her eyes were the same piercing shade of green they had always been, flawed only in the way of gemstones.

"Want to dance?" Ivy asked. "I assume that's why you're here."

The old gauntlet, thrown once more. Shame sliced through her, followed by a cauterizing hatred that stopped the wound from bleeding. The smart thing to do would be to walk away. That was what the Lillian she'd worked hard to become would do. *Should* do. Looking at Ivy, however, she saw a flicker of something as old as their enmity and wondered at it with a clarity that had nothing to do with liquor. The hatred in her belly purred with delight.

"Sure," she said. "Why not?"

Ivy followed Lillian into the crowd with her mouth dry and a pounding in her ears that might have been the bass. Lillian's muscled legs went on forever in those jeans, aided by the heels, which didn't really seem Lillian's style, and the sway of her hips. Her dark hair was pulled up and gathered in a twist Ivy longed to undo, and when Lillian turned back around to face her, lips full beneath their gloss, Ivy had to swallow.

The Lillian Lee she had known, as a rule didn't show cleavage. Ivy had documented her entire wardrobe one year out of boredom. None of them were anything like this top.

Lillian at twenty-one had been cute. At twenty-three she'd been hot. Now, at thirty-one, she was stunning—or maybe Ivy just hadn't been willing to admit she'd noticed before now. The woman in the skanky red dress cut eyes at her a few yards away, clearly annoyed she'd stolen Lillian away, and on the far side of the room, visible for a moment through a shift in the crowd, she saw Stormy look around.

Her attention was snatched back by Lillian. She'd raised her hands and closed her eyes, for all the world looking like she was lost in the music. Ivy moved with her, keeping their bodies close but not touching, and taking advantage of Lillian's closed eyes to study the curve of her cheeks and the bow of her upper lip.

This was a terrible idea. She had told herself she wouldn't go out up until the moment she'd received Stormy's text, and even after, for a whole five minutes she had been sure she'd stay at home alone with her dog and her failing body. Then the pain had spiked and instead of making her feel tired, as it usually did, she'd felt reckless enough to call an Uber and pop more of her pain meds than she should have. Now, here she was, dancing with Lillian again.

Lillian's lashes fluttered open as she pulled the pin from her hair and let it fall in a tousled mass around her shoulders.

Sweet hell. She was unprepared for the smell of her shampoo or the way her hair softened her face. Her hands found Lillian's waist and rested there, lightly, though she wanted to grip her hard enough to leave the imprint of her fingers on her skin. Lillian didn't pull away.

The music changed to something with a faster, more insistent beat. Ivy, who had spent much of her teenage and college years in clubs, recognized the switch. The DJ wanted everyone on the floor. Lillian's body shifted beneath Ivy's hands, and her fingers tightened, pain forgotten as Lillian's skin burned her through the sheer fabric of her top.

Lillian's arms were still above her head, and she leaned into Ivy's hands, as trusting as the ballerinas Ivy had trained with before she'd convinced her parents to forgo ballet in favor of more riding lessons. Though perhaps, she amended, trusting wasn't the right word. It implied Ivy had control of the situation, which was so far from the truth it was laughable.

She wasn't laughing.

Lillian turned away from her, still allowing Ivy to hold her, and let their bodies touch. Desire arced through Ivy along the same paths the nerve pain usually took, but with far more pleasant results. Her hands dropped to Lillian's hips, sliding over the fabric of her jeans and down her thighs before she remembered who she was dancing with.

She didn't care. Couldn't care. Lillian's hair was smooth against her cheek, and the skin of her neck was close enough to brush with her lips, thanks to her heels. She did. Lillian's body responded with a shiver that made Ivy's eyes close as she struggled to control her breathing. Then Lillian began to dance in earnest, and it was all Ivy could do to stay upright.

Lillian dropped her hands and rested them on top of Ivy's. She waited for her to pull her hands away, flinging her off in disgust, but instead Lillian slid her palms up and down her knuckles before finding the exposed strip of skin between the hem of Ivy's dress and the tops of her boots, which came to just above the knee. Fingertips skimmed over her thigh. Unable to stop herself, she bit Lillian's neck, tasting her sweat. The way her skin yielded beneath her teeth, firm and warm and real, was intoxicating. She deepened the bite as Lillian dug her nails—short, as ever—into the meat of her thigh, and she nipped the muscle at the base of her neck before working her way back up to Lillian's jaw. Lillian was supple fire in her arms—and she knew how to use her ass. Ivy pulled her closer, then abandoned her grip on Lillian's hips to feel the flare of her waist again and the softer skin of her stomach. She could hear Lillian's breathing in her ear, as ragged as her own.

Another song faded in, and then another, before Lillian turned around again. They didn't look at each other; Ivy was intensely aware of the fragility of this moment, though there was nothing fragile about Lillian. She felt impossibly solid beneath her palms as she ran them up Lillian's back and over her shoulders, then into her hair, bringing their foreheads together. Lillian slid her thigh between Ivy's and pulled her closer.

Ivy couldn't help the whimper that escaped her lips as Lillian's leg pressed into her. The world vanished behind the backs of her eyes. She kept them shut, feeling Lillian's hands on her own hips and her own waist, thumbs pressing into the line just inside her pelvis. Her hands were now buried in Lillian's hair for support, and she had the sense that if she let go, she might slide bonelessly to the floor. She wanted Lillian's touch everywhere—her ass, her back, her breasts and her legs, and she wanted to rub herself shamelessly against Lillian in this crowded room, heedless of the proximity of their colleagues or the fact that this was the woman she'd once vowed to push in front of the nearest bus. That level of abandon, however, was a line she wouldn't cross even in her current state. She danced with Lillian like an adult who, if she lacked self-respect, at least had morals.

Then Lillian kissed her.

She didn't see it coming—courtesy of her shut eyes—and so she had no time to stifle the sobbing sound that mewled up in her throat as her lips parted to accept anything and everything Lillian Lee was ready to give. Lillian's lips moved over hers, taking their time. Ivy was aware she had pressed herself as close to Lillian as it was possible for her to get while remaining vertical, and that Lillian's hands on her ribs were doing more of the work of keeping her upright than her own legs.

She didn't care. Lillian took Ivy's lower lip in her teeth and drew slowly away, stealing Ivy's breath as she went.

She opened her eyes to find Lillian looking at her. Color stained her cheeks, and her lips were still parted from their kiss, but there was flint in her gaze. Ivy longed to strike herself against it.

"Lil?"

"I'm just fucking with you, Ivy," she said as she pulled away. "Why, did you like it?"

Lillian gave her a sharp-edged smile over her shoulder as she cut through the crowd and out of sight.

Lillian searched for her friends in the crowd, avoiding elbows and heels as best she could with her vision blurred. It wasn't the alcohol. She felt as if the past had superimposed itself on the present. Everywhere she looked, she saw two scenes: the club and a smaller party years ago in a friend's Ithaca apartment. It had been cold then, too—December in Upstate New York, right after finals. Everything had smelled like cheap booze and stress sweat as the veterinary students mingled and yelled to be heard over the bass beat. They'd each convinced themselves they'd failed their exams and would soon be the latest to drop out, ground to dust beneath the med school machine. Her friends had danced as they shouted at each other in the endless reiteration of the same exam questions. She couldn't take it. She downed her drink, unsure of what number it was, and moved away to find a drink and someone to talk to who wouldn't make her relive the horror of the afternoon's last test.

Ivy stood with her group of friends between Lillian and the drinks. Her scant top showed the smooth muscles of her shoulders, and her hair fell in blond ripples down her back. Light glinted off the golden strands. Somehow this seemed important. She stared at Ivy's hair until the other woman turned around with a frown.

"What, Lee?" Ivy crossed her arms and gave Lillian her best "why is the carpet speaking?" look.

"Nothing." She turned to go.

"No really, what? Bad exam?"

"Fuck you, Holden."

Ivy's eyes had a glaze to them that might have warned her if she had not been hammered.

"Try me, Lee," she'd said, though her gaze was unnaturally glued to Lillian's lips.

Morgan, ever her protector, swooped in at that moment and put a hand on Lillian's shoulder.

"She's good, Donovan," Ivy said, sounding irritated. "We're just dancing."

And they were—though more to the rhythm of their argument than the music.

"I'm good," Lillian told Morgan. Morgan shook her head and sauntered back to her other friends.

They shot exam questions at each other as the songs changed. Forgetting that this was exactly what she'd been trying to get away from, she warmed to her subject. Physiology was her weak point, but as Ivy fired answers back, some of the nausea receded. Ivy had chosen the same answers. Odds of them both being wrong were low.

"What about that cat question?" she asked at last. She didn't need to clarify. It was the question that had everyone sweating. Instead of answering, however, Ivy spun until her body was flush with Lillian's. They'd moved to a corner of the room away from their respective friends, and she placed her hands on Ivy's hips instinctively as she moved with her.

She'd danced with plenty of girls before. None of them had felt like this in her arms. Ivy leaned back into her and let Lillian take her weight. Exam questions fled her mind. Everything fled her mind. All that remained was the floral scent of her perfume.

Ivy turned around, flushed and wide-eyed, and something in Lillian snapped. She didn't protest when Ivy grabbed her hand and pulled her into the next room. The door shut. Music pounded through the walls.

"What—" she said before Ivy kissed her. She tasted like sweet wine and cloves, and her hair was honeyed silk in her hands. When they resurfaced, both rumple-haired and breathless, their lips bruised and puffy and Ivy's eyes more open and vulnerable than anything she'd ever shown Lillian before, she felt like molten glass.

"Ivy?"

"Come over to my place? Please?"

It was the please that had done her in, she reflected as the club came back into focus around her. She'd sounded so genuine. So real. A lie, of course. After a night she still dreamt of with alarming regularity, made all the worse by the longing that shadowed her for days after, Ivy had made her true feelings plain.

Nothing they'd whispered to each other beneath the moon had mattered. When the sun had risen, the Ivy Lillian knew returned.

"Get the fuck out of my house, Lee."

She'd been used.

"Who was the sexy blonde?" Stormy asked when Lillian found her friends again.

"Didn't get her name." If her friends hadn't noticed she'd been dancing with Ivy, she wasn't going to tell them. Morgan, at least, had definitely been distracted—the way she looked at Emilia would have been nauseating on someone Lillian didn't love. Stevie was too short to see over the crowd, so unless she'd gone to the bar or the bathroom, Lillian thought she was safe there, too. That left Angie and Stormy. Angie pouted, suggesting another get out of jail free card had found its mark. Stormy, however, was studying her out of narrowed eyes.

Shit.

"Lillian had a sexy blonde?" Stevie asked. Morgan and Emilia broke apart to stare at her, and she prayed the music would swell into a sudden and earsplitting crescendo. It didn't.

"Yeah she did," said Stormy.

"Where did she go?" Stevie craned her head to see over the crowd, which was a futile pursuit. Lillian scanned the way she'd come but saw no sign of Ivy. Disappointment and relief mixed with the cocktail in her stomach.

"Did you get her number?" Angie asked.

"Nope."

"Why not?"

"She wasn't my type."

"She sure looked like your type," said Stormy. "Ever heard of leaving room for Jesus?"

"You're Jewish."

"You're bad."

"What I am is tired. Any chance you want to head out soon?"

"Sure." Stevie rolled her shoulders. "My ass is sore."

"In a minute. Lil, grab a breath of fresh air with me?" said Stormy.

Lillian followed Stormy outside on wobbly legs. Squats had not prepared her for dancing like that. Nothing could have prepared her for dancing like that—not with Ivy. Her victory didn't change the fact that the places Ivy had touched her still tingled, or that her hands had memorized the way Ivy's ass had felt in that dress. *When did I touch her ass?* And Ivy's mouth on her neck—she breathed in the cold night air, choking on the cloud of cigarette smoke from the smokers clustered outside the door, and tried to clear her mind while Stormy bummed a cigarette off a grungy hipster with an easy smile.

"You shouldn't smoke," she said.

"You know I don't. But it's cold as fuck out here. Want to tell me why you were making out with Poison Ivy?"

"Not particularly."

"I thought you said you hated her."

"I do."

"That's not what it looked like."

"I can hate her and still . . ." she trailed off.

"Want to jump her bones?"

"Crude, but yes." She sagged against the wall. "I told you things were complicated."

Tonight proved that unequivocally. Walking away from Ivy was much, much harder than she cared to admit to herself. The tether between them tightened with each step.

"That's what she said, too."

Lillian froze. "What do you mean?"

"She came into the brewery yesterday and I asked her what her deal was."

"What? Why?"

"You're my friend. I was curious."

"You're nosy."

"I was right," said Stormy.

"About what?"

"She's into you."

"Ivy Holden is not into me." Even she could hear the bitterness in her words.

"Your hickey says otherwise."

"I do not have a hickey. I'm a doctor, not a sixteen-year-old."

"Tell that to your mirror."

Lillian felt the spot on her neck where Ivy's lips had been and frowned. Then, as she stared at her friend, her frown deepened. "Did you tell her to come out tonight?"

Stormy took a drag of her cigarette and exhaled away from Lillian before answering. "Yes."

"What the hell?"

"You can't honestly be mad at me. I saw you. You had a good time."

Lillian found herself speechless with rage for the second time that night.

"Oh. Shit," said Stormy. "You are mad."

"Yes."

"Lil—"

Lillian left her to finish her cancer stick and shoved her way back inside, where, with one look at her face, the rest of her friends wordlessly made for the coat check. Ivy was nowhere to be seen.

Victory.

As they drove, she leaned her head against the windowpane and let the cold glass leech the flush from her cheeks. She'd won, yes—but at Ivy's game.

Chapter Five

Sunday dawned with a full body ache that started in each of her pressure points and worked its way outward. Darwin burrowed deeper into the crook of her neck and grumbled in his sleep, not keen on rising early unless pitched out of bed, and she breathed in the sweet smell of sleeping dog. He always smelled a little bit like maple syrup.

A gray morning sent shreds of mist rising off the river, and the clouds looked like they were thinking about snow, if not in the immediate future, then as a worthy possibility for tomorrow or the next day. Black branches swayed slowly against the gray-white of the sky.

Lillian. She touched her burning fingers to her lips and then traced the nerve pain along her jaw and down her numb neck, the pain forgotten as she remembered what it had felt like to kiss and be kissed by Lillian Lee.

"I'm just fucking with you, Ivy."

She'd earned that a hundred times over. And yet, there was only so much a person could fake, and Lillian's pulse had beat just as quickly as her own. That hadn't all been anger, had it?

Would it matter?

I am not hate fucking my coworker, she told herself as the idea spread like warm honey through her limbs. Not today, anyway. Today she needed to focus on reclaiming her nerve endings for less thrilling pursuits than their current pastime, which combined electric shock therapy with freezing numbness. No one had told her numbness could hurt. It seemed obscenely unfair.

"Why, did you like it?"

She had. Too much.

And yet, she didn't think working with Lillian after this would be a problem. In so many ways, it would be easier than the way things had been going. They were even now, and it wasn't like things between them could have gotten any worse. If anything, they'd just leveled up their game, and she'd always been good at playing with high stakes. The only part about last night she regretted was seeing Lillian dancing with another person. The molten jealousy that had poured down her throat rose again as she recalled the proprietary way that woman had looked at Lillian.

Lillian was hers, whether to torment or to touch, and the depth of that jealousy unnerved her.

Unnerved. She wished she could unnerve herself. Literally. She fumbled for the gabapentin she kept by her bed and popped an extra two before flopping back down, exhausted by the effort. Her doctor had warned her that moving would likely trigger a flare-up, but that with luck it would die down like the others after a few weeks or months. In the meantime, she would lie here until the drugs took the edge off, force herself to eat and drink something, and then slather her body in whatever cream did the trick today. Sometimes the medicated nerve cream worked, while other times over the counter IcyHot at least changed the sensation from biting ants beneath her skin to the tingling the menthol promised on the label.

She groaned as her phone rang.

"Hello?" she said, recognizing the number of the barn manager where she stabled her horse.

"Hi, Ivy? It's Kelly. I just wanted to let you know I pulled Freddie from pasture this morning. He got kicked real bad by Moose, and he's favoring the left hind."

"Swelling?"

"Some. Mostly above the stifle."

"Keep him on stall rest. I'll be in soon."

She hung up and breathed slowly out through her nose, then pushed the covers back and propelled herself out of bed.

The full-length mirror in her bathroom greeted her. She glared at her body. Toned muscle and smooth, pale skin covered the screaming nerves beneath, hiding the illness that was stealing her life. People lived with MS for years and years before it became debilitating, she knew, but the thought of those years—waiting for the damage to worsen, knowing there was no reversing it—left a coppery taste of fear in her mouth. She wrapped her arms around herself and stared at her eyes in the mirror. She was alone in this, and she always would be, trapped in this body until it failed completely. All the money in the world couldn't buy her way out.

The barn was quiet when she pulled up. A few cars sat in the lot, but the barn aisle was empty when she walked in. Horse heads popped out over several stalls, including Freddie's black nose.

"Hey, baby," she said to him as he thrust his muzzle into her chest. She eased into his stall and brushed some shavings out of his mane. His hide was nicked with bites, and the kick on his hind had left a half moon cut with significant swelling. He let her probe it with the patience of years.

"How's he looking?" asked Kelly from over the stall door. Kelly was a broad woman with thick dirty-blond hair she kept in a perpetually messy bun. She was also the reason Ivy had chosen this stable; Kelly radiated confidence and horsewomanship, and Freddie loved her.

"Have you tried putting him out by himself?"

"That's next. I thought Moose would go easy on him, but . . ." Kelly trailed off as she stroked Freddie's head. "I don't know what's going on with the herd. I'll change up the pasture rotations, though."

"Thanks." Ivy rested her cheek against Freddie's neck. "How's your baby?"

"Psychotic." Kelly was training a green colt with more speed than sense, and Ivy enjoyed watching her work when she happened to be in the barn. "He's going to break a leg."

"Freddie was like that once." She stroked his bay coat, feeling the velvet of his winter fuzz against her burning hands. Animals helped more than any medication. "Now he's a perfect gentleman, aren't you?"

"I just wish the rest of the herd would agree. Our turnout is limited, and he looks so sad out there by himself." Kelly paused. "I looked you up the other day. You were brilliant in the USEA intercollegiate series."

Pride for her horse swelled inside her. "All Freddie."

"Whatever you say. Do you still compete?"

"I don't have much time." Freddie arched his neck around to lip at her belt. She pushed him gently away. "And I don't want to ruin him over fences at his age."

"Dressage circuits," said Kelly. "He'd be stunning."

"He is."

Kelly nodded and gave Freddie a parting pat. Ivy leaned her head against his flank and let the brain fog descend again as Kelly's boots sounded on the padded concrete, growing more distant with each exhale.

Lillian listened to the sound of the greenhouse fountain trickling over the rocks she'd hand selected from the coast and wondered if she would ever feel tranquil again. Hermione lay curled in her lap. Muffin usually avoided the greenhouse in daylight, finding it too warm, but Circe munched hibiscus flowers in her sand enclosure. Their presence barely took the edge off the buzzing knife of anger and something else, something less definable, that sawed her each time she breathed. Her anger at Stormy at least made sense. But her feelings about Ivy? Those defied logic.

She'd thought she'd gotten over the pull of Ivy's body, replacing it bit by bit with more hatred. It didn't matter that she'd won their most recent battle, pulling the same trick Ivy had pulled on her years ago. It couldn't matter, not once she'd seen the longing in Ivy's eyes or heard Ivy's breath catch when she kissed her.

Ivy wanted her. Ivy wanted her with the same intensity, the same melting, irrevocable need that had driven them together again and again, each clash as satisfying as it was wounding. And if Ivy still wanted her, that meant Lillian couldn't fool herself into believing the night they'd shared was some sick game on Ivy's part.

It *had* meant something to her.

She breathed in the humid air of her greenhouse and tried to capture some of its serenity. The sharp scent of leaves and flowers mingled with the subtler scents of earth and water, but they did not restore her equilibrium. She didn't know if anything ever would. Ivy's roots ran too deep. They'd sent hairline fractures into the bedrock even here beneath her greenhouse, the one place she could always count on to ground her.

An hour later found her on the road toward Bath. Her dogs slumbered in the backseat of her Subaru Crosstrek as she took Route One through the coastal towns of mid-coast Maine. When she pulled into the driveway of her parents' small colonial, situated within walking distance of Bath Iron Works, where one of her mothers worked, Hermione perked up. She knew where her royal presence was most appreciated. Muffin, who believed all humans existed for butt scratches and ear rubs and did not discriminate, exhibited her usual enthusiasm for arriving at any destination where she'd been fed in the past. Lillian let the dogs out of the car to hop around the yard and knocked on the green front door.

Her mother opened it and promptly scooped Hermione into her arms and kissed the dog on the nose. Her other mother, Daiyu, shouted a greeting from the kitchen.

"Hi ma," Lillian said. "Glad to see I'm still your favorite."

June Lee held Hermione up for a second kiss and ignored her only child. Muffin barreled past to where Daiyu was presumably preparing something to feed hungry dogs. Lillian heard her mom greet the mutt with an exclamation of how fat Muffin was getting, followed by a series of pet names that should have embarrassed even the most shameless of golden retrievers. She kicked off her shoes and slid into a worn pair of house slippers before padding down the carpeted hallway to the kitchen.

"Mama," she said to Daiyu. "Muffin is not fat. She's fluffy."

"I watched that comedian on Netflix. I know what "fluffy" means."

"Of course you did."

Daiyu's chin-length hair framed her face, and she tucked a dark strand behind her ear as she hugged her daughter. "You look tired, *xiao moguai.*"

"I didn't sleep well," Lillian admitted.

"I'll make some tea." Daiyu busied herself with the pot, leaving Lillian to examine the production taking place on the counter. Suet, bird seed, molds, pinecones, and a jar of peanut butter lined the countertop.

"Feeding the squirrels?" she asked.

"Not this winter. I have a new system. Those rats won't get a single nibble."

Daiyu's battle with the squirrels was legendary, even at the veterinary hospital where she worked as a technician. It was also futile. Lillian secretly believed Daiyu's efforts to protect her bird feeders were only breeding wilier squirrels.

"What is it?"

"Fishing line."

"Didn't you try that a few years back?"

"She did," said June, entering the kitchen with Hermione nestled on her hip. June wore her hair cropped short and graying, but she was still handsome. Stevie liked to call her a silver fox, which amused June and mortified Lillian. Age was chiseling her where it was softening Daiyu, as if it was determined to distill them down to the essence of their natures. It always surprised people when they found out June had carried Lillian instead of Daiyu—though the whiteness of Lillian's skin should have been a clue.

Sunlight filled the kitchen and glinted off the stainless-steel molds Daiyu pressed her mixture of suet and birdseed into. The smell of steeping oolong filled her with some of the contentment she'd been lacking since Ivy Holden had arrived in Seal Cove.

"Why aren't you sleeping?" Daiyu asked. "Brian?"

Her mothers had liked Brian, though June had always held herself a little aloof, as if she didn't think he was good enough for her daughter.

"No," she said. She'd hardly thought about Brian, which she couldn't entirely attribute to avoidance. Her breakup had been transcended by Ivy.

"Work?" June guessed.

"Sort of." She perched on the counter, earning a disapproving look from Daiyu. "Ivy."

June's frown clouded her features. Daiyu tutted in displeasure. Lillian had complained bitterly about Ivy all through vet school, and her mothers shared her animosity.

"That girl has no business making your life harder than it is," said June.

Except Ivy wasn't a girl anymore. Something about her had changed—grown even, and she didn't trust herself around it.

"What did she do?" asked Daiyu.

She thought about telling her moms the truth, but wavered. They wouldn't understand. *She* didn't understand. Reason and her feelings for Ivy were like water and clay. One ran right off the other.

"She's . . .distracting."

June snorted. "You're not in school anymore. She is not your competition."

"She was never your competition. You're a better doctor and a better person than that privileged . . ." Daiyu trailed off and pursed her lips.

Ivy symbolized everything about America that Lillian hated. Her privilege—courtesy of her race, her good looks, her wealth, and her cultural capital—was everything her moms had fought against their entire lives. They'd raised Lillian to succeed in a world that wanted nothing to do with her or her family, doubly stigmatized by ethnicity and sexuality, and she'd done it. Ivy, meanwhile, had merely set one foot in front of the other on the red carpet the world rolled out to greet her. She could not tell her parents about the other half of her feelings for Ivy. Not only would they not understand, they would potentially see it as a betrayal.

"I just needed to get away for a few hours," she said instead.

"Good. Your mother could use a hand with her birds," said June.

"Not fair. You just don't want to help."

"So suet me."

Daiyu and Lillian groaned at the pun. She grabbed the teacups to serve her family and tried to forget about Ivy and the way her lips had yielded beneath her own, or the way Ivy's body had melted into hers when she'd parted her legs, Ivy's hands tangled in her hair and her breath coming fast and hot into Lillian's mouth as Ivy surrendered control for the first time in the entirety of their feuding relationship.

The tea did not quench her sudden thirst.

Ivy left for work Monday morning with enough time to stop into Storm's-a-Brewin'. Her first appointment was an in-clinic case, which would put her in direct proximity to Lillian. She whistled at Darwin as she opened the door of her truck for him.

Lillian thought she'd won the last round.

Ivy, however, had other ideas.

Stormy smiled at her as she took her place in line behind a motley assembly of patrons. She flexed her hands in her coat pockets to try to dispel some of the lingering weakness. Yesterday had been bad; today, however, would be better. Or at least, it would be if the power of thought had anything to do with it.

"What can I get for you?" Stormy asked when she reached the counter.

"You told me I should try the dark roast."

"And I just brewed a fresh pot."

"I'll also take your medium roast."

Stormy's eyebrows rose, and she tilted her head. "Trying both?"

"Bringing one for a friend."

"A mutual friend?"

Ivy handed over her card without answering.

"Whatever you do, don't tell her I told you it's her favorite, or that she sprinkles cinnamon on top and takes soymilk but no sugar. I'm already in trouble."

Ivy didn't ask why Stormy was in trouble with Lillian. She suspected the answer had everything to do with Stormy's impromptu invitation to the club, which, judging by Lillian's reaction, Stormy had not shared with her friends. Aware of the pressure from the line behind her, she accepted the to-go cups and did not ask Stormy why she had issued the invitation in the first place, or why she had just given her instructions for how to fix Lillian's coffee.

Second-guessing Stormy's motives wouldn't get her anywhere. *She's Lillian's friend, not yours.* The reminder chilled her, despite the hot coffee in her hand. She was alone here, which had been what she wanted. It was too late to wish for something different. Instead, she focused on something more achievable: conquest by coffee.

Ambulatory fell to Morgan today and the clinic truck was already on the road. The rest of the hospital staff was there, however, including Lillian. Ivy was disappointed to see that her car was out of the shop. She ordered Darwin to heel and pushed through the back door, coffee cups in hand.

Georgia greeted her with her usual good humor. Ivy asked after her mother, who, she was relieved to hear, was doing much better after her ordeal in the hospital. Kidney stones were no joke, though Georgia managed one or two at her mother's expense, imitating her mother's crush on her surgeon.

"Is Dr. Lee here?" she asked.

"In the treatment area with a drop-off."

Ivy strolled through the clinic and into the treatment area, affecting her best nonchalant gait. Lillian was examining an African gray parrot with gentle hands, and Ivy leaned in the doorway to watch as Lillian carefully plucked a blood feather from beneath the parrot's wing.

"Good morning," she said when Lillian finished.

Lillian's shoulders stiffened, but there was a warily triumphant cast to the set of her jaw, which Ivy had vivid memories of kissing less than forty-eight hours previously.

"Good morning."

"Coffee?"

Triumph faded to confusion, then irritation, which made Ivy smile. She'd been right: Lillian *had* thought she'd won.

"You brought me coffee?"

Sensing the curiosity of the assistant, Ivy fixed a professional smile on her face. "I can see if Georgia wants it. It's Stormy's medium roast."

"That's . . . very kind of you."

"Is that a yes?" She waved the coffee in a half circle.

"Yes." Lillian drew out the syllables in her hesitation.

Ivy set the coffee on the counter and threw Lillian what she intended to be a careless smile. It faltered under Lillian's eyes, and she found herself clutching her own cup of coffee too tightly.

"Dr. Holden?" Shawna asked.

She jumped, spilling coffee on her hand. She hissed at the pain of the hot liquid against her raw nerves.

Lillian was at her side and plucking the drink from her hand before she had time to register her movement.

"Run that under cold water. Stormy's coffee is hot." She steered Ivy toward the sink. Lillian's grip on her shoulders was authoritative and nothing like the hands that had slid over her body as they danced. She shivered all the same as she opened the cold water tap and thrust her scalded skin beneath it. An involuntary hiss escaped her. The cold triggered an unpleasant numbness, which spread past her wrist and into her forearm.

"Want me to return Grayson to his parents?" asked the assistant who had been left with the parrot.

"Please, and tell them I'll be in shortly."

"Your first appointment is outside," Shawna said when Ivy turned away from the sink. "I'll get them unloaded."

"Thank you," said Ivy.

In the quiet that followed, she pulled her hand out from the water and patted it dry with a paper towel. Lillian remained beside her. It was harder to meet her eyes than it should have been. Her hand hurt in a way that promised a long and unrelenting day, despite her earlier optimism, and that was nothing she needed Lillian to see.

"Are you okay?" Lillian asked.

"Yes."

Lillian took her hand and turned it over. The familiarity in the gesture cemented her feet to the ground. She couldn't move. She could barely breathe.

"It looks all right," said Lillian as she examined the skin. "And serves you right. You do know that, don't you?"

She looked up. Amusement, anger, and something almost tender filled Lillian's face.

"I don't know what you're talking about." Ivy let her gaze flicker to Lillian's lips. She saw the flush that crept across Lillian's cheeks, and satisfaction drowned out the pain.

"You know exactly what I mean."

They had only a matter of minutes before someone else wandered to the back, and mindful of the clinic security cameras, she checked their angles before speaking.

"But I really don't. Stay late tonight and explain it to me?"

"What—"

"Oh, and Lillian?" She used Lillian's full name, enjoying the way it felt in her mouth. Lillian's flush deepened. "I did like it."

With that, she pulled away and left Lillian standing there. She forced herself not to look back with a new appreciation for Orpheus.

The day passed in a steady stream of patients. Lillian saw appointments on Mondays and procedures on Tuesdays, which meant, in reality, that on Mondays she squeezed procedures in during what was, in theory, her lunchbreak since she was nearly always booked up. Under no circumstances would she be staying late tonight to talk with Ivy.

Stormy's text message didn't help.

SA: *Respecting your space, babe, but let me know when you're ready to talk. Want to apologize and buy your love with chocolate stout.* <3

An apology would mean talking about what had happened, which would mean acknowledging that while Stormy had set the weekend's events in motion, it had been Lillian and Ivy who determined its course. She wished she could talk to Morgan. Morgan would do her best to understand, but her friend had been distracted since Emilia entered her life, and she was too close to the problem. Angie would also understand, but Lillian found herself reluctant to bring it up. What would she even say? I want to fuck the woman I've hated for years, and yes, I am also fairly sure I still hate her? Plus, she's my coworker? That wasn't healthy. It was downright destructive. And Angie would probably tell her to go for it; self-destruction was basically her MO.

She was barely able to concentrate on her last appointment. By the time she discharged the guinea pig and finished her paperwork, her hands were sweating, and she had to ask Georgia to repeat herself several times. Danielle was off-clinic today, which meant if she stayed after hours, she would be alone with Ivy.

Which she was definitely not going to do.

"I'm taking off unless you need me," said Georgia.

"I'm all set. Is anyone still here?"

"Equine, I think. Want me to check for you?"

"No thanks. I'll double-check before I lock up." She gave Georgia what she hoped was a confident smile.

"Have a good night, Dr. Lee."

The sound of the door clicking shut echoed in the empty hospital. Lillian tapped her fingers on the counter and stared at the computer. All her paperwork was done. There was absolutely no reason for her to stay, and every reason for her to leave.

A different door opened and closed. Footsteps on the clinic floor made their way from the barn entrance to where she waited, every muscle in her body tense.

"Hey," said Ivy. The clinic polo worn by the large animal staff clung to her frame, and Lillian flattened her hand on the counter to keep herself from fidgeting.

"I was just about to head out," she said.

Ivy shrugged and didn't move, nor did she stop staring at Lillian.

"How's your hand?" she asked to fill the silence. Someone needed to tell Danielle those polos were a criminal offense. Morgan and Stevie left them strewn around the house, and since she often picked up after them, it was an easy leap to imagine how Ivy's body would feel beneath the soft cotton.

"Fine," said Ivy.

She cast around for something else to say. "Thank you for the coffee."

"Any time."

"But you shouldn't have."

"Why not?" Ivy asked. "I was there. You drink coffee. I grabbed you a cup."

"You didn't buy coffee for the rest of the staff."

93

"Want me to?"

Lillian glared at her. Ivy Holden could buy coffee for the entire hospital for the rest of the year and think nothing of the expense. "That's very generous of you."

"Not really," said Ivy. "But if that's what it takes to get you to drink it . . ."

"You can't do this."

"What, buy you a drink?"

"Yes."

"Why? Afraid you might like it?" Ivy's voice dropped into a low, mocking register.

Lillian stood and pushed her chair back so suddenly it rolled into the cabinet opposite. "Whatever this is—"

Ivy cut her off. "You know exactly what this is, Lil."

"No, I don't."

"You sure?"

"Goodbye, Ivy." She grabbed her bag and cut through the nearest exam room to get to the safety of her car.

"Lil," Ivy called from behind her. "You forgot your jacket."

She paused in the middle of the room and looked back. Ivy held her coat out to her, and the light from the doorway framed her against the darkness of the room. Her lean silhouette posed a challenge. Light played along the curve of her waist and haloed her blond hair, suggesting the very paths Lillian's hands wanted to explore. But there was also arrogance in that posture. Ivy knew Lillian wanted her. Knew, and mocked her.

Anger licked the same depths as desire. Somehow, despite pushing Ivy away at the club, she still felt like prey. Ivy would not win—even if that meant denying herself. She moved to take the jacket just as Ivy shut the door.

The exam rooms had softer lights than the rest of the hospital, designed to soothe as well as illuminate. Lillian opened her mouth to demand Ivy stop fucking around, then swallowed her reprimand. She was alone in a room with Ivy, who was looking at her with a dare her body longed to accept.

"Ivy," she said, half plea, half curse. Ivy set Lillian's jacket on the counter and reclined against it. To get to her clothing, Lillian would have to either ask again or reach around Ivy. Half of her demanded she throw Ivy against the counter and sink her teeth into that smile. The other half urged flight. The muscles in her body trembled with indecision. Ivy's smile widened.

Don't play, she warned herself.

"May I have my coat?"

"Sure." Ivy made no move to give it to her. The taunt in her posture was now unmistakable. If Lillian seized her jacket and fled, she'd lose the upper hand she'd gained at the club. *And if I stay . . .* If she stayed, there was only one way this would end.

Do I want to go there again?

Want was the wrong word. She wanted it. She wanted it too much, and there were thorns in Ivy's eyes.

"Scared?" Ivy asked.

"Fuck you."

"I think you want to."

The burst of heat felt like fury as she closed the space between them and shoved Ivy hard against the counter with her hips while her lips found Ivy's mouth. Ivy's response was immediate. She laughed low in her throat, a sound that made Lillian want to scream. Ivy didn't get to control this.

Ivy didn't get to control *anything.*

Her fingers buried themselves in Ivy's hair, and she tossed the clip that bound it to the ground. Ivy's laugh turned into a moan as Lillian tangled her hands in the thick blond waves, using her grip to hold Ivy still as she parted her lips with her own. Ivy pushed back against her. She used the counter as leverage until Lillian was forced a staggering step backward. Ivy caught her around her waist with one arm, and braced herself against the nearest wall with the other as they collided with it. The impact wasn't enough to hurt, but it did momentarily stun her, which was all Ivy apparently needed—she pinned Lillian's hands to her sides and raked her teeth down the sensitive skin just above her shoulder.

Her knees threatened to give out as her breath came hard and fast. Ivy nipped her sharply—half goad, half promise. She cried out, not in pain, but because the sensation sent a shockwave through her that demanded some kind of release. She tried to break free of Ivy's grasp, but it was hard to fight when her skin had grown hypersensitive to every brush of Ivy's mouth. Ivy's tongue found the groove above her collarbone. She shuddered, no longer capable of coherent thought, and shut her eyes as Ivy pulled down the collar of her shirt.

Ivy's lips skimmed the hem of her camisole. She was vaguely aware Ivy's fingers were on the buttons of her blouse, undoing one at a time, but the fact that her hands were now free was secondary to the shuddering breaths wracking her body as Ivy's mouth worked lower and lower. When Ivy yanked her shirt off her shoulders, following the motion with a bite, however, the surge of desire triggered instinct. She grabbed Ivy by her belt and pulled her closer. The heat between them built as she grabbed a handful of Ivy's hair once more. Ivy's green eyes were unfocused, but they sharpened as Lillian pivoted them, guiding Ivy by her hair until she had her back against the counter where they'd started.

"Get up."

Ivy obeyed. She relinquished her grip on Ivy's hair and tugged her shirt out from her work pants, using the height of the counter to her advantage as she revealed the smooth skin of Ivy's stomach. Memory flashed: *snow, a stumbling, drunken run from Natalie's party, hand in hand, and then the strobing lights of passing cars through an unfamiliar window as Ivy lay beneath her.*

Stop.

This was not then. This was now, and right now Ivy shivered as she ran her hands up her sides. Her touch was light; she wanted to scratch her, to dig her nails into the thin muscles covering her ribs and the curvature of her hips. She wanted to mark her. She wanted to see the evidence of her touch on Ivy's pale skin, and she wanted Ivy to see it, too. She wanted to stain her so deeply Ivy couldn't shrug it off or walk away.

Ivy tried to fumble with Lillian's hair tie. She raked her nails down Ivy's back. Ivy cried out as she wrapped her legs around Lillian to draw her in closer. The feel of her skin giving beneath her nails was even more intoxicating than she remembered. She did it again, and again

Ivy whimpered, arching into the touch. Ivy's lace bra met first her gaze—only Ivy would wear something like that to work—and then her teeth as she teased the nipples half-visible through the sheer fabric while her hands continued scratching their manifesto.

"Oh God, Lil."

The strong muscles of Ivy's back tensed beneath her hands as her teeth dragged over her nipple. Her mouth found the swell of breast above the lace. She traced the cleft between with her tongue, then bit down hard. Ivy's hips jerked. She heard a thud as Ivy's head made contact with the cabinet behind her.

She bit and sucked past Ivy's full breasts and down along her side, leaving marks behind. They filled her with a savage satisfaction. If it hurt, Ivy made no move to stop her. Shirtless, the dark green lace of her bra stark against her pale skin and her hair tumbling around her shoulders in a heavy sheet, Ivy's beauty destroyed her. She stood, staring, and was therefore unprepared for Ivy's counterattack.

Ivy slid from the counter and tore Lillian's shirt from her back. Her hands were warm as she splayed her fingers over the skin above Lillian's hips and turned her around so her back was to Ivy. She let Ivy ease her camisole over her head, the memory of the club clouding her senses as Ivy's fingers undid the clasp of her belt, then the button, before sliding back up her stomach and to her breasts.

Lillian's bra was simple and practical. Ivy unsnapped it, letting it fall as she cupped Lillian's breasts and rolled her nipples between thumb and forefinger. She felt the moan building inside her and bit her lip, but it broke free anyway, need transformed into sound. Ivy's lips were on her ear, tracing the outer shell and then covering it to whisper, "I want you, Lillian. Fuck, I want you."

She reached over her shoulder to hold the back of Ivy's neck as she leaned into her body, Ivy's words echoing in the spaces between her atoms. Ivy's tongue flickered over her ear in the wake of those words. Her knees momentarily gave out. One of Ivy's hands still held her breast, but the other slid into the top of her pants, brushing the fabric of her underwear while she teased her ear with her tongue, making a promise she desperately hoped Ivy intended to keep. It occurred to her, very dimly, that they were in an exam room, and that tumbling Ivy to the floor would be unhygienic. The unfairness of that fact was wiped clean by Ivy, who dipped her hand lower, still over the fabric, and into the wet heat at Lillian's center.

Blues and greens swirled in the corner of her vision. She hadn't been touched in months by anyone other than herself, and she'd forgotten—how had she forgotten?—the way it felt to be stroked by another person, to melt into the touch, to lose herself entirely beneath the hands and mouth of someone she desired.

Even if that person was Ivy.

Lillian's breath came in gasps as Ivy held her, and the feeling of Lillian in her arms, letting her hold her, trusting her to keep her upright, was mesmerizing. Lillian's nipple hardened against her palm, and lower down—she didn't bother biting back her moan as she eased Lillian's underwear aside to stroke the delicate skin around her opening. Lillian's body shook as she arched into her hand.

How many times had she lain awake imagining this? Remembering this? She felt Lillian's desire building as she teased her, Lillian's hair against her face and her ear—she'd always liked Lil's ears, unpierced and perfect—pressed against her lips. She wanted to fuck Lillian now, right here, and she wanted to wait, drawing this moment out.

"Ivy, please," said Lillian as Ivy passed over her opening for the fifth time, dragging her fingers up to part around her clit, arousing without satisfying. The sound of Lillian begging closed like a fist around her heart. A growl rose in her throat: possessive, hungry. She released it into Lillian's ear. Her ecstatic shudder sent a mirrored thrill through her own body, and she licked the delicate shell before answering, tasting her words.

"No."

Lillian uttered a wordless curse and twisted, breaking free of Ivy's hold and crushing her mouth to hers. *Lil*, she had time to think, before Lillian stole her breath and her willpower and anything else not securely lashed down as she kissed all the light from the room and gathered it between them. Whining, blinding need drowned her. She fumbled for something to grab onto, finding the edge of the counter, and was aware that Lillian was undoing her pants as she fell back against the smooth wall. Lillian took Ivy's lower lip between her teeth and bit down. The pain sparked a cascade effect that sent desire spilling over as Lillian's hand slipped into her pants and under her underwear and into her.

She screamed into Lillian's mouth as the feeling of Lillian Lee inside her, moving, stroking where she needed it most built and built. Lillian didn't break the kiss. The weight of Lillian's body kept her standing, and Lillian buried her hand in her hair again, the tugging following the same rhythm as Lillian's fingers. She clung to her, arms around her neck, and her tongue entwined with Lillian's as Lillian took control. She felt her climax rising to meet her demands, and whimpered when Lillian stopped without warning, pressing into her and pinning her desire against her fingertips. Ivy's eyes flew open as Lillian smiled against her lips.

"Don't stop, Lil," she said. "Please."

"I never thought I'd hear you use that word."

"Lil—"

Lillian pushed deep inside her, then slowly withdrew, leaving Ivy shaking and gasping in frustration.

"Oh fuck," she said, still clinging to Lillian. "Oh fuck Lil, no, please."

"Why?"

"Lil, I swear to god, oh shit—" A shudder took her by surprise, and she rode it out, needing Lillian inside her again.

"You made my life hell." Lillian brushed her clit with the tip of her finger.

"You made mine hell, too," Ivy said between gasps. "More than you know."

"Tell me."

"I—" she couldn't speak with Lillian poised just above her clit, the barest hint of pressure resting against her, and Lillian's hold on her hair unflinching. She felt she might split open, unmade in a clinic exam room while Lillian laughed at her. "I wanted you."

"When?"

She jerked her hips, desperate for Lillian's touch, but Lillian pulled her hair and she trembled to a halt.

"Since second year."

Lillian parted her folds. Her touch was languorous, and lacked the urgency Ivy ached for. Lillian's lips were bare centimeters away from her own. Every time she tried to reach them, Lillian pulled away.

"Second year?" Lillian's voice rose. The brief show of vulnerability almost brought her to climax.

"Yes."

It had been long before that party, though she hadn't wanted to admit it to herself.

"Tell me why I shouldn't walk away from you right now, Ivy Holden."

"Because," said Ivy, breathless. "You want to fuck me."

Lillian searched her face with her brown eyes. Her lashes brushed her cheeks each time she blinked, and Ivy couldn't read her expression. Lillian's bare chest rose and fell against her own. She longed to taste that skin again.

"That's not a good enough reason."

"Isn't it?" Ivy managed to capture Lillian's lips for a second before Lillian pulled away, only to tilt Ivy's head back and kiss along her neck, her lips and teeth exquisitely rough. She didn't answer Ivy's question. That didn't matter. All that mattered was that Lillian's mouth was claiming her, and that the torturously slow rhythm of her fingers was increasing, skimming and then plunging in a way that turned the world red behind her eyelids. Her left leg had hooked itself around Lillian's waist at some point, and she used its leverage to ride Lillian's hand harder, her neck nearly as sensitive as her clit beneath Lillian's tongue.

"Lil?"

Morgan Donovan's distant voice broke through the insistent pulse at her core. Lillian straightened, still inside her, and met Ivy's eyes with shock writ large across her features.

"My car," said Lillian. "She knows I'm here."

Which meant she would come looking, and if nothing else, she'd notice the light on in the room and turn it off.

"Go," Ivy said, hating Morgan.

Lillian withdrew slowly, leaving Ivy shaking, and threw on her shirt and jacket before shoving her camisole and bra into her bag. Ivy struggled with her own shirt. Her hands refused to cooperate, though at least this was from thwarted desire and not nerve damage. Lillian reached for the door handle and shut off the light.

She ducked behind the table and rested her face in her hands as Lillian left her alone in the dark.

Chapter Six

"Surprised to see you still here," said Morgan as Lillian rounded the corner.

"I was just finishing up paperwork." She shoved her hands in the pockets of her pants to hide the evidence of Ivy's desire.

"Good. Come to Stormy's with us," said Stevie.

Stormy. She was still angry at her friend. More than that, however, she needed to get home and change into clothes that didn't smell like Ivy's perfume, because if she didn't, she was going to find herself in Ivy's driveway later on that night. Going out didn't fit into that plan. "Not tonight."

"Come *onnn*," said Stevie. "I need a baked good, and you and Angie haven't made anything in ages."

"We have a perfectly functional, fully stocked kitchen," she reminded her. "You are capable of baking things yourself."

"But am I?" said Stevie. "The last time I tried I lit the stove on fire. Also what happened to your hair?"

"My hair?" Lillian reached up to feel her head. Loose strands met her fingers, and she had a sudden image of how rumpled she must look. "Oh. Yeah. I got bored. Paperwork."

"You got bored," Morgan repeated. "You okay, Lil?" Her eyes drifted around the clinic, and Lillian realized Ivy's things were still on the counter.

"You know what? Yes. Let's go to Stormy's." She needed to get them out of here before Morgan came to conclusions she wasn't prepared to address. "Maybe she has some leftover muffins."

"Or scones." Stevie said. "I love absconding with scones."

Scones were not what she wanted in her mouth. She trailed behind Stevie, hesitating at the door. Ivy's perfume clung to her skin as well as her clothes, and her hands smelled like Ivy—sharp and sweet at the same time, like her namesake.

"Lil, c'mon."

The sanctuary of her car came as a relief. She rested her head against her steering wheel as Morgan and Stevie piled into Morgan's truck across the lot. At least Ivy's truck was parked behind the building out of her friends' sight.

"Holy hell," she whispered to her knees. "What am I doing?"

"Boifriend," Stormy sang out as they entered. Her expression faltered when she saw Lillian.

The pub was mostly empty. Several students with laptops and lattes lounged at the tables, but only a few people sat at the bar. It was, after all, a Monday night in November.

"Got anything with chocolate?" Stevie asked as she slid onto a barstool and leaned on her elbows to stare up at Stormy hopefully.

"You bet your sweet blond ass I do," said Stormy. "What are you in the mood for?"

"Carbs."

"Pain au chocolate?" Stormy's French, Lillian noted, was terrible.

"Yes."

A chocolate croissant appeared in front of a gratified Stevie as Morgan and Lillian took their seats beside her.

"How's Emilia?" Lillian asked Morgan.

"Good." Morgan's face broke into a broad smile. Lillian's heart warmed. Seeing Morgan happy took the edge off the turmoil in her

103

own life. Morgan deserved happiness, and Emilia was a wonderful human.

Emilia. She could talk to Emilia about Ivy. Emilia had no connection to the practice, and she hadn't known Lillian in vet school, which made her a safe repository for the emotions boiling inside her. Stormy, who she might also have turned to, had betrayed her trust—she glanced up at that moment to see Stormy staring at her with an anguished expression—which ruled her out.

"What can I get you two?" Stormy asked.

"Hot cider," said Morgan.

"You do know I only keep that on the menu for you, right?"

"That's why I love you."

"And you, darling?" Stormy turned to Lillian. Her eyes brimmed with apologies, but Lillian was unmoved.

"I'm all set. I had some of your coffee this morning."

Stormy blushed, and Morgan glanced between them with a crease of confusion between her brows.

A soy hot chocolate appeared in front of her a minute later. Lillian sighed and accepted it. Stormy was a meddler who needed to feed and hydrate everyone around her, which made her perfectly suited to her job, even if it sometimes made her difficult.

"I am so not ready for winter," Stevie said as she washed down her croissant with a hot chocolate of her own.

"You should take Olive skijoring," Morgan suggested, referring to the horse Stevie had adopted over the summer. "It would be good for her hind end."

"Skijoring?" Lillian asked.

"Skiing, but pulled by a horse or dog."

"Like waterskiing?"

"Yes," said Morgan.

"Horse people are insane."

Stormy made a noise of agreement, then blew out a breath. "Lil, I need to talk to you."

Morgan and Stevie blinked at Stormy's tone.

"Stormy—"

"Please."

Lillian slid off her stool and stepped around the counter, cursing Stormy for her lack of subtlety under her breath. Stormy ordered Morgan to man the bar and tugged Lillian into the back. Shelves of coffee beans, cups, baked goods, and kegs of beer lined the walls, along with the fridges, stove, and dishwasher. Stormy leaned against a keg and hugged her arms around herself.

"Lil, I'm so sorry."

"Are you?"

"I am. I should have told you I invited her."

"You shouldn't *have* invited her."

"Lil—"

"You know how much I—" she broke off. She couldn't bring herself to say, "hate her." "You know what she is to me."

"Actually, I'm not sure I do." Stormy's apologetic tone took on a more assertive timbre. "You talk about her all the time, and she clearly gets under your skin."

"Because she likes to drive me crazy."

"Devil's advocate, here, but it looked like you drove her crazy, too."

"Don't."

"Look." Stormy chewed on her lower lip. "She came in here the other day and she just seemed really sad. She asked about you. I'm a bartender. I see people like her all the time, and I know when someone feels shitty about something they've done, and I know when someone wants someone."

"What do you mean, she looked sad?"

Her heart should not have twisted at the words.

"She doesn't know anybody here except the people at Seal Cove. All her people are summer people, and she's about to spend a winter in Maine with no friends."

"How do you know she has no friends? She's probably part of some country club somewhere."

"Maybe. But you know I can't resist beautiful sad faces."

"You should try harder."

"You're mad at me, and I respect that. I'm sorry for surprising you. But I'm not sorry about what happened after. That was all you, honey."

Lillian slid to the floor against the fridge. "Please don't tell anyone."

"I won't."

"I don't want Morgan to know."

"Morgan's your best friend."

"Just . . . keep it a secret?"

"I have so far."

"Thank you."

"You still mad at me?"

"Yes."

Stormy squatted down to Lillian's level and held out her hands. Her dark red nail polish matched her lipstick. "I just want you to be happy. You've been so sad, and we just established how I feel about that."

"And you thought setting me up with my arch nemesis was the cure?"

"Judging by the teeth marks on your neck, which were definitely not there yesterday, I'm gonna say yes."

"You do understand hooking up with my colleague is unprofessional?"

"You're two consenting adults. You're not her supervisor, and you don't write her checks. The worst that can happen is things are awkward and awful, which you've basically said is already the case."

"She's a rich girl with no concept of privilege."

"So educate her." Stormy made a lewd gesture before grabbing Lillian's wrists and lifting her to her feet. "I really am sorry, Lillian."

"I will forgive you on one condition."

"What?"

"You don't do anything like this ever again."

"What if I know what's good for you?"

"Stormy."

"Okay. I promise not to meddle in your love life for a whole year."

"I said 'ever.'"

"A year and a day."

Lillian sighed. "A year and a day, then."

Stormy lifted herself on her toes, took Lillian's face in her hands, and kissed her on each cheek. "Done. Now explain to me why you're not wearing a bra."

Ivy trotted Freddie around the indoor arena, missing the skylights in her Colorado facility as one of the overhead lights flickered. Freddie floated over the sand footing. She loved his trot; some horses had jarring trots which were impossible to sit to, but not Freddie. His gaits had always been smooth, and the further along he came in his training and the more she learned his rhythm, the more he felt like an extension of her body.

Today she wove serpentines through the freshly dragged ring, her reins loose in her hands as she focused on her seat and legs. If she wanted to keep riding—and nothing was going to come between her and horses—she needed to prepare for the days when her body was less cooperative. Right now, for instance, she had hand warmers shoved in her riding gloves to combat the icy numbness that had been plaguing her all day at work, and her mind was foggy. She'd wanted nothing more than to go home and fall into bed, but that cycle was dangerous.

Besides. Lying in bed would only result in thoughts of Lillian, and that ground was heavily mined. Several days had passed since they'd hooked up at the clinic. She'd been on ambulatory since then, but not seeing Lillian was just as torturous as being in her presence.

Freddie flexed his neck as she turned the last serpentine into a circle, spiraling him tightly in, then out, keeping his full attention on her. The simultaneous complexity and simplicity of the task calmed her. Her body knew what was required of it. Despite its betrayals, it responded, and she managed to concentrate on the movement of her horse through the haze that wanted to envelope her completely. This haze was not the product of pleasant fantasy. It buzzed at the corners of her vision and made a wreckage of her thoughts. Wading through it took most of what she had. At least on horseback she didn't have to formulate complete sentences to clients.

She switched to a cooldown when sweat darkened Freddie's shoulders and let him amble around the ring. Another rider had joined them, and Ivy smiled in greeting as the younger girl put her mare through her paces. The horse was a grade mare, her bones raw compared to Freddie, but she responded to her rider's commands with enthusiasm. Ivy reminded herself this was not a show barn, but a small private stable in coastal Maine.

Her body felt tired and rejuvenated by the time she dismounted and led Freddie back to his stall. He bumped her arm as they walked, lipping the sleeve of her coat. She gave him a gentle reprimand.

"Nasty cut he's got there."

Morgan emerged from a nearby stall with her eyes fixed on the partially healed gash on Freddie's hindquarters.

"He's not fitting in with the herd here." She tried not to dwell on the parallels between their situations and avoided Morgan's gaze. Lillian wouldn't have told her anything, would she? The way she'd rushed out of the exam room, horror on her face at the prospect of discovery, suggested otherwise. For her part, she didn't know how she felt about what might happen if anyone found out about whatever was going on between them.

"I'm sorry to hear that."

"Thanks."

She took a step toward Freddie's stall, hoping to cut the conversation short. A muscle spasm rippled through her thigh. An electric jolt of pain followed and traveled into her foot, seizing the muscles all the way down. Her leg gave out beneath her in surprised agony. She managed to catch herself on Freddie's saddle before her momentum carried her to the ground, but she heard the sound of Morgan rushing to assist her past the whimper she'd barely managed to contain.

Deep breaths. Her forehead rested against Freddie's saddle. Leather, soap, and horse filled her senses. The pain receded, leaving her foot numb, and she straightened.

"Ivy?"

"Charley horse," she said, rubbing her leg. "I'm fine."

Morgan looked like she didn't quite buy the excuse. "If you need a second, I can throw Freddie in his stall for you."

"No, we're good." She tested her weight on her left leg. It held, though shakily. "Probably didn't drink enough water today."

Morgan's scrutiny made her skin prickle with terror. She would rather Morgan find out about Lillian a thousand times over before she found out about *this*. Not yet. There were years, potentially, before anyone had to know about the weakness eating at her nervous system. Years where she wouldn't have to deal with pity.

"Really, I'm fine."

"Sure."

Morgan backed up to let them pass. Ivy led Freddie forward with gritted teeth, trying not to grip his reins for support.

The second spasm sent her sprawling.

Morgan was at her side before she had fully registered what was happening. Freddie snorted but remained still, his training, as ever, impeccable, and the cold cement floor pressed through her breeches and penetrated her down vest to wrap around her torso. Meanwhile, the pain in her leg continued as the nerves seared and the muscles contracted. She clutched it with the arm not bent beneath her until it calmed, and the pain again resolved into something manageable. Manageable, she reflected bitterly as she let Morgan pull her into a sitting position, was an ever-expanding definition.

"Are you hurt?"

"No." She winced as she snapped at Morgan. "Sorry. No, I'm okay."

"Hang tight." Morgan bustled Freddie into his stall and removed his bridle and saddle with brisk efficiency, then returned to her side. "How's your leg?"

The leg in question was begging for amputation, but she didn't say that. At least it was her left, and not her right. That would have made driving difficult.

Driving. She clenched down on that fear. So far, her condition had not caused severe vision problems, though that was always a risk in the future, nor had it limited her ability to move around. *And it won't.*

"Ivy?"

She couldn't muster a lie. "It—It's felt better." The admission spilled from her lips and she fought a nearly irresistible urge to weep. "I must have pulled something."

"I can get you some ice."

She didn't need ice. She needed to be home with her gabapentin and a soft blanket and her dog.

"I'll be okay. Really."

Morgan squatted, hands on her knees and her gray-blue eyes searching Ivy's face.

She pushed herself to her feet and locked her knee to keep her leg from giving out a third time. Carefully, trying not to show just how unstable she felt, she made her way to Freddie's stall, grabbed a brush, and slipped inside. She kept one hand on the bars of the door as she groomed the areas stiffened with sweat, then, once she was satisfied he was taken care of, limped down the interminably long aisle and out the door to her truck. Morgan walked beside her. Their silence was companionable, though Morgan's steadying hand on her elbow grated. At least Morgan seemed to intuit Ivy didn't want to talk.

"Thanks."

"No problem." Morgan backed away as Ivy shut the truck door.

"Fuck," she said to the empty cab. "Fuck, fuck, fuck." The November night pressed around her and narrowed her vision to her headlights, which lit an uncertain path down the potholed road to her rented house. She couldn't even call it home.

Lillian didn't see much of Ivy that week, and the clinic felt strangely empty without her. *Not a good sign.* Missing Ivy couldn't mean anything good. Instead, she listened to clients bitch about not having enough money and did her best not to take it personally when they accused her of being selfish for not treating their pets for free.

"Nobody *made* him get a golden retriever," she said to Georgia in the break room. "If you don't want to deal with cancer, get a breed that doesn't die from cancer ninety-nine percent of the time."

"You should show him your student loan bill," said Georgia. "I keep saying you should post it in exams rooms, along with your salary. That would shut them up."

"But would it?" She munched on a carrot stick, snapping it in half with more violence than was necessary. "Some days, I regret my job."

"What would you do instead?"

"Something that paid well, didn't follow me home, and that people actually appreciated."

"Does that exist? Because sign me up, too."

"Touché. I just hate seeing cases like that. I can't give his dog free chemo. We'd go bankrupt, and it's not like I would ask him to do his job for free."

"If this is Jack Wilson, you don't want him doing his job, period. He messed up our plumbing a few years back," Georgia said with a scowl. "And his truck is slathered in NRA stickers."

"Lovely."

"I like Dr. Holden."

The non sequitur made Lillian instantly suspicious. "Great."

"She's been good to Shawna. You can tell a lot about a doctor by how they treat their techs." She gave Lillian a warm smile. "Like you."

"Ivy's professional."

"Mhmm." Georgia's smile widened, and Lillian decided it was time to leave the break room for the comparative safety of her next appointment.

Unfortunately, her next appointment was waiting in the very same room where she'd fucked Ivy, and the memories made concentrating on her job extremely difficult.

She texted Emilia toward the end of the day, desperate to talk to someone.

"Cold and dark," Emilia said when Lillian got out of her car in Emilia's driveway. "My favorite running weather."

Decked out in reflective gear and with spotlights around their foreheads, also known as the world's least fashionable headbands, they set off down the backroads along the river. Lillian searched for a way to broach the subject of Ivy. After a quarter mile and zero inspiration, she settled for the blunt truth.

"I want Ivy Holden."

"What?" Emilia skidded to a stop and turned to face her, temporarily blinding her with her flashing headlamp. "*Want* want?"

She filled Emilia in on the details of recent events, including their encounter in the clinic. "I need you to tell me I'm being an idiot and that I should stop before this backfires."

"Hang on. I'm still processing. This makes so much sense, though. I knew there was some weird energy between you two when we ran into her on our run."

"It's always been like that."

"How does she feel?"

Hot. Wet. Perfect.

"I have no idea. Everything she does is so calculated. This could just be a long con."

"That seems . . . unlikely."

"It would be right up her alley." The shame of that long-ago party surfaced briefly, and she quelled it.

"Even if she moved back here just to torment you, that says a lot about the level of her obsession."

A car zoomed past them, leaving behind the smell of exhaust. Lillian started walking but did not break back into a jog. "She's not obsessed with me."

"Why not? You're gorgeous, smart, and almost as fast as me," Emilia said with a playful shove. "Have you tried talking to her?"

"We don't talk. We fight."

"What do you want out of this then?"

What *did* she want? She shook her head in the darkness. "I don't know. Maybe I'm just rebounding."

"That's possible." Emilia didn't sound convinced. "Actually, now that I think about it, your dynamic with her is a little bit like a relationship with an ex. You hate each other's guts, but you keep sleeping together anyway."

"I'm not sleeping with her."

"But you want to?"

Lillian didn't answer, which was answer enough.

"Before you do anything, you should try getting to know her better. Maybe she's changed."

"What am I supposed to do, invite her over for dinner?"

"That's not a bad idea. She's part of the clinic now, and you could hang out in a group setting. That way you can't kill each other, or . . . well, you know."

"Can you do me a favor, though? I haven't told Morgan about this, yet, and I'm not ready to."

Emilia hesitated, then nodded. "I won't mention it to her. Can I ask why you don't want to tell her?"

"Honestly? I'm not sure." She listened to the sound of her sneakers on the freezing gravel. "Morgan dealt with me complaining about her all through school. It just feels strange. Angie and Stevie don't know anything either."

"They won't hear it from me. Ready to run again?"

"Always."

They set off at a jog, their breath steaming in the cold night air, and Lillian felt lighter than she had since Ivy Holden had arrived.

"A potluck?" Ivy reeled from the invitation.

"Yeah. Bring whatever. It's a clinic Friendsgiving. Thanksgiving, only without the genocide and the smallpox blankets," said Stevie.

"But—"

"Lil asked me to invite you." Morgan eased the winch of the trailer down to unhitch it.

"Oh."

She was so taken aback that she stood staring at Morgan until Morgan straightened, the trailer unhitched and the clinic truck free from its weight. Stevie undid the chains and hooked them around the hitch with deft fingers.

"I'll do a meat dish, but Lil's a vegetarian, so there will be options," Morgan continued.

"Lil will probably put together some sort of sign-up sheet because she's anal like that," Stevie added.

"If you don't want to cook, you can always bring wine. Stormy—not sure if you know her, she owns Storm's-a-Brewin' and she's a good friend—will hook us up with beer. She's not part of the clinic, so she won't be there, but we buy from her." Morgan favored the trailer with a critical look as she checked the tires.

"Do you do this every year?"

"Usually." Morgan patted the trailer and headed for the clinic's barn, calling back over her shoulder, "and it's very casual."

A potluck. Ivy looked around at the leafless trees and tried to take

113

stock of her emotions. A potluck meant she'd get to spend time with Lillian outside of work, which was complicated in and of itself. Seeing Lillian had gotten harder, not easier. Her throat dried out every time she caught sight of Lillian's hair, and her body, already unreliable, went weak with want. At least her leg hadn't given out again like it had at the barn. Her fingers brushed her thigh, nervously testing to make sure the leg would hold her weight. She couldn't afford to fall like that here. It was bad enough Morgan had witnessed her fall once.

Sure enough, a sign-up sheet appeared the next day, written in Lillian's neat script.

Ivy put her name down for wine. Cooking was something she did because she had to, and even then she did it rarely, preferring to order in. She had so little energy left over at the end of the day. Expending it on an activity she found irritating at best was a less than desirable option.

"Hey, stranger," said Stormy that evening as Ivy slid onto a barstool. "What can I get you?"

"Small cup of your dark roast." *And advice.*

"Excellent taste."

Stormy served the coffee in a squat red cup with a pleasingly thick handle.

"I wanted to thank you for the invitation to the club the other week," she said, schooling her features and tamping the creeping blush back down her capillaries.

"My pleasure." Stormy winked, and the blush overpowered her defenses. "Glad you had a good time."

"Can I ask you something?"

Stormy paused in the middle of refilling whipped cream canisters and waited.

"What do people wear to a potluck?"

"You've never been to a potluck?"

"Not—" She broke off. It wasn't that she hadn't been to a potluck before. Rabbit Island had them regularly, but those doubled as casual cocktail parties, and she strongly suspected the gathering at Bay Road would be a different sort of event. "Not for work."

"Wear something casual. Lil's crowd is laid-back."

"Casual." She could do casual.

Stormy eyed her over the row of whipped creams. "Like jeans."

"Got it." She took a sip of coffee and let the quiet murmur of the café's few customers wash over her. "So, did Lil figure out you invited me the other day?"

"I'm still doing penance. I'll be covering her bar tab for a year."

"Sorry about that."

Stormy shrugged. "I invited you. And all things considered, I'd say it was worth it. She looked like she had fun."

Ivy choked on her coffee and spent the next thirty seconds coughing. Stormy passed her a cup of water.

"The way I see it, if I don't get to play meddling bartender, then what's the point?"

Ivy arrived at 16 Bay Road with several bottles of very nice wine, a cowl-neck sweater dress to combat the frigid air, and a racing heart. She tried to calm the latter. This was just a dinner with her colleagues. She'd been to hundreds of gatherings where far more was on the line, usually with her mother whispering a litany of who's who in her ear. The only difference was Lillian would be at this one. *Lived* here, in this sprawling white farmhouse with smoke curling from the chimney against the darkening sky.

Several cars already filled the driveway. She recognized them from the practice and took a steadying breath before setting foot on the wrap-around-porch and knocking on the front door.

A curvy brunette she recognized from Lillian's Instagram answered.

"You must be Ivy," the woman said, motioning for her to come in.

"Yes, nice to meet you . . .?"

"Angie. I used to work at the clinic, and now I run the boarding facility."

Ivy shook Angie's hand and followed her out of the foyer and into the kitchen.

She stopped. The large kitchen opened into the living room, which was separated by a bar and a massive fireplace. The white cabinets and gleaming hardwood floors were partially blocked from view by the assembled party and its attendant dogs—all of whom came skittering towards her—but the warmth radiating from the place brought a lump to her throat.

"Dr. Holden," said Georgia, greeting her with a smile.

Lillian, who stood behind her, turned at her words. She wore a simple black sweater paired with a red scarf and jeans, and her hair was down and free around her shoulders. Ivy's pulse skittered.

"Where should I put the wine?"

"I can take it." Lillian eased past Georgia and took the bottles from Ivy with a forced smile, but her hand lingered against Ivy's fingers. "And sorry about the dogs."

Ivy glanced down to examine the waiting animals. She recognized the German shepherd as Morgan's dog, Kraken, but the other three were new to her. A brindled pit bull smiled up at her with a wiggling butt, and beside him, a massive, fluffy, three-legged monster of a mutt flattened her ears.

"Kraken, Marvin, Muffin, and Hermione," Lillian said.

Ivy counted, but only saw three dogs. "Am I missing one?"

"Behind you." Lillian placed her fingers on Ivy's wrist and pointed. Distracted by the touch, it took Ivy a second to turn and see the Italian greyhound, also a tripod, hopping by her feet.

"Oh my goodness," she said. "You are precious."

"The tripods are mine," said Lillian. "Don't let them fool you. The little one is the monster."

"Isn't that always the case," said Ivy, thinking of Darwin back at her house, who was no doubt plotting his revenge for this abandonment. "This is your place?"

"Yes. Stevie, Angie, and Morgan live here, too."

"That sounds . . . crowded."

"We can't all have trust funds." Lillian's gibe lacked her usual venom. "You look nice, Ivy."

Ivy found herself wishing she'd worn something cooler. The cashmere dress felt suddenly stifling as her face, neck, and chest flushed at the compliment, and the blush deepened when Lillian smirked.

"Thank you," she managed.

"Help yourself to anything you want. Food's on the table, and drinks are in the kitchen."

"Lil—" she stopped. She had no idea what to say to Lillian, except that seeing her made something in her throat swell and she wanted nothing more than to stare at this woman—a woman she'd hated for years—until the stars faded.

"Ivy," said Morgan, appearing at Lillian's side and swinging an arm around Lillian's shoulder.

Always swooping in at the wrong moment. "Hey, Morgan."

"This is my partner, Emilia." Morgan beckoned to someone out of her range of sight, and the woman she'd run into on her jog weeks ago smiled at her.

"Yes, we've met." Emilia's smile held far more warmth than Morgan's.

"I ran into Lillian and Emilia on a run the other day," Ivy said.

"Pun intended?" Stevie, who was passing by with a drink, shot Ivy a wink.

"Never," said Ivy, who, as a rule, thought puns were the lowest form of humor.

Lillian laughed. The sound curled around her heart, and she watched Lillian's mouth soften. Her dark eyes met Ivy's in a moment of solidarity. She was vaguely aware of Morgan's scrutiny, but she didn't care.

The evening passed in a blur of conversation, wine, and not enough solid food. She eventually ended up ensconced in an armchair by the fire with a large black cat on her lap, pinioned by his claws. Most cats would have fled for safety and solitude during a gathering of this size, but the enormous purring animal had an authoritative glint to his green eyes that Ivy recognized; she saw it often enough in the mirror. She stroked his head with the tips of her fingers.

"Oh my god." Stevie froze as she entered the living room. "Ange, come here."

Ivy looked up to discover Stevie staring at her with wide blue eyes.

"Oh wow," said Angie when she popped her head around the fireplace. "You're still alive."

117

"Yes?" said Ivy.

"Lil, come here," Angie said.

Lillian, who had been chatting with Emilia, turned. Her eyes also widened. "You're petting James."

"Is that his name?" asked Ivy.

"I call him the devil's familiar, but yes, technically it's James," said Stevie.

"He doesn't normally . . . make friends." Angie pressed a hand to her mouth to hide a smile. "I need to draw this."

"Take a picture," Stevie told her, pulling out her phone.

Ivy searched for Lillian's eyes. They met hers, and Lillian drifted toward her with raised eyebrows. "I didn't take you for a cat whisperer."

"I like cats," said Ivy. James butted his head against her hand. "And I like this cat."

"He seems to like you."

"I take it that's unusual?"

"Angie found him in a dumpster a few years ago. He was totally feral, and let's just say he still has his moments."

"He's a sweetheart."

"Only you would say that, Poison Ivy," said Lillian, but like her earlier jab, this one also felt gentle.

"It isn't fair, you know," Ivy said as Lillian perched on the arm of her chair. "Poison Ivy is so easy. What am I supposed to call you?"

"My mother calls me 'Silly Lilly.'"

"You should not have told me that."

"Why? I can hardly see you saying it." Lillian's perfume wafted over her.

"You might be surprised, Silly Lilly." Ivy paused. "Okay, you're right. It doesn't have much sting, and I feel really weird now."

"And it isn't like you've ever needed help insulting me."

"You made it easy," said Ivy. "Not my fault."

"It's a pity you're trapped in that chair."

"Why's that?"

"I was going to offer to show you around the house."

"I could move James." James chose that moment to extend his claws, and she reconsidered her position. "Or not."

118

"Too bad." Lillian's voice promised things Ivy would gladly have endured a tiger's claws for, had she not wanted to draw attention to the fact she was staring up at Lillian Lee with naked longing.

Lillian couldn't tear her eyes away from Ivy. Her charcoal gray dress accented her pale skin, and her hair spilled down her back. She sat curled in Lillian's favorite chair with James laying claim to her lap, and all Lillian wanted to do was straddle her, cat be damned, and finish what they'd started.

A hand touched her back. She jumped.

"How's it going?" asked Morgan.

"Fine," she said. Morgan glanced at Ivy, then back at her. "We're getting along for a change."

"Did Angie spike the punch with something?"

"Maybe catnip," she said, pointing at James.

"Or predators stick together. Can I talk to you?" Morgan didn't wait for a reply and pulled her toward her greenhouse. She looked over her shoulder to find Ivy still watching, her green eyes full of liquid desire.

"What's going on?" Morgan asked when the greenhouse door was shut behind them and the glass muffled the sound of the party.

"Nothing's going on."

Morgan shoved her hands into the pockets of her jeans and stared at Lillian with an expression that said "bullshit" more clearly than if she'd spoken aloud.

"I'm fine," said Lillian.

"She'll hurt you again."

"What?" Lillian froze in the act of pruning a dead flower from a hanging plant.

"Ivy."

"Ivy can't hurt me."

"I'm not an idiot, Lil. I know something happened between you two at Cornell. Fuck, everyone knew."

Lillian crushed the husk of the petunia in her fingers. The dark greens filling the edges of her vision swam in the light from the door. "Nothing happened," she said, but the lie sounded weak even to her own ears.

"You're not acting like you. The last time that happened was when you were dicking around with Holden."

"I never—"

"I get why you didn't tell me. I'm just worried about you."

She met Morgan's slate gray eyes and said nothing. Morgan's frown faded, and her broad shoulders relaxed as she searched Lillian's face. Morgan knew her well enough to know admitting what had happened would have meant admitting how much it had hurt her, which could only have been possible if she cared about Ivy.

"What are you going to do?" Morgan asked.

"I'm going to be professional." She let the flower fall to the floor in a sprinkle of dust. "We work together now. Nothing's going to happen."

"You sure?"

"I'm sure. Besides, you were the one telling me to give her a chance."

"I was talking about working together. Not . . . you know."

"Gross."

"Pro tip," said Morgan. "Try not looking at her like she's a buffet."

"You're an ass."

Morgan's warning sobered her, however, and she did not return to Ivy's side. Instead, she wandered into the kitchen and chatted with Danielle Watson, Georgia, and Shawna while her mind strayed continuously back to Ivy.

Was Morgan right? Could Ivy hurt her again, or had they grown up enough to move past that? Did she even *want* to move past that? This new game they were playing had higher stakes than the taunts they'd thrown at each other in school. Yes, the underlying dynamics remained the same, but the rules had shifted. More was on the table. Quite literally, she thought, remembering how it had felt to have Ivy's legs wrapped around her in the exam room.

But since when did she play games? Her hands strangled the wine glass. She didn't gamble. Every risk she took was calculated to the nearest degree, and she did not enter into games where the stakes were higher than she could afford. She had no safety net. Stability was sexy—not *this*. The person Ivy turned her into was reckless, and that was dangerous.

"... explain why it is called Rabbit Island?"

She turned to see Angie and Ivy, who had finally been freed from James' clutches, enter the kitchen. Ivy's cheeks were flushed from the heat of the fire and the wine Angie was liberally pouring into her empty glass. Lillian made a mental note to find her keys and call her a ride if she finished that drink.

"It's shaped sort of like one," said Ivy.

"Are there rabbits on it?"

"No. Just these little shrew things and mink."

"Mink?" Angie squealed in delight. "They are so cute!"

Ivy smiled, her skin porcelain against the flush of her cheeks and her lips—*not a buffet*, she reminded herself.

"What happens to the island in the winter?" Shawna asked. She, too, had apparently been eavesdropping—or had been drawn by Angie's squeal.

"It's closed. They shut off the water, which means they don't want people out there. Fire hazard. Work crews go out to work on houses, though."

"That sounds absolutely frigid," said Lillian.

"They have space heaters, but yes. Not a job I'd want."

"Why don't they work in the summer?" Angie asked.

"Because," said Lillian, "rich people don't want their vacations interrupted by construction."

"It does get in the way of cocktail hour."

"Speaking of," said Lillian, "the wine is wonderful. Would I have to sell an organ to afford it?"

"Depends on the organ." Ivy shifted her weight, and Lillian wondered how she had ended up standing next to her again. Angie studied them with interest. Lillian saw her fingers twitch as if sketching. *Great. I've become fuel for comics.*

"Not the liver," Angie said, and somewhere Stevie laughed.

"Kidney?" Lillian wondered, not for the first time, if Ivy had been

121

born with perfect eyebrows or if she'd just had them sculpted for so many years they grew in that way.

"Or you could just let me buy you another bottle."

Angie's eyebrows, which were only slightly less immaculate, sky-rocketed.

"The thing about rich people," Lillian said for Angie's benefit, "is they think their money can get them whatever they want."

An unfamiliar emotion flickered in Ivy's eyes. "Not always."

What was *that*?

Ivy cut off her reflection by raising her glass in a toast. "But good wine? Yes."

"Have you ever been to the island during the winter?" Lillian changed the subject before she grew any more distracted by the wine staining Ivy's lips.

"No. I've seen photos and it looks absolutely freezing." She paused and leaned back against the counter, tilting her head. "Why, would you come with me?"

She issued the invitation so quietly Lillian doubted anyone had heard. Angie had gotten into a heated debate with Shawna about which organ she'd donate for money, and no one else was paying them any attention.

"Is that an invitation?" she said, just as quietly.

"It could be."

"Then sure, why not. I'd love to be inspiration for a horror novel."

Ivy's smile was quick and bright. "Meet me at the dock by seven on Sunday," she said. "There are only two boats. One there at seven, and one off at three."

"So we'll be trapped on an island without running water or heat for . . ."

"Eight hours. Pack a lunch, Lee."

"You're insane."

"So don't come."

"That's not—" Lillian broke off in frustration, which rekindled Ivy's smile.

"That's not, what?"

Lillian took a chance and put her hand over Ivy's on the counter.

Their bodies hid the gesture from sight and the contact deepened the flush on Ivy's pale neck. "That's not what I meant."

"No?"

She dug her thumbnail into Ivy's wrist and Ivy's breath caught in her throat.

"Lil," she said, and the need in her voice was unmistakable.

"I'll see you Sunday."

Sunday. Three days. Plenty of time to call it off, Ivy thought as she finished her exam on a yearling colt. He tried to nip her sleeve, but she pushed his head away and scratched his mane to distract him.

I'm the one who needs a distraction.

She also needed a cup of coffee. They'd worked late into the evening, thanks to a series of emergencies, and she and Shawna both were dragging.

"Want to grab some coffee before the next one?" she asked Shawna as they loaded the truck.

"Desperately."

"My treat."

Shawna flashed her a smile, and Ivy wished Lillian would react that positively to such an offer. She finished up her paperwork as they drove, her mind conjuring images of Lillian each time she blinked. Shawna kept the truck running as she ducked into Stormy's for their order.

The smell of freshly brewed coffee replaced the damp chill off the winter ocean. She inhaled deeply, only to have her breath hitch as she took in the café's occupants. Lillian stood at the register chatting with Claire, one of Stormy's employees. Ivy let her eyes linger on Lillian's ass before taking her place in line behind her.

Lillian didn't turn around, but Claire glanced up, alerting Lillian to the presence of another customer with the shift in her attention. Lillian moved automatically to the side. "Sorry," she said in the habitual way one apologized to a stranger in public. She still hadn't looked up.

"No need to apologize, Dr. Lee."

Ivy watched with satisfaction as Lillian realized exactly who waited behind her. Lillian's cheeks pinked, and she chewed on her lower lip.

"How can I help you?" asked Claire.

"Two dark roasts. Large, with room."

Claire turned to pour, leaving Lillian and Ivy to stare at each other. She remembered the feel of Lillian's nails digging into her wrist and felt a blush spread across her own cheeks—and farther south.

Lillian recovered first. Nodding at the coffee streaming from the carafe, she said, "And here I took you for the latte type."

"I like pumpkin spice just as much as the next girl, but Stormy's coffee is *good*."

"Everything Stormy serves is good. Her scones are the reason I run." Lillian stroked the large glass jar holding the day's remaining scones.

"Blueberry or cinnamon?"

"I don't discriminate."

"Good to know." Ivy moved closer to the bar, ostensibly to pay for her coffees. Lillian didn't pull away, and her dark eyes caught the sheen of the polished wood like cognac.

"If you start bringing me scones—"

"That's awfully presumptuous, Lil."

Lillian's blush deepened, and her eyes narrowed the way they always did before she launched an attack.

"And I'll take three scones," Ivy said to Claire. "Whichever ones you grab."

"Sure thing." Claire scooped the scones with a pair of tongs and made to put them in the same bag. "Oh, that last one's for Lil. You can bag it separately."

Lillian looked, for a moment, like an artist's rendition of frustration—mouth open, eyebrows contracted, face reddening by the second—and then she laughed. "You're incorrigible. You do know that, right?"

Ivy touched Lillian's elbow fleetingly and gave Lillian her best smile. She knew it was her best because her mother had instructed her daughters to practice smiling in front of a mirror in preparation for admissions interviews and dinners with important people. She and Madison had done as instructed, but they'd also worked on a few expressions *not* intended for members of congress. This smile was one of them, and Lillian's pupils dilated in response. Ivy glanced at Lillian's lips, remembered they were in a coffee shop, and scooped her order off the counter, sans one scone.

"See you later, Lee."

Lillian replayed her encounter with Ivy as she scanned the page of her book that night, not taking in a word. Sighing, she started from the top of the page and tried again. The mystery novel was by one of her favorite authors, and the detective had just discovered she was being stalked by the killer. It should have gripped her; instead, all she could think about was Ivy.

Something had shifted. She couldn't pinpoint the exact location, or what, if anything, had been dislodged, but she'd felt the tremor beneath her feet as her anger at Ivy for yet again using her wealth as a weapon had dissipated into amusement.

And what if Ivy *wasn't* wielding wealth with the intent to harm? What if she had simply wanted to buy her a scone, knowing—and liking—how much it would irritate her? Logically, that made more sense than an Ivy who wanted to humiliate her by flaunting her privilege, especially considering the smile she'd given her right before she left. That smile had taken up residence in her body, and she found herself wondering if the batteries in her vibrator had enough charge to get it out of her system.

She shut her book. Muffin lay sprawled across her bed while Hermione curled up on her pillow, nose buried beneath her paws, and she'd drawn the curtains over her windows to trap the warm yellow light from her lamp. Houseplants hung from the ceiling in baskets. Their shadows cast strange shapes on the walls. She reached for her bedside drawer and removed the notepad and pen she kept there for emergencies like these.

"Pros," she said to the room, making a column on one side of the paper. "And cons." At the top, she drew a doodle of an ivy leaf, spiraling the vine down the dividing line until she felt like Angie with her comics.

Starting with the cons seemed easier. Getting involved with Ivy would reopen old wounds, had the potential to go catastrophically wrong, could make things awkward at work, and came too soon on the heels of her breakup with Brian. Plus, Ivy made her lose her cool, was insufferably privileged, and had already hurt her badly. She refused to think about just how badly, which was another con in itself. Satisfied she'd gotten the list off to a decent start, and jotting *blond* down for good measure, she turned to the pros.

The pen creaked beneath her teeth. She hadn't even realized she'd been chewing on the end. Another habit she'd thought she'd broken herself of, revived thanks to Ivy Holden. She was lucky she'd never smoked, or she'd no doubt pick that up again, too.

Pros. There had to be at least one pro besides *really fucking hot*. Didn't there?

The white space taunted her.

Hot, she wrote.

Really hot went beneath it. She refused to add *smells amazing and has unfairly soft skin*, because that would mean admitting she'd noticed.

I won't have to worry about getting to know a stranger on a dating app. There. That was a solid pro, not that she had any intention of actually dating Ivy. Just . . . what? Fucking her?

Yes, said her body.

"I'm an adult," she said aloud. Neither of her dogs offered comment.

She makes me feel dumb and talk to myself, she added to the cons.

Normally, lists made her feel better. More in control. She weighed the columns and bit the pen so hard it cracked. The problem, she knew, wasn't the list itself. It was that no matter how many items she added to the con side, there was a part of her that didn't care. She couldn't think straight around Ivy.

We both know it's a terrible idea. She wrote this slowly under both columns, because it was true, and because the fact that they each knew it was stupid hadn't slowed them down. If anything, by unspoken agreement, it had made things easier. Getting involved with Ivy was like throwing a stone at a window to see what would happen. She knew the glass would shatter and there would be a price to pay, but hurling the rock felt so damn good.

Chapter Seven

"This is a very bad idea," Ivy said to Darwin as she pulled his sweater on over his head. He licked her face, undaunted. Ivy considered the knapsack she'd packed with wine, bread and cheese, an extra sweater, water, and her medications. Going out to the island for a day hike was one thing. Going out to the island for a day hike with Lillian Lee was quite another. They'd be together for an entire day in the cold. *Almost forgot.* She shoved a box of hand warmers into the bag, too. The last thing she needed was her hands giving out on her. The challenge she'd issued in a haze of wine was exactly the reason why people didn't drink around their enemies—even enemies who were no longer enemies, precisely, but something much more insidious.

Lillian had dressed warmly in a winter jacket, scarf, hat, and gloves, a testimony to her familiarity with what happened the minute the wind came off a freezing ocean. A steaming thermos of coffee was clutched to her chest, and she also wore a day pack, along with a sturdy pair of hiking boots and thick warm socks over a pair of thermal leggings.

The handful of men and women queuing up at the ramp to board the ferry eyed them with interest. All were clearly headed to the island to work, along with a load of lumber, and they nodded without engaging Ivy in conversation. Clouds tumbled overhead, blown by a stiff late November wind. Snow was in the forecast; she burrowed her hands deeper into her down jacket and closed the distance between her and Lillian.

"Good morning," she said.

"Good morning."

Awkward silence stretched while Darwin darted around the dock looking for crumbs and rodents. Ivy searched for something to say. "I should have asked earlier. Have you ever been to the island before?"

"No. Monhegan, yes, but not Rabbit or Mouse or any of the other Rodentia."

"It won't be as nice, obviously, with everything shut down and no leaves."

"Ivy," said Lillian with mock concern, "are you worried I won't like your ancestral hive?"

"You're hilarious." She nudged her. "Now get on the boat."

They stayed in the ferry's sheltered lower deck along with the work crew, who chatted about the weather with a reverence she had once scorned and now understood. Weather was everything in a coastal town. Today, the wind had whipped the ocean into swells that sent the boat slamming down into each trough. Lillian grabbed the back of the seat in front of them and turned a startled face to her.

"If it was going to get really bad, they wouldn't take the boat out. I've been on rougher seas than this."

"'Been on rougher seas.' Who are you?" Lillian shook her head and looked out the window, which was streaming with seawater, at the passing coast. The storm gray of the waves and the overcast sky reflected each other as the ferry surged forward. Along the shore, the evergreens looked nearly black, and the rising sun was nothing more than a hazy smudge of gold behind the clouds. Ivy's heart caught in her throat at the bleak beauty of it. This was where she'd grown up; here, and at the private schools she'd attended. Her parents' home in Connecticut, which they'd sold years ago, was just the place she'd spent the occasional holiday.

And she was taking Lillian here—the girl she'd once fantasized about mutilating with a scalpel. The dissonance of her thoughts hit her

129

like a wave of nerve pain. Darwin wriggled in her arms. She loosened her grip on him, aware she'd been squeezing him too tightly. *What the hell am I doing?*

Lillian leaned closer to the window to study the boat's wake. Her red scarf covered her chin but not her lips, and her hair stuck out from beneath her hat, trapped between hat and scarf in a tumult that might have been comical if it hadn't made her want to tug the hat from Lillian's head and smooth the strands behind her ears. She looked eager, almost excited as she watched spray slam into the pane. Ivy had never seen her look like that. Well, except for their first spay lab, but Ivy had cut that excitement short herself when she'd told Lillian she'd bet one thousand dollars she couldn't find both ovaries.

She kept her mouth shut this time.

The ferry ride took twenty minutes compared to the half hour it filled in the summer, when it also doubled as a harbor tour, and the island loomed large and cold out of the fog. Ivy hadn't ever seen it quite this bare of leaves. She'd been up late in the season before, but never at the end of November.

"I was joking about that horror novel," said Lillian as she shot Ivy a look. "But can I just say that if you're going to kill me, this is exactly the kind of evil-looking place I'd imagine you'd choose."

"Rabbit isn't evil," Ivy said. "It's winter."

"It looks like the kind of place where things might come out of the mist and . . . I don't know. Eat us."

"The mist will clear," Ivy said, irritated. "Will your brain?"

Lillian's smile brought out the dimple in her left cheek—*that* was a look she was more familiar with. Getting under her skin had always made Lil smile like that.

The work crew let them disembark first. Darwin led the way up the ramp with Ivy close behind. His short legs blurred as he sped off up the sidewalk, pausing only to sniff the dry yellow grass along the side of the leaf strewn path. A snowflake drifted past.

"Snow won't stop the boat from coming back, will it?" Lillian asked.

Ivy turned to see her staring at the retreating ferry. Its wake churned white against the blue-gray water.

"Depends." She plucked Lillian's sleeve and walked backward up the path. "Would that frighten you?"

"You," said Lillian, whipping around and glaring before bursting into laughter, "are such an ass."

"The ferry will come back for the work crew. As long as we're down here by three thirty, we'll be fine."

"You said three. You said the boat leaves at seven and three."

"From the harbor. It will get here at three thirty. Three twenty, more like. Here, I'll set a timer on my phone if that will make you calm down."

"Did you just tell me to calm down, Ivy Holden?" Lillian took a step toward her and Ivy backed up faster.

"Yeah, I think I did."

"Take it back."

She turned and broke into a jog, leaving Lillian to curse and chase after. Her backpack slammed against her spine, probably due to the bottle of wine, but she ignored the pain and sped up. Closed summer houses bordered the sidewalk as it wound around the cove. Plywood covered windows, and the chairs that usually dotted the porches were stored inside homes or beneath the porches themselves. The empty faces of the cottages watched impassively as she flew past.

She slowed when the incline increased and the wine bottle made a renewed effort to bypass her spine and batter its way through her ribcage. Lillian stumbled to a halt beside her and pulled her scarf down. Their mingling breath steamed in the air.

"This is where you spent your summers?"

They stood on a hill overlooking the cove where Ivy had grown up swimming and playing in the sand with Madison. The mist didn't obscure their view of the ocean or the mainland to the south, and the whitecaps dotting the waves looked like drifting snow.

"I mean, it was a little warmer."

"No wonder you grew up expecting the world."

"What does that mean?" Ivy said, though she knew exactly what Lillian meant.

"Nothing. Which one of these houses is yours?"

"It's on the other side."

131

"Are you going to make me jog there, or can we walk?" Lillian tugged her hat off after the scarf and shook her hair out. Ivy stopped her from putting it back on with a hand to her wrist.

"We can walk," she said. Her voice came out in a whisper.

Lillian looked up just as a snowflake settled on her lashes. They'd left the work crew far behind, along with everyone else they knew. This was the most alone they'd ever been.

"Good. Because you know I'm faster than you."

"Are you, though?" said Ivy.

"I definitely am." Lillian linked their hands together and nodded up the path. "But I'll let you take the lead this once."

"Really." Ivy phrased it as a statement instead of a question.

"Since you're planning to bury me out here? Sure. The shame won't get back to my family."

"Will you stop comparing my favorite place in the world to a mausoleum?"

"This is your favorite place?" Lillian's voice lost its mocking edge.

"Yes."

Lillian's hand tightened around hers, and they both glanced down at their interlocking fingers.

Lillian pulled away first.

Crows shrieked overhead as they entered a short stretch of pine woods.

"I swear it isn't usually this ominous," said Ivy.

"They're just startled to see people. Did you know crows are so smart researchers have to wear masks to run studies on wild specimens? Crows can pass facial information about humans to birds who've never seen them, which is more than we can do about them."

"Bird nerd."

"They have excellent problem-solving skills, too."

"You're not scared of crows, but you're afraid of mist?"

"I am not afraid of mist. I have a healthy respect for setting. If I wander into a scene from a horror movie, I notice." The pine tree nearest them swayed in the wind, and Lillian pointed at it.

"Fine. I will prove to you this is not the opening to whatever movie you're playing in your mind." Ivy pointed up the path. "Through here is the most spectacular view you've ever seen."

"Like you know what I've seen," said Lillian, but her hand brushed Ivy's, and the corner of her mouth quirked in a smile.

Ivy turned them down a footpath slick with moss and icy rocks. "Careful," she said as she navigated the trail. The pines overhead echoed the sound of the crashing surf. She inhaled the scent of pine and saltwater and felt some of the lassitude that clung to her body shred and blow away like fog. The path curved. She paused with her hand outstretched to stop Lillian.

"Oh." Lillian breathed the word as she stared out over the cliff. The island formed a small inlet here, and the granite bluffs towered above it. They stared down at the waves crashing on the rocky shore. Shallow caves hollowed by countless millennia of surf were hung with icicles of frozen spray, and the sun chose that moment to peek through a thinning layer of cloud, illuminating a swirl of snow and an iridescent glimmer rising from the turning tide. Ivy took it in with a cursory glance before turning her attention back to Lillian. Her lips were parted slightly in awe, and the refracted sunlight sparkled in her eyes.

Ivy felt like the water below. Lillian was a cliff she'd been dashing herself against for years, and she'd worn patterns into Lillian just as surely as she had parted and reformed around the narrow bulk of Lillian's body, sliced by rock and barnacle but still whole. They were always going to end up here, she thought as Lillian caught her staring. She was always going to bring her to this place, and what happened next hardly mattered, just as what had happened before mattered only in the grooves it had left in each of them. Ivy didn't fully understand what that meant yet. What she did know was the grooves were there, and her future was a dark tunnel she did not want to look down, and so she wouldn't, so long as Lillian occupied her present.

Darwin barked at a gull off to her right. The sound echoed oddly off the cliffs, and then was lost in the wind and the waves. She didn't break her gaze. Lillian's hair blew around her face. Ivy reached out and let it slap against her fingers, aware of how close she stood to Lillian and how cold the air felt on her own cheeks. She smoothed the strands behind Lillian's ear and touched the curve of her jaw with her thumb. Neither of them spoke. The space between them pulsed with the surf.

She wanted to drag them both beneath it to a place where words were little more than bubbles of air floating unheard to the surface.

> *And so, all the night-tide, I lie down by the side*
> *Of my darling—my darling—my life and my bride,*
> *In her sepulchre there by the sea—*
> *In her tomb by the sounding sea.*

Unspoken was the understanding they were separate here from their shared past. On this cliff, where the sun had been replaced with shadow and the wind scattered a gust of briny snow over the rocks, they were nameless, and Ivy pressed her lips to Lillian's with a tenderness that cut her more deeply than any accusation Lillian had ever thrown her way.

Ivy's lips were cold against her own, as were the tips of Ivy's gloved fingers where they cupped her face, but her mouth was warm when she parted Ivy's lips with a soft exhale. There was no ferocity to this kiss, no desire tinged with vengeance. Ivy moved slowly and carefully, each brush of her lips and tongue gentle and deliberate and somehow crueler in its gentleness than the tug of war they'd played out before. She kissed her back with the same slow strokes. Their lips touched briefly, then separated, tongues barely brushing, and the more slowly they moved, the more deliberate the touch of teeth to lower lip or tongue to tongue, the more Lillian felt herself exposed. Around them, the empty shells of crabs littered the rocks, dropped by gulls to break them open.

She felt like that. Except, unlike the crabs, she would gladly give herself to Ivy. Would offer everything, in this moment, so long as Ivy's lips remained on hers and the wind tried and failed to gust between them. She held Ivy in her arms. Ivy's wool jacket was damp with spray, but she could not feel it through her gloves, and Ivy's hair was a shock of white-blond against the black of her coat and the dark green of her scarf. Her perfume mingled with the smell of the ocean and snow and pine sap. Lillian understood, as Ivy's hands tangled in the hair at the back of her neck, that she would no longer be able to dissociate any of those smells from the others. She'd smell Ivy every time a breeze blew off the water, and she'd have to get rid of Angie's favorite pine candles unless she wanted to think of how soft Ivy's lips were when they weren't fighting.

She opened her eyes as Ivy pulled away. Ivy's irises were as dark as the pines behind her in the overcast light, and they pinned her there at the cliff's edge, until an emotion she had no name for swelled in her chest and forced her to look away.

"I want to show you more," Ivy said, and held out her hand.

She took it. There was no universe in which she would willingly hold Ivy Holden's hand. Here, though, in this place where the outside world had no context and they were separated from their world by ocean and sky, she enclosed Ivy's fingers in her own and drew them into the warmth of her pocket. Ivy smiled, brief and sweet, and something like breaking glass shattered past the edge of Lillian's hearing.

Darwin bolted back up the footpath to the sidewalk and waited with a wagging stub of a tail for them to ascend. They moved carefully. It would have been easier going if she released Ivy's hand, but releasing it would mean acknowledging she held it at all, and she wasn't ready for that.

Back on level ground, it was easy to fall into step beside Ivy as they wound along the rocky coast and through a forest dusted with the first of the snow. The moss grew so thick that when she stepped on a patch that had reached out to claim the sidewalk, her boot sank into it without a sound. She stopped and knelt to examine it without relinquishing Ivy's hand.

It hadn't frozen yet, which she found remarkable, given the moisture content, and the tiny fronds that made up the organism bore equally tiny crystals of ice. A few fruiting bodies poked hopefully up through the greater mass of green. She rested a gloved fingertip against one. Life fascinated her. Animals were her livelihood, but there was something about the stubborn frailty of flora that entranced her. This moss was trod upon, frozen, and deluged with rain and wind and drought, and it lived on. Certain grasses thrived when grazed upon, depending on the sharp points of herbivore hooves to aerate the soil and the snip of teeth to encourage growth in both shoot and root. Weeds flourished in the wake of industry. So many of those same weeds were edible—a coincidence she found ironic every time she thought about it. Dandelion, burdock, plantain, chickweed, cattails, pigweed, thistles. All forage humans brought with them in the wake of destruction. What had grown in the spaces left by Ivy's wake? And how long had she fed on that bitterness?

She glanced up from the moss to see Ivy crouching beside her, green eyes intent on Lillian's face.

"I have a terrarium with that moss," Ivy said. "You'd probably like it."

"Maybe." They were both speaking in the same hushed tones. Lillian found it hard to breathe this close to Ivy, and she worried that if she kept staring into Ivy's eyes, she'd fall off a precipice she would not be able to climb back up.

"Can I show you more?"

She nodded and rose to her feet.

The island sloped downward as they left the forest. Houses watched them, but she was more interested in the plants growing along the path. Bay laurel. Faded blueberry. Thorny Rosa rugosa. She periodically paused to examine an unfamiliar leaf.

"What are you looking at?"

"I'm not sure, but this is bay laurel. Like the cooking spice."

"Really?" Ivy's fair brows knit together, and she leaned in to stroke the shrub.

"It's everywhere here."

"I know what blueberries and blackberries look like. That's about it."

Lillian identified a few more of the plants around them. Ivy's breath tickled her cheek as she looked over her shoulder to follow the lesson.

"You're into plants *and* birds?"

"Yes."

"That's . . .actually kind of cool." Ivy crushed a bay leaf and inhaled before moving on. Lillian followed her down a sandy path to a rocky beach. Pebbles rolled beneath her feet as she slid down the eroded footpath past the exposed roots of a copse of wind-blasted pines. Waves foamed over boulders and surged through tide pools crusted

136

with ice and dark brown seaweed. Blue gray water stretched out to distant islands and the endless horizon beyond. Beside her, Ivy shivered as the wet wind needled their faces. Lillian looped her arm around her. Ivy didn't pull away. Her body felt surprisingly small, here by the sea, like she might dissolve into spray if Lillian let her go. Perhaps they both would. The wind stripped pretentions, leaving something elemental in its passing, and the longing to swallow the world stopped her breath. Waves crashed. She'd gladly break apart with Ivy, Aphrodite returning to foam, lashing the coast in loving libation. Anything to feel this keenly alive.

They were playing at something that could not be maintained off this island. Whatever this was—this sudden tenderness, this affectation toward friendship—it was permeable. Reality would seep through like it always did. Ivy was still the girl she'd hated, and even if that changed, she was still her colleague and the last person on earth Lillian wanted to feel this thorny, budding thing for. But she couldn't take her arm away.

"It's so different in the summer," Ivy said. "Now, it looks angry."

The ocean roared in reply as snow fell on the waves.

It looks like us.

Darwin barked and chased the sea foam as it tumbled over the rocks. Ivy called him back and suggested they hike on, launching into a story about a game she used to play with her sister by the water's edge. Her voice grew increasingly animated. Lillian could picture a tow-headed child and her sister scrambling up rocks and searching for crabs beneath the seaweed draping the tidepools like hair. This picture of Ivy was different from the woman she knew: Wilder, slightly feral in her bare feet and salt-stiff clothes. She tasted the edge of a yearning Ivy's voice barely contained: the need to be alone sometimes, without society's eyes. It was more relatable than she liked.

"You were free here," she said in a low murmur.

"What?"

"Nothing. What kind of shells wash up on these beaches?"

The island was small enough that they were able to walk the shoreline in a few hours. By the time noon came and went, Lillian was hungry and chilled and ready to rest somewhere out of the wind.

137

"I used to think about you when I was here," Ivy said as turned down a sidewalk. "I never wanted to. But . . ."

She trailed off, and the wind filled in for the rest of her words.

"Did you fantasize about pushing me off a cliff?"

"Sometimes. Mostly I'd think about how much you'd hate it."

"What part?"

"This." Ivy pointed up at a house. The trees around it had been cleared to give it an unrestricted view of the surrounding islands and the horizon beyond, and the white porch and dark wood shingles commanded the panorama with an architect's eye.

"Is this yours?"

Ivy nodded and drew her toward the steps. She took in the immensity of the cottage as she mounted the stairs to the porch. Arches delineated the sweep of it, framing the view and holding up the house's second-story balcony. Leaves had gathered in the corners, but she could see, as if someone had set up a projector, how this place would look in summer: rocking chairs filled with people drinking white wine and gin and tonics, perhaps sipping on light beer and talking about politics and stocks or whatever it was that got discussed in places like this. She pictured Ivy in a summer dress, or perhaps in white shorts and a preppy blouse, laughing at a joke that was, more likely than not, borderline racist in some way, and the bubble that had surrounded them all morning popped. Yes. She would have hated this. *Did* hate it.

Ivy's smile was bittersweet when Lillian at last turned back to her.

"I didn't realize other people didn't have summer homes until I was seventeen," Ivy said. "I get how fucked up that is. I really do."

"Do you, though?"

"I went to private schools. My friends were all like me, and the scholarship kids came with us on vacation, so I never saw their houses. I remember getting my friend Beck drunk on a yacht. He'd never been on a boat before, and as he was throwing up and crying and cursing me out, I finally got it. He hated us."

"Poor little Ivy," said Lillian, unmoved.

"I thought I was different from my family because I wanted to be a veterinarian instead of a lawyer or a surgeon or a congresswoman. And then I met you."

"Just stop." She didn't want to hear Ivy's next words. She wasn't going to be this woman's societal awakening—wasn't going to *let* Ivy make her into that.

"What?"

"Just—I'm not here for your life story." The words came out harsher than she'd intended, and she'd intended them to wound.

"Then what are you here for?"

She didn't respond.

"This is me, Lil. I'm privileged. I enjoy it. I like nice clothes and nice cars and nice houses, and I like that doors open for me."

"They open for you because they shut on everyone else."

"I know." Ivy set her bag on the ground and opened it, pulling out a bottle of wine and a corkscrew. She uncorked it and drank straight from the bottle before passing it. "My family's money is from oil; did you know that?"

Lillian shrugged. She'd googled Ivy, but she wasn't about to confess to it.

"They fund the think tanks, which keep the fossil fuel industry pumping, and my cousin has one of those climate change bunkers. He's on the board of Exxon. I am a product of colonialism and genocide and the actual destruction of this planet, and—" Ivy broke off and raked her hands through her hair. The eyes she fixed on Lillian were wild. "I hate it, and I love this place, and I love—" she broke off again.

"I don't know what you want me to say, Ivy." White guilt was her least favorite brand. She had grown up enjoying the privilege of her own white skin while Daiyu dealt with micro-aggressions and, more than a few times, outright aggression. Ivy had no idea what it was like to watch a parent suffer like that. Lillian had served as a shield when she could, but ultimately it was a divide she never could cross. Daiyu stood on one side, while she, with her white skin, stood on the other. Her anger folded in on itself. She recognized the anguish in Ivy's voice. She too knew what it was like to resent her privilege. An unnerving thought surfaced: could this be part of why Ivy had always gotten to her? Were the similarities between them greater than she wanted to admit?

"I don't want you to say anything. I just want you here. With me."

She opened her mouth to shoot Ivy down out of reflex and then hesitated, because the look on Ivy's face didn't belong to the girl she knew. It wasn't haughty or smug or even full of desire. It was raw and vulnerable and wounded.

"Why?"

"Hell if I know." Ivy paced to the railing and stared out at the ocean. Lillian set down her own bag and joined her.

"Let's not talk about that," she said.

"About what?"

"This." She rested her shoulder against Ivy's.

"Lil—" Ivy twisted so that her back was to the railing, and the vulnerability parted to reveal a question that Lillian did, at least, have an answer for. She kissed her, not gently this time, but hungrily, angrily, as if she could erase Ivy's words and the stain of truth they'd left behind. Ivy whimpered and clung to her. Her hands fumbled with the zipper to Lillian's jacket, and Lillian bit down on Ivy's lower lip. *How can I want sweetness and destruction from the same person?* She wanted to break Ivy down into atoms and ether, and she wanted to feel the wholeness of her in her arms.

She yelped when Ivy's hands slid beneath her sweater. "Your hands are *cold*."

Ivy pulled her closer. "You're really, really warm, though."

"Not anymore." She shivered as Ivy slid icy hands over her rib cage, cold and desire fighting for supremacy.

"Let's go inside."

Ivy shouldered open the door to the house to reveal a large dark room. Dust cloths covered the furniture, but the wide wood planking of the floors gleamed in the dim light let in by the unshuttered windows. Lillian's gaze was drawn at once to the fireplace. The hearth was huge. Gray stone that looked like it came from the island itself took up most of the wall, and the iron grate was wrought in fanciful curves that cupped a laid fire. Ivy went to it immediately and felt along the mantle for a box of matches. Lillian studied her as she bent to light it.

"Are you allowed to light a fire in the off season?"

"Definitely not."

"Will you get in trouble?"

"Only if the island manager happens to be walking past, which is highly unlikely."

Lillian didn't press the issue. She wanted to be warm.

She wandered while Ivy tended to the fire. The furniture beneath the dust cloths was as ornate as the fire grate and didn't look particularly comfortable. A massive staircase led to the second floor, and she touched the dark, polished wood as she investigated the dining room, a second smaller living room with a woodstove, the sunroom, and finally the kitchen. She found another staircase toward the back of the house. *Servant stairs*. Stairs for people like her. She was about to climb them when Ivy caught up with her.

"Exploring?" Ivy asked. She'd taken off her coat, and while she looked chilled, her windblown hair and cream-colored sweater offset the red of her lips.

"Do you mind?"

"Not at all. I'll give you a tour."

She started up the stairs, giving Lillian an unobscured view of her legs and ass. The simmering anger began to bubble into something else.

"Most of these are guest rooms. My parents sleep in the master suite with the balcony, and my sister and I sleep in the back." She opened doors into rooms with white sheets draped over all the furniture, but Lillian could easily see how in a different season sunlight would stream in over the fourposter beds. Ivy's room had a view of trees and sky, as well as water. Waking up in that bed would be like waking up in a dream. She did not want to be awed. And yet she couldn't be otherwise.

"Let's go get warm." She had to get out of this room. It wasn't just the promise of power revealed by the unobscured views; the bed was giving her ideas.

"Sure."

Ivy watched Lillian turn on her heel with an ache in her stomach. She'd seen the emotions that had flickered over Lillian's face, and they lingered in the room like ghosts. She wanted her to love it here even though she knew that was impossible. The island was the one place she felt truly herself. She and Madison had run barefoot over these shores while Prudence let her guard down, content to allow her children this modicum of wildness. If Lillian could see that side of her, would some of the ice in her gaze melt?

Probably not.

At least the fire was warm. She pulled a thick wool blanket out from a chest and spread it on the hearth. Darwin, who was no stranger to comfort, settled in the center of immediately. Lillian shed her jacket and sat cross-legged next to the dog while Ivy arranged the food she'd brought on an end table she'd procured from beneath a sheet. Cheese, bread, and fruit. Her hands were stiff as she broke open the wrapping around the cheese. She needed to warm up but sitting near Lillian without something to do with her hands was too daunting.

"Does your cousin really have a climate bunker?"

"Yep. I've seen it. It's like an underground mansion."

"That's—"

"Incredibly hypocritical," Ivy said before Lillian could get angry again. "But also interesting from an engineering perspective, and pointless."

"Pointless?"

"Would you live in a bunker?" Ivy settled by the fire and tried not to show how desperately she needed the warmth.

"I don't know. Maybe."

"I couldn't."

"Are you claustrophobic?"

"I like the sky," said Ivy. "And I don't think we deserve to hide underground."

"That's not what I would have thought you'd think."

"Has it occurred to you that you might not know what I think about everything, Lee?"

"Has it occurred to you that I might not care?"

She didn't flinch at Lillian's tone. "Then why are you here?"

Lillian looked away. The firelight turned her brown eyes golden and played across her skin. They both knew why they were there: to finish what they'd started, whatever it was. Lillian didn't answer the question this time, either. Ivy hadn't expected her to. They ate in silence, both watching the flames.

"You started this," Lillian said after a while. "Do you remember? You were such a dick that first day at orientation."

"And you fainted."

"I don't like heights."

"You were fine today on the cliff."

"I was ten feet from the edge, not climbing a ladder. There's a difference."

"I was nervous at orientation," said Ivy.

"That doesn't give you the right to be a bitch."

"Yeah. I really was a bitch to you." Ivy knew it had been the truth then, even if she'd grown in the intervening years.

"Recognizing the problem is the first step toward recovery," said Lillian.

"Why would I want to recover? I don't need people to like me. I need them to do what I want."

"What about common courtesy?"

"It doesn't exist. It's a social construct that keeps women lower on the ladder."

Lillian opened her mouth, then shut it.

"Bitch Feminism," Ivy continued.

"You're . . . not wrong. But you can be tough and still be a decent person."

"Maybe. But think how boring school would have been if we'd been decent people."

"I am decent," said Lillian.

"Are you?" Ivy leaned forward and stroked Lillian's scarf, pressing her hand through the material against Lillian's collarbone before pulling away. "Because I'm not the only bitch in this room."

Lillian's cheeks flushed. "I would have been your friend if you'd let me."

"You hated me the minute you saw me," said Ivy.

"That's not—"

"Come on. Admit it."

"No."

"Why? Worried you'll hurt my feelings?" She was always surprised how low her voice got when she was teasing Lillian.

"You don't have feelings."

"That's not entirely true," said Ivy.

"Prove it. Tell me about the last time you felt something."

Ivy held her eyes as she answered. "Today. On the cliff, with you."

Lillian searched her face and then reached for Ivy's scarf, pulling her closer and forcing Darwin to scramble for safety as she tumbled into Lillian's lap. Lillian's hands and clothes were fire-warmed and hot to the touch as she clung to her shoulders, half in her lap, half sprawled across the hearth. She tried to right herself, but Lillian kissed her with a fierceness that disabled thought. She wrapped her arms more tightly around Lillian's neck. One of Lillian's hands gripped her hip and the other cupped her cheek, her nails digging into skin through cashmere, all the while keeping her lips upturned to Lillian's. She couldn't breathe. Not because Lillian's tongue brushed hers and stole her breath, but because the unspoken answer to the question she hadn't asked coursed through her bloodstream.

She'd felt something on the cliff, and Lillian had too. She felt it in the roughness of Lillian's teeth on her lips and in the way her hand covered the curve of Ivy's hip, protective, assertive, simultaneously holding her up and pinning her down. Ivy trembled. It started in her stomach, a fluttering that spread along her bones until she shook all over, wracked by years of wanting *this*.

Lillian pulled away. Ivy gasped and opened her eyes to find Lillian staring at her in concern.

"Are you all right? You're shivering."

She couldn't speak. She reached for Lillian instead, tumbling them onto the blanket and bearing them down with the weight of her body. Lillian exhaled softly, the sound almost a moan as Ivy sought her lips and then the line of her jaw, nipping the skin along it until she came to Lillian's neck. Lillian's hands slid beneath Ivy's sweater and along her back, hot and sure, holding her closer. She bit down. Lillian did moan this time, and the sound sent a white heat through Ivy that dispelled the shaking and left her hungry. A part of her worried that marking Lillian's skin would leave her in an awkward position at work. That part was small and easily ignored, and Lillian gasped as Ivy worked her way down, leaving behind bruises that filled her with a tenderness that made her want to scream.

She tugged Lillian's scarf off. The cloth fell to the floor, where Darwin was quick to take advantage of this new bed. She straddled Lillian as Lillian's sweater and shirt followed, leaving her half naked before the fire. Lillian's simple black bra shimmered in the light of the flames, and the line that ran down Lillian's stomach caught shadows like spilled ink. Ivy paused, letting the clothes fall from her hands, and took Lillian in. Lillian let her. Her black hair was flung across the blanket, and her eyes—she would never really be able to look away from those eyes—were half veiled by her lashes.

"You're gorgeous," she said in a whisper that cut her throat.

And then she raked her nails down Lillian's sides as Lillian had done to her that day in the clinic. Lillian arched her back and cried out, twisting her hips up into Ivy and turning her head to the side, her lips parted and flushed. Ivy repeated the motion, dragging her nails up over Lillian's ribs, counting them as she went, her thumbs tracing the tense line of Lillian's abs as she bucked beneath her. Red marks left a testimony to her passage, and in them she read their entire history.

She undid Lillian's bra with hands that blissfully obeyed her. Lillian's nipples, darker than Ivy's, were hard and perfect and she scratched her again as she leaned in to kiss them.

Hands grasped her hair and held her as her tongue traced the curve of Lillian's breast, circling the center until Lillian forced her over it. Then, unable to continue teasing with Lillian's body urging her on, she took her nipple in her mouth.

"Ivy, oh my god, Ivy."

Lillian, saying her name. Lillian, arching into her, begging with hips and hands and ragged gasps as her teeth and tongue claimed her body, roughness the only way she knew how to be with this woman.

Lillian's fingers released her hair long enough to pull Ivy's sweater, shirt, and scarf off all at once, but Ivy didn't let her take back control. She kept her hands on Lillian's breasts, rolling her nipples between her fingers as she bit Lillian's ribs. Lillian's cry was lower this time, a primal sound that undid something inside her, though she hadn't thought there was anything left to undo. Her lips found Lillian's hips and the dip between, and the leggings were hardly a barrier as she pinned Lillian's legs with her weight.

"Lil," Ivy said, tasting her through the fabric. She eased the hem of the leggings down, exposing the gentle slope of her hips and the soft skin beneath her belly button, smooth against her lips. Below, where Ivy wanted to be, Lillian's dark hair was neatly trimmed. She kissed that, too, not biting, but simply brushing her lips over the surface. Lillian tensed, her whole body poised as Ivy drifted lower. One stroke of her tongue. Lillian shuddered, her breath coming faster, and Ivy observed, transfixed, as Lillian's chest rose and fell above the skin she'd marked.

Lillian's leggings were now in her way. She tasted Lillian again, sliding through her and over her, her own desire a living thing, and tugged on her pants. They slid down slowly, and she had to move to pull them off entirely. When she finished, Lillian lay before her, and she found she couldn't move from where she knelt at her feet. *I'll remember this forever,* she thought. *And I'll never look at this fireplace the same way again.*

Her hesitation gave Lillian time to move. She sat up in a fluid fall of tangled hair, and Ivy gasped as she was pushed against the warm stones of the mantel. Lillian fumbled with Ivy's belt and together they removed her jeans and socks, leaving Ivy in her underwear with stone digging into her spine and Lillian in her lap, holding her wrists as she returned the kisses Ivy had left on her body.

The exquisite agony of pain and desire flooded her nervous system. Lillian seemed to know instinctively where she was most sensitive, and Ivy saw blue behind her eyelids when Lillian bit into the muscle of her shoulder. The sound she made might have been human; she didn't know, and she didn't care. Her body no longer belonged to her. The softness of Lillian's lips and the sharp edge to her bites caressed her neck and down between her breasts. Lillian undid her bra, temporarily freeing Ivy's hands—not that she had any willpower left to put them to use—and the blue light splintered her vision as Lillian took her nipple in her mouth. The gentleness of her tongue was a promise and a taunt. She struggled to free her hands, which had been pinned again, only to hear Lillian laugh.

"I need to touch you."

"You've had your turn."

"I—fuck, Lil."

Lillian dragged her teeth over her nipple. Electricity jolted directly to Ivy's clit. She struggled harder, desperate to touch Lillian, to feel the skin of her hips and her ass and the flare of her waist, the hard muscle of her thighs, anything—everything. Lillian turned her attention to Ivy's other breast. She licked the curve, tracing the swell where it met her ribs and sternum, coming close but not quite closing on her. Her lips just brushed the nipple. Ivy writhed against Lillian's grip, her head flung as far back as rock would allow, her chest canting toward Lillian's mouth and every centimeter of skin dying for her touch. When it came at last, Ivy nearly did, too.

Lillian released one of her wrists. This knowledge seemed distant and unrelated to the feeling of Lillian's mouth until she felt Lillian's hand slide between their bodies and under her underwear, fingers warm as they rested against Ivy's center. Lillian broke away from her nipple and kissed her neck again, tenderly this time, and she turned her face to meet Lillian's.

Heat pooled in her abdomen as Lillian stroked her, teasing her opening and running up and around her clit. She parted her lips, and Lillian claimed her mouth the same way, driving deeper with every stroke, pausing sometimes to tease and lick and suck as her hand brought Ivy closer and closer to the brink. The trembling that had come over her earlier returned. Everything in her body felt loose, like she might break apart into base matter as Lillian found her rhythm. Lillian's other hand still held her wrist, and that grip seemed to be the only thing grounding her as Lillian brought her over the edge. She screamed, and the sound echoed in the empty house as the fire crackled behind her and Lillian Lee didn't stop.

"Lil, please—" she said, her body hypersensitive to every touch. Lillian responded by slipping one finger inside her. Her body spasmed around it, tightening, and she let Lillian turn her until she was on her back on the blanket with her underwear on the ground and Lillian's mouth on her clit. She clutched the ledge of the hearth and her own hair as Lillian's tongue, relentless, brought her to a second climax with a ferocity that lifted Ivy off the hearthstone, her legs wrapped around Lillian's shoulders, and Lillian's name flaying her throat as she repeated it until it felt like the only word she had ever known.

Lillian stroked Ivy's side, her fingertips skimming over the pale skin and the red marks left by her teeth. They marred the creamy white of her skin, and looking at them broke something in her chest. Ivy lay in her arms. Ivy Holden, green eyes closed and her body limp, lay in her arms. She should be running, but instead she memorized the small scar just above her hip and the freckle on her thigh and wondered if she had ever seen anything this beautiful. The sound of Ivy saying her name still lingered in her ears.

One of the bite marks encircled Ivy's shoulder. Another marred her left breast, and still more lined her ribs and neck and—*oops*—even her jaw. A mark for every insult they'd ever traded, every hurt they'd ever caused one another. Her own body bore a matching constellation.

Ivy's eyes fluttered open. She smiled, a crooked thing that lifted one corner of her mouth. Lillian hadn't seen that expression on her face before. It tugged at her own lips as she stroked Ivy's cheek. She wanted to say something, but she was afraid of what might escape if she opened her mouth, so she stayed silent as Ivy caught her hand and kissed the center of her palm. The motion looked unconscious, natural in every regard, and yet it burned.

My poison ivy.

Ivy reached up to touch Lillian's face. She pressed her fingers to Lillian's lips and her crooked smile deepened as she traced them. Lillian felt the touch in her marrow.

"Your lips have always gotten to me," Ivy said. "You used to drive me crazy when you chewed on those fucking pens."

"You said it was a gross habit." She remembered the taunts, and the way Ivy stared at her—only now she saw it in a different light.

"I said a lot of things I didn't mean."

Ivy's hand drifted down Lillian's sides and over her ass. Lillian shifted as desire followed, and Ivy, noticing, nudged her leg between Lillian's. Ivy's thigh pressing into her brought her body fully awake. Her hips moved without her permission, riding Ivy as fingers explored the curve of her ass and the cleft between. She half fell across Ivy when she lifted her body to meet Lillian's need. Her hair curtained their faces. Ivy's eyes looked black in the shadow and she pulled Lillian close, hands on hips and ass, urging her on. Lillian's breasts brushed hers as she rocked to Ivy's rhythm, unable stop herself from succumbing to the irresistible pull of Ivy, Ivy, Ivy—

She didn't realize she was speaking aloud, half sobbing as Ivy brought her to climax. Just before she came, Ivy captured her mouth with hers, and Lillian gasped out a string of expletives mingled with praise. Ivy rolled her gently over, cradling her head. She closed her eyes to catch her breath. They flew open again when Ivy, stretched out beside her in the wrong direction, closed her mouth over her clit.

It was the same thing she'd done to Ivy. That didn't make the shock any less intense, or the almost painfully sensitive skin any less on fire. Ivy lifted Lillian's leg and half turned her hips so she was ensconced between Lillian's thighs. Her tongue circled her, easing her back up and then taking her down, firmly in control, and her whole body tensed as Ivy's tongue swirled in increasingly small, tight circles. Her thighs tightened around Ivy as she came again. The orgasm made her head spin, and the firelight threw strange shadows across the room. Ivy turned her the rest of the way over until she lay on her stomach. The blanket was slightly scratchy against her cheek and smelled like wool and mothballs, but above those scents she smelled Ivy's perfume. She inhaled it in gasps as her body shook.

Ivy lay down on top of her and kissed her ear. Lillian tried to move, but her body was weak with the aftermath of Ivy's touch, and Ivy felt right lying there, her weight a comfort and a warmth. Ivy deepened her attentions to Lillian's ear, reminding her of all the times she had whispered something cruel to her during a lab that required close contact, and how, even then, she'd been sharply aware of the feeling of Ivy's breath and the heat of her body.

"Oh god," she said as Ivy's hand parted her from behind and slid inside her. She hadn't thought she had strength to move, but Ivy's

149

fingers slid in and out of her, slowly, and Ivy nipped her ear with precision as she whispered, "you're not done yet, Lillian."

"Ivy, please, I can't, oh shit, oh, holy shit—"

Ivy bit her shoulder, sharp enough to hurt, sharp enough to cleave a path from Ivy's mouth to Lillian's center as she lifted her hips and fucked her.

The fire died as they lay beneath another blanket, legs and arms entangled, Lillian's head on her shoulder and her heart in Lillian's hands. She breathed in the smell of Lillian's hair. It flooded her system like a drug. Maybe that's what she should tell her doctor. *I need a prescription of Lillian Lee.* Not that she would ever tell Lillian about her condition. She shut down that line of thought and focused again on the simplicity of lying by a fire with a woman she—*no, don't even think it.*

Her phone alarm went off. Lillian propped herself up on her elbows, hair mussed, and reached for it.

"We should get going," Ivy said reluctantly.

"Yeah." Lillian looked down at her, and Ivy saw the closeness that had grown between them start to fade.

Darwin stirred from the nest he'd made of their clothes and watched with canine interest as they dressed and packed up their bags. Ivy scattered the remains of the fire until only glowing coals remained.

"Can we leave it like that?"

Ivy dug out a water bottle and poured it over ashes. The last coals went out in a hiss of smoke and steam, and she shut the flue.

"Now we can leave it." She felt like she'd poured water over more than ashes. The warmth that had accompanied Lillian's embrace felt doused as well.

They walked down to the dock in silence. There was no point talking about what had happened. Not here. Not yet. She did pull Lillian into the shadow of a pine tree to kiss her one more time before they got to the landing, but when she opened her mouth to ask *what happens next?* she couldn't form the words.

150

"Where are the workers?" Lillian asked as the dock came into view.

Ivy looked around. Lillian was right. The work crew and any equipment that could not be left out in the cold overnight should be here already. Instead, the dock was empty save for a gull. Snow blew sideways off the ocean, and Ivy took in the size of the swells and the whitecaps with a growing sense of unease.

"Give them a few more minutes. Here." She led Lillian to the shelter of the boathouse and watched the path, trying not to let panic override her senses. The work crew should have been down here ten minutes ago. Something was wrong.

"Ivy—"

"I have the right time," she said, cutting Lillian off. That wasn't the issue. The issue was the size of the swells and the color of the sky, which was storm gray and full of snow. The ferry might have come early, she realized, and the captain, knowing Ivy was an islander, might have assumed she had gone to stay with the island manager. It was not his job to find day hikers.

Minutes ticked by, and three thirty came and went. No workers trickled down to the dock, and no boat cut through the storm. By three forty-five Ivy knew they were in trouble.

"What's going on?"

"The ferry must have come early because of the storm. The weather wasn't supposed to do this when I checked the forecast."

"The weather never does what it's supposed to do here," said Lillian. "Will it come back for us?"

Ivy hesitated. She didn't want Lillian to worry, but she also couldn't conceal the reality of their predicament. "No."

"What?" Lillian started for the door to the boathouse, as if she might hail a ferry like a taxicab.

"Lillian—"

"What are we going to do? We can't stay out here. My dogs—I work tomorrow—"

"The ferry will come back in the morning. We'll make it to work on time." *Barely.*

"And if we freeze to death?"

151

"We'll go back to the house and light the woodstove. There's probably some cans of soup somewhere, and my mom hoards bottled water. We'll be okay, Lil."

"Nothing about this is okay." Lillian paced the dock. Wind snatched at her scarf and snarled her hair. If they didn't hurry, the house would be too dark for them to find anything, and Ivy needed to move before her own panic overruled her.

"I'm sorry."

Lillian whirled. "Did you plan this?"

"Did I plan what?"

"To trap us here? Is this some kind of sick joke?"

"No!" Ivy took a step back, floored by the vehemence of Lillian's words. "I swear to god. I had no idea the weather was going to do this. If you want, we can go to the island manager's house. There's electricity and heat."

And I'll never hear the end of it from my mother.

Lillian's snarl softened. "You mean we're not alone out here?"

"The manager lives here year-round. We're okay. I promise." A particularly strong gust of wind hurtled into them. She took hold of Lillian's gloved hands. "Let's get into shelter and come up with a plan, okay?"

"Okay." Lillian blinked as snow frosted her lashes.

They walked quickly back, Darwin darting around in his constant search for shrews, and Ivy lit the first candle she could find.

"Let's get the woodstove going. We can close off the sitting room, which will keep it warmer, and I'll grab some of the down quilts from upstairs. Can you see if you can find anything to eat in the kitchen?"

"Sure."

She lit a second candle and handed it to Lillian, then headed for the woodpile outside the kitchen door. Snow had piled up in inches beyond the reach of the back porch, and she filled the log carrier with kindling and enough logs to last them several hours, though she'd need to make a few more trips to get them through the night. Her fingers fumbled the logs in their gloves. The stress had triggered a small flare. Her hands felt like they were wearing electric mittens, and they prickled every time she moved them. It didn't matter.

Back in the sitting room with its antique furniture and squat stove, she crumpled newspaper and laid the fire as she'd been doing for years. *Make a house for the flame*, her father had told her. She'd never had to lay a fire for her own safety, however, and the chill of the room and the growing howl of the wind jeered at her attempts. She blew on the small flame until the paper caught. The wood floor was hard and cold beneath her knees. When the kindling burned at last, she exhaled, and turned around to find Lillian studying her.

"I found some soup," Lillian said, holding up a can of what looked like lentils. Ivy couldn't see the label in the gathering dusk.

"Good. We can heat it up once the stove gets hot enough. Will you keep an eye on the fire while I go find some quilts?"

"Of course."

The formality of Lillian's tone sent splinters into her heart. Why had she thought things would be any different? They'd done what they came here to do, hadn't they? And now they would go back to how they'd always been—perhaps a touch more polite, but still something less than friends. She didn't want that.

She tried to think of what she could say to express this need for something different as she searched closets for quilts and dragged couch cushions in front of the woodstove, making a nest that they could divide or share. Water she found in the pantry, the bottles frozen but easy enough to thaw, and a small pot and two bowls for dinner when they grew hungry. There was still wine and plenty of bread and cheese to make a full meal, and while the septic system had been winterized, nobody would mind if they went to the bathroom in the woods behind the house—not that the prospect was particularly appealing in what was fast becoming a squall. They would be fine. In the morning, the ferry would take them back to the harbor, and no one ever needed to know what had happened here.

Lillian chewed on her lip, which was bruised and swollen from kissing Ivy, and stared at her phone. The cold had nearly killed the battery, and she had no way of charging it. That left her very few options. Biting down on her lip hard enough to risk splitting it, she composed a text to Angie.

LL: Stuck on Rabbit Island with Ivy overnight. I'm fine, but can you feed the dogs? And don't say anything to Morgan. I'll explain when I get back. Thank you. <3

This would be so much fun, she thought darkly as she pictured the look on Angie's face. She didn't have a choice. Hermione and Muffin needed dinner and breakfast, and Angie would take care of them. With any luck Morgan would be staying with Emilia and she wouldn't ever need to confess she'd gotten stranded on an island with Ivy—or why she'd been there in the first place.

Ivy tossed a pile of quilts down the stairs and followed with her candle. The soft glow lit her face, making her look like something from a Wyeth painting against the wood-paneled walls.

Ivy.

Lillian looked away. She was raw and exposed here, huddled before the fire in her winter jacket, and she didn't know what to say. A part of her had hoped fucking Ivy would get her out of her system. Maybe it would have, if she'd been able to leave, but that option seemed less and less likely. Ivy didn't meet her eyes as she pulled the cushions off one of the sofas and laid them on the ground.

"Couldn't you just move the sofa?"

"It's the world's most uncomfortable couch. We're better off this way."

Lillian helped her arrange the cushions and accepted the quilt Ivy offered her, wrapping it around herself. Ivy shut the door to the wood-stove and watched through the small window to make sure it caught the draught from the chimney, then nodded with apparent satisfaction. Bundled side by side, they both stared at the flames through the glass and waited for the room to warm.

"I'm sorry," Ivy said. It was her second apology of the afternoon and, coincidentally, only the second time in their lives Ivy had apologized to her. "I really had no idea this would happen."

"I believe you." The wind rattled the windows, reminding her that this house was completely uninsulated from the cold, and that they had fifteen hours before they could leave. Fifteen hours in Ivy's company.

She wanted to be back in front of the fireplace with Ivy's arms around her, and she didn't know how to ask—nor did she know if she should. The momentum that had carried them here had broken along with their enmity, leaving her adrift.

"Do you want to play cards or something?" Ivy glanced at her out of the corner of her eyes, her quilt a puff of expensive cotton and goose down around her shoulders. Her tone suggested cards was the last thing she wanted to do, and Lillian couldn't help smiling.

"Let's play a different game."

"Like what?"

Lillian cast around her mind for the games she'd played while bored at friend's houses growing up. "Two truths and a lie."

"Seriously?"

"Why not?"

"Hang on." Ivy shed her chrysalis and left the room, returning with a bottle of gin. "Okay. Now we can play."

"There's still a little wine—"

"I am not telling truths without something harder," Ivy said as she uncapped it and took a sip.

"Fine. I'll go first." Lillian considered the very short list of personal truths she wanted to reveal to Ivy and instantly regretted her choice of game. "I'm an only child. I'm really good at soccer. I once swallowed a golf ball."

Ivy shifted on the cushions to face her. The bite mark on her jaw was half hidden by shadow, but she knew it was there. "I know you're an only child," Ivy began. "You might be good at soccer, but swallowing a golf ball is too weird, so I'll go with soccer as the lie."

"Wrong. I played varsity soccer and I've never swallowed a golf ball, but Morgan did when she was a kid. Your turn."

"Okay. I hate spiders, I have nightmares about earthquakes, and my friends in elementary school called me Hivey because I was allergic to so many things."

"You don't have nightmares about earthquakes," Lillian guessed.

"I do. We were in one, once, while visiting friends in California. I like spiders. Go."

"Give me a minute." Lillian paused, then leaned forward. "I wanted to be an astronaut when I was a kid, my first kiss was with a boy named Ernie, and I used to wait to leave class so I could walk behind you."

Ivy raised an eyebrow. "Why did you want to walk behind me?"

"It's two truths and a lie, not two truths and an explanation. Guess."

"Please tell me you didn't kiss a boy named Ernie."

"I did," said Lillian, remembering. "His full name was Ernesto and he was really sweet."

"What did you want to be when you were a kid, then?" Ivy asked.

"A marine biologist."

"Of course you did."

"One of my moms was in the Navy. I wanted to work with Navy dolphins. Your turn."

"Fine. My first kiss was my cousin Brianna, I've always wanted to be a vet, and I had your schedule memorized all four years of school."

Lillian considered the list. "It's gross you kissed your cousin, which I think is true. I don't think you've always wanted to be a vet. Did you really have my schedule memorized?"

"I did. It wasn't intentional, but . . ." Ivy shrugged. "My cousin was a year older than me. I was twelve. We were bored. My mom caught us later that summer, which was a nightmare."

"Did she have a problem with you kissing a girl?"

"No. She had a problem with me kissing my cousin. She assumed we were just experimenting, so I didn't have to come out to her until later. I wanted to be an Olympic equestrian when I was younger."

"Shocking." Lillian had her next trio of answers ready. "I love blondes, I've never smoked weed, and I haven't been sane since you started working at the clinic."

Ivy toyed with a strand of her very blond hair. "I know you've smoked weed. I've seen you do it."

"When?"

"You and Morgan, after finals in the orchard."

"What were you doing there?"

"None of your business. So that means you don't like blondes, but I drive you crazy?"

"Correct. Your turn."

Ivy frowned. "Wait. What's wrong with blondes?"

"Everything is so easy for you. Do you know how much I hate how much I—" She cut herself off before she could finish the sentence with *like you*.

"You weren't easy for me, if that makes you feel better. And you've been driving me crazy for years, Lil." Her voice cracked.

"It's your turn."

"I hate the way you smile. I love your hands. I want to buy you things, and I know you hate it when I do."

Lillian wondered if the room was warming up or if the flush in her face was due entirely to Ivy's words. "You don't love my hands."

"I think I just emphatically proved how much I do."

"Okay. Um . . ." She searched for two more truths, but the recent memory of how her hands had felt on Ivy's skin made it difficult. "I'm out of things."

"Tell me about your boyfriend."

"Brian?"

"Yeah. What was he like?"

"You really want to talk about my ex right now?"

Ivy passed her the gin. "I'm curious."

"Don't be. Brian—wait. How do you know about Brian?"

"Your Insta."

"You creeped on me?"

"Like you've never done that."

She had, of course. She'd gotten better about checking up on Ivy over the intervening years. Initially, she'd stalked her profile frequently. Meeting Brian had helped wean her off the habit, which usually corresponded with low moods. She knew enough from her infrequent checks, however, to turn the tables.

"I'll tell you about Brian if you tell me about Kara."

The mischief left Ivy's eyes. "Kara was great. We broke up. I came here. That's about it."

"Is that why you came here? To get away from her?"

"No."

"Then why—"

"What happened with Brian?"

157

"Long distance got too hard. It happens." She paused and listened to the fire. Had distance been the issue? She'd assumed so, but the assumption didn't fit here as well as it had on the mainland. The shadows cast by that relationship shifted to match a different shape. "Brian was stable. We had the same goals, and he supported my career choices and didn't get in my way."

"Sexy."

"Some things are more important than—"

"Than sex appeal?" Ivy smirked.

"Brian and I understood each other. We were partners. He should have been *safe.*" Her voice cracked on the last word.

Ivy didn't make a joke at that. Her lower lip twitched instead into a slight frown.

"What happened with Kara?" Lillian asked to forestall further comment.

"We . . . wanted different things."

Ivy took a long pull of gin, wiped her mouth with the back of her hand, and shifted her position on the cushions so only six inches separated them. "Let's play a different game."

Ivy's lips, like hers, were swollen from the hours they'd spent kissing, and she could detect the botanicals in the gin on her breath.

"I told you about Brian."

"Trillium."

Angie's comic flashed into her mind before she remembered. Trillium. Their safe word. Backing down where Ivy was concerned defied instinct, especially since she'd just revealed so much about herself, but the pleading in those three syllables weakened her resolve. She'd let her off the hook, this time.

"A game, then. What did you have in mind?"

"Let's pretend nothing exists outside of this room." The howl of the wind picked up, as if to emphasize Ivy's words. "No past. No future. No Seal Cove."

"No consequences?"

"No consequences." Ivy let the blanket slide off her shoulders as she leaned in to kiss first one corner of Lillian's mouth, then the other. Lillian tilted her lips up for a third kiss, but it didn't come. Ivy had paused a bare centimeter away. Her eyes, lit by the woodstove, had never looked so green.

"I'll play."

"Good," said Ivy. "Now take off your shirt."

"I don't take orders, Holden."

"Really?" Ivy slid her hands up underneath the hem of Lillian's sweater and lifted. She let her take it off. Her undershirt remained.

"I didn't take it off. You did."

"I know." Ivy's thumbs brushed the curve of her breasts through the cotton, pausing just above her nipples. The slight pressure hit her dead center. "But you'll take off this one."

"You sure?"

"I'm sure." Her thumbs moved in slow circles, still barely making contact through the cloth. Lillian's breath quickened, and the inhale brought Ivy's touch close enough to make her gasp.

"You'd be surprised how stubborn I can be."

"Not really." Ivy pressed down and dragged her thumbs over her nipples.

She squirmed, then leaned back on her hands, breaking the contact. Ivy smirked and pulled her own layers of clothing off in one move, leaving only her bra. Her hair cascaded over her shoulders. Firelight teased honeyed hues from its waves, and Lillian fought to hold her position. What she wanted to do was bury her face in that hair and kiss the skin beneath. Ivy's bra, which was uncharacteristically simple with only a hint of dark green lace along the straps, created a generous expanse of cleavage. Teeth marks stood out starkly against her skin.

She longed to leave more.

Ivy straddled her slowly. Her thighs, still clothed, held her body over Lillian's lap. "Take your shirt off."

"No." She looked up at Ivy and settled back on her elbows. Ivy followed. Her hair fell around their faces, smelling of wood smoke and snow as well as her shampoo. She breathed it in. "God, you smell good."

Ivy laughed low in her throat, then closed her lips over Lillian's ear and ran her tongue around its curves. Desire licked her like flame. She was dimly aware she was on her back now, Ivy pinning her to the floor

159

as she kept up her relentless campaign, occasionally pausing to nip at Lillian's earlobe before returning to undoing her one stroke of her tongue at a time. Her hips pressed up into Ivy, and she struggled to free her hands so she could pull Ivy closer. Ivy raised herself out of reach. Her breaths were coming in shuddering gasps now, and when she moaned, Ivy moaned too. The vibrations of Ivy's desire against her ear sent every nerve in her body into high alert. Every place Ivy touched sang with it, and she turned her head to capture Ivy's mouth with her own. Ivy's kiss was hot and deep, her tongue teasing as she stroked her the same way she'd stroked Lillian's clit only a few hours before.

And then Ivy pulled away.

Lillian didn't even have breath to beg. She stared up at Ivy, pleading with her body.

"Take off your shirt."

"I don't think I can."

"That's too bad."

Ivy sank onto Lillian's hips and reached behind her to undo her own bra. Lillian struggled to sit up, lured by the shadows flickering over Ivy's skin and the weight of Ivy against her.

Ivy buried a hand in the hair at the back of Lillian's head and lowered her back down. Bracing herself on one arm, Ivy leaned over her again. Ivy's breasts brushed hers, taut nipples hard against her own, and she thought of how much better they would feel without a barrier. Ivy rocked back and forth, slowly, her breasts swaying with her.

Fuck it.

Lillian yanked the shirt off her head as best she could with Ivy's hand still in her hair, then fumbled at her bra. She swore, and Ivy's hair caressed her bare skin until her bra came unsnapped at last. She shimmied it off one shoulder, aware Ivy had no intention of releasing her, and let it fall to the other side.

The warm skin of Ivy's nipples brushed her own as Ivy rocked a little faster. Breath rasped in her throat. The prickle of pain at the base of her neck from her straining hair follicles eased into pleasure as Ivy's breasts met hers, again and again, their soft weight a promise and a taunt.

"I told you you'd take it off eventually."

"Shut up."

"Will you take off your pants if I ask nicely?"

"I want you to do it," she said, arching her back.

Ivy lowered herself fully and the metal of her belt buckle pressed into the cloth of Lillian's leggings.

She lost herself to Ivy's lips. Now that Ivy had freed her hands, she stroked the skin of her back and the curve of her ribs, feeling the raised flesh where her nails had marked her earlier. She did not claw at her now—not yet, at least. Ivy shivered when she touched her lightly. She experimented with tracing the dip along her spine with her fingertips. Ivy bit Lillian's lip in response and moaned.

Sensing an opportunity, she tumbled Ivy onto her back. Ivy didn't fight her, and lay with her golden hair spilling around her, waiting. She undid Ivy's belt and the top button of her jeans, sliding the zipper down one centimeter at a time. Ivy raised her hips for her to pull the pants off.

"Do you want me to leave your socks on?" Lillian asked. "It *is* cold."

"Don't be an ass."

She parted Ivy's legs after she had removed the rest of her clothing and kissed the skin of her inner thigh. Ivy's hand found her hair again. She ignored Ivy's insistent tugs and worked down instead of up, tasting the skin behind her knee and along her calf. Ivy's other leg wrapped around her shoulders. She turned and kissed that one, too, sucking hard enough to leave more bruises as Ivy's breathing intensified.

She gave Ivy's clit one long stroke before she settled across her stomach. Ivy's moan of frustration nearly made her rethink her trajectory, but not quite. Instead, she took Ivy's breasts in her hands, pressing the skin between them down with her thumbs so that she could take both of Ivy's nipples in her mouth at the same time.

"Lil," Ivy gasped as her whole body bucked.

Lillian raked her tongue across Ivy, teasing and pulling with lips and teeth while Ivy writhed beneath her. She moved her hips in time, loving the feel of Ivy's nails digging into her arms and shoulders and scoring new lines over the old.

"Why. The hell. Do you still. Have pants on." Ivy managed in

161

between gasps.

"Because," she said, letting the breath from her words pass over Ivy's nipples. "You haven't taken them off."

Ivy's laugh, while still throaty, was so genuine she lifted her head to look at her.

"What?" Ivy asked.

I've never heard you laugh like that.

Instead, she said, "Are you going to do something about it?"

"Depends on if you let me breathe."

"So you want me to stop?"

"God no," said Ivy with a groan. "But you really need to lose the leggings."

"Sounds like a you problem."

Ivy scoffed and snapped the waistband of Lillian's pants. "I can make it both of our problems."

"Or you could just take them off." She rolled off Ivy and lay beside her, watching the fire play across Ivy's skin.

Ivy turned on her side, head propped on her hand.

"I could put my shirt back on," Lillian threatened.

"Don't you dare." Ivy sat up so quickly she nearly burned herself on the woodstove. Lillian grabbed her elbow and tugged her out of harm's way.

"Easy, Holden."

"I'll show you easy."

Lillian's leggings, underwear and socks were peeled off her in a smooth motion that, though she would never admit it aloud, impressed her. Heat from the stove radiated across her bare skin.

"Was that so hard?"

"Surrender is always hard."

"You're surrendering?" she asked Ivy as she entwined their fingers and pulled her back down beside her.

"Temporarily."

She opened her mouth to make another comeback, but Ivy stopped her with her lips. A vicious gust of wind rattled the window-panes. It was easy to pretend, as Ivy had suggested, that the world ceased to exist beyond the wind and the walls. The ocean might extend for thousands of miles in every direction, leaving them marooned here without fear of rescue.

"I want you," she said as Ivy slid inside her. "I want you so damn much."

Chapter Eight

She woke from a dream of winter to add wood to the stove and found Lillian's arms around her beneath a mountain of quilts. Lillian's measured, sleeping breaths stirred her hair, and when Ivy moved, Lillian tightened her hold in her sleep.

A reflex, she told herself. Still, she hesitated before making another attempt to rise. She could feel Lillian's heartbeat against her back, and their legs were tangled together, her feet resting in the curve of her lover's, thighs warm alongside her own. The room, however, was cooling rapidly. If she didn't disentangle herself soon, the fire would go out completely. She eased Lillian's arm away from her chest, careful not to let a draft of cold air under the blankets, and reached for a log. Lillian murmured something as she tucked the blankets around her but didn't wake. She opened the door to the woodstove and blew on the coals until they glowed again, refusing to think about what could have happened had she not awakened. Then again, the looks on the faces of everyone who knew them when it was discovered they'd died in each other's arms would be priceless. She pictured Morgan's stunned expression and smiled to herself.

The fire took a while to catch. Unwilling to risk it going out, she sat up to wait, shivering in the cold. Lillian's cast-off sweater lay nearby.

She pulled it over her head and inhaled the smell of Lillian's skin. Behind her, Lillian burrowed closer in the instinctive way of sleep, her hair black as blood across the quilt. She smoothed a strand behind her ear, careful not to wake her. Lillian's lips were slightly parted. She remembered those lips on her skin and remembered how her name sounded leaving them.

Don't think about it. Not yet.

As well forget it was winter. Whatever happened next, she could not fool herself into thinking things would go back to the way they'd been.

"What is this?" she asked Lillian, so quietly the words barely stirred the air. "What are we doing?"

Lillian couldn't possibly have heard her, but she stirred, a line creasing the smooth skin of her forehead. "Ivy?"

"I'm here."

Lillian's eyes opened. The dim light caught them, and Ivy stilled, arrested by the simple pressure of that gaze.

"Come back."

Lillian lifted the quilt. Ivy slipped beneath it and let Lillian pull her close again, aware, as she had not been earlier, of how her nerve pain had quieted as if granting her a brief respite—as if even her tortured immune system had calmed in Lillian's arms. Not that *calm* was the right word. What she felt was deeper, and she did not have a word to describe how right it felt to lie there with Lillian's lips pressed to her hair and her hand tucked against Ivy's chest, their bodies acknowledging in sleep how intertwined their fates had grown.

None of this made sense.

On the other hand, perhaps it *did* make perfect sense, she reflected the next morning as they huddled on the ferry for warmth, roused by the last one percent of battery on her phone and the alarm she'd set the night before. Both had just gotten out of relationships. Both knew the other's limit. Why not do whatever it was they were doing and spare innocent people the fallout? It wasn't like they could hurt each other any more than they already had.

Beside her, Lillian watched the black waves rise and fall behind the fogged glass.

"Crazy storm last night," said the ferry's captain.

"It was."

"Must have been real crazy on the island."

"Yeah."

She pressed her hands between her legs to keep from touching Lillian. Darwin curled up on the seat beside her, content with his lot. Nothing out of the ordinary had just happened for him, save for getting fed bread for dinner. The captain shot sideways looks at her periodically, but he did not ask what had compelled her to weather a small blizzard off the coast. She hoped he wouldn't mention it to the island manager.

The ferry brought them into the harbor at 7:40, leaving them barely enough time to get to the clinic, let alone home. Lillian drummed her fingers on the seat in front of them as the ferry pulled into the wharf.

"Do you have an eight o'clock?" Ivy asked.

Lillian nodded. She'd thrown her hair into a messy braid, but it was clear she'd wakened in a hurry.

"My first appointment isn't until eight thirty. I can pick you up a coffee."

"Thanks. I need to run home. I can't see appointments dressed like this."

"Make sure you grab some cover-up."

"Right. This—" Lillian didn't finish whatever she was thinking, for the ferry shuddered to a halt and she took off with an, "I'll see you at the clinic."

Ivy tipped the captain as she followed.

The fastest shower of her life and a drive at uncomfortable speeds down the snowy roads brought her to Stormy's. She waited in the short line with an odd lightness in her chest.

"Did you survive the potluck?" Stormy asked.

"Potluck?" *Right.* Impossible to believe that had been only a few days ago. "Oh. Yeah. It was good. Two dark roasts and one medium."

"Medium, hmm? It went that well?"

She couldn't help the smile tugging at her lips under Stormy's good-natured teasing.

"Maybe I'm making up for bad behavior."

"Oh, I hope it was bad." Stormy poured the three coffees into to-go cups and set them on the counter. "Come tell me about it later?"

The overture of friendship, tossed so lightly, hit her like a javelin. She was desperate, she realized as she took the coffee, for someone to talk to about Lillian, and she couldn't very well call up her friends from Colorado. They wouldn't understand, and they still hadn't forgiven her for leaving on such short notice with only a vague explanation.

"I will," she promised Stormy, and left the café with a grin spread across her face and the tray of coffees for her, Lillian, and Shawna clutched to her chest.

Lillian relented after the twentieth text message and agreed to meet Angie for lunch at Stormy's café. Despite the panicked rush that had started her day—she *hated* running late—things had gone smoothly. Ivy had delivered her a coffee with cool professionalism broken only by her lingering eye contact, and none of her appointments had complained about the cost of treatment. Most of her rechecks had even complied with her instructions, which was a small miracle.

Now she faced the gauntlet.

"Well?" Angie asked as soon as she joined her in line.

"Can I order food first?"

Angie huffed and turned to the menu. "Let me guess. Seasonal salad?"

"You say that like it's a bad thing."

"It is when there's grilled cheese on the menu."

"You," Stormy said when the older woman in front of them stepped aside to wait for her beverage, "and I need to talk."

"Oooh," Angie said, waggling her eyebrows at Lillian. "You're in trouble."

"Can I get lunch instead of the Spanish inquisition?"

"Sí. But only if you tell me why Ivy Holden bought you coffee this morning."

"Probably as an apology for holding her hostage on Rabbit last night," said Angie.

Stormy's jaw dropped. "You were on Rabbit last night? Wasn't there, like, a blizzard?"

"Yes. That's why we got stuck."

"Back up." Stormy glanced between Lillian and Angie. "Why were you there in the first place?"

Lillian looked over her shoulder, hoping to use the line as an excuse to evade the question, but there was nobody behind them.

"It's a long story."

"Then give me the condensed version." Stormy put her hands on her hips and waited.

"You cannot tell Morgan. Or Stevie. Or my moms."

"My group chat with the Momma Lees is where I dump all my gossip though," said Angie with a pout.

"I'm serious. I don't . . .I'm not sure what's going on."

Waking up with Ivy in her arms, golden hair and golden skin warm against hers beneath the quilts, her body sore from sleeping on the floor and from the activities that had led them there, and every ache a gift. The smell of Ivy's hair. The curve of her cheek. Her breasts, soft and heavy in her hands as she rolled her over to kiss her in the white light of dawn.

Her friends sobered at her tone of voice.

"Okay. We promise. Let me get you lunch, and I'll have Jill cover for me. What do you want?"

They placed their orders and found a table. Angie put her chin in her hands and stared at Lillian, looking pensive.

"What?"

"Sometimes you surprise me, Tiger Lily."

"You and me both."

"Why can't we say anything to Morgan or Stevie?"

"Because Stevie will tell Morgan, and Morgan—She won't understand. And I'm not ready to deal with that yet, because *I* don't understand."

"Fair."

"Your food will be up in a minute," Stormy said as she joined them. "Are you okay, Lil?"

"I don't know."

"After you hooked up with her in Portland, I—"

"Wait, you hooked up with Ivy in Portland?" Angie asked.

Lillian dropped her head into her hands while Stormy filled Angie in.

"Damn, girl, I can't believe you set them up."

"I'm still mad at her for that," she said from between her fingers.

"Okay. So. You kissed at the club because Stormy is an evil genius, but you hate her, and now you spent the night with her on Rabbit. Did anything happen?"

Ivy, straddling her. Ivy, teasing her. Ivy, eyes wide and green as she came in Lillian's arms.

"Um."

"Hey." Stormy peeled her hands away from her face and took one in her own. Angie took the other, squeezing her fingers.

"What am I doing?" she asked her friends.

"We don't know," said Angie. "But if you tell us, we can talk it out."

"I don't process," she remembered Morgan telling her that summer when Lillian confronted her about her feelings for Emilia. She'd scoffed at Morgan at the time, but now she understood. She'd never had a problem talking to her friends about Brian. Something about Ivy, though, made her want to clam up and sink deep into the cold mud of the sea floor.

Could it be the fact that you've been talking about how much you hate her for years?

"I . . ." she swallowed and tried again. "I slept with her."

"Holy shit," said Angie.

"And?" said Stormy. "How was it?"

"It was . . ."

Angie leaned forward. "Good? Awful? Mind blowing? I'm going to need to change the whole comic, you know."

"It was . . . good," she said, settling for an adjective that was so far from satisfactory she wanted to laugh.

"Scale of one to ten, one being Brian."

"Brian was good in bed, Ange."

"Whatever. He dumped you, so I hate him."

Stormy reached out and took her chin in her other hand and tilted it toward the light. "Is that a hickey?"

169

"Absolutely not."

"It absolutely is."

"I've never seen you with a hickey," said Angie in delight.

"Nor will you." She slipped her hands free of theirs and pulled out her makeup case. Flipping open a mirror, she dabbed more liquid cover-up on her jaw and neck, embarrassment painting her cheeks. She snapped the mirror shut.

"Are we talking a seven? Nine?"

"Also, how did you not freeze to death?" asked Stormy.

"There was a fireplace and a woodstove."

Angie passed a hand over her brow in an imitation of a swoon. "That's legit romantic."

"There is nothing romantic about me and Ivy."

"Just cozying up together in front of a fire, on an island, in the middle of a snowstorm, with only each other for warmth? You do realize people write fanfic about things like that, right?"

"I don't read fanfiction."

"Your loss," said Angie. "Clearly."

"Are you going to keep seeing her?"

"I have to, don't I?" she said to Stormy. "We work together."

"Are you going to keep *sleeping* with her?"

"I don't know."

"Do you want to?" Angie asked.

She hesitated, the words *I don't know* refusing to leave her lips. She did know. She knew without a shred of doubt she wanted to sleep with Ivy again. Not just fuck her, but sleep with her, her arms around Ivy's waist and their breath falling into rhythm.

Which is a very, very bad sign.

Perhaps sensing she was either unwilling—or unable—to answer, Stormy cleared her throat. "Okay. Let me get this straight. You were rivals in vet school, but you're both doctors now, and mature, intelligent, professional women. Does the past matter?"

Waking in Ivy's apartment. The cool cotton of Ivy's duvet against her cheek. The way the pillow smelled like Ivy's shampoo. And Ivy, sitting up in bed, her arms around her knees, staring straight ahead. Her hair fell in a rumpled wave down her naked back. A lock curled around the blade of her shoulder, while another brushed the channel of her spine. *So vulnerable. So different than the Ivy who tormented her across a lab table.*

"*You're perfect, Lee,*" Ivy had whispered late last night, her hand deep enough inside Lillian to brush her soul, while snow drifted past a streetlight out the window. She'd felt perfect. She'd felt whole. She'd felt, in other words, like someone else, because those women couldn't be Ivy Holden and Lillian Lee. They were sworn enemies. They were not . . . whatever this was.

Except her body called her bluff. Two years of obsessive hatred had memorized every inch of Ivy. She could pick her footfalls out of a crowd, knew the many timbres of her laugh and what each meant, knew the feeling of Ivy's breath on her ear, whispering an insult, standing too close. Knew what Ivy smelled like after a shower, after the gym, after an exam when stress-sweat defeated her perfume. Those weren't things you knew about someone you wanted hit by a bus. Those were things you knew about some-one *you* wanted.

And now, here she was in Ivy's bed, and there Ivy was, haloed by the rising sun. She sat up. Ivy stiffened. Swallowing her trepidation, she reached to lay a hand on Ivy's cool shoulder.

Ivy's voice cut the hope out of her with all the surgical finesse of a chainsaw.

"*Get the fuck out of my house, Lee.*"

"The past always matters," said Angie.

"Yeah, but—"

She cut Stormy off. "We work together. It's a bad idea."

"Why, because things could get worse than they already are?"

Their food arrived on the bar, sparing her the need to answer. She rose before either of them could object and retrieved her salad and Angie's grilled cheese. Her friends had their heads together when she returned.

"We've decided," Angie announced.

"What have you decided?"

"That you should quit while you're ahead. Tell Ivy it was fun while it lasted and go back to being weird and bitchy about her all the time."

She sensed a trap.

"Yes. And then I'll date her," said Stormy. "Because she is *fine.*"

"Since when are you into femmes?" asked Angie.

"Since whenever I feel like it."

"Please do not date Ivy Holden," said Lillian.

"Why not?"

"Because—" She paused. Both Stormy and Angie waited, their gazes predatory. "Because she has a mean streak, and I don't want you getting hurt."

The memory of that distant morning was too fresh. Ivy could be all sweetness when she wanted to be, which was clearly the side she'd chosen to show Stormy, but that didn't change what lay beneath. Poison coated the luster of her leaves. It was one thing for Lillian to touch her, knowing she was poison, but she would not let her friends.

"That's definitely the reason," said Angie in mock seriousness. "Don't you think?"

"Absolutely. It has nothing to do with the fact that she can't stand the thought of me and Ivy boning—"

"Stop." She stabbed her fork into a fat slice of radish and glared.

Stormy held her hands up in surrender. "Relax. You're right. She's not my type."

"What we really decided," said Angie in a gentler tone, "is you've been messed up since Ivy got here, and everything makes much more sense now."

"What part of this makes any sense?"

"You're repressing some serious emotional shit about that girl."

"What Angie means, in case 'emotional shit' isn't clear enough, is you have feelings for Ivy. Very complicated feelings. And if they haven't gone away in the last six years, they are certainly not going to go away now that you've slept together. You don't get an easy out from this."

Her salad wilted in her stomach. She eyed the radish still speared on her fork and felt just as impaled. "I know. I just don't know what to do about it."

"What if you gave her a chance?"

She looked at Stormy, some of the anger from the night at the club still lingering. They didn't know Ivy like she did. People didn't change that drastically in just a few years. Stormy, however, was right about one thing: she was in it now, and there was no easy way out.

"How do I give her a chance?"

"Some people do dinner," said Angie. "Instead of nearly freezing to death."

"I need something that doesn't involve money so she can't lord it over me."

"What about a concert? Something fancy and classical that requires you to wear a black dress. And you could buy the tickets ahead of time. Or you could take her to the Boothbay botanical gardens, or for a sleigh ride, or . . . hot tubs! Sleigh ride then hot tubs!"

"So, like . . . date her?"

Angie patted her consolingly. "For a doctor, sometimes you're surprisingly thick."

"If I do that, I'll have to tell Morgan eventually."

"Yes?" said Stormy, drawing the word out into a question.

"And she is not going to like it."

"She's not your mothers."

Lillian could feel all the blood draining from her face. "Oh no. I forgot about them. They'll kill her. Like, actually kill her and bury her body in a bog if they find out I'm seeing her."

Angie and Stormy blinked.

"Why do I feel like there's more to this story than you've told us?" asked Angie.

"There isn't," she said too quickly to be believable. "Whatever. I'll deal with Morgan and my moms when there is something to deal with. Right now I need to eat and get back before I'm late for my next appointment."

"Well, well, well," said Stormy when Ivy took a seat at what was beginning to feel like her stool at the bar. "What can I get you?"

"Something decaf. I need to sleep tonight."

"Any chance that's because you didn't get enough sleep last night?"

"I have no idea what you're talking about," she said, adopting an airy tone.

"Mhmm. Something to eat?"

She ordered a bagel and lox and rested her elbows on the bar to watch Stormy work. Stormy did her best to please her customers, and it was clear who were regulars from the jokes they exchanged. Ivy was lucky the town had a place like this. She'd noted a few of the other bars, which seemed to cater to very different clientele.

"It's funny," Stormy said as she circled back around with a frothy beverage. "Don't you think? You and Lil crossing paths again."

"Yes, my abs are sore from laughing."

"I'm sure that's the reason they're sore." Stormy winked. "Talk to her recently?"

"Had lunch with her today."

The room felt hot and close suddenly, and the soft music jarred her ears. "Oh."

"We had a fascinating conversation."

Do not ask what it was about. Do not ask what it was about. Do not— "What did you talk about?"

"Plants."

"Plants?" She sipped her drink, not tasting it.

"Yes." Stormy flipped a cloth from her apron and scrubbed at a circle of condensation on the bar. "Lilies. Types of ivies. Whether or not the two could grow in the same garden."

She clutched the warm mug. "Lil's a gardener, right? What does she think?"

"She's worried," said Stormy.

Ivy looked at her hands and tried to sound nonchalant. "She should be. They're both poisonous to dogs and cats."

"The urge to make a terrible joke about pussies and bitches is strong, but I'll have you know that I, a mature adult, have overcome it."

"I'm not sure that counts as overcoming," said Ivy.

"Little victories. How are you liking Seal Cove? You've been here almost two months."

"It's nice."

"Not exactly a ringing endorsement," said Stormy.

"It's November in Maine."

"I actually love November." Stormy gestured at the dark sky beyond the café windows—only a few lights in the harbor breaking the black. "It's so melancholy and bleak and moody."

"Exactly."

"You never had a goth phase, did you."

Ivy laughed. "No. Prep school uniforms made it rather difficult."

"I'm sure you could have found a way."

"I could have, but investigators would still be looking for my body after my mother murdered me. Goth daughters are harder to show off to conservative senators."

"I'll bet."

"And you?"

"The darkness in my soul shines through no matter what I wear," said Stormy. "Are you sticking around for the winter holidays?"

"No. My family takes Christmas seriously."

"You know," said Stormy, pausing her work to concentrate fully on Ivy. "We usually hold a Holiday Thing. I'm an atheistic Jew and none of the rest of us are religious, so it's very chill, plus Lil's mom will make moon cakes for the Lunar New Year. You should come."

"Didn't you get in trouble the last time you invited me out?"

"Hazard of the job."

"I don't think Lil wants me crashing something like that."

"Well, I happen to like you, so I'm inviting you as *my* friend. Fair?"

"I'm flattered."

"You should be. I don't pick up just any strays."

Ivy had never been called a stray in her life, but as she felt the warmth of Stormy's smile soothe the ache in her chest, she decided the term fit. She'd fled Colorado with her tail between her legs and had wound up here, sniffing around Stormy's bar for human connection.

"Thanks," she said, embarrassed and grateful in equal parts.

"I'll text you the details."

It wasn't Stormy who texted her the next day, however, as she worked up a case of colic on a nearby farm. She checked her messages when she got back in the truck, fingers stiff with cold and snow spitting down from a leaden sky.

LL: *I have two tickets for the Portland Philharmonic Orchestra. Interested?*

Her chapped lips split in the wake of her grin. She recognized the challenge. Classical music wasn't something she particularly enjoyed,

175

which Lillian knew. If she accepted, it would show Lillian she cared enough to sit through something she didn't love. If she refused, or suggested a different event, she'd show Lillian she wanted to spend time with her, but not make sacrifices to do so.

Clever, Lee.

IH: *Can I buy you dinner first?*

Lillian's response came later that day.

LL: *Yes, but I get to choose the restaurant.*

IH: *It has to have napkins on the table.*

LL: *Paper, or cloth?*

IH: *The fact you have to ask is embarrassing for you.*

LL: *Because you're a snob?*

IH: *Because cloth is better for the environment, and I thought you cared about the Earth.*

LL: *Cute. I'll pick you up at 5 on the Friday after Thanksgiving.*

IH: *Have my schedule memorized?*

LL: *Don't flatter yourself. It's on the hospital calendar.*

IH: *Sure.*

LL: *See you then, Holden.*

Lillian's family celebrated Thanksgiving passively. Daiyu didn't like turkey, so they cooked two Cornish game hens instead: one each for Daiyu and June, and a tofurkey for her. The tofurkey was more of a joke than a sincere attempt at celebrating genocide, but, smothered in vegetable gravy, it wasn't half bad.

"You seem happier," Daiyu said as she passed a basket full of warm pumpkin bread. Muffin raised her snout from beneath the table to sniff the baked goods, true to her namesake.

"Work is going well." She tried to keep her voice level so she didn't betray the giddiness she felt every time she thought of Ivy. "As much as I hate to admit it, having another vet on the staff again is helpful."

"Even if it's Ivy?"

"She's a good doctor. I'm trying to overlook the rest."

"Working with people you don't like is part of life," said June.

"You've been lucky so far at Seal Cove. Take Randall."

She bit into the warm bread as her mother launched into a rant about one of her coworkers. The story involved a crane, which made her shudder. It defied reason that June could work several stories in the sky while she could barely climb footstools. Thinking of heights brought her back to Ivy. Which also defied reason.

She was going to go on a date with Ivy Holden.

Willingly.

After dinner and the necessary kitchen cleanse, which was difficult on loaded stomachs but eased by June's liberal hand with the beer, they collapsed on the couch. Daiyu rested her head on June's shoulder, and June kissed her wife's graying hair. Lillian, who had curled up in her favorite armchair with Hermione snuggled against her, felt a pang of love and jealousy. She wanted the kind of love her parents had. Deep. Simple. Present. Ivy didn't fit into that picture.

On the other hand, she'd just gotten out of a four-year relationship. She deserved a chance to sleep with whomever she pleased, and dating Ivy for a while was—

A terrible idea.

Hermione let out a long sigh from her narrow snout and burrowed deeper into her lap. No matter how she looked at it, dating Ivy, if she could call what they were doing dating, would only end badly. Stormy and Angie may have pointed out things were already going badly, but they didn't know the full extent of the damage Ivy Holden could inflict on her. The old wound was still there. Even as she thought this, an image of Ivy sitting beside her at the Portland symphony rose in her mind.

"What are you smiling about?" asked Daiyu.

"Dinner."

Her phone buzzed in her pocket. She pulled it out, hoping it wasn't from the clinic, and opened an image from Angie. This time, the smile turned into a laugh. Angie had finished a strip of her Poison Ivy comic, and she studied the panels, admiring Angie's skill. Poison Ivy, wrapped in noxious green leaves, fought Tiger Lily. Sentient plants rose to aid them both, vines wrapping around legs and arms and the frame of the panel itself. In the last several, the characters engaged in a wrestling match that got progressively more intimate, until Tiger Lily had Poison Ivy pinned beneath her. She zoomed in on the speech bubble.

You don't have the guts to kill me, said Poison Ivy.

There's more than one way to win, said Tiger Lily, and in the next panel—

"Good god," she said aloud, then typed a message to Angie.

LL: *This is straight up porn.*

AD: *You liked it.*

LL: *My boobs are not that big.*

AD: *But hers are.*

"What do you want to watch?" June asked.

"Whatever you want," she said, trying to look away from the comic on her phone screen.

Angie had a point. She remembered firelight falling over Ivy's breasts, and, despite her distended stomach and the presence of her mothers on the couch, felt her body react.

AD: *You're welcome.*

LL: *Shut up.*

The drive to her aunt's house in Connecticut was uneventful. She sang along to the radio and tried not to think about the promise she'd made to herself.

I'll tell them.

She pictured her mother's ashen face; her father's stunned expression; the horror as the realization their perfect, golden daughter had a flaw sank in.

I have to tell them eventually.

But did she? How long could she hold out before the disease made the decision for her? How long could she stand the loneliness eating her from the inside out?

I am not lonely.

That, however, was a lie too far, even for her. Madison knew, but Madison was one person. An important person, but she couldn't ask her sister to be everything for her. She'd moved closer to home because her doctor told her she might need help, and she'd decided she'd rather have her family's help than Kara's.

I'll tell them. I will.

But who was she explaining to? Herself? The therapist she didn't have, though she probably needed one?

Then there was Lillian. She skipped through her playlist, looking for something to distract her. Lillian, try though she might to convince herself otherwise, wasn't just a rebound. Ivy might be a rebound for Lillian, though, and she couldn't afford to lie about that to herself, either. What she felt for Lillian hadn't dimmed in the intervening years, and now—

Nope. Don't go there.

She wasn't fit for a relationship. Not like this. She had nothing to offer Lillian—if Lillian even wanted something from her beyond a chance to burn off old grudges. Plus, the sex. That had always been good. She remembered Lillian's mouth on her body, taking both her nipples between her teeth at once, and searched for a faster song.

Cousins greeted her with hugs and gossip the minute she got out of her car. Her shoulders sent sparks of pain down her arms from driving for several hours, but she ignored the pain and returned their affection. The cousins closest to her in age, Brianna and Mark, pulled her into the room that had always been their lair growing up; a pool table, bar, and huge flat screen TV were the main perks.

"Where are Keith and Sarah?" she asked, not seeing their partners.

"In the kitchen, I think. Your parents are there, too. Drink?"

"I'm good for now."

"Ellen's kids are nightmares. I wish she'd brought their nanny," said Brianna.

"And don't even get me started on—"

"There you are." Madison swooped into the room and down on Ivy, pulling her to her feet and into a hug. "Mom's looking for you."

Shooting her cousins an apologetic smile, she let Madison lead her back into the main house.

"She's not wrong about Ellen's kids. Fucking nightmares with legs."

"Maybe they'll put the kids' table in another room."

"Let's hope so. What's new with you?"

"Got trapped on Rabbit the other night."

Madison halted, her mouth open. "No you didn't."

"Sure did. Don't tell anyone."

"What were you doing out there?"

"The ferry came back early. I missed it."

"Were you alone?"

She shrugged, and a smile tugged at her lips. Madison cackled.

"You're *bad*. Anyone I know?"

"No."

"Good for you. You didn't burn the place down, did you?"

"Pretty sure you would have heard about it if I did."

Richard and Prudence deposited kisses on her cheeks when she entered the kitchen. Prudence's hands were cool and dry on hers, and she smelled like Chanel and cinnamon. Her father held a potato peeler in one hand and wore a goofy grin.

"We could use your scalpel expertise," he said, gesturing at the mountain of peeled potatoes beside him. Ivy accepted a knife and started chopping, listening to the chatter around her as her aunts and uncles and her cousins and their spouses and children milled about the large kitchen. The potatoes were cold, and her knife hand was weak from nerve pain, but she persevered.

The holiday went as it usually did. The conversation wandered from stocks to pop culture to politics and to the children, who were shunted to a far table not because there was no room at the massive, many-leaved oak dining table, but because Ellen's spawn didn't know the meaning of the words "be quiet." Ellen looked like she'd been dragged behind a semi over gravel for several miles. Her husband, meanwhile, dominated discussion whenever possible, and Ivy rolled her eyes at Madison as he went down a conservative rabbit hole.

"How's your bunker?" she asked, unable to bear it any longer.

Prudence, sensing conflict, interrupted. "Ivy, could you pass me the cranberry sauce?"

"They've upgraded since the last data set came back from Exxon's scientists," he said. "Now that we know there is a possibility of anoxic events, they are rethinking the filtration systems."

"Of course." She marveled at how he seemed completely un-aware—or at least uncaring—about the hypocrisy of his statement. Then she pictured him and his wife locked in a bunker colony with their children, presumably without their nanny, and stifled a snort of bitter laughter. Lillian would explode with righteous anger if she heard.

Her imagination provided her with an image of Lillian sitting beside her, white-knuckled on the silverware, which, of course, really was silver, jaw clenched as Ellen's husband continued his detailed explanation of climate bunker engineering. As ludicrous as it was to imagine Lillian here, and as much as Lillian would hate it, she couldn't help wishing she could reach for her hand beneath the table.

The opportunity to talk to her parents came sooner than she liked. After dinner, as the football game blasted from several TVs and clean-up finished in the kitchen, her mother and father motioned her and Madison to join them for a moment in an empty sitting room.

"It's so good to see you girls," said Prudence.

Madison groaned and clutched her stomach. "I'm going to burst, mother. You won't see me much longer."

"That's my girl," said Richard. "Taking after her daddy."

"Now that you're both in driving distance, we wanted to talk to you about the summer."

As her mother launched into plans for the summer season on Rabbit, Ivy began to sweat. This was it. Both her parents were here, and she had Madison beside her. She wouldn't get a better chance until Christmas. Which . . . *No. I do it now.*

"Actually," she began when Prudence paused for breath, "there is something I wanted to talk to you about."

Three pairs of eyes turned to her. Her mother's green ones. Her father's gray. Madison's aquamarine, full of compassion and the under-standing of what was coming next.

"I have MS," she opened her mouth to say. What came out, how-ever, was something totally different. "I'd like to throw a party. For the clinic. In the summer."

Madison's brows knit together in confusion. Her mother's brow crinkled in a different sort of expression entirely. "Really?"

181

Are they the right sort of people? She could hear Prudence's thoughts as clearly as if she'd spoken aloud.

"Really." Her voice firmed as the idea took form. Lillian in a cocktail dress. Lillian on the porch, sun on her shoulders. Stormy could cater, and perhaps she could convince Lillian to spend the night, assuming things hadn't blown up entirely by then.

"Oh. Well. That sounds lovely."

"Great idea," said her father. He put a quelling hand on his wife's arm.

There were two kinds of rich people, she imagined telling Lillian. Those who were hyper-conscious of wealth and class, and those who were too rich to care. Her father fell into the latter category, and right now she loved him fiercely for it.

The prospect of a date with Lillian kept the pain at bay for the days following Thanksgiving and her failed attempt at confessing her condition to her parents. It buzzed at the edge of her perception, but she found it easier than usual to ignore.

She laid several outfits on her bed Friday afternoon. Her favorite black dress. Tight slacks and a sheer blouse. A dark green dress she knew looked amazing against her skin. A suit, because putting a power move on Lillian did things to her imagination that she wished would stop.

"What do you think, Darwin?"

Darwin was busy rolling around on the thick rug at the foot of her bed, sending a fine mist of terrier hairs into the air. She considered her options. Clothing sent messages. Her mother had drilled that into her at a young age, and while she'd resented it as child, she'd grown to appreciate her mother's intuition. The right outfit opened doors. The only question was what kind of door she wanted to open tonight.

Her cocktail dress dipped modestly in the front but swooped low down her back, inviting touch. The long-sleeved green dress, on the other hand, showed a generous amount of cleavage—not enough to cross the line into trashy, but enough to draw and hold the eye. She remembered the feeling of her breasts brushing Lillian's and shivered.

Then there was the suit. Perfectly tailored, it would be another gauntlet. *I'm in charge,* it said as it lay on the bed. *And I know exactly what I want to do with you.*

Which was far from the truth.

She wished she had someone she could talk to. Stormy was too close to Lillian to truly confide in, and Madison was too cutthroat in her love life to offer sound advice. Her mother, of course, was out of the question, and her friends in Colorado were probably still angry at her, since she'd barely reached out. She was on her own.

Not the slacks.

Which left the suit and the two dresses. She stepped into the black dress. It came to just above her knee, hugging her hips, and she arranged her hair to fall over her shoulders as she surveyed herself in the mirror. The black brought out the gold strands in her hair. She turned to look at herself over her shoulder, approving of the way the dress showed off the curve of her waist and the smooth skin of her back. Sexy, but classy.

Maybe.

The green dress was warmer, which, considering the weather, was a point in its favor. She stroked the skin above the neckline, imagining Lillian's lips and teeth instead of her hand, and how she'd let Lillian push her back against a bed, or a wall, or—

Focus.

The suit turned her into a different person. That was what she loved about fashion. The minute she slid her arms into the sleeves of the jacket, she felt confident. Competent. In this outfit, she'd be the one shoving Lil up against her front door, heedless of the snow, whispering an invitation in her ear as she eased her key into the lock.

Would power or vulnerability better serve her?

She knew the answer. The green dress seemed to stare back at her, luring her into surrender. Vulnerability would prove to Lillian she was willing to listen, willing to put some of their past behind them. It was the right choice. She fingered the hem of her blazer and wondered what Lillian was thinking at that moment, and if she, unlike Ivy, had any idea what they were doing.

Chapter Nine

Lillian pulled into Ivy's driveway and stared. The house was quint-essential New England with its shingles and cozy windows, and the pines and leafless deciduous trees sheltered it from the wind off the Damariscotta River. At five o'clock, the sun was just setting, and it cast long shadows over the leaf strewn ground. She got out of her car with her heart in her mouth.

Still time to back out of this.

Her strides covered the distance between her car and the door too quickly. She hesitated, hand raised to knock. Her peacoat cut the chill from the air, which meant the trembling in her legs had a different cause. *This is such a terrible idea.*

The door opened before her knuckles touched it.

"Hey."

Ivy stood in the doorway, dressed in a casual suit of dark gray wool and a white shirt she'd left unbuttoned just enough to hint at cleavage. The slim-cut suit pants made her legs look like they went on forever, and the designer black boots beneath radiated control. The heels on Lillian's feet looked flimsy in comparison, and the way Ivy's hands were tucked into the pockets of her slacks, and the tousle of her hair around her shoulders, robbed her of speech. Mascara and a subtle lipstick were the only visible signs of makeup. An Ivy that looked like this could get away with anything, so long as she kept staring at Lillian the way she was now.

"Ready?" Ivy asked, reaching for her coat with her lips curved in a suggestive smile.

She nodded and stepped back to let Ivy pass.

I'm in trouble, she realized. *So, so much trouble.*

In the car, Ivy rested her hand on Lillian's thigh, her thumb brushing over the fabric of her tights. She gripped the wheel and focused on the traffic on Route 27, and did not part her legs for Ivy's fingers, even though her body ached for it.

"How did you get into classical music, anyway?"

"One of my friends growing up. Her mom taught piano, but my friend didn't like playing, so her mom taught me, instead."

She did not point out that her parents could not afford to give her lessons. Ivy squeezed her thigh and she squirmed in her seat, clamping down on a groan.

"That's sweet."

To keep her composure, she continued talking. "Then later I taught myself. They left the practice rooms unlocked at school and I'd play whatever sheet music I could find lying around or online."

"Do you have a piano now?"

"No."

"Why not?"

"I don't really have time, and since I don't own my own place yet, it seemed like a bad idea."

"Why don't you own?"

"You have a lot of questions." Her voice rose on the last word as Ivy slid the hem of her dress up higher.

"Maybe I want to get to know you better."

She chanced a glance away from the road and caught Ivy's eye. Was she serious?

"I don't own a house because, unlike you, I have a massive student loan debt I want to get paid down before I take on a mortgage."

"What kind of house would you want?"

"Something cozy," she said, forgetting to guard herself. "With a

185

library room and a big garden and a greenhouse."

"I can see you in a place like that."

"What about you? Mansion on the water?"

"I like where I'm at now. Besides, it's small enough I can keep it clean myself, and Darwin loves chasing the Roomba. Anything bigger and I'd have to get a house cleaner."

"Putting money into the local economy."

"Trickle-down economics at its best," said Ivy. "Kidding. Although ultimately I want something with a barn for Freddie, for when he's fully retired."

Horses. She seized on the topic. "How is he liking Maine?"

"He's not."

"Colorado is cold too, though."

"It isn't the weather." Ivy shifted in her seat, and the coy tilt of her lips slipped into a frown. "The other horses won't leave him alone."

Animals, provided they were not Seal Cove clients, were a safe topic, and it got them to Portland. She found street parking near the restaurant she'd selected: The Blue Crab.

"You can parallel park as long as it's a standard?" Ivy said.

"As if you can drive stick at all."

"You don't know. Maybe I've learned."

She raised an eyebrow at Ivy. "Have you?"

"I have to keep some secrets from you, Lee."

Ivy got out of the car, and she followed, avoiding a pile of gray slush.

"Here." Ivy held out her hand. She took it, allowing Ivy to pull her onto the sidewalk, and winced as a gust of wind barreled down the city street. Ivy's laughter tickled her ear as Ivy wrapped an arm around her and steered her toward the restaurant door.

"Reservation for Lee," she told the hostess.

"I'm impressed," said Ivy. "There are tablecloths."

"You did say you were paying." She meant the jab to sting, but Ivy just laughed again.

They were led to a table in a corner. She shrugged out of her coat and heard Ivy's breath catch.

The dress she'd chosen for tonight had sat in the back of her closet for a long time. She couldn't remember when she'd purchased it, or why, but when she'd sent Angie a panicked text and summoned her to her room for approval, Angie had blinked rapidly and immediately pulled her phone out of her bra to snap a photo.

"I need evidence you can look this banging."

It was a simple, thin-strapped black evening dress. The material probably cost about as much as one of the buttons on Ivy's jacket, but the way Ivy was looking at her, her hand still on the back of the chair as if she'd forgotten how to sit down, made it priceless.

"Everything all right?" she asked.

"You clean up nicely," Ivy said. Her tone was lightly mocking, but her eyes continued drinking Lillian in.

"I'll try not to be insulted by the implication I require cleaning up." She sat and pulled the wine list toward her.

Ivy plucked it out of her hands. "No offense, but I'm choosing the wine. Pinot noir or merlot?"

"What if I wanted white?"

"Do you?"

"No."

Ivy glanced at her over the menu. "Please let my extravagant up-bringing do some good."

"I am perfectly capable of choosing what I want to drink."

"Of course you are. Which is why we're going to try several." Ivy smiled at their waiter, who had appeared in time to overhear the end of their conversation. He vanished, only to return moments later with the three bottles Ivy had requested, the French pronunciations rolling off her tongue.

"Tell me which one you like best. You seemed to like the pinot I brought over the other day."

The waiter's expectant presence made a derisive comeback impo-lite. Instead, she accepted the proffered glass and breathed in the smell of the wine as she'd seen Ivy do.

"This is one of my favorites," said the waiter. "Can you smell the currants?"

"Yes, and is that cherry?" Ivy asked.

The waiter beamed.

Lillian smelled wine. Good wine, but just wine. Then it hit her tongue.

She'd had nice wine before. Stormy maintained the best wine could be found for $14 if you knew what you were looking for—and Stormy did—but this was different.

"What do you think?" Ivy asked her.

"It's good."

An understatement. She licked the last drop of it off her lips and eyed the bottle.

"This one has more of an oaky finish," said their waiter as he poured the next wine into their glasses, and he waxed poetic about the last, a French red from Burgundy, which seemed to mean something.

"Your pick," Ivy said.

She wondered if this was some kind of test—Ivy's way of proving how much more she knew about the world, and how provincial Lillian was with her blue-collar upbringing and her thrift store clothes.

"The first one."

"An excellent choice. I'll leave the bottle?"

"Please," said Ivy.

He removed the rejected wines and left them to peruse the dinner menu.

"Do you enjoy that?"

"Tasting wine? Yes. I do."

"I detect a hint of cherries," Lillian said, mimicking Ivy's earlier words.

"Can't you?"

"Years of clinic cleaning products have ruined my nose."

"I told you the other day. I like nice things." Ivy poured their wine as she spoke, and Lillian felt her eyes on her bare shoulders.

A warm loaf of bread soon joined them, and she drizzled olive oil into a small dish, watching Ivy do the same. The oil clung to Ivy's lips. She wanted to lick it off, pushing Ivy back in her chair and straddling her lap, and she also wanted to toss a glass of red wine onto Ivy's spotless white blouse to prove a point. Neither were appropriate behavior for a restaurant. Instead, she studied the vegetarian side of the menu without seeing it.

She'd chosen this restaurant because while it served delicious food in a classy environment, the cost of most plates amounted to the price of the symphony tickets. Ivy could not outspend her. She had not, however, anticipated the wine list. Naively she'd assumed they'd drink by the glass. The bottle sat between them, taunting her.

Let it go, she tried to tell herself. *So what if she's rich? It's not like you're dating her. You're just . . .*

What the hell *were* they doing?

"Ivy—"

"Thank you. For inviting me out." Ivy reached her hand across the table, and she took it, thrilling at the touch despite herself. "Can we just enjoy this? For now?"

She weighed Ivy's words and what they might mean. *This. This* was the two of them, not fighting, for the first time in years. *This* was the heat building from within the fragile cage of her chest and spreading through her body whenever Ivy touched her. *This* was the memory of disaster.

Keep it light.

"Okay," she said, squeezing Ivy's hand.

Ivy's answering smile lit the table with its glow.

The theater chairs, though cushioned, were threadbare, and the metal frame dug into Ivy's seat bones where the stuffing was thinnest. She adjusted her coat on the back of her chair to better support her spine. Around them, a crowd of mostly older people shuffled and flipped through the glossy pages of their programs. Lillian perused hers, too, and Ivy studied her profile. The clean line of her jaw; the curve of her forehead; the slight bump in her nose, which would have been an imperfection if it hadn't accented the cheekbones that ran parallel.

"I've waited years to hear this Rachmaninoff concerto performed," Lillian said. If she was aware of Ivy's scrutiny, she didn't show it.

"What's special about it?"

"You'll see. Or hear, rather."

Three hours of music. Already her body protested the uncomfortable chair and the slightly sour smell of the older man on her other side.

"I should take you to Carnegie Hall," she said, trying and failing not to compare the two venues in her mind.

"Portland's an easier commute than New York City."

"True, but New York—"

The lights dimmed, cutting her off. The susurrus of paper and voices stilled. Lillian leaned forward slightly in her seat, and Ivy draped her arm around the back of Lillian's chair, damning the armrest both for cutting into her hip and for separating them. As the orchestra began tuning their instruments to the conductor's baton and the music swelled to fill the hall, it occurred to her that while she had been dragged to symphonies and plays and other cultural events as a child, hating the long hours sitting still, Lillian's family would not have had subscriptions to theaters. This was a thing Lillian had decided to do for herself as an adult, not because her parents thought it looked good for the family, but because she loved it.

Of all the things to spend her money on.

Then again, as the notes of the first piece electrified the air and Lillian's lips parted in expectation, perhaps she'd denied symphonies their due. The chords that watching Lillian struck in her were worthy of whatever dead genius the musicians on stage brought back to life with bow and horn and reed.

Lillian leaned back into her arm when the second movement started. She stroked the bare skin of Lillian's shoulder with her thumb. In school, they'd competed for everything, even going so far as to try to best each other in the gym. She remembered watching Lillian lift and taking note of the weight so she could up her game. Those days seemed far away here in the theater. They could be anyone. Two women, out on a date, who perhaps met for the first time over a dating app, or at work. They could put the past behind them.

Morning. The sun waking her in her bed in the Ithaca house, bright on her white quilt. Lillian, stirring, her hair dark against the pale blue sheets, and panic rising in Ivy's chest to meet her.

"Ivy?" Confusion in Lillian's voice, as if she couldn't quite believe she'd woken up in Ivy's bed—could not believe what that implied. "Are you okay?"

Not confusion, then. Concern. She realized her hands were wrapped tightly around her bare knees, her body hunched around the raw thing that had taken up residence in her chest. She wasn't even hungover. That, at least, would have provided her with an excuse as to why Lillian Lee was in her bed, and might even have wiped her memory of the night before. Of how good it had felt to touch her, to kiss her, and how Lillian's hands had broken something open inside Ivy.

"Get the fuck out of my house, Lee."

Lillian's expression flashed from shock to hurt to bitter resentment, and then, at last, into hatred. She gathered her clothes and pulled them on, jamming her hat over her tousled hair and glaring at Ivy the whole time, as if there were no words to encompass the depth of her rage. And there weren't words. Not for that, and not for the way Ivy was crumbling.

Things could have been so different. Her palm cupped Lillian's shoulder, all smooth skin and rounded muscle and heat. What if she'd asked her to stay? If, instead of kicking her out and spending the day screaming into her pillow, she'd made them coffee and sat on her couch with Lillian's head in her lap while rare Ithaca sunlight glinted off the snow?

These seats really were desperately uncomfortable. They hit every pressure point in her body. She thought of the pills in her purse and wished she could take one—or three. It was the nerve pain, she told herself, and not the pain of memory. *I am not the person I was then.*

And yet, how different was she, really? Hadn't she run away from Colorado rather than face the reality of her condition, just as she'd pushed Lillian away when confronted with the magnitude of everything her feelings for Lillian represented?

Fate's a real bitch. She'd run from one monster into the jaws of another. This monster, however, smelled like jasmine and had just put her hand on Ivy's thigh.

"Here it comes," Lillian said as the orchestra stilled in preparation for the next piece.

Piano chords filled the theater, striding up and down the minor scale. She could tell Lillian was holding her breath, and she nodded sharply as the strings joined in a rising torrent. Ivy watched her. Her eyes were closed, and she swayed a little with the music as her fingers shifted on Ivy's leg. *She's playing along,* she realized as she timed the movement of Lillian's fingers to the piano notes.

The music swelled and ebbed, guided by the pianist, and the notes seemed to hover in the air, plucking strings in her chest. Then they tumbled back into the dramatic rhythm of the concerto as the horns announced their presence.

Intermission surprised her. She could have remained like that for days, her eyes on Lillian, the pain in her body singing along with the notes. The brightening light in the theater felt like an affront. Lillian exhaled slowly, and her lips curled into a private smile.

"Worth the wait?" Ivy asked her.

"Yes."

She'd meant the music, but the way Lillian said yes, heavy with bliss, reminded her of the night they'd spent on the island, and she wondered if Lillian, too, was thinking about wasted time.

"What did you think?" Lillian asked.

"It was . . .powerful."

"Isn't it? I remember the first time I heard it. I didn't know anything about composers—who I was supposed to know and what I was supposed to think, and I found the sheet music for "Concerto No. 2 in C Minor" in a practice room and pulled it up on my phone." Lillian blushed and glanced away. "I sound like such a nerd."

"You've always been a nerd. It's cute."

"Shut up."

"So, you listened to it, and then what?"

"I felt like the piece was mine. Like it spoke to me. And if you make fun of me for that, Ivy Holden, I will murder you right here."

She laced her fingers through Lillian's. "I won't."

Truth be told, the piece *was* Lillian's, and would be linked indelibly with her in Ivy's mind for the rest of her life.

"Did you like it? I know classical isn't your thing."

"Shh." Heedless of the older man to her left grumbling to his wife about the temperature of the room, she leaned in and brushed Lillian's lips with hers in a kiss that tasted like the sweet, lingering notes of the concerto.

"It wasn't bad," she said when she pulled away. Then, because the inadequacy of the statement hung in the air between them, she added,

"It was beautiful."

She took advantage of the intermission to use the bathroom. Ensconced safely in a stall, she opened her purse and pulled out the small bottle of water she kept for emergencies like this and popped two gabapentin. Who cared if it made her drowsy? The alternative was intolerable. Her body thrummed with pain. She knew the signs. If she didn't stop it now, she'd soon be incapacitated, and there was still half a concert to go.

And after that?

Exiting the stall, she saw her reflection in the mirror. The make-up she'd applied to hide the dark circles beneath her eyes had faded. Opening her purse again, she dabbed on a little more concealer. The night was only getting started.

Music hummed in her veins as she drove. Ivy had her head tilted back on the seat, and the light from passing cars lit her in alternating flashes of white and red. She looked tired—more tired than the lateness of the hour called for. Shadows limned her eyes beneath the brush of lash against cheek.

"Are you okay?"

Ivy smiled with her eyes closed. "I'm trying to remember how that piece you like goes."

Lillian sang a few bars, and Ivy joined in, picking it up quickly.

"I like that part there, where it goes up and down. Can you play it?"

"On the piano?"

"Yeah."

"It's been a while, but yes."

"Will you play it for me?"

"I don't have a piano."

"Someday then."

Someday implied a future where she and Ivy were close enough to allow for such things, and she wasn't sure she was ready to think about any day beyond this one and possibly the next where Ivy was concerned. But the quiet plea in Ivy's voice tugged at the tangled emotions she felt whenever she looked at the woman in her passenger seat, and so, in a voice as quiet as Ivy's, she agreed. "Someday."

The drive passed in a companionable silence after that. Ivy did not slide her hand between Lillian's legs as she had on the way into Portland. Instead, she linked their fingers together on the armrest and let the simple contact say what Lillian felt sure neither of them was willing to put into words. Ivy's hand was warm, and the pressure of her fingers as the road unspooled beneath the headlights grounded her. She walked Ivy to her door in the safety of that silence, and when Ivy glanced over her shoulder, holding the door open, she stepped inside.

Darwin greeted them with Jack Russell enthusiasm, circling and barking before jumping into Ivy's arms. Ivy let him lick her face, then encouraged him outside to do his business. While they waited for him to return, she asked, "Can I get you a glass of wine? Or tea?"

She sounded almost shy.

"Tea would be wonderful."

Lillian shrugged out of her coat and gazed around the house. Ivy flicked the lights on as they entered while Darwin skittered at their heels and smelled of snow. Warm pine floors and large windows overlooked the dark river; a cozy living room with woodstove and fireplace opened into a small but well-appointed kitchen; tasteful landscape paintings hung on cream-colored walls; and a lobster pot swung by the coat rack, disturbed by the coat Ivy tossed over a hook. In short, it was a quintessential Maine cottage, and she was surprised at its simplicity.

"Nice place."

"I know." Ivy put the kettle on and tossed her blazer over the back of a kitchen chair. "I'd buy it in a heartbeat if it was for sale."

"The view of the river must be spectacular in the daylight."

Ivy looked up from the stove. *Stay and find out*, her eyes seemed to say, but the unspoken invitation reminded Lillian of another morning years and miles past. She hugged her bare arms, feeling the chill. The flirtation in Ivy's gaze faded into concern.

"Are you cold? I can lend you a sweater. Or grab you a throw."

"I saw one on the back of the couch. I can get it."

"Not that one, unless you want to choke on a cloud of Darwin.

Hang on." Ivy left the kettle to its own devices and opened a cupboard in the adjacent living room, pulling out a light gray blanket. "Here."

"Thanks. I should have brought a cardigan. I don't know what I was thinking."

That wasn't entirely true. She'd been thinking about how she looked in the dress, and what Ivy would think of her, and the heat those thoughts generated had rendered a cardigan obsolete in that moment. Now, however, she shivered as Ivy draped the blanket over her shoulders. The night they'd spent on the island had been unplanned, an accident she could write off as poor weather and poorer judgment. If she spent the night again, she'd have no such excuse.

And she wanted an excuse. Desperately.

The blanket was sinfully soft. Cashmere, no doubt, or some other expensive fiber. It slid over her skin and warmed her immediately.

"What kind of tea would you like?" Ivy asked as she stepped back.

"What do you have?"

"Honestly I don't even know." Warm kitchen lamplight backlit her blond hair as she peered into a cabinet.

Lillian made her way over and immediately understood the problem. Tea lined several of the small shelves, profuse to the point of excess and lovely in their little tins.

"Why do you have so much tea?"

"My mother sent it as a housewarming thing."

"Did she buy out a shop?"

"She probably went online and just selected one of everything. I don't even know what half of these taste like."

"You haven't tried them?"

"I like tea, but not that much. It would take me a month to try just half."

"You could open Ivy's Tea Salon." This close, she was once more aware of the smell of Ivy's shampoo, delicate and floral, and beneath that the heady musk that clung to her skin.

"You sure you don't mean Poison Ivy's Tea Salon?"

"You weren't that poisonous tonight."

"There's still time." Ivy turned to face her and reclined against the counter, grinning.

"Not much. It's almost morning, technically." The microwave clock read 11:45, but her body felt buzzed and awake and her fingers itched to undo the buttons of Ivy's blouse.

The kettle's shriek started low and rose as they ignored it, until Ivy huffed and snatched it off the burner. Freed from the spell of Ivy's eyes, Lillian selected a sachet of a rose and strawberry herbal blend and dropped it in the blue ceramic mug beside Ivy's, which contained a sachet of ginger. The aromas blended surprisingly well as the hot water suffused the dried leaves.

"Want to sit? I promise this couch is more comfortable than the one on Rabbit."

She did not particularly want to sit, especially after that flash of memory, but the tea smelled heavenly, and she wasn't clear on the best way to segue into the positions her mind had helpfully conjured. Shrugging her assent, she entered the living room.

The couch was indeed a significant improvement. She sank into one corner while Ivy took the other, leaving an uncomfortable gap between them that Darwin was quick to occupy. She loosed a silent thank you prayer for dogs and searched for something to say.

"Do you miss Colorado?"

Ivy toyed with the edge of the tea sachet before answering. "Yes."

"What do you miss?"

"The mountains, mostly. My house. Friends, of course, and I liked my old clinic."

"Then why leave?" She was genuinely curious this time, and not angry. Something about Ivy's sudden appearance in her life felt wrong—not because she resented it, but because Ivy was clearly hiding something, and whatever it was felt connected to the circles beneath her eyes.

"It was time for a change. How did you end up here, anyway? You're a specialist. You could have gone somewhere with better pay."

Another evasion. She let it go for now and took Ivy's bait.

"What makes you think Seal Cove doesn't pay well?"

"It's a small practice on the coast of Maine, not a referral hospital in Portland."

"Morgan was here. Besides. Not everything is about money."

She'd been offered positions elsewhere. They'd offered significantly higher starting rates, but she'd been unable to accept in the end. Staying near her moms, where she could care for them and they for her, was ultimately more important, and Morgan was a known entity. After vet school, where Ivy had made her feel like she didn't belong, that had been too tempting to turn down.

"Just Morgan?"

Was that jealousy in Ivy's voice?

"I value my friends."

"Clearly, since you live with so many of them."

"Just because—"

"Were you and Morgan ever a thing?"

The question stunned her. "Morgan? As in Morgan Donovan?"

"Do we know any other Morgans in common?"

"No, and no. Morgan's like a sister to me. Why?"

"I always wondered." Ivy shifted on the couch. "You were so close."

"We were roommates, then and now. What about you and that girl—what was her name? Adele?" She recalled the redhead with distaste. One of the polished girls who clung to Ivy like the vine of her namesake, Adele had been especially nasty to Lillian whenever she had the opportunity.

"I almost forgot about her. We were sort of a thing, but it didn't last."

"Because she was a pit viper?"

"No. You actually."

"You . . . told her about what happened?" She took a sip of scalding tea and hissed in pain, which was still better than meeting Ivy's eyes.

"Of course not. I just . . . lost interest. The timelines overlapped."

She didn't need to ask which timelines. There was only one that mattered.

"I'd apologize for ruining your fling, but you don't deserve it," she said.

"I know." Ivy tucked her legs up beneath her. Steam wreathed her face from the mug clutched in her white-knuckled hands. Silence pulsed between them. At last, Ivy let out a shaky breath, then asked, "Will you spend the night?"

The confidence that radiated from her earlier had broken. She looked small and fragile in her white blouse. Lillian had dedicated a significant portion of her adult life to wishing she could reduce this woman to the kind of vulnerability displayed before her now. She'd longed to crush her, scoop up the remains, and run them through a blender. Instead, confronted with the reality, she felt a rush of an emotion she refused to analyze or name. What had Angie and Stormy told her? *There is no easy out.* If she said yes, she was committing to something, and she wasn't foolish enough to believe it was just one night. Once was an accident. Twice could be shrugged off as coincidence, but three times was a pattern, and patterns were hard to break. Scratching Darwin behind the ears, she set her mug down on the coffee table and took a deep breath.

"I'd like that."

"You have a woodstove *in your bedroom?*"

Ivy paused at the door and considered the room. Her bed, piled with quilts and pillows and topped with the best mattress money could buy, faced the small red-enameled cast iron stove in the corner. Windows overlooking the water framed it, and she crossed the plush carpet to light the fire she'd laid in it earlier that day.

"I like being warm," she said. "And so does Darwin."

The overstuffed armchair covered in a shimmer of white hair beside the stove proved her point. She glanced at the book she'd left open on the arm to make sure it wasn't anything embarrassing, then turned around to face Lillian.

Lillian, here, in her bedroom. The glow of the fire and the ambient cast of the lamp by her bedside glimmered in her dark hair. The throw was still tucked around her shoulders, and she stood, looking around the room, her eyes quick and assessing.

What does she see?

Her bedroom wasn't anything special. Well, the king-sized bed and the woodstove were special, but the decorations could have belonged to anyone. Pale curtains. An oil painting of the harbor. The only visible personal touch was the photo of her and Freddie on her bedside table. She'd picked up before going out, anticipating this moment, but she hadn't pictured how Lillian would look standing in the middle of it. She hadn't anticipated how absolutely *stripped* it would make her feel. Her pulse sped up as panic dried her mouth.

Fucking Lillian—the word sounded coarse in her mind, but she refused to substitute another—should have been simple. They had a history. There was a score. The stakes had been set and broken years ago, and in a twisted way, that had made her safe in Ivy's mind.

Safe was the last thing she felt now.

"Lil," she said, her voice catching on the name, "I—"

She what? She was sorry? She wasn't ready? What could she possibly say that would convey any of the things currently shredding her from the inside out?

Lillian did not come to her rescue.

Okay then. Truth time.

"I kicked you out that morning because I was scared."

The words crawled out of her like the slimy, cowardly things they represented. Lillian crossed her arms over her chest.

"Scared of what? You were out."

"Not—not that."

"Then why?"

"You're just . . .so different from me."

"Different how?"

Lillian's expression closed, and Ivy's heartbeat sped up further. How to explain? How to adequately express the panic that, then and now, Lillian's proximity triggered?

"There were things about my family I didn't want to think about. Things about . . . about myself I didn't want to think about. Being around you—it was easier to hate you."

Part of the truth, but not the whole of it. She didn't know how to tell Lillian that when she'd looked down at her sleeping face that long-ago morning, she'd realized she was never going to get over Lillian Lee.

And she'd been right. Looking at her now, watching suspicion cloud her eyes and twist her lips, the urge to run clawed at her throat. Ivy was a Holden. Holdens were cool, collected, and always in control.

Holdens married senators and lawyers. Holdens did not fall in love with Navy brats who wore secondhand clothes and looked at Holden money like it was covered in blood, because Holdens pretended their money was clean. She knew how privileged she would sound if she put any of those things into words.

Since then, she'd read. She'd listened to the people put at risk by her family's business interests and donated as much as she could without compromising her quality of life to causes in direct opposition to her family's operations in pipelines, tar sands, lobbyists, and war.

It wasn't enough. She'd never be clean of that guilt, and as long as she surrounded herself with people like Lillian, she'd be reminded constantly of the harm her bloodline continued to wreak. She had never hated Lillian. She had hated how she felt around Lillian: vulnerable. Out of control. Complicit.

Holdens did not fall in love with Navy brats.

Her earlier thought came back to her with the force of a sledgehammer.

Oh. Oh no.

"That's such a cop-out, Ivy."

A cop-out? She struggled to remember what she'd said. Something about how hating Lillian was easier than thinking about other things. Things like how she'd been in love with Lillian for years. Her ears rang. Her limbs were numb. The room itself seemed to tilt.

"I know," she said, because that seemed like an appropriate response.

"Do I scare you now?"

She met Lillian's gaze and answered honestly.

"You terrify me."

The trembling started in her legs. Her knees shook, and she sat on the edge of her bed as it passed through her body and down her arms to her hands, then up through her chest and into her jaw. Her teeth chattered. This wasn't MS. This was something much worse. This was—

Her eyes welled up.

Her lower lip trembled.

No, please no, I don't want to cry. Not now. Not in front of her.

But the pressure, once it found a crack, sought release.

"Hey." Lillian closed the gap between them and took a seat beside her. "Ivy—"

Hearing Lillian say her name that tenderly broke the valve wide open. She buried her face in Lillian's neck and sobbed.

"I'm so sorry. I'm so sorry for everything," she kept repeating, no matter how many times she tried to clamp down on the words. It was as if words, like the sobs wracking her shoulders, were convulsive. She couldn't stop them or even slow them down. The blanket absorbed most of her tears, and Lillian wrapped her arms around her and pulled her closer, stroking her hair and rocking her gently. She did not deserve this kindness. She did not deserve this compassion. She was a worm. A maggot. Something filthy and diseased, and Lillian was bright and perfect and whole. If Ivy truly cared for her, she'd let her go, but she'd done that once already and she knew she did not have the strength to go through that again.

That wasn't quite true, either. Letting Kara go had been hard, yes, but had she really run from Kara? Or had she run *to* Lillian? Lillian kissed the tears from her cheeks when the sobs finally subsided.

"Let's get you to bed, okay?"

She nodded and let Lillian unbutton her blouse and lead her to the bathroom, where Lillian found a washcloth, drenched it in warm water, and handed it to her to scrub her face. Red rimmed her eyes in the mirror and her skin was blotchy and puffy. *I'm a mess. A total, absolute, mess.*

Then her eyes caught sight of the medicine bottles by the sink, and she froze. Lillian had seen them too. The prescriptions told a story to anyone with a medical degree, and she grabbed them and hastily tumbled them into a drawer. Lillian said nothing.

Ivy stood, panting and ashamed, and wanted to scream at the entirety of creation for the injustice of this moment. Lillian placed a soothing hand on her waist.

"Let me get you a glass of water. I'll be right back."

Mute, she nodded.

When Lillian left, she gripped the edge of the counter and stared into her wild eyes, bright green against the bloodshot whites, and considered bashing her forehead into her reflection until the mirror lay shattered in bloody pieces around her.

She couldn't tell Lillian about her condition. If she hadn't been able to tell Kara, then confessing her weakness to Lillian was out of the question. She'd already revealed the depth of her inadequacies. And yet, what was one more? Lillian had already seen the very worst in her. It could hardly matter.

Except then passion would turn to pity, and she needed Lillian. Needed the heat from her gaze, whether it was hate or lust or something in-between.

Tepid pity would break her.

Ivy's kitchen lay in darkness as Lillian padded down the stairs in her stockinged feet. Her mind tumbled over itself as she scrambled to process everything that had just happened. Ivy, in tears. Ivy, confessing. Ivy, shoving those pill canisters into a drawer before she could get a good look, but she'd seen enough to know something was wrong. People didn't hide medications without reason, and the ones she'd seen were not prescribed for potentially embarrassing but ultimately manageable conditions like irritable bowel syndrome. They suggested systemic damage. Sparks of fear burst in the corners of her vision. Ivy, however, clearly did not want to talk about it, and one look at her face had told Lillian that asking would cross a line. She'd let her guard down tonight and shown Lillian more than she'd ever expected to see, but it was obvious those pills had represented a bridge too far. She had no choice but to respect Ivy's privacy—for now.

Finding cups required opening only three cabinets. Filling two with tap water, she took a moment to gaze out the window at the stars over the river. Orion hung above them, his bow pointing toward distant galaxies and constellations.

His arm must get tired.

The absurdity of the thought was a measure of how far off course the night had gone. Not that she'd known what to expect. Perhaps that, once arriving at Ivy's, they'd tumble into Ivy's bed for another night like the one they'd shared on the island. Definitely not that Ivy would dissolve into tears in her arms and apologize repeatedly for everything she'd ever done to Lillian. Ivy's absolute dissolution had made it impossible to gloat or even feel mild vindication. The other woman's pain was palpable beneath her hands as her ribs shook with sobs and she clung to Lillian, curled in on herself like a broken thing.

She tore her eyes away from the stars and headed back upstairs.

Ivy waited cross-legged on her bed in an oversized sleepshirt. Her eyes were puffy and the tip of her nose was red, as were the two bright spots of color in her cheeks, but she breathed slowly and met Lillian with a sad little smile.

"Drink this."

Ivy obeyed.

"Do you . . . do you want me to go?" she asked.

Ivy shook her head. "This wasn't how I expected the night to end," she said in a voice roughened by tears. "I'm sorry. I had a really nice time with you."

Lillian scooted closer to her on the bed and tucked an errant strand of hair behind Ivy's ear. "It was always going to be messy."

"I was kind of hoping you would be the messy one."

"Give it time." Her heart clenched at how small Ivy looked, hunched in her sleepshirt, lashes still damp with tears. She'd never thought of Ivy as fragile, just insidious, like a weed.

"Do you want to borrow something to wear?"

Clothing would offer a layer of protection for them both, as well as comfort.

"Sure. Which drawer?"

"Top left."

She left Ivy on the bed and rummaged through the drawer she'd indicated, noting and mentally cataloguing the lingerie her fingers skimmed as she pulled out a loose, silky T-shirt, and trying and failing not to imagine how Ivy might look dressed in lace.

"Can you unzip me?" she asked Ivy.

Ivy rose and, barefoot in just a shirt, brushed Lillian's hair to the side as she eased the zipper down her back.

"Thanks."

Warm hands gently tugged the straps over her shoulders. She let Ivy pull the dress down, assisting when the fabric strained over her hips, and stepped out of it as it fell to the floor. She hadn't worn a bra, and Ivy's hands skimmed along her bare back and down her sides, pausing at the hem of her tights.

"Are you going to sleep in these?"

She was glad some of the ironic tone had crept back into Ivy's voice. "Absolutely not."

Before she could pull the sleepshirt over her head, Ivy turned her around. Lillian was an inch taller, which didn't amount to much, but it did mean Ivy had to tilt her head up very slightly. The kiss she gave her was sweet and lingering, and she tasted salt on her lips as she ran her hands through Ivy's tousled hair.

The sleepshirt, when Ivy eventually let her pull it on, was even softer than the cashmere blanket. It flowed over her skin, managing to be both silky and warm. She immediately contemplated stealing it. Ivy tossed back the quilts and slid into the bed, turning off the light as she did so. The remaining glow came from the woodstove, and as Lillian slipped beneath the sheets, she felt like they were once again back on the island with only the storm outside.

Ivy nuzzled into her and tucked her head beneath Lillian's chin. They breathed together for a long while, listening to the wood crackle in the stove and the pine trees whisper outside the windows. It had been a long time since she'd held someone like this. Ivy fit into her arms with an ease that triggered multiple alarm bells. She silenced them and murmured into Ivy's hair.

"I didn't take you for the little spoon."

"Shut up."

A dog barked somewhere far away.

"Hey Ivy?"

"What?"

Ivy's words warmed the skin of her chest through the shirt, and her body stirred in response.

"You're not the only one who needs to apologize."

"I started this." Ivy's lips had moved closer to the taut skin around her nipple, and Lillian's hand tightened around the blond locks currently vining through her fingers.

"I judged you, too."

"Oh yeah?"

Ivy's breath was hot and close, and Lillian fought not to pull her closer still.

"I said to myself, 'There's a blonde with an attitude problem.'"

Teeth raked her, light and teasing, and she bit her lip. It did not quite muffle her moan.

"You weren't wrong," said Ivy.

"No, I wasn't."

Ivy nipped the curve of her breast and dragged her nails lightly down Lillian's side and over her ass. She shuddered. Part of her wondered if she should ask Ivy whether she was ready for this, considering the emotional output of the last hour. Another part of her was wet and aching for Ivy's touch, and as Ivy's fingers slid over her ass and between her thighs, brushing her through her underwear, she fought to stay sentient.

"Are you sure you're up for this?" she managed to gasp.

Ivy took her nipple in her mouth through the fabric in response.

"Holy hell, Ivy."

She felt Ivy's smile against her skin. Hands tugged at her underwear. She wriggled out of them, then urged Ivy to do the same. Ivy stroked her thigh and the curve of her ass, sliding her fingers up over her hip and then down, her thumb skimming the crease between thigh and center. Electrified by the touch, she rolled over onto Ivy, parting her legs with her body. She could feel Ivy slick against her as she kissed her neck and bit her shoulder, rocking her hips and gasping each time Ivy pushed back. Nails dug into her as Ivy urged her on, her heels digging into the back of Lillian's thighs like spurs.

The heat of her pressed into Lillian. Beneath her, Ivy's lips parted, and a flush crept up her chest and into her cheeks. Her breasts rose and fell rapidly, moved by her breath and the motion of their hips, and Lillian watched, awed, as the color in Ivy's face heightened and she bucked, faster and faster, until her body shook.

"Lil."

She felt Ivy come against her, and her vision swam as her own need drove her on, pushing Ivy over the edge. Ivy cried out Lillian's name again, arching her back to grind into her, and Lillian kissed her cheeks and lips and jaw, wanting to taste all of her.

"May I?"

She didn't understand the question, at first. Her body trembled on the brink, and all that mattered was Ivy and the places they touched. Places like where Ivy's hand had slid between them, cupping her, stroking her opening and rendering her helpless.

"Yes. Please, yes."

Ivy's fingers, inside her. Ivy's mouth, sharing her breath. Ivy's hips, rocking against hers, guiding her hand deeper and deeper. She felt each curl of finger through her entirety, as if Ivy stroked every nerve, and she let herself be rolled onto her side. Sheets tangled in her fingers as Ivy increased her tempo. She twisted, needing Ivy deeper, needing more, bypassing the point at which she would normally have come and climbing higher.

"Harder, please, Ivy."

She screamed as Ivy obeyed. The shadows on the ceiling burst into streaks of color as an orgasm unlike anything she'd ever experienced ripped through her, shaking her loose from her bindings and growing as Ivy sped up, pushing her as she'd always pushed her, until she convulsed around her hand and begged her to stop.

Slowly, Ivy subsided, extracting tremors with each stroke. Lillian released her hold on the bedding and fumbled for her, finding it hard to see, let alone breathe. At last she found a shoulder and a face, which she turned toward her own. Ivy's tongue danced over her lips and she cried out again, Ivy still inside her, her body hypersensitive to touch.

"I want to kiss you."

"You are."

"Not there."

She laughed, or at least she tried to. The breathy sound that escaped her lips could have been anything. "I don't think—that was incredible—I—oh god."

Ivy ignored her attempts at protest and pulled up her shirt to kiss down her stomach, which seemed to have grown new nerve endings, then took her swollen clit in her mouth.

She worked her gently, sucking in long, even pulls, rolling her tongue over the tip and barely moving the fingers inside her—just a hint of pressure, pushing her clit deeper into Ivy's mouth. She'd never been sucked like this. Didn't know it was a possibility. Ivy's teeth and tongue and lips pulled her, tugging her back into that land of twisting, colored shadows, gathering Lillian to her until the whole of her was concentrated in that pulsing, aching center. She thought she might be crying, or screaming, or both. Her cheeks felt wet. Ivy pulled again, holding her, teasing her, while Lillian tangled her hands in her own hair and writhed in abject need.

The first orgasm had nearly flattened her.

The second one came on like a summer storm. She felt it building, clouds boiling over the horizon as Ivy moaned into her, curling her fingers deeper, demanding Lillian rise higher. She'd hooked one leg over Ivy's shoulder, but the other leveraged her hips, asking, begging Ivy for more. And Ivy gave and took and drew her out like Orion's bowstring before letting her snap in a kaleidoscope of shadow and light.

Chapter Ten

Ivy wandered into Storm's-a-Brewin' for a cup of something hot, feeling slightly pathetic at the relief she felt seeing Stormy behind the counter.

"My favorite bunny," Stormy said. "Is it cold out there or what?"

Ivy hadn't noticed the temperature of the December air. Her insides had been burning steadily since last night, and she felt almost feverish.

"Uh, yeah. Cold."

Stormy gave the quiet coffee shop, which contained a handful of middle-aged women gathered around a table and the usual high school students, a quick glance and then turned her full attention to Ivy.

"Are you okay?"

"Yes," she said instinctively, and then, "no."

"Ah, yes. *That* feeling. I know it well. Sit."

Ivy sat. Stormy put a hot cup of something that smelled like lavender and warm soymilk in her hands and leaned on the bar. Her thick curls fell around her face, framing her smile.

"What's bothering you?"

"Oh, you know. Everything."

"Maybe I should have given you something harder to drink. The lavender is supposed to be soothing, but I can always pour you a tall one."

"I'm not sure that would help, either."

"Then it really is serious."

The feverish feeling continued and, half delirious, she looked into Stormy's face and wondered how much she could trust her and what it said about her that a bartender was her only friend. Even if that wasn't entirely true, the fact that she hadn't called any of her old friends in months was also telling, though whether it spoke to the quality of those friendships or her own insecurities, she couldn't say.

"Have you ever had a secret that would change everything if other people knew? I mean absolutely everything, every part of your life."

"You mean besides my role as Wonder Woman?" Stormy's expression was serious despite the joke. "No, I haven't."

She poked the foam on the top of her drink, considered the absurdity of both the action and her last statement, and stared at the foam peak now clinging to her finger.

"Sorry."

"For what?"

"That was kind of a big thing to say."

"It's not the craziest thing I've ever heard. Not even the craziest thing I've heard this week. Apparently, Stevie knows a guy who adds diesel to his beer because, and I quote, 'it's the American thing to do.' Carries a flask of it around. Something about supporting pipelines."

"*What?*"

"I know, right?"

"That's—wow. Super disturbing."

"So you're good."

"That's a pretty low bar."

"I live to lower bars." Stormy tapped the bar between them and made a cymbal sound. "Anyway, I'm sorry you're dealing with that."

She appreciated that Stormy didn't ask questions, even as the urge to confess overwhelmed her.

You did this to yourself. This is what you wanted, remember? Anonymity. Punishment for leaving Kara. Reap the rewards of isolation, bitch.

She really needed to have a chat with her internal monologue about its tone one of these days.

"I never thought I would be this person."

"What person?"

"The kind of person who spills their guts to a bartender."

"Hang on." Stormy ducked into the back and emerged a few minutes later with her coat.

"Jill will cover for me for a bit. She owes me hours. Let's get out of here."

"To where?"

"You have a horse, right?"

She nodded.

"Let's go see him."

Seeing Stormy in the barn brought a smile to Ivy's lips. Her attire was entirely wrong—Doc Martins paired with thick leggings and an octopus-patterned knitted sweater dress beneath a battered peacoat, the whole affair topped with a handmade red hat and a bulky scarf. A teenage girl in jodhpurs raised her eyebrows until she saw Ivy watching her. Ivy gave the girl her best Valley Girl glare, and the child paled and retreated into a stall.

"This is my boy."

Freddie poked his long head out of his stall at the sound of her voice.

"He's so handsome." Stormy let him sniff her hand, then stroked his muzzle.

"Do you ride?"

"Me? Hell no. I like horses, but I'm afraid of heights, and they're too tall. But I love to kiss their noses." She illustrated her point by planting a smooch on Freddie's. He twitched his lip and nudged Stormy, hoping for a treat.

"He's a real slut for kisses."

"Can't say I blame him. Have you met Stevie's horse?"

"No, I haven't."

"Olive's a real sweetheart. She needs a friend, though. I've been trying to convince Angie to get a goat, but so far no luck."

"Is Olive stabled at the house?"

"Yep."

An idea flashed across her mind. She discarded it immediately. There was no indoor arena at 16 Bay Road, and Freddie was accustomed to luxurious box stalls. Moving him just because he was lonely and not getting enough pasture time was ridiculous. It was December. He'd be fine. And she did *not* need another excuse to see Lillian.

"I thought the barn was a doggy day care."

"It is. Morgan built a shed for Olive. It's cute and cozy."

And cold. Freddie turned his dark eye to her and she stroked his cheek.

"Now that we're not in the bar, I'm not your bartender," Stormy said. "Congratulations. You're no longer pathetic."

Ivy laughed and rested her weight against Freddie's stall door. "Fair enough."

"You don't have to tell me your secret, but I need to ask. Is it going to hurt Lil?"

"I don't see how it could."

Her condition wouldn't hurt Lillian, but it might repulse her. Which shouldn't matter. *I am not in love with Lillian.* And Lillian certainly was not in love with her. They'd had a nice date, and then Ivy had fucked everything up by crying and then making love to Lillian like it was the only thing in the world that mattered, which was so fucking stupid she could cry.

This was why she'd left Colorado. She wasn't a fit partner for anyone. Kara, who loved the outdoors and travel, had deserved so much more. Which is why she'd left, sparing Kara the agony of deciding whether she wanted to slow down or move on.

Is that true? Or did you run away before Kara could look at you with pity?

"Ivy?"

She looked at Stormy, doubt thudding in her chest in place of a heartbeat. Yes, she'd run. Right into the arms of her enemy. But why? Because she wanted to punish herself? Because Lillian already despised her, so she couldn't possibly disappoint her? Or because she'd never gotten over the stricken look on Lil's face the morning Ivy had ruined everything?

"I—"

You what? What are you going to say, you spineless scrap of shit?

"Oh god." She covered her face with her hands and hoped no one but Stormy was watching. Freddie lipped her in equine concern, and she rested her forehead against his neck.

"Hey." Stormy rubbed her shoulder in soothing circles. "It will be okay."

But it wouldn't. She'd be lucky if she was able to work, let alone date, and she couldn't ask anyone to sign up for her baggage. Not when things were so uncertain. Her doctor had told her she could hopefully expect to lead an almost normal life, potentially for years. Someone else might have bought that. She knew there were no such guarantees. Treatments might improve. Her condition might hold off. Or she could find herself incapacitated and unemployed and living with a caretaker. She could not dump that onto someone she cared about.

Which was why Lillian was perfect, she reminded herself. Lillian didn't want anything from her. That was clear by the way she'd been hiding their . . . whatever it was . . . from Morgan. Lillian was rebounding. Ivy could be a rebound. It didn't matter if she got hurt in the end. She was already hurting. She would be hurting forever because the only thing she could truly count on was the certainty of pain.

She couldn't tell any of that to Stormy.

Steadying herself against her horse and the worn wood of the stall, she forced a smile. "You see? I really am a mess."

"Again, I've seen worse."

Perhaps a small truth was in order.

"I've never been this person before."

"What person?"

"The kind of person who falls apart."

"You WASPs. It's like you think repression is a virtue. You know what repression is? It's dumb. D-U-M-B."

"But it feels so good."

"Just 'cause it's tight don't make it right," said Stormy.

"Thank you for that visual."

"Seriously though. Can I give you some professional advice?"

"Sure."

"The longer you try to hold yourself together, the bigger the explosion, and the more civilian casualties."

Casualties like Lillian.

Lillian hummed to herself as she scrubbed her dinner dishes in the white farmhouse sink. Lemon-scented dish soap frothed beneath the sponge, and she could hear Stevie and Angie arguing good-naturedly about something in the living room. A car door shut outside. She glanced out through the window and saw Morgan hopping out of her truck, her sable German shepherd, Kraken, at her heels.

"Hey, stranger," she called out to Morgan as the front door opened.

Kraken raced around the corner to greet her. Morgan followed at a more sedate pace, and Lillian heard the thud of her kicking off her boots in the mudroom. She resumed scrubbing. There was something so satisfying about the way soap frothed under hot water. The heat of it penetrated the rubber gloves she wore to keep her hands from drying out as she dug into a particularly stubborn bit of burnt sauce.

"I need to talk to you."

Morgan's voice, right behind her shoulder, made her jump.

"I'm listening."

Morgan turned off the hot water. Sighing, Lillian removed her gloves, crossed her arms, turned, and withered beneath Morgan's accusatory stare. She had a good idea about its cause.

"What the hell, Lil?"

"What the hell, what?"

Morgan wore her work outfit: a monogrammed fleece pullover and Carhartt work pants, which were streaked with horse slobber. Keeping her voice pitched low, presumably so Angie and Stevie wouldn't hear her, she dropped the bomb Lillian had been dreading.

"You do know Ivy's place is on the way to Emilia's, right?"

"Is it?" Playing dumb was . . . dumb, but she wanted to put this conversation off for as long as possible.

"Your car was in her drive this morning."

She wiped her hands on the dish towel for something to do with them, even though they hadn't gotten wet. Morgan put a hand on her shoulder and looked down at her with her eyebrows drawn in concern.

"What were you doing there?"

She could tell Morgan it wasn't any of her business, because it wasn't, but one look into Morgan's stormy eyes suggested that would get her exactly nowhere. Which was bullshit. Morgan hadn't enjoyed her friends prying into *her* love life just a few months ago.

"Nothing's happening. I needed to talk to her about a case."

"At six in the morning? On your day off?"

"I don't need to be interrogated about—"

"She wrecked you."

This silenced her.

Morgan let go of her shoulder and mussed her mop of curly hair, frustration evident in the lines around her mouth. "You told me nothing was going to happen."

She chewed on her lower lip until she tasted blood. The shame of that long-ago cold run back to the apartment she had shared with Morgan flooded through her again. She'd felt used. Dirty. Betrayed by Ivy and her own body, and by the feelings warring in her chest. So different from how she'd felt leaving Ivy's this morning.

"I get you don't want to talk to me about this, and I want to respect that. You know I don't like talking about my own shit. But if you're sleeping with her again—"

"I'm not," she started to say, but the words died in her throat, and all that came out was a croak. She turned away from Morgan and dried the edge of the sink, refusing to meet her eyes. The warmth that had stayed with her since she left Ivy's house cooled by degrees kelvin.

"I'm not going to let her hurt you again."

"It was never that simple, *dad*."

"Lil."

She forced herself to look into her friend's face, and despite Morgan's protective words, the compassion she saw there melted her resolve.

"I can't help it. She messes me up."

"I know."

"I'm sorry I didn't tell you."

"Don't apologize. Like I said, I get it, and nobody lets anything stay a secret around here." Morgan cast a dirty look toward the living room as she spoke, and Lillian laughed.

"Don't blame them. Stormy's the real issue."

Morgan snorted. "You don't need to tell *me*."

"Remember when Emilia first got here?"

"And none of you would leave off about her? Yeah, I remember." Morgan's frown smoothed into a smile, as if she couldn't even pretend to be annoyed even though, at the time, she'd been impossible to live with.

"Do you think you could have stopped yourself from falling for Em?"

"You can't compare Emilia to Ivy."

And yet, there were striking similarities, now that she considered the comparison. Both women had arrived in town unexpectedly. Both had family ties to the area. Both were running from something.

But Emilia hadn't previously broken Morgan's heart.

"Are we talking about my favorite Poison Ivy?" Angie asked, appearing in the kitchen with her black cat purring in her arms.

"No," said Morgan at the same time Lillian said, "Yes."

Morgan narrowed her eyes and glanced between the two of them.

"What do you mean, your favorite Poison Ivy?"

"Oops." Angie winced at Lillian, clearly just remembering Ivy was a forbidden topic around Morgan. "Nothing. Love to hate her. That's all. Also Stormy invited her to Holiday Thing."

"What?" Lillian and Morgan said in unison.

"She didn't tell you?" Angie said to Lillian.

"No."

"Awkward." Angie began backing out of the room.

"Wait. How long has this been going on?" Morgan asked Angie.

"That's my cue to leave." Angie darted out of Morgan's reach and vanished into the living room, where Stevie immediately began interrogating her in a heated whisper.

"Um."

Morgan raised an eyebrow. Lillian exhaled slowly and surrendered to the inevitable.

"A few weeks. We hooked up at the clinic and then I got trapped with her on Rabbit and then we went to dinner and the symphony and I spent the night at her place, and I know I'm an idiot and I don't know what to do," she said in a rush.

"You got trapped with her on Rabbit? Why didn't you call? I could have come to get you."

"Your boat was out of the water."

"I would have put it back in if I'd known."

"In a blizzard?"

"You were out there *that* night?"

"I survived."

"Do I even want to know how you stayed warm?"

Lillian's cheeks heated, and Morgan shook her head, a grin tugging the corner of her mouth. "Was it good at least?"

Lillian sagged against the counter and groaned. "Oh my god, yes."

"Better than Brian?"

"Why does everyone always hate on Brian?"

"Because he should have paid you more attention, and I still think you should have dated that lobsterman instead." Morgan's grin spread further. "You know which one I'm talking about."

Lillian laughed, remembering a summer several years ago when they'd been younger, Morgan had still been with her ex-fiancé, and a handsome lobsterman had done his best to get Lillian to go out with him each time they ran into him in town.

"Sexy Sean?"

Morgan moved her hips suggestively, and Lillian swatted her. "Stop it."

"Wait a minute. Back up. You hooked up in the clinic?"

"Can we not talk about that?"

"The blonde at the club. That was her, too, wasn't it?"

"Stormy invited her."

To Morgan's credit, she didn't look offended Lillian had kept this a secret from her.

"Is this a 'fuck and get it out of your system' thing, or something else?"

"Definitely the first option."

Morgan's eyes suggested she saw through the lie, but she didn't press it. This left her feeling, not the relief she'd expected, but a roiling uncertainty that Morgan's worry was more than well-founded; it was rooted as deeply as the apple trees in the farmhouse orchard.

"I don't have feelings for her. It's just . . . complicated."

"Sleeping with her isn't going to make it any simpler."

"I know. But if I'm not . . ." Not what? Fucking her? Hooking up with her? Neither phrase adequately described what had happened the night before. "If I'm not doing whatever this is, then I want to actually murder her. I can't find a middle ground."

"She's only been here two months."

"And I haven't been touched by anyone in over six, okay?" Her voice rose and broke, and silence radiated from the living room. "I know it's a terrible idea. I know it's going to end badly. And I'm doing it anyway."

Stevie and Angie applauded from the other room.

"Then I'm here for you," said Morgan, and Lillian gave her a shaky smile.

"Thank you."

Lillian didn't text her that week, though they saw each other at work, and Ivy resisted the almost claustrophobic need to reach out. The unfamiliar feeling crawled under her skin. She'd gone years without texting Lillian Lee. Nothing had changed. She reread their previous exchange for the hundredth time, then shoved her phone into her pocket.

"Ready for this next one, Dr. Holden?" asked Shawna.

"Let's hope so."

Flurries skittered across the truck's windshield as they pulled into the small dairy. An older man in a plaid jacket greeted them at the barn doors, and they followed him inside to the parlor. The heifer in question was an older Jersey cow with a dished nose and large, gentle eyes.

"She's my best milker," said John.

The problem was immediately evident. Swelling covered her left flank, and when she stepped into the stall and placed her hand on the hot, tight skin, probing a small, puckered area closer to the spine, she nodded.

"Looks like an abscess. We should be able to take care of it for you today."

Shawna gave a subtle fist pump out of the farmer's sight. "Is it gonna be a good one?"

"Only one way to find out."

Normally the prospect of relieving an abscess would have cheered her up, too. They were relatively simple to treat, satisfying, and left the animal feeling immediately better. She wished she could apply the same practice to the hot, infected bubble of shame inside her.

She'd fallen apart in front of Lillian. Fallen apart didn't even halfway cover it. She'd spoiled their evening by breaking down, and it didn't surprise her that Lillian hadn't wanted to talk since.

"Oh, wow," said Shawna.

Ivy feigned enthusiasm as she flushed the abscess and removed a foot-long splinter from the wound.

"This would be the problem," she said, tossing the stick on the ground.

"She got out the other day. I checked her over, but she seemed fine. Just a scratch." John's mouth quirked down.

"It was probably part of a longer piece, and this broke off inside. We got it out, which is what matters."

He patted the cow and murmured something into her brown ear that sounded like an apology. Shawna hid a smile. She wrote him a script for some antibiotics, provided he tossed the milk, and instructions for wound care, and had made it halfway down the aisle before a high-pitched squeak stopped her in her tracks.

"What was that?" asked Shawna.

"Goddamn barn cats," said John. "People keep dumping them. I paid to have three fixed already this year."

"Sounded like a kitten."

Cows turned their heads in mild interest as John pushed his way past a stanchion, knelt, and straightened, cupping a calico scrap of fur in his weathered hands. Wordlessly, he held out the bundle.

A scrawny kitten lay stunned in his palms, its foreleg twisted at a horrific angle.

"Got stepped on."

Ivy took the kitten, who remained in shock, and tenderly investigated.

"Humerus feels shattered."

"I can take care of it," said John in a heavy voice. "Got a .22 in the feed room."

There had been a time in her life when the prospect of hearing a man talk about shooting a cat would have horrified her. Farm life, however, required tough choices, and she could tell that John, for all that he clearly loved his cows, was not going to shell out money to send an unwanted kitten to surgery.

"We'll take her with us." At his concerned look, Ivy added, "the clinic will take care of it."

She could cover the cost of euthanasia out of pocket. The kitten mewled in her hands, and she cradled it closer to her body.

"I can get you a box."

The kitten rode back to the clinic on the cab floor in a cardboard box lined with straw.

"Poor thing," said Shawna from behind the wheel.

Ivy watched the frail ribs rise and fall. By its size, it could be anywhere from six to twelve weeks. Malnutrition made it hard to tell. The dilute calico coloring was more tortoiseshell than calico upon closer examination, and its worm-like kitten tail ended in a tuft of orange. *Definitely infested with worms. And fleas.* Maybe someone at the clinic would be interested in adopting it and paying to have the leg amputated, provided there was no internal damage. Cats did well as tripods, especially with front limb amputations.

Tripod. Lillian's dogs were tripods, which brought her thoughts back to their owner, just like everything else in this town. The kitten chose that moment to lift its head and stare at her, opening its mouth in a silent meow.

One surgery, one flea and tick treatment, a douse of dewormer, several vaccines, and multiple doubts later, she arrived home with a small cat carrier in her hand. The clinic had provided a loaner litter box, and she'd taken a few cans of food for her newest mistake.

"Darwin, I'm sorry."

Darwin sniffed the carrier suspiciously. He'd met many cats over the years, including Kara's, but this unexpected delivery of feline fluff was clearly more than he'd bargained for, especially on a night when his dinner was late and he'd been denied his usual evening cuddles. She set the kitten up in the downstairs bathroom with towels, food, water, and a litter box it probably didn't know how to use, and shut the door.

IH: *I just adopted a kitten.*

Her sister's response was disturbingly fast. Madison always had her phone on her.

MH: *Pictures or it didn't happen.*

She sent a photo of the kitten post-anesthesia, its tongue sticking out and its shoulder shaved and dotted with suture. A series of emojis assaulted her screen as Madison released the nonverbal equivalent of a squeal.

MH: *Wait. It's missing something.*

IH: *Can't sneak anything past you.*

MH: *What happened to its leg?!?!?!?!*

IH: *Cow.*

MH: *I will love it forever. It just became my new favorite sister. It is a girl, right? When can I come see her?*

IH: *It's a girl and you can come whenever.*

MH: *See you in three hours.*

IH: *It's eleven o'clock.*

MH: *Fine, this weekend?*

IH: *Sure.*

MH: *Love her all night long for me.*

IH: *Definitely leaving her locked in the bathroom.*

MH: *OMG YOU'RE A MONSTER*

Yawning, she clicked her phone screen off and headed upstairs. It buzzed in her hand. Expecting more accusations of animal abuse from Madison, who had never owned so much as a houseplant but loved lavishing attention on the pets of others, she glanced down at her screen.

LL: *What's this about you taking home a tripod?*

Her heart should not have been capable of the kind of leap it gave as Lillian's name lit up the screen. She fell backward onto her bed, still dressed, and curled around her phone. Darwin leapt up beside her, circled, and flopped down on her pillow.

IH: *It's really creepy you already know about that.*

LL: *Angie knows everything. Don't ask me how; she doesn't even work there anymore.*

She sent Lillian the same picture she'd sent her sister, suddenly overcome with affection for the kitten in her bathroom.

IH: *She could be yours.*

LL: *Angie's cat would eat her.*

IH: *James? I like him. He's sweet.*

LL: *Only you would think so.*

Darwin sighed deeply behind her and she thumbed the screen, lingering over Lillian's name.

"It's too early for this much snow," said Angie when Lillian entered the kitchen. Outside in the predawn black the wind howled, and snow plastered itself to the screens beyond the kitchen windows. She wasn't sure whether Angie meant too early in the season or too early in the morning, but either way she agreed. At just past six o'clock, it was still dark as pitch, and Hermione shivered in her arms. She'd need to put her doggy snowsuit on before letting her outside.

"Ew. What the hell is that white shit?" Stevie asked, emerging rumpled and bundled in a flannel bathrobe that dragged along the ground.

"Did you steal that from Morgan?" Angie said, noticing the robe too.

"It isn't like she even sleeps here half the time. She won't miss it."

That was probably true. Morgan spent more and more of her nights with Emilia, and if the winter kept on like this, she suspected Morgan's inevitable move would come sooner than any of them had predicted. Cold weather made people want to nest. Unbidden, an image of Ivy's bed danced in the steam rising off her coffee.

"Speaking of sleepovers, what's up with you and Ivy?"

Stevie brightened at Angie's question and folded up the sleeves of the robe to free her hands enough to grab a coffee mug of her own. The smell of Stormy's coffee beans permeated the kitchen and lulled

Lillian into a good enough mood to answer, aided by her under-caffeinated condition and the ease with which her own thoughts had already gone there.

"I'm not sure."

"But you slept there last week after your date."

"I did."

"Be honest. Blondes do it better, don't we?" said Stevie. Angie flicked her with hot coffee from her mug, and Stevie shielded herself with Morgan's robe.

"When are you seeing her again?" asked Angie.

"Probably today at work."

"You're so boring. Ask to go see her kitten."

"Yeah, ask if you can pet—"

Angie clapped her hand over Stevie's mouth, thankfully stopping the lewd comment at the gates. Stevie bit down, eliciting a squeal and a smack from Angie. Lillian topped off her coffee and reached into the foyer to grab Hermione's snowsuit from its hook.

"Sorry munchkin, but out you go."

Muffin, protected by several inches of thick fur, barreled out the back door. Hermione hunched on the doorstep and squinted accusingly up at Lillian as snowflakes landed on her snout. She nudged the little dog with her toe. "You have to go so we can check on the green-house. You like the greenhouse."

Hermione waded grudgingly into the snow. Stevie's dog, Marvin, materialized from behind her and launched himself into the growing drifts. Lillian laughed at the outrage on Hermione's face and wished she had thought to take a photo of it to send to Ivy.

The impulse worried her. She'd shown restraint over the past week, sobered by Morgan's concern. Rushing into something with Ivy was a potentially catastrophic idea, even if she'd found it hard to sleep every night since. Memories of Ivy crowded her thoughts.

A gust of snow blew into her face, mercifully cooling her core temperature. Hermione skittered inside a moment later, and, shedding a fine mist of snow, the other two dogs followed. She shut the door on the blizzard and hoped neither Ivy nor Morgan got called out today, knowing full well that the hope was futile, and headed for the greenhouse.

"Stevie, tell Morgan to drive safely," she said when she returned to the warmth of the kitchen to peel the snowsuit off Hermione and replace it with an indoor sweater.

"Yes, mom."

"When are you seeing Ivy again? And work doesn't count." Angie, undeterred, waited expectantly for an answer.

"We don't have anything planned."

"Why not?"

"I invited her out last time. It's her turn to make a move."

"And she hasn't?" Angie's face fell.

"No."

"Hasn't it, like, only been a week?" said Stevie.

"Exactly. It's been a week. I thought you said it went well?"

"The words we overheard were 'oh my god.'" Stevie's imitation of Lillian's response to Morgan's question about whether or not the sex had been good was eerily accurate. She blushed.

"Sometimes slow is good."

Angie snorted in disagreement.

"Remember that we'll kick her ass if you need us to," said Stevie.

"I can handle Ivy."

"I bet you can."

"Ange—"

"What! I'm just happy you're getting some action."

She suddenly wished her friends hadn't brought Ivy up. It wasn't that she'd expected Ivy to call, but Ivy had given no sign she wanted to see Lillian again. No text. No lingering at the clinic to catch her as she got off work. Lillian had been the one to reach out in the end when Angie had heard about Ivy's kitten from Georgia.

Why did you expect anything would be different this time?

Of course Ivy hadn't called. People called Ivy. She was probably used to men and women throwing themselves at her, eager for her attention and her body and her money. Lillian wasn't that person. Spending two nights together didn't tie her to Ivy in any way. Clearly Ivy didn't think so, either, or she would have at least *texted*, instead of waiting for Lillian to make a move. Sure, Ivy had invited her to the island, but that was after Morgan had invited her to their Friendsgiving

223

potluck, and it had been more of a challenge than a planned date.

Date. That was the problem. She'd let Angie and Stormy talk her into inviting Ivy out for a date, and now here she was, feeling jilted and used. She blocked the image of Ivy sitting red-eyed and vulnerable on her bed. Maybe she'd misread things. Or maybe a part of her wanted to misread things, because the alternatives were too loaded. And what if Ivy hadn't reached out because she was embarrassed about breaking down? She knew how she would feel if Ivy had caught her in a similar emotional state. Her anger dimmed. Perhaps it fell on her to reassure Ivy she cared.

Except the last time Ivy had opened up to her, she'd pushed her away with a viciousness that had left a ring of scar tissue around her heart. Going through that again wasn't an option.

If Ivy wanted her, she could damn well come and get her.

Madison arrived that weekend with a bottle of champagne and a crushing hug. Ivy reeled from the embrace and held her sister at arm's length.

"What's up, Mads?"

"Your sister," Madison said, drawing out her words for effect, "made partner."

"Oh my god!" This time, it was Ivy clasping Madison tightly, and she even managed a squeal of excitement. "That's huge!"

"I'm the youngest partner the firm's ever had."

"And you're a woman."

"Breaking that glass ceiling, baby. Speaking of glasses . . ." Madison waved the bottle of champagne.

Ivy pulled two flutes out of the cupboard and braced herself for the pop of the cork. Darwin darted after it, and she pried it from his jaws while Madison poured them healthy servings of bubbly.

"To you," Ivy said as she raised her flute in a toast.

"And to you, for moving close enough to celebrate with me."

"Right now, I'm glad I did."

"Right now?" Madison's eyes narrowed, and Ivy kicked herself for the slip.

"Want to see the kitten?"

Her diversion worked. Madison set her drink on the counter and looked around expectantly.

"She's in here. She's not supposed to move too much yet, so I have to keep her in the bathroom."

The kitten chirruped the moment the door opened and hopped toward Ivy, her cone unbalancing her.

"Oh she is the cutest little gremlin. You have to keep her. What's her name?"

"I haven't gotten that far yet."

Madison dropped to the floor, heedless of the spilled cat litter, and let the kitten pounce on her fingers. "How are you feeling?"

She looked down at her sister, who was still petting the kitten, and shrugged. "Okay."

"Like, okay okay, or okay as in you feel like shit but don't want to tell me?"

"Can we talk about you being made partner?"

"My job is much less important than my only sister's health."

"I'm fine. Really. I knew I'd have a flare-up when I moved, and I'm managing."

"How's work going?"

"So far it's been good." She didn't mention her suspicions that Shawna knew something was wrong, or that Morgan had seen her fall in the barn, or that she was sleeping with a coworker.

"Have you seen Paul and Claire yet? I thought they were in Portland. Or Brunswick."

She'd forgotten all about Paul and Claire, friends from Rabbit, and Madison seemed to guess this, because she asked, "So who *have* you been hanging out with?"

"People from work."

Madison stood and steered her out of the bathroom and toward the couch, grabbing their drinks and the bottle on the way. The woodstove radiated heat, and the latest storm had left a sheet of glittering snow on the ground outside. Sunlight glinted off the water. The river hadn't frozen yet, and waves caught the evening and reflected it back at the sky.

"Have you talked to Kara?"

She shook her head.

"I still think you should have told her why you left."

"Would you, if you were me?"

Madison considered the question for a moment. They'd been raised in the same environment, and they both knew showing weakness wasn't an option. "That isn't the point. You never gave her a chance."

"A chance to what?"

She pictured Kara, blond and blue-eyed and dressed for the mountains, whether it was hiking or skiing or biking or trail riding, her body a beautiful machine. Ivy had loved that about her—Kara's energy, her enthusiasm, her optimism that there was something exciting just around the next bend or over the next ridge. She couldn't ask her to slow down. Kara deserved someone who could keep up.

"A chance to decide if she wanted to stay with you."

"It wouldn't have worked."

Madison took a sip and studied Ivy over the flute rim but didn't pursue the interrogation. "Tell me about your coworkers then."

"They're nice."

Her hand strayed automatically to her phone, but still nothing from Lillian since their exchange the other day. She'd started and deleted at least twenty messages since then. All had sounded hollow, and the situation hadn't been helped by a surge in late-night veterinary calls. It seemed like each time she opened a chat to invite Lillian over for a drink, her phone rang with another emergency, and on the nights she had off, she slept, exhausted and aching and panicked that Lillian was slipping away. She couldn't lose her again; nor could she stand the thought of Lillian's pity.

She steered the conversation away from Seal Cove and back to Madison's promotion. The excitement she felt for her sister wasn't feigned. Madison was driven, and she deserved the recognition. She couldn't help hearing Lillian's voice in the back of her mind, however, pointing out it was always people like Madison who got ahead: rich women with family connections. Familiar resentment flared. This was why Lillian was a bad idea. They were too different, and while this no longer frightened her, she recognized differences that wide were hard to bridge. The class barrier was more like a cement wall. Scaling it required grit and being prepared to tear your skin on the barbed wire up top.

"Are you coming to Florida for Christmas?"

"Yes."

"Good. You could use some sun. You look like a vampire."

They settled in for an evening of bingeing old shows on Netflix and laughing at inside jokes. Ivy relaxed in her sister's presence, grateful for the visit and the company of someone who didn't care about who she'd been in vet school.

Did I make a mistake, coming here? She asked herself as she let Madison pour her more champagne. *Should I have gone to Boston instead? Or Portland? Someplace no one knows me?*

Instead, she'd latched on to Seal Cove like a limpet, and she didn't want to know what she'd discover if she examined that decision too closely.

"Mads," she said, seizing on an idea. "Are you still friends with that guy who went to Berklee?"

"Damien? Yeah, why?"

"I have a question about pianos."

December's early snowstorms melted with a warm front that turned the backyard at 16 Bay Road into a dog-churned soup and splattered cars with salt and slush. Lillian glared at the gray sky, hot in her coat, and tried to shake her foul mood. Today had not been a good day.

It had started with a series of unpleasant appointments, where she'd plastered a smile on her face and listened to clients reciting information they'd gleaned from the underbelly of the internet, and had ended with the discovery that Brian had posted a photo of his new girlfriend—sorry, *fiancée*—on Instagram. Which served her right for hiding in the bathroom for a few minutes in between appointments, scrolling through social media in search of cute animal content.

Four years. Four years of back and forth, each devoted to their careers as well as each other, or so she'd thought. Four years of giving him space to finish his PhD. Four years of long-distance calls, drives to Rhode Island while he was at Brown, and spending most nights alone. She'd given him the freedom they'd both claimed they needed, asking virtually nothing, waiting for the time when they could be together in a more concrete sense, and within months of leaving her he'd decided to commit the rest of his life to someone else?

He'd found true love, and all she'd found was Ivy.

She dug in her pocket for her car keys, the lights of the clinic bright behind her in the dark, and swore under her breath. Ivy. Ivy, who had also run from her because she wasn't enough. The memory still hurt with the same ferocity. Six years had elapsed since then. Six years since she'd realized the animosity she'd felt toward Ivy masked something else, only to have Ivy throw it back in her face.

The hatred she'd felt afterward was real enough.

"Lil, wait up."

Her fingers closed around her keys just as Ivy's voice pierced her thoughts. She turned in time to see Ivy slow from a jog to a walk, jacket open in the unseasonable warmth, her blond hair whipped by the damp wind. The lurch of her heart against her breastbone didn't ease the sick twist in her gut.

"Hi," Ivy said as she halted before her.

"Hi."

Ivy's face fell at her tone, but Lillian made no move to soften it. When had Ivy ever shown consideration for her feelings? The rational part of her brain recognized the unfairness of the thought. She shut it down. She didn't want to be fair. Life wasn't fair, so why should she be? Brian was her proof. She'd made the safe decision, choosing stability and dependability over the tumult of emotion Ivy promised, and when she'd been with Brian, she, too, had felt stable and dependable. The person Ivy turned her into boasted neither of those qualities.

Which terrifies you, doesn't it?

"It's been a crazy week." Ivy's excuse was as pathetic as her own fears.

"Sure."

Ivy searched her face with those terribly green eyes. "Anyway, I wanted to ask you if you'd like to have dinner with me."

Her anger melted fractionally, but not enough to relent. "I'm pretty busy."

"Oh." Ivy dropped her eyes and studied the slush at their feet. "Well, let me know when you're free?"

The car keys bit into her palm. Glancing around to make sure no one was watching, which, considering the darkness of the parking lot and the weather, seemed unlikely, she sagged against her car. Her pea-coat would have salt stains on it, but she didn't care. Ivy's vulnerability stole the heat from her anger.

"I'm sorry. I had a really shitty day. I'd like to have dinner with you."

Ivy's smile should have bathed the entire lot with light. "What are you doing tonight?"

"I was planning on drinking a bottle of wine by myself," she admitted. *And burning Brian's things.*

"What about splitting a bottle?"

"After today, I might need my own."

"I have a few lying around."

"Of course you do."

"So?" Ivy held out a tentative hand.

She stared at it, wanting to stay angry, but unable to resist the memory of Ivy sleeping in her arms. Their fingers interlocked in the space between them.

"Your hands are freezing," she told Ivy.

"I've been on the road all day."

She abandoned her keys and put her other hand over their clasped ones, chafing Ivy's cold skin to warm it up. Ivy edged closer, almost shyly, and Lillian wanted to laugh at herself for how easily her resolve broke around this woman. It didn't matter whether that resolve was to remain professional or calm or aloof—all Ivy had to do was shift the position of her shoulders, and Lillian lost it.

"How's your kitten?"

"Come see for yourself."

She pulled into Ivy's driveway an hour later, dressed in her softest pair of leggings and a long sweater. Hardly elegant, as Angie had kindly pointed out when Lillian asked her to watch the dogs, but she didn't owe Ivy anything. The strength of the bitterness still welling up from the fiancée-shaped-wound in her chest surprised her. Had she wanted to marry Brian? Had she thought that was where they were headed? Her hands gripped the steering wheel too tightly.

It doesn't matter. You're here on a date. You have options, too.

Ivy Holden wasn't an option, though. Not really. Lillian still didn't know *what* Ivy was to her, and that uncertainty, she admitted, probably had just as much to do with her unstable mood as Brian. Ivy met her at the door. Like Lillian, she'd clearly gravitated toward comfort, though she didn't want to hazard a guess at the price tag on the black jeggings encasing her legs, or the dark green-and-red plaid button-up.

"Come in."

A fire blazed in the living room despite the warm front, though she supposed fifty degrees wasn't exactly toasty, and her nose picked up the smell of warm bread. She followed it into the kitchen. Ivy put on a pair of oven mitts and pulled a rustic loaf out of the oven.

"Did you bake that?"

"I wish. Picked it up from a local bakery, though, if that counts?"

It smelled incredible. An array of soft cheeses perched on a cheeseboard, and she was grateful she hadn't yet cut cheese out of her diet.

"Something to drink?"

"Sure. Let me help?"

"Wine is on the counter. I figured I'd pick up a few bottles in case one wasn't enough for you. There's a—shit."

Lillian turned from the wine in time to see Ivy, who had started slicing the bread, clutching her hand.

"Are you hurt?"

"No," Ivy said, blood oozing from between her fingers and giving evidence to the lie.

"Come to the sink." She guided Ivy toward the faucet and turned on a stream of water. Ivy released her injured hand, and Lillian hissed in sympathy at the deep cut on her forefinger.

"I'm such an idiot."

Lillian glanced at her face, alarmed by the viciousness in her voice. "You cut yourself. Not a big deal. Serves you right for having expensive knives."

Ivy shook her head with her lips pressed into a thin white line.

"Does it hurt?"

"Not yet."

Water washed away the worst of the bleeding, but she needed something to wrap it with.

"Where can I find gauze?"

"I've got some in the downstairs bathroom."

"Keep that under the water."

She found the medicine cabinet easily enough and pulled out the supplies she needed. Ivy still looked livid with herself when she returned.

"May I?"

Ivy removed her hand from the water, and Lillian dried and bandaged it as gently as possible.

"At least it's your left," she said, trying to bring some color back into Ivy's blanched face. "Work isn't going to be fun, though."

She didn't mention the other activities it would impair.

"Yeah."

"Hey." She cupped Ivy's cheek and sought her eyes. Ivy met hers reluctantly. "It's not a big deal. Last summer, Morgan put her hand flat on a grill. Burned the hell out of it because she was too busy drooling over Emilia."

"Are you implying I was drooling?" A small twitch at the corner of Ivy's mouth might have been the beginnings of a smile.

"No." Not that she would have minded. "But I think I'll cut the rest of the bread."

Something pounced on her foot as she reached for the knife. She looked down, expecting Darwin, and instead saw a dilute tortoiseshell kitten scampering away.

"Was that . . .?"

"She'll be back. This is her favorite game. Having three legs doesn't slow her down at all."

Sure enough, fur rocketed around the corner of a cabinet for another drive-by assault on Lillian's socked foot.

"She's doing well then?"

Ivy did smile this time. "She's a hellion."

"How did you end up with her?"

She finished slicing up the bread while Ivy explained about the cow and the shattered humerus, and helped her carry the food and wine into the living room. Ivy didn't seem to have any qualms about eating on her couch. *She can probably afford to have it professionally cleaned.*

"You must think I'm an absolute mess," Ivy said when she finished relating the kitten's misadventures. "First . . . the other night . . . and now I almost chop off my finger."

The attempt at self-deprecating humor didn't fool her. Ivy stared at her wounded hand as if she wanted to hack the whole thing off.

"Remember when you sliced through the body cavity in anatomy lab?"

Ivy straightened in outrage. "That was totally you."

"Was it, though?"

"You're lucky I'm injured, or I'd—"

"You'd what?"

"Throw bread at you."

"Don't waste it. This bread is delicious. I'd be fine eating just this for the rest of my life."

"Wish I'd known that before I picked up a squash soup and a salad," said Ivy.

"No, I'll take those, too."

Ivy grinned. "I like your appetite."

"So," Lillian said a little while later as she sat back, stomach full and lips sweet with wine, "you and Stormy seem to be getting along."

"She's been kind to me."

She studied Ivy. She'd expected her to make an offhand comment about the café or Stormy's personality—not that Stormy had been kind to Ivy, as if she were a stray cat Stormy had left milk out for by the back door.

"Does that surprise you?"

"She's *your* friend."

Right. And Lillian's friends had been operating up until recently under the assumption she and Ivy hated one another.

232

"Well, she likes meddling."

"I've been meaning to talk to you about that. She invited me to your winter holiday party, but if you'd rather I not—"

She held up her hand to stop Ivy. "Of course you're invited. They all know now anyway."

Pink flushed Ivy's pale cheeks. "Even Morgan?"

"She saw my car parked here the other day."

Ivy's mouth rounded in an O of amused horror. "She didn't."

"She absolutely did. Cornered me as soon as she got off work."

"Unsurprising." Ivy laughed hollowly. "She told me not to fuck with you when I first got here."

"What?"

"In a nice way."

"That wasn't her place."

"She cares about you. Also, I don't remember her being that ripped at school. The woman is jacked. I was a little intimidated, which you are not allowed to tell her."

"You? Intimidated?" Lillian couldn't picture it.

"I said a little, not a lot."

"Still."

They fell quiet, and she sensed the inevitable questions rising in them both.

"Everyone knows?"

"Yeah. Well, just Morgan and Stevie at work."

Another pause.

"What are we doing, Ivy?"

Ivy gave her a half smile and pulled her knees to her chest, empty wineglass dangling in one hand. "I don't know."

"Me either." She finished her own wine and watched the last drops run down the side to pool at the base of the bowl. "Is this a mistake?"

"I don't want it to be."

Again, that aching vulnerability in Ivy's voice. She wished Darwin weren't between them. At the same time, she was grateful for the neutral zone his small body provided. History had shown she did not make sound decisions where Ivy was concerned.

"What do you want?" she asked Ivy.

It had to be Ivy who took the first step. She would not put herself out there again until she knew where Ivy stood.

"I want—" Ivy's voice broke. "I want you."

Such simple words, but she reeled, the whole room spinning, as things that had rattled around for years fell into place. Brian didn't matter. His new fiancée didn't matter. Those things couldn't matter in a world where Ivy saying *I want you* soothed a wound so deep she'd mistaken it for a part of herself.

Ivy waited for her to respond.

"How?"

Inadequate. Hardly a response. But she needed to know. *How* could Ivy want her, after throwing her away? *How* did Ivy want her now, in what capacity, to what degree, and *how* the hell was she supposed to deal with any of this? *How* could they move forward? What would that even look like?

"I want to be with you."

Her breath hitched in her throat. She looked away from Ivy, away from the words she'd wanted to hear six years ago and had convinced herself she'd left behind. Wanting to be with Ivy was impossible. It would never work. It would—*fuck.* She wanted it. Oh, how she wanted it.

"Really?" She sounded so stupid. So weak.

"Yes."

Ivy reached across the couch, bridging the gap where Darwin lay sleeping, his small paws twitching, and took her hand.

She squeezed it with the force of all the things she did not know how to say and smiled like the fool she knew herself to be. Ivy's answering smile finished what the wine had started: she fell, drowning in green.

Chapter Eleven

She led Lillian into the stable by the hand. The warm front persisted, but she still wore thin gloves to keep her hands from stiffening in the damp and chilly air. Lillian's bare fingers warmed hers through the fabric.

The barn smelled like horse and hay and fresh pine bedding. Rubber mats lined the central isle, reducing the chill of the cement and the sound their boots made as they walked past stalls of drowsing, munching, and curious horses. Noses thrust over wooden doors, for the pastures had turned to mud and the barn manager had elected not to turn the horses out for fear of losing too many shoes to the sucking, icy muck. Gentle whickers of greeting followed them. Even the overhead lighting was soft, which she appreciated. The fluorescent bulbs were not as harsh as some of the barn lights she'd endured over the years, and the stable radiated warmth and cleanliness. Freddie recognized her footsteps and poked his head over his door. His ears pricked forward and his lips twitched as if he could already taste the treat she'd brought him.

"He's a huge baby," she said as Freddie bobbed his head in anticipation. She pulled an oat cake out of her coat pocket and handed it to Lillian, who, holding her palm out flat, smiled as Freddie lipped it up.

That smile banished the lingering chill.

Lillian stroked Freddie's muzzle and scratched the wide, flat plane of his cheek. "He's gorgeous."

Freddie bumped Lillian's chest, and, laughing with unrestrained pleasure, Lillian scratched the itchy spot beneath his forelock and let him rub his eye against her. He'd learned to be gentle over the years, and while some horses might accidentally knock a human over while vigorously using them as a scratching post, Freddie knew his own strength.

"I'd love to watch you ride," said Lillian.

Ivy looked down at her jeans. "I'm not dressed for it."

"People ride in jeans." Lillian looked her up and down with a boldness that left heat lingering in its wake. "Though I wouldn't mind seeing you in breeches."

"I'll remember that."

"Please do."

They were the only people in the barn, save for one of the ubiquitous teenage girls that barns attracted mucking out a stall at the far end, and Ivy took advantage of the quiet evening. She pushed Lillian against the stall door with her hips and gripped the bars on either side of her head, the bite of the metal cold even with her gloves. Lillian glanced around them once, then hooked her fingers into Ivy's belt. Ivy's breath caught on a groan as Lillian kissed her. She still couldn't believe they were doing this, whatever *this* was, and how good it felt to lean into Lillian's mouth. Freddie retreated into his stall and resumed browsing for missed stalks of hay.

The slam of a car door broke them apart. Color highlighted Lillian's cheekbones, and her dilated pupils reflected Ivy's.

"I was serious about watching you ride."

Ivy had ridden competitively most of her life, and yet no hyper-critical judge or disdainful competitor had ever made her stomach swoop with nerves the way settling into the saddle with Lillian Lee looking on did. Freddie twitched his skin in a warning that if she didn't pull herself together, her nerves would make him jittery. *Deep breaths.* She inhaled through her nose and exhaled through her mouth, gathered her reins, and urged him into a walk with her seat. He complied and set off at a working walk with an ear cocked back, waiting for her next command.

The butterflies subsided as she warmed up, though she was still hyperaware of Lillian, who sat on the small risers on the far end. Freddie's strides loosened with each pass. She moved him through his gaits, as usual checking for signs of stiffness or lameness, and, satisfied, decided it was safe to show him off.

She did not jump him anymore, but a part of her was glad of it as he bowed his neck and came onto the bit. She asked for turn-on-the-forehand and hindquarters, half-pass, shoulder in, piaffe and passage. Freddie was built for dressage, and she thrilled at his responsiveness. He came alive between her seat and legs, carefully contained power rippling through his haunches on the pirouette. His gait, always smooth, was nearly flight in extension, and while she knew the years and years of training that had gone into this moment, as they passed along the mirrors, she appreciated how effortless his movements appeared.

Breathing hard, and not wanting to bore Lillian, though hacks like this made her want to ride forever, she slowed him to a walk, scratched along his mane, and raised her eyes to meet Lillian's across the wall separating the risers from the arena. The sheer admiration on her face almost convinced her to repeat the whole thing over again.

"I'm not a horse girl, but that?" Lillian waved at the ring. "That was . . . wow, Ivy."

She stroked Freddie's neck again and bit her lip to keep from smiling too widely at the compliment.

"I didn't see your hands move at all. How did he know what you were telling him to do?"

"It's dressage. Part of the point is subtlety—and control. The least amount of pressure necessary is the right amount."

"I like that." Lillian straddled the divider, moving slowly so as not to spook Freddie, and perched close enough for Ivy to reach out her hand and brush a gloved thumb across her chin.

"You should try it some time."

"The last time I was on a horse was a friend's birthday party when I was twelve."

Ivy slid off Freddie and uncinched his girth, setting the saddle on the dividing wall by Lillian.

"What are you doing?" Lillian asked.

She didn't answer, and, glad to see Freddie had hardly broken a sweat, she swung on to his bare back. It was a trick she'd taught herself years ago that required momentum and upper body strength to execute. The fact she succeeded today in front of Lillian, after an extended lapse in practice, was a small mercy.

His warm back soothed the muscles of her thighs. She rarely rode bareback, these days, but it was bliss in the wintertime. Freddie leg-yielded at her command until he stood parallel to the wall.

"Get on," she told Lillian.

"Absolutely not."

"Please?"

"I don't have a helmet."

She unfastened hers and passed it to Lillian, who took it and stared at it doubtfully.

"I won't let anything happen to you."

"You can't guarantee that," said Lillian. Ivy remembered her fear of heights and warred with the desires to push Lillian and to let it go.

"Please?" she asked again.

Lillian wavered. Perhaps she didn't want to back down, or perhaps she, too, had remembered their very first meeting. Or, and she hoped this was the case, perhaps Lillian had thought about how it would feel to sit with her arms around Ivy's waist.

"Okay."

"Slide on behind me. He won't move."

Freddie twitched an ear as Lillian draped a leg across his back and then with a muffled whimper settled into place. The arms around Ivy's waist closed, vise-like.

"Breathe," she told Lillian. "We won't move until you're ready."

Lillian took a shaky breath and Ivy suppressed a laugh. Freddie waited patiently.

"Don't do anything crazy." Lillian's breath tickled the back of her neck.

"I just want to show you what it feels like."

She took them into a walk, her body tuned into Lillian's seat, adjusting her own position and Freddie's to keep them centered. "Let your hips move with him, and with me. Yeah. Better."

"God, we're high."

"I've fallen more times than I can count."

Lillian stiffened. "Is that supposed to make me feel better?"

"It doesn't hurt as much as you'd think. And I haven't fallen in years. Freddie's pretty chill these days." She decided not to recite statistics about riders who'd ended up paralyzed or dead after bad falls.

"Can we not talk about falling?"

"Sure."

"Thank you."

"Are you breathing?"

"Yes." Lillian said the word into Ivy's ear, and she shivered, wishing suddenly that Lillian was riding her instead of Freddie.

"There are different types of walks. This is just a walk, but I'm going to move him into a collected walk. Let me know if you can tell the difference." She closed her fingers slightly on the reins, tilted her seat, and put the barest pressure on his sides.

"It feels . . . I'm not sure. Like he's ready for something?"

"Exactly. And this is an extended walk." Freddie lengthened his strides at her request.

"Oh it's faster."

"Sort of."

"Definitely."

"He's extending his stride, that's all. This is a faster walk." He picked up a working walk, and she paid careful attention to Lillian's position. After a half circumference around the arena, Lillian relaxed.

"Okay, this isn't terrible."

"Want to try a slow trot?"

"Isn't that the bumpy one?"

"The bumpy one?" she teased.

"It's been a while since I had to learn this."

"Freddie's trot isn't bumpy. Breathe, then hold on to me."

Freddie picked up a slow, floating trot. Lillian slid to one side but corrected herself before Ivy had to halt, and their hips moved together as she wove serpentines down the arena. Lillian's arms loosened their death grip on her waist and settled over her stomach, sending a low heat through her abdomen.

"Horses aren't usually this smooth, are they?"

"No. Freddie's special. Hold on."

She put him into a half-pass, and then a leg yield, and Lillian exhaled shakily. "This is a lot harder than you're making it look, isn't it?"

"Yes." No point in lying, even for modesty's sake, and she wasn't going to downplay their hard work.

Eventually, after showing Lillian a few more dressage moves, she settled into an easy walk around the arena and enjoyed the warmth of Lillian's body against her back and the press of her knees into her thighs. Lillian trusted her enough to get on a horse, despite her fear of heights. She wasn't sure which thought warmed her more: the trust, or what it might imply. Their first meeting came back to her. She smiled at the memory of Lillian's eyes flashing behind her bulky glasses. Would Lillian have climbed the ropes if she hadn't goaded her?

And here she was again, pushing Lillian out of her comfort zone. She wondered if she should feel guilty before discarding the thought. Let people like Brian and Morgan coddle Lillian Lee. She knew better. Lillian wanted to be pushed.

Her legs shook when they hit the ground. *I just rode a fucking horse.* Freddie's back seemed even higher now that she knew what it felt like to sit astride it, but she didn't have long to ponder her feat of bravery. Ivy dismounted after her and tangled a hand in the hair at the back of her neck, Freddie's reins in the other, and kissed her deeply. Her body responded to Ivy's tongue with an immediacy that demanded they leave the barn at once.

Ivy pulled away too soon. She gasped, and Ivy grinned, nodding toward the exit. "Grab the saddle?"

She complied. The saddle pad was cool to the touch, chilled from its time away from Freddie's back. He'd been pleasantly warm and surprisingly comfortable. His spine hadn't dug into her seat, nor had he been painfully wide. And Ivy—she glanced over at Ivy, who was watching her out of the corner of her eye. Ivy had felt strong and solid in her arms, totally in control in a way that might have pissed her off even a few months ago but instead made her want to bite the skin above her collarbone. Ivy was hot on horseback. The total concentration on her face as she'd put Freddie through his paces and the obvious trust the horse had in her hands was hypnotic. She could have watched Ivy ride for hours.

Ivy took the saddle from her and rested it on the saddle rack by Freddie's stall door. Freddie stood in the crossties, large brown eyes liquid and gentle.

"Here." Ivy handed her a curry comb. Remembering a few things from school, she moved it in circles over his hide while Ivy followed behind her with a bristled brush. His dark bay coat gleamed beneath the attention.

Once he'd been groomed out and put away, Ivy grabbed the saddle, bridle, and tack box and led the way down the hall back to the tack room.

"It's heated," she said as the door shut behind them.

"So is the indoor," said Ivy. "Which is why I'm boarding here. The barn is pretty well insulated, too, so it doesn't get that cold, especially with the horses in."

The tack room was spacious as well as warm. Trunks and saddles gleamed with polish, and the smells of leather and saddle soap replaced the smells of hay and shavings. She hadn't examined Ivy's saddle closely while carrying it. Now, comparing it to some of the others, she could tell it was high quality. Ivy slipped a cloth cover over it, wiped the bridle and bit down with a cloth, and hung it on its hook. Her tack box went into a trunk. Lillian stopped her from shutting it to peer inside.

Leg wraps. Saddle pads. Ointments and salves. Fly spray. Fly mask. Horse shampoo. More brushes and combs. Spare barn boots. And, lying on top of a sheepskin saddle pad, a riding crop. She picked it up and turned it over in her hands.

"Don't get any ideas," said Ivy.

"Like what? This?" She took the crop by the handle and brought the leather tip up to rest beneath Ivy's chin, tilting it. Ivy's lips parted

241

in a sharp inhale.

"Take off your coat."

Ivy unzipped her jacket and set it on her trunk, her eyes never leaving Lillian's face. Her sweater clung to her curves, and she trailed the crop down Ivy's throat, tracing one collarbone before letting the tip dip into her cleavage. Lillian could feel her trembling through the shaft as she followed the curve of breast to ribcage and back. Ivy's nipples hardened beneath the cashmere.

She put slight pressure on the center of Ivy's chest with the crop and pushed. Ivy sat on her trunk, gazing up at Lillian in silence, though her lips were parted and flushed. The sight thrilled through her. Carefully, afraid of hurting Ivy even as a part of her fantasized about what it might be like to bring the crop down across her bare ass, she flicked Ivy's left nipple with the leather tip. Ivy's hips jerked on the trunk and she leaned back, bracing herself on her hands and giving Lillian more room to maneuver. She repeated the motion, surprised at how good it felt to stand over Ivy with what was essentially a weapon in her hand.

Well, maybe she shouldn't have been that surprised. They'd fought for most of their relationship. *All is fair in love and war.*

She drew a line between Ivy's nipples. When she reached the right nipple, she circled the taut skin, memory erasing the fabric barrier. Ivy's breath hitched when the crop touched her. Lillian flicked it over the tented fabric. She clamped her jaw shut on a groan as Ivy's head tilted back, the long line of her neck exposed and her mouth open. She flicked her again, harder this time, and Ivy's hands tightened on the edge of her trunk as her legs fell open.

Lillian hadn't done anything like this with Brian or any of the other men and women she'd been with. She'd had good sex, but nothing that soaked her instantly in a barn tack room. *What am I doing?* She thought, but the sound of Ivy's ragged breathing made it impossible to second-guess herself or feel self-conscious. Ivy's eyes dared her to go farther. To risk. To live fully in the moment. She flicked her a third time, relishing the way Ivy's body responded, lithe and coiled and as contained as her horse had been.

Her eyes followed the leather as it trailed down Ivy's hip, and she used the crop to lift the hem of her sweater. The undershirt beneath had been tucked into her jeans for warmth. *Rude.* She travelled along the edge of Ivy's belt and watched her stomach tighten through the thin cloth. Pausing at the buckle, she tapped the clasp. Ivy shuddered and bit her lip to keep quiet. She tapped it again, wanting to watch Ivy struggle for control. A whimper escaped Ivy's lips. Rewarding her—*or me, if we're being honest*—she dropped down along Ivy's zipper until the tip of the crop lay against her center. Ivy's eyes were half-lidded, and the sound of her breathing filled the room. Lillian traced the seam of her jeans down to her knee, then her calf, then back up and over the spot where her clit lay and down the other leg.

"Lil—"

She tapped the tip of the crop against the denim. Ivy bucked. Her own breathing was equally ragged now, and she couldn't remember ever wanting anyone the way she currently wanted Ivy. She'd be willing to risk a charge of indecent exposure just to touch the crop to Ivy's center, watching her wet the leather. The image stole her breath. She hadn't thought she was into things like this, but she'd fuck Ivy Holden with the thick end of the crop right now if she asked. And those eyes didn't just ask. They begged. She stepped closer, pulling the crop up and away to tease her nipples again, noting the flush spreading across the exposed skin of Ivy's chest. She pulled the fabric down and watched, shamelessly, as the crop dipped into Ivy's cleavage.

"Fuck," she said under her breath.

Ivy's shaky laugh was all the answer she seemed capable of giving. The swell of breast against the dark leather and the stray lock of blond hair falling over Ivy's shoulder printed themselves indelibly on her mind. Ivy had a freckle above her right nipple. She memorized this, then caressed Ivy's cheek with the crop before flipping it so that she held the shaft instead of the handle. She wanted to touch Ivy with her other hand, but something about the way Ivy sat, nearly prostrate before the touch of the crop, stayed her. Instead, she brought the handle down between Ivy's thighs and swore, reverently, as Ivy closed her legs around it and moaned her name. She pressed it into her. Ivy's hips moved with the slow rhythm, and then her eyes flew wide open as the latch on the tack room door lifted.

Lillian dropped the crop and stepped back, pretending to examine

Ivy's saddle cover while Ivy tried to look like she was putting on her shoe. A middle-aged woman and her daughter entered and waved cheerily at Ivy. She smiled in a passable attempt at normalcy.

"Good to see you, Jean," Ivy said as she stood and grabbed her coat. "Ring's all yours tonight."

Lillian avoided eye contact and fled the room after Ivy. Outside in the empty aisle, Ivy collapsed against her in a fit of silent laughter. Lillian felt like they were sixteen, nearly getting caught making out in an empty classroom, and the laughter that bubbled out of her throat was lighter than any she'd heard leave her own lips in years.

"Come on." Ivy took her hand and, with a look that should have started a fire in the hayloft, towed Lillian out of the barn and toward her car.

Ivy's appointments ended on time. She stopped by Storm's-a-Brewin' on her way home, because while she was on call tonight, which meant she could not invite Lillian over, the painful tightness in her chest needed release. It wasn't until she sat at the bar and waved at Stormy that she understood the tightness wasn't MS or the crushing weight of keeping her condition a secret. She was happy. Irrepressibly, obliteratingly happy, and trying to contain it was causing her physical pain.

"I need some shades if you're going to come in here glowing like that," said Stormy.

"Hello to you, too."

"What can I get you? Wait. Never mind; I want you to try this." She pulled a small round bottle out from beneath the bar.

"Is it beer?"

"Nope. Cider. Just got a batch back from my brewer. These are apples from Angie's place. Small batch. Prepare to have your mind blown, and it's a low alcohol content, so no need to worry if you're on call. Just try a sip."

Stormy practically bounced behind the bar, and Ivy relented. "I'll try it."

The squeal of excitement from her friend was worth any nerve pain the cider triggered, though she hadn't experimented enough with cider to know for sure if it would bother her the way beer did. Stormy popped the lid and handed it back.

"It's not a sweet cider," she said, frowning as if she'd just realized this might be a problem for Ivy. "But it's crisp."

She took a sip. The cold cider crested on her palate, and the biting taste of winter apples flooded her taste buds.

"Holy shit, this is delicious."

"Really? You're the first to try it. Besides me and my brewer, obviously."

Flattered more than she could express, she took another swallow. One of the reasons she'd never enjoyed cider was because most of the ciders she'd tried had a cloying sweetness that stuck to her throat and left her hungover. This was different. Crisp, as Stormy had promised, and slightly floral. *And grown in soil tended by Lillian Lee.* That thought, more than anything else, gave the cider its flavor.

"You should be proud. Can I buy a case?"

"Of course!"

"And I've been meaning to ask. The island could use an infusion of good beer. Do you ever cater events? I could hook you up."

"I've done a few small things locally, but nothing high end."

"If you want to, let me know, and I'll bring some of your beer to Rabbit this summer. Not the cider though. That's mine."

"Deal. Although I wouldn't want to get you bunnies all hopped up."

Ivy stared at her, deadpan, until Stormy laughed at her own terrible pun. "I take it back."

"Too late."

"I hear things are going well with you and Lil?"

She couldn't quite hate how easily that made her blush, or how quickly the happiness threatened to overwhelm her again.

Stormy raised her eyebrows. "That's a yes."

She nodded.

"And she accused me of meddling. Hah. I know what I'm doing."

"Don't tell her that," said Ivy.

"Don't *you* tell her I said that."

245

"I would never."

"Your reputation notwithstanding, I believe you."

Lillian leaned back into Ivy's couch and stroked the kitten, still unnamed, sprawled across her thigh.

"Close your eyes," said Ivy.

"Do I trust you?" she asked, and though the question was in jest, there was a part of her that wished someone would answer it.

"I don't know. Do you?"

"What will you do if I close my eyes?"

"Don't you think that defeats the purpose of a surprise?"

"Is it a good surprise?"

"I think it is," said Ivy.

"Will I?"

"I hope so."

"Will it hurt?"

"What kind of surprise would hurt and also be something you would like?" Ivy paused, perhaps recalling their adventure in the tack room, then smirked. "Lee, I didn't think you had it in you."

"Not what I meant." She folded her arms across her chest. "And you have no idea what I have in me."

"Falafel, pita, and wine." Ivy checked them off on her fingers.

"Fine. I'll close my eyes, but don't make me regret this."

"First you have to stand up."

Lillian removed the kitten, stood, and held out her hands. "Okay. Closing my eyes now."

Ivy towed her gently across the floor. She could tell they'd left the living room by the diminishing warmth of the fire, and her feet brushed over the edge of a thick carpet.

Ivy's breath warmed her ear. "You can open your eyes now."

It took her several heartbeats to figure out what she was seeing. The room was a study, of sorts. Bookshelves lined two of the walls, and a window seat occupied a third. The yellow light of a corner lamp illuminated the object in the room's center.

"Ivy, what is this?"

A piano stood on an oriental rug. Black wood reflected the lamplight in waves, and she moved forward to touch it. Not just any piano. A Steinway baby grand. Her fingertips left faint prints on the veneer.

"Do you like it?"

"I don't understand."

"Check out the sheet music."

Her eyes focused on the sheets arranged on the music rack. Rachmaninoff's Piano Concerto No. 2 in C Minor. The piano had to be one of the smaller baby grands made by Steinway, but that hardly mattered. Restored or new, a piano in this condition cost well into the five digits.

"You didn't tell me you had a piano."

"I didn't, then," said Ivy.

The prickling started in her fingers and moved over her shoulders, down her back, and across her scalp. Air refused to flow normally into her lungs and instead rattled in her ears.

"But you don't play piano."

"No, but you do. And it's gorgeous, isn't it? I thought, 'why not?'"

She spoke like a piano was a decoration. An accessory. Something closer to a vase than an instrument.

"Why not?" She repeated Ivy's words in a voice that sounded nothing like her own. Ivy hadn't appeared to notice, or else she was too busy admiring her newest possession to realize something was wrong.

"Yeah. I spoke to one of my sister's friends. He told me this was one of the best pianos I could find in the States.

"Exactly. And you don't even play."

A frown creased Ivy's forehead. "Why does that matter?"

"You just went out and bought a piano."

"I wanted to hear you play."

"That's—" She touched the lid with the reverence it deserved. A reverence Ivy would never show it. *Could* never show it, because she was too used to quality to recognize it.

"Lil?"

"This is a mistake." She backed away from the piano. From Ivy. From everything she'd allowed herself to hope for. Ivy had said, *I want you*, and this is what she had meant. Possession. Something that could be owned and discarded, much like she'd thrown Lillian away before.

"What's a mistake?"

"The fact you have to ask that. The fact you can just buy a piano and expect me to fall in love with you without—without knowing the first thing about me."

Ivy's face, already pale, whitened to chalk.

"This is what you do." Her voice grew stronger, more certain as her anger came to a crescendo. "You have no idea what it's like for the rest of us. Do you think you can just buy me? That, what, I'll forgive you everything just because you've thrown enough money at me?"

"Like *you* know the first thing about money."

"See? That's what I'm talking about. You think you're better than me. You always have."

"Bullshit. You're just as bad. You think poverty gives you moral superiority, but you're not poor anymore, Lee. You're a doctor. Welcome to the middle class."

"Like *you* know anything about the middle class."

"And you freak out the minute someone tries to do something nice for you."

"Nice? Nice is dinner. Nice is a picnic, or a shoulder rub, not a fucking *Steinway*. You could have at least gone with a Yamaha, or a—"

"You hate when I buy you drinks. You hate when I buy you anything. You're the one with the money problem, not me."

"Name one thing in your life money can't fix. One thing, and I'll—"

"I have MS, Lillian."

She choked on her next retort.

Ivy trembled across from her, gripping the piano for support. Ire radiated from her tense shoulders.

The meds on Ivy's bathroom counter made sense now. Terror for Ivy opened its mouth to swallow her. She balanced on a tightrope of fury over the pit. Just as she had on the ropes course, she willed herself not to look down. The fall waited. Except this time, there was no harness to catch her, and no way to climb back out.

Her feet gripped the rope.

"Thank goodness you have good health care, then." The cruelty in her words shocked her at the same time as it thrilled her. Something dark and liquid and hot clawed at her insides, and when she opened her mouth, it spoke with her voice. "Tough luck. But you'll never have to worry about supporting yourself. You'll never have to worry about affording your medication."

"That's not—"

"When pretty rich girls get sick, it's tragic. When poor girls get sick, it's a drain on the health care system. How is that fair?"

"How is that my fault?"

"It's not an excuse."

"I'm not saying it's an—"

"You can't just throw that out there and expect me to overlook everything else."

"I'm not!"

"You *are*. You broke my heart, Ivy, and now that you're broken, I'm finally good enough? You're settling? No. I'm not going to be your consolation prize."

The sound of her own panting breath filled the silence between them. She knew she was being irrational. That was the problem: nothing about her feelings for Ivy was rational. Everything that should have been tempered by reason came out plasma hot. Around Ivy, she was unpredictable. Unstable. Cruel. Ivy made the world too bright. She made her want things she couldn't have.

Things like pianos. Music. Passion. Ephemeral joys that might fade with the dawn.

Ivy's body, wasting.

Ivy, dying.

No.

Tears streamed down Ivy's face, but her eyes were cold when at last she spoke. "I think you should go."

She turned her back before her own tears had a chance to fall.

Chapter Twelve

Florida heat hit her face with the smell of flowers and cut grass. She inhaled, grateful to be out of the cold, but the sun could not warm the chill that had settled into her chest since Lillian had walked out of her house. Again.

"You're so pale," said Prudence.

"There's my girl." Her father shouldered past her mother to envelope her in a hug. His cologne, subtle and familiar, lingered when he held her at arm's length to look her over. "Nothing a little sun can't cure, right?"

Her parent's Naples house sat directly on the beach. Sandpipers darted in and out of the waves past the salt grass growing on the low dunes, and the evening sun bled into the ocean. Her winter clothes felt heavy and cumbersome.

"Is Madison here yet?"

"She's walking the beach, on her phone as usual," said Prudence. *As if she's one to talk.* Prudence might have recently retired, but she never strayed far from her own phone. Committees and board meetings had dominated her life when Ivy and Madison were children, and all that had changed since was the nonprofit status of the callers.

She rolled her luggage to a guest bedroom and changed into a light sundress, briefly wishing Lillian could see her before remembering Lillian wouldn't want to see her, regardless of how she looked in the dark blue cotton.

"I'm not going to be your consolation prize."

Her stomach clenched, and she met her eyes in the mirror, gratified at the anger blazing out of them. Anger she could deal with.

"Mom looks like she spent the last month in a tanning bed. It's atrocious." Madison strolled into her bedroom without knocking, a glass of white wine in one hand and her eyes finishing a roll.

"Was that the first thing she said to you, too?"

"Yes. I told her I didn't want to get skin cancer. Or wrinkles."

"Dad looks good, though."

"I know. He finally shaved off that disgusting goatee," said Madison.

"Right. His Brad Pitt look." Ivy faked a smile at the memory.

Madison's eyes, now that they had finished circumnavigating their sockets, settled on her. "You do look like shit, by the way. No offense."

"I'm not sleeping well."

"Don't expect to sleep better here. Dad's snoring is unbelievable. Come on."

Madison beckoned her out of the bedroom, and she followed her down to the patio. A bottle of wine waited, accompanied by cheese and crackers and their parents. She filled them in on her new life in Seal Cove while the sun finished setting and mosquitoes made their move. Bug spray stung her nostrils as her father passed the can around.

"It will be so nice to have you close by this summer," said Prudence.

"We'll have to get you a boat," said her father.

She pictured Lillian's reaction to those words and grimaced.

"What? It's perfectly logical, and considering your hours it makes sense."

"You'd look hot in a Pershing."

Just what she needed. A fucking yacht. Lillian would—

No. It didn't matter what Lillian thought because Lillian had slammed that door in her face.

"Ivy is perfectly capable of choosing her own boat," said Prudence, interrupting a heated debate between Madison and Richard.

" . . .*everyone* has a Regulator," Madison said before quelling beneath her mother's stare.

"Ivy's always made up her own mind, anyway."

She smiled at her father. He meant it genuinely now, though there had been a time when Ivy's independence was a sore point. An uncharitable part of her wondered if he would be secretly glad she'd gotten sick. It would put her back in his court, dependent on family money. *"If you'd become a surgeon,"* she could hear him saying, but she hadn't, and fighting imaginary battles was a waste of time.

"How is that woman you went to school with? What was her name—a flower, wasn't it? Lily? Rose?" asked Prudence.

Ivy stilled. "Lillian."

"The one you hate?" Madison perked up at the prospect of drama.

"She hasn't changed." *But I wish the subject would.*

"It does seem a shame you ended up working with her." Prudence refilled her wineglass and waved the bottle. Ivy covered her drink with her hand, but the rest of her family accepted.

"It's a small field."

"It isn't that small," said Richard. "I feel like I see a new vet hospital opening every day."

"She isn't making your life difficult, is she?" Prudence asked.

"No." The breeze off the water might as well have come from Seal Cove, it was so frigid. None of the others shivered. "I'm going to grab a sweatshirt. Anyone want anything?"

Lillian surveyed the living room. Her favorite people filled it, digging hands into bowls of snacks and sipping festive drinks while the fireplace crackled merrily and a cold December rain slicked the windows. It might turn to snow later, or perhaps sleet. The weather app on her phone changed its mind every few minutes, and in the end it didn't matter. Anyone who needed to crash here would have a bed if the roads got bad, or at least a couch. She counted: Stormy, Morgan, Emilia, Stevie, and Angie, along with Georgia and Shawna and a few other clinic people. Plenty of room, and plenty of food. Veterinary gods knew she'd made enough. Cookies and spiced breads and pies and latkes and dumplings and her mom's sweet rice balls and moon cakes, not to mention the casseroles and sweets provided by the guests. They'd hardly made a dent. The counters looked like they might collapse under the weight.

"Get out of the kitchen," Angie ordered from the living room.

"Just a second." Something was in the oven. Blanking on what exactly, she opened the door. Stevie's pigs-in-a-blanket or whatever those tiny hot dogs wrapped in canned crescent rolls were called. She reached for the tray, recognized she wasn't wearing an oven mitt just in time, and remedied her mistake without burning anything.

"I thought Dr. Holden was coming," someone said as she emerged from her fortress of baked goods. She retreated again under the pretense of getting another drink. Mulled wine couldn't dull the sharp sting of that name.

"She's in Florida with her family for a few days," said Shawna.

"Generous of you to cover," Georgia said, presumably to Morgan.

"Not really. I'm taking a week off this spring and said I'd cover the holidays if she covered that."

"Where are you going?" asked Stormy.

Sensing a shift toward safer conversational currents, Lillian made a second attempt at reentry.

"She's going to New Zealand with Emilia," said Stevie. "And she doesn't even like *Lord of the Rings*."

"There is more to New Zealand than a bunch of long-ass movies."

Angie, Stevie, and several other voices pounced in outrage. Lillian took a seat beside Stormy and warmed her hands on her mulled wine.

"I'm worried about Dr. Holden."

Dammit, Shawna.

"Why's that?" Morgan zeroed in on the comment with a sharpness that instantly aroused Lillian's suspicions. She had told her friends she'd had a fight with Ivy but had left out a few key details.

"She just seems off."

"We all have off weeks," said Georgia.

"More off than an off week."

"How?"

Shawna hesitated before speaking. "She's been . . . clumsy."

Morgan frowned. "Did she put you at risk?"

"Not at all. She's very careful, and I like working with her. Forget I said anything."

"Didn't you say you saw her fall a while ago at her barn?" said Stevie.

Morgan shot Stevie a look, suggesting Stevie hadn't been supposed to share that information.

"Anyone hungry?" Lillian hadn't realized she'd stood up until her wine slopped down her wrist. Ignoring it, she put on her brightest smile. "There's way too much food, and Ivy isn't here to help us, which means more responsibility for the rest of you."

"Careful. She's fattening us up to eat us," said Angie.

"I knew she was a witch. Look at all the shit she grows in her greenhouse." Stevie narrowed her eyes. "And her familiar is clearly Hermione."

"Don't insult her, or she'll put a bag of live wasps in your pillow," said Angie in a stage whisper.

Lillian cracked a smile. "Morgan, please take these two with you on vacation and drown them in the East Australian current."

Stormy pulled her back down to her seat on the couch, ignoring Stevie and Angie. "No more food. You've stuffed us already. Give us time to digest."

The conversation shifted back to Morgan's upcoming vacation. Stormy put her hand on Lillian's arm, drawing her attention.

"Do you want to talk about it?"

"There's nothing to talk about. I thought she'd changed. She hasn't."

If only it were that simple.

Christmas was a comparatively relaxed affair. Unlike Thanksgiving, where they gathered with the rest of the clan, Christmas had always been reserved for immediate family and grandparents, back when the senior members of the family were still alive. Now it was just the four of them. She didn't miss going to midnight Mass.

"Sometimes I wonder if I should have moved to Cali," said Madison from her beach chair. "This is so nice."

"I like the cold." Ivy lay on the sand, only a towel between her and the hot earth. She liked the way it felt against her back, and she could ignore the tickling feet of insects if she pretended they were simply symptoms of neuropathy. The ocean beat the shore a few yards off, and the cries of seagulls drowned out the voices of the other beachgoers. They could have chosen to lounge by the pool, but this was nicer.

"We should sail back to Boston. Spend the winter here, hit the water in the spring, and you can take the boat from Boston to Maine."

"Mmm," she said. Sun warmed her eyelids and an ocean breeze stirred the fine hairs on her stomach. It reminded her of Lillian with a sharp pang. "I should have moved to Boston."

"I know. I told you that."

"There's still time. If this job doesn't work out, I'll think about it."

She heard the creak of Madison's chair and opened her eyes to find her sister staring at her.

"What?"

"Are you okay? I'm not talking about your body. I mean you." She tapped Ivy gently on the forehead.

"I will be."

And she would be. She'd return the piano, focus on work and reducing stress, and forget about Lillian Lee. Just because she hadn't managed to forget about her in the years that had elapsed between vet school and now didn't mean she couldn't persevere. Success would come eventually.

Or she could swim out into the ocean and let the current take her where it wished.

They'd been so close. To what, she didn't know, but she wanted it with a fierceness that bit into the heart of her. She closed her eyes again. Behind her lids, she replayed the scene in the study, feeling Lillian's rage pour over her again and again and again.

"When are you telling mom and dad?"

Still thinking of Lillian, she started. "Telling them what?"

"About your MS."

"Oh."

"Yeah."

Fearing her parents' disappointment seemed pointless, now. "Tonight."

"Wow. Okay. Can I help?"

She took her sister's hand and squeezed it. "Just be there for me if Mom freaks out?"

"Always."

They gathered as a family to watch the sunset, Darwin periodically rising to chase gulls and sandpipers and small lizards. Madison kept shooting meaningful glances in her direction, which made it difficult to enjoy the colors streaking the horizon. She wished, absurdly, that Lillian was beside her, and flinched anew with rejection. At least her parents wouldn't react like *that*. What was pity compared with the loathing in Lillian's voice? What was anything?

"Mom? Dad?"

Her parents turned to look at her. Prudence's expression sharpened immediately at her tone, and she reached for Richard's hand.

"What's up, buttercup?" said her father.

Breathing deeply, she looked at her parents' faces, memorizing them in this last moment before everything changed. Then she spoke.

"I have MS."

She stroked Darwin in the wake of her announcement. Her mother stared at her. Shock bleached her tanned features and brought out the fine wrinkles around her eyes and mouth. Ivy saw her swallow several times before she finally managed to speak.

"Oh my God," she said at last. Richard remained silent.

"It's not as bad as it sounds," said Madison.

"How can it not be as bad as it sounds?" Her mother's voice was hoarse.

"My doctor doesn't think I have primary-progressive MS. I could be basically fine for years."

"This is why you moved. I should—how—no one in the family— Why didn't you tell us sooner?"

"I didn't want you to overreact."

Her mother's short laugh had a hysterical edge to it. "I think I am reacting appropriately to finding out my daughter has a debilitating condition."

"It doesn't have to be debilitating."

"Are you sure you have it? We can get you a second opinion. Rick, say something."

Her father's expression was distant, and his lips did not move.

"I've already had one. The MRI results are in line with the disease progression, and my symptoms align with the diagnosis."

"Your symptoms?" Prudence's voice cracked.

"Yeah."

She didn't want to talk about this. She didn't want to have this discussion at all. Seeing her mother's reaction had always been going to make this more real, which was the reason she'd put off telling her. The panic she'd been keeping tamped down for months writhed in her stomach. This was not the end. She would not let this be the end.

"Are you . . ." Prudence broke off, and Ivy knew she was trying to remember everything she'd ever heard about multiple sclerosis. "Do you have trouble . . . you know. With the bathroom?"

"No, mom." This really was the last thing she wanted to discuss. "I just have pain sometimes."

"Are you sure?"

"I am sure I have pain."

"Are you sure it's MS?" Her mother chafed her hands along her slacks, rubbing the material and pressing her palms into her thighs. It didn't stop her body from shaking.

"I'm sure." She used her gentlest voice: the one she reserved for telling clients their animal had a terminal condition.

Prudence began to cry.

"Mom, I'm okay."

"You're not. You're not okay." Her sobs intensified. Ivy sat where she was, unable to give her mother any comfort as her dreams for her daughter's perfect future shattered around them both. Madison picked at the label on the wine bottle.

"Prudy, stop." Her father spoke at last, gathering himself and focusing his eyes on Ivy. "What do you need from us?"

"Nothing, right now."

He nodded. "You've got the family behind you."

The family, and all that entailed: money, resources, love. She thought of Lillian's accusations and felt a jolt of hate. How dare she undermine this support with her judgment? What did she want Ivy to do, suffer alone on principle? These were her people, and they loved her and she loved them—fiercely; unconditionally. In that, they were no different from any other family. Even Lil's.

"Thank you," she said to her father, and the protective set of his mouth almost managed to warm her.

Daiyu's eyes felt as sticky as the rice balls Lillian had stuffed her face with on her arrival.

"What?"

"You look sad."

"I'm not."

"Don't try that with me. That might work on your other mother, but I," said Daiyu, throwing a loving glance at June across the table, "am not a fool."

"Really?" said June.

"Things aren't going well at work."

"Is it that Ivy girl?"

Daiyu's guess was too close to home. She dropped her eyes to her plate. "No."

"Is she giving you a hard time?"

Trust her mother to see through the lie.

"She bought me a piano."

Daiyu and June exchanged confused glances, but their confusion couldn't possibly outweigh her own. Why had she said that? What the hell was she thinking? Her moms never needed to know about what had happened, and there was absolutely no reason, short of her own idiocy, for them to find out.

"Why did she buy you a piano?" asked June.

She looked around the dining room for an escape route. Nothing came to her rescue.

"Lillian?"

To her profound horror, her lower lip began quivering. *Not enough sleep.* She willed herself to regain composure.

June studied her. "I thought you two didn't get along?"

"We don't."

Daiyu and June exchanged another glance.

"It seems to me," Daiyu began, "there are one or two things missing from this story."

"She's trying to buy me."

"What did you do to make her think you might be for sale?" asked June.

"I didn't do anything!"

"Your mother didn't mean to imply this was your fault," said Daiyu with a glare for June. "We're just curious about why a woman you've hated since school is buying you expensive gifts."

"And why that has you so upset you haven't touched your food—"

"Except for rice balls," Daiyu added.

"—or talked about anything except her since she arrived, even Brian."

"Who has a fiancée," Lillian said, hoping that would change the subject.

"Oh sweetie," said Daiyu. "He never deserved you."

"Was it a nice piano?" asked June.

"A Steinway."

"Is that a nice piano?" June addressed the question to Daiyu, who shrugged.

"You've always wanted a piano."

"That's not the point."

"Of course it isn't." Daiyu reached across the table, her elbow dimpling the tablecloth, and took Lillian's hand. "What happened between you?"

She did not want to tell her mothers about the tenuous *thing* that had blossomed briefly and then died. She did not want to remember with this knifing acuity how Ivy's face looked lit by firelight, or how it felt to hold her, or how her heart constricted when she thought of

259

Ivy—graceful, confident, haughty Ivy, falling in a barn or struggling in front of Shawna.

"I made a mistake," she said.

"That is nothing to be ashamed of." Daiyu's hand was warm and firm around her own.

"I'm still confused about the piano," said June.

"Lillian is in love with Ivy," said Daiyu.

"What? No, I'm not—"

"How did you get that from a piano?"

"And Ivy cares for Lillian, but our daughter is stubborn, like you."

"She's a spoiled rich girl who thinks money can solve all her problems," said Lillian, panic tinging her words.

"Is that why she talked about her all the time in school?" June asked Daiyu, ignoring Lillian.

"Yes."

"Stop." She yanked her hand out of her mother's, and stood, shaking, her breath coming in sharp gasps. "I am not in love with her. She doesn't understand the first thing about me, or us, or what it's like to have to work for something. She's always trying to use her money to show how much better than me she is. She orders me drinks and buys a fucking Steinway just so that she can hear me play Rachmaninoff after I took her to the symphony, and she thinks that's okay? She thinks that can make up for the fact that—"

She broke off, aware she was shouting and that both her mothers were staring at her with wide eyes.

"When you were little, before your mother got a job working at the Ironworks and when I was just a veterinary assistant," Daiyu said in a quiet voice, "we lived out of our car in the summer and rented a motel room in the winter. I did housekeeping after my vet shift. We scrounged and scraped and eventually we built a life so you could have something better."

"I know."

"We did not raise you to believe poverty was a virtue."

This sounded too close to Ivy's words. She shook her head, preparing to argue, but Daiyu steamrolled on in quiet, measured tones.

"If the only reason you hate this girl is because she has what you

260

do not, and you are afraid to accept generosity, then we failed."

"That isn't it. She didn't earn her money; her family—"

"The rich in this country rarely earn their money. When I came here as a girl, that was the first thing I realized. You are a doctor, Lillian. We couldn't have even dreamed you'd make it this far."

Shame sat heavily on her tongue. June had run away from home at sixteen after coming out to her parents, who had threatened to send her to conversion camp. Daiyu was an immigrant and the daughter of immigrants who had spent years waiting for their green cards. Her parents had met and fallen in love when June was eighteen and pregnant. They'd sacrificed so much.

"Has she hurt you?" June asked.

Mute, she shook her head.

"Been cruel?" asked Daiyu.

"Not . . . not since school."

"And in school, were you cruel to her, too?"

"Aren't you supposed to be on my side?"

"I have watched you put your happiness aside for too many years," said Daiyu. "Your drive is wonderful, but you've always put work first."

"Because—"

"Don't interrupt your mother," said June.

"When you started seeing Brian, we were worried. Not because he was a bad man. We liked him. But because he was so far away. It was like you did not want to risk yourself. You've always played things safe, and I wondered about Ivy. When you talk about her, even though you are angry, you come alive."

"And," said June, shooting Lillian a reproving look, "you are allowed to have nice things. If a rich girl wants to buy you a piano, you let her."

"But she doesn't appreciate—"

"Then make her appreciate it. You care about this woman, don't you?"

She didn't answer Daiyu.

"Invite her here for dinner."

"No. Absolutely not."

"Are you sure—" June asked Daiyu, and Lillian felt a surge of hope

June, at least, would see reason.

"We will decide if she is worthy of you."

"This isn't the fourteenth century," said June.

"Be quiet. I know how to judge white people's intentions. Invite her here. Don't throw something away just because you're scared of losing it."

"Don't throw something away because you feel you don't deserve it, either," June added.

Lillian stared at her mothers, looking back and forth between them as if sense might arise from the absolute madness of their suggestion the longer she waited. Invite Ivy Holden into their home? She shook her head. They didn't understand. Ivy wasn't just a woman from a different background. She was cruel, mercurial, and even if she hadn't shown those qualities in the last few months, Lillian knew they were there. She couldn't forget.

She couldn't forgive.

Ivy, inside her, breathing her name in wonder as they lay in her bed in her house in Cornell. Ivy, stroking her hair, whispering "I've wanted to do this for so long." That same Ivy, only hours later, kicking her out. That was the Ivy she'd seen in the study.

"I can't." She hated how her voice cracked on the word. Pushing away from the table and her mothers' anxious expressions, she stumbled out of the kitchen and toward the backyard, where a blast of winter air froze the tears on her cheeks.

She'd never been so grateful to be airborne. Darwin curled up on her lap in their seat in first class as Florida dropped away from the plane's windows. The man beside her had his head buried in his laptop, and she rubbed Darwin's soft ears between her fingers. Aloft, she could pretend she was free, bound neither to Maine nor to her family. She could be flying anywhere.

I don't have to go back. There were other jobs. Other clinics. Even some in Maine if she wanted to stay close to Rabbit like she'd planned. There was always Europe, too. France could be nice. She could brush up on her French and stay in the family apartment in Paris. Or she could move to Boston to be near Madison. Taking advantage of the in-air Wi-Fi, she opened the veterinary job portal she'd used to find the Seal Cove opening and scanned the listings. Several practices near Boston were looking for equine veterinarians, and one or two in Maine.

Fuck Maine. She'd leave the state. It was called Vacationland for a reason. Nothing tied her there, and the health care in Boston was better anyway. Lillian could have Seal Cove. While she didn't love the idea of leaving the clinic in the lurch, that wasn't her problem. Morgan could go fuck herself, too. Freddie would be happier in a new stable, maybe with a herd who didn't beat him up. She could start over. Again.

She saved a few jobs and closed her eyes, feeling Darwin's ribs rising and falling as he slept. Sure, she'd miss Stormy. The woman had grown on her. But she could make new friends. That had never been difficult.

Lillian's face formed from the dots behind her eyelids: beautiful, but twisted with anger, betrayal, and fear. Sick anguish twisted her down to her DNA. How could she have thought they could ever move beyond their pasts? It wasn't just their time at school. Lillian might not believe her capable of understanding where she'd come from, but she could see the pain their class difference caused her. Sometimes those barriers were insurmountable.

I will not be your consolation prize.

She'd been foolish to allow herself to hope for any other outcome. If Lillian believed Ivy considered her as little more than a *prize*, then nothing had changed. She still saw Ivy as a selfish rich girl. Worse, a damaged rich girl. Spoiled goods.

It was worse than pity.

Pain unfurled through her limbs. Not MS—that pain she could handle. This pain tasted like pine and salt and Lillian's scorn, and she curled around her dog in the airplane seat and endured it because she had no other choice.

Snow spat down from the sky in brittle flurries, amounting to nothing but still managing to sting her face as she walked across the parking lot and to the clinic. Lead had settled permanently in her stomach. A week had passed since she'd fled Ivy's house. Mechanically, her eyes scanned the parking lot for Ivy's truck. Nothing. She must be on ambulatory, which meant Lillian wouldn't see her. It should have been a relief. She should not have felt crushed by her absence.

The day stretched into a series of appointments without end. Owners, deep in the post-holiday doldrums, complained about bills and animal ailments that refused to heal. She did her best to keep her tone level as she internally screamed at them for their lack of compliance. Only one case brightened her day. A girl with white-blond hair in a flawless braid proudly presented her new pet boa, despite her mother's terrified expression, and Lillian knelt to explain the snake's nutritional and habitat needs to the enthusiastic child.

"You don't have to feed live mice," she said, watching the mother pale further.

"That's good," the woman said. She sounded faint.

"I read mice can scratch snakes. But won't dead mice be boring?" The girl's green eyes beseeched her, and her heart twisted as she thought of another pair of green eyes.

Am I the mouse here, or the snake?

She was still brooding over this question when she arrived home to find Angie perched on the kitchen island.

"Hey," she said. "What are you doing up there?"

"Trying to decide what to make for dinner."

"Let's go to Stormy's." Lillian spoke without thinking, unable to bear the prospect of cooking. Cooking was another thing she'd never had a chance to do for Ivy. "I'll text the others."

"Thank god. I really didn't want to cook. Have you heard anything from her?"

"No."

Angie slid off the counter and opened her arms.

"I don't need a hug."

"Liar."

"Fine." She let Angie squeeze her tightly and let out a shaky breath. She would not cry over Ivy.

"Let's go now. They can meet us there," said Angie. "You need something sweet."

They fed the dogs, then drove the short distance to the harbor and parked close to the warm lights of Storm's-a-Brewin' and jogged across the wind-stricken street. Her scarf blew over her face and she tugged it down with a gasp of cold as Angie pulled her into the shelter of the shop. The aroma of roasting coffee beans filled her nose, washing out the smell of salt and snow, and she searched the surprisingly crowded shop for Stormy.

Ivy sat at the bar with her head bent in conversation with their friend.

"Uh oh," said Angie as she followed her gaze. "Do you want to leave?"

She shook her head. Of course she wanted to leave, but this was her place. Her friends. Ivy could get the fuck out if Lillian's presence bothered her. "Let's get a table."

Angie chose one far from the bar, and Lillian put her hand on the back of a chair facing away from Ivy. She hesitated. As much as she didn't want to watch Ivy chat up Stormy, she also didn't want to turn her back on her. What if she came over? She opted for a chair that allowed her to watch the bar out of the corner of her eye.

Stevie, Morgan, and Emilia arrived a few minutes later.

"So glad we're not on call tonight," Steve said as she collapsed into the chair next to Angie. "It is cold as balls out there."

"Gross." Angie wrinkled her nose at the expression.

"I may need to get a treadmill," Emilia said as she took the seat next to Lillian.

"Just borrow mine whenever you want."

"But don't bring Morgan. I've been enjoying not having my cheese stolen," said Angie.

"You miss me," said Morgan with a grin. Her arm rested around Emilia's shoulders, and jealousy ate at Lillian's momentary pleasure.

She was happy for Morgan, but her shoulders ached where Ivy's arm had lain.

"Whatever. At least I don't have to hear you getting it on," said Angie. "No offense, Em."

"None taken." Emilia didn't even blush.

"Yeah. Some of us haven't gotten laid in ages," said Stevie.

"There's more to life than sex."

All eyes turned toward her.

"The bitter spinster speaks," said Stevie, and in a high mock-British accent, added, "I shall never marry, for I have forsaken all love save for that of my dogs and my vibrator."

"Shut up, Stevie," said Morgan, glancing at Lillian with concern in her gray eyes.

"Oh." Stevie flushed. "Sorry. I didn't mean to be a dick."

"And yet," said Angie, "so often you are."

Angie and Stevie fell to squabbling while Emilia and Morgan turned worried faces toward her.

"How are you doing?" Emilia asked.

She still hadn't told them the whole truth. Her eyes wandered across the room to where Ivy still sat at the bar. Her shoulders were slumped, and Stormy periodically reached out to touch her hand sympathetically.

"I'm okay."

It was true. Sort of. The hours she'd spent looking at medical studies and research on multiple sclerosis, and the additional hours she'd spent staring at Ivy's social media accounts aside, she was fine. She had a job she loved and amazing friends and that was more than some people ever found.

"Have you talked to her?"

"I don't have anything to say."

Ivy got up a few minutes later and avoided looking at Lillian as she headed for the door. She watched her leave. The gust of cold air that briefly followed her exit fell on her cheeks like a slap.

"I want to talk to you," Morgan said as they prepared to leave an hour later. Emilia, perhaps sensing the kind of conversation it was best to give a wide berth, joined Angie and Stevie at the bar with Stormy.

Lillian and Morgan remained at the table.

"About what?"

"Ivy." Morgan didn't beat around the bush.

"What about her? You were right. It was a bad idea."

"I'm worried about her."

"What?" This took her by surprise.

"Shawna told Stevie some things. I know you're fighting—we'll get to that—but I need to ask you something: Is she okay? Health-wise?"

The question too closely echoed her own thoughts.

"Why would I know?"

Morgan stared at her, unamused by her deflection.

"It's . . . it's not my place to say," she said at last. Angry as she might be, she couldn't bring herself to out Ivy's condition.

"Do we need to be worried? As a clinic?"

"No." Heat filled her chest. Threads from the message boards she'd glanced at flashed across her memory. MS patients worried about losing their jobs, worried about discrimination, worried about when the next flare-up would occur, decimating their ability to function. No wonder. If Morgan, who was generally tolerant, protective even of others' weaknesses, was willing to write Ivy off at the first sign of sickness, then they had every right to be concerned.

"Are you sure?"

"She's a good veterinarian."

"That's not what I'm saying. If there's something going on, then the clinic needs to know."

"Or we could see if she needs help, instead of moving to replace her."

"I didn't say anything about replacing her."

"It sounds like that's where you were going."

"Lil—"

"I don't want to talk about this."

"Okay. We don't have to." Morgan ran her hand through her short hair and looked at her with a bemused expression.

Her tear ducts prickled ominously. "I'm sorry. I just—I don't know."

267

"What did she do this time?" Morgan's voice was gentle.

"It . . . it wasn't her. It was me." She paused, but Morgan waited for her to continue. "I freaked out on her. She—Morgan, I don't know how to be around her sometimes, and I hate her, and—"

She couldn't continue. Her mother's words echoed in her skull. *Lillian's in love with Ivy.* She wasn't. Couldn't be. That would be *so dumb.*

"Dammit," she said, and let her head fall into her hands.

Ivy had rooted within her like her namesake. She felt the green, pulsing strength of those roots around her heart and the tendrils that burrowed through her bloodstream with each breath. She couldn't uproot her without internal damage. Moreover, she didn't want to. Ivy's brightness might cut, but it also illuminated. The world without her ebbed and flowed in muted grays.

Morgan rubbed her shoulders as she sobbed in the middle of the coffee shop, understanding crashing over her like the frozen surf beyond the steamed glass windows.

Chapter Thirteen

Stormy's words rattled around the empty cab of Ivy's truck. "Do what's right for you," she'd said, her hand warm on Ivy's at the bar and her brown eyes full of empathy. "That's all we really can do."

The problem was she didn't *know* what was right for her. She knew what she wanted, and look where that had gotten her. Alone and sick and stupid. She started the engine and turned into the empty street.

Reaching out to other clinics hadn't brought the relief she'd hoped. Seal Cove had started to feel like home, despite everything that had gone wrong. She liked her house. She liked her view of the river. She liked her clients and the hospital staff, and she liked Stormy's café and the small community she'd built for herself over the last few months. Moving here, however, had been just another mistake. Putting down roots in poisoned soil never would have worked. Better to pull out now, vegetal metaphors and the person they reminded her of be damned. It was time to move on. She sagged at the prospect of the work involved. Interviews. Getting to know a new hospital. Moving, potentially, if she couldn't find a new job close by. And, of course, the inevitable flare-up that would follow.

She fought the wind for control of her scarf as she got out of her truck and let herself into her house. The kitten pounced on her boots as she fumbled them off. Not even this made her smile. She was just so *tired*. Of fighting with Lillian, of running, of her failing body and her diminished dreams.

The vibration in her pocket didn't register for a moment. Vibrations and odd sensations were a regular occurrence, and it wasn't until she remembered she'd put all non-clinic calls on silent that she reached for her phone.

Lillian, read the caller ID.

Her thumb hovered over the accept icon. Her heart flopped, once, not daring to hope. She tried to tell herself not to pick up. Lillian had made her position clear. There wasn't anything else to say.

There also wasn't anything even resembling a choice.

"Hi."

"Ivy?"

"Yeah." She waited, listening to Lillian's unsteady breathing on the other end.

"I . . . I was hoping we could talk."

"I'm listening."

"Maybe not on the phone?"

"I'm on call tonight."

"Oh. Tomorrow?"

"Sure."

"Can I make you dinner?" The pleading note in Lillian's voice tugged at the barriers she'd tried to build since their last fight. She didn't know what this meant. Dinner was more than a conversation. It was . . . what? A peace offering?

"Trillium," Lillian said into Ivy's silence.

Trillium: the safe word they'd jokingly agreed upon, she remembered, and she cradled the phone against her cheek even though nothing about this felt safe. "Okay."

"Come over at seven?"

"Okay," she said again.

"Okay. Cool. Um . . . okay. Bye?"

"I'll see you tomorrow, Lil." She forced herself to hang up before either of them could say anything else, and sank to the floor of her foyer to rest her head against her knees.

Her hands shook as she chopped the eggplant into cubes. The white flesh oxidized almost instantly, but that wouldn't matter once she'd sautéed it in the honey, ginger, and soy sauce simmering in her wok. Other vegetables lay in neat piles on her cutting board, and the rice cooker counted down the minutes until seven o'clock. Ivy would be here soon.

And then?

A chorus of barking dogs announced tires on gravel. The knife clattered to the cutting board from her suddenly nerveless fingers. The house was empty. Morgan was with Emilia, and Angie and Stevie were off doing who-knew-what, probably with Stormy, though since Morgan was on call, Stevie—*it doesn't matter where they are.* She reined in her racing thoughts and wiped her hands on a towel, smoothed her hair behind her ears, and then undid the motion with a nervous shake of her head.

Ivy waited on the front step. Purple circles underlined her eyes, and she looked like she hadn't slept well in a week. Even her hair, normally sleek and hydrated, seemed lank in the porchlight. The effort of not reaching out to her was almost physically painful. She'd wanted Ivy to hurt, but not like this. She looked defeated. There was no sweetness to the victory.

"May I come in?"

"Oh. Right. Sorry." She stumbled backward to let Ivy into the foyer and scolded the dogs, who took advantage of the enclosed space to corner their victim.

"No Darwin?"

"He's at home with the cat."

"Dinner will be ready soon. Can I get you something to drink?"

"I'm okay," said Ivy.

"Tea?"

"Sure."

Even her voice sounded defeated. She turned away from Ivy to hide the emotions wreaking havoc on her expression and led the way back into the kitchen. A small fire burned in both hearths. The kitchen blaze crackled and let loose a shower of sparks as she passed. James slept on a faded blanket before it. He cracked one green-gold eye at the sound, then resumed his nap.

She'd set two places at the kitchen table. Ivy sat in the proffered chair and stroked the dogs gathered around her. She followed the movements of those slim fingers, remembering the way they'd slid through her hair. Hermione jumped on her two hind legs and pawed Ivy with her only forelimb until Ivy succumbed and picked her up. The little dog's obliviousness to the human tension deepened her own longing.

She put the kettle on and stirred the eggplant, adding Five Spice as needed. The aromatic scents of spice and oils filled the kitchen, and she lost herself momentarily in the work. Cooking, unlike Ivy, was predictable. You added the right ingredients in the right order at the right time, and usually things worked out. Love was different. She'd done all the right things with Brian, but the meal had soured in the pot before she could taste it. Her mother's words haunted her. Had she really played things safe? If Brian hadn't called things off, would she have ultimately ended up dissatisfied? Picturing him as a dish was easier than contemplating what to say to Ivy. Brian was mild. Healthy, maybe, but unchallenging. Ivy was sharp spices and new combinations that burned and bit and brought every single taste bud to life.

The fire popped. Oil sizzled. Her spoon scraped the sides of the wok. When the kettle went off, she brewed two cups of ginger tea with a dash of brown sugar and set one in front of Ivy.

Ivy looked up from Hermione and searched her face. What did she see? Was her terror obvious, or had she managed to hide it behind years of never reaching farther than the nearest rung?

"Thanks."

Nodding, she turned back to the stove and finished up preparing the meal. Steam fogged her glasses. She took them off. They wouldn't be much help if, as her tear ducts warned her, the evening went as she feared.

"Here." She placed the bowl of rice and vegetables before Ivy and sat, her own plate sending tendrils of steam to the ceiling.

"It smells amazing."

This was the longest phrase Ivy had uttered since her arrival.

"You look like you haven't been eating well."

Ivy ignored the comment and took a bite, blowing on a slice of eggplant to cool it. Lillian watched her face change as she chewed. Caution faded, and awe replaced it.

"Lil, this is—wow."

Pride in her cooking dispelled some of the dread. "It was one of my favorite dishes growing up."

"I can see why." Ivy took another bite, this time with more enthusiasm. Light came back into her eyes and Lillian didn't press any conversation on her as Ivy devoured the food on her plate. Ivy could afford to eat out whenever she wanted, but the way she shoveled food into her mouth suggested home-cooked meals were a rarity. It felt good to give her that.

"There's more," she said when Ivy finished.

"More—oh." Ivy glanced at her empty plate and shrugged almost sheepishly, as if she hadn't realized she had polished off her serving. "Maybe in a minute."

Lillian set her own utensils down and wished she hadn't eaten anything.

"Ivy," she began, her throat thick. "I—"

Apologizing to Ivy had always been impossible.

"It's okay. I get it," said Ivy.

"Get what?"

"This was always going to be messy. You deserve someone who can be there for you. Who doesn't do . . . what I do. You know."

"That's not—"

"I never saw you as a consolation prize, for what it's worth."

Lillian flinched, remembering the words she'd flung at Ivy. "I didn't mean that. I mean, I did, at the time, but not . . . not like that."

"Then like what?"

This was it. This was the thing she needed to say. She felt the way she had during her first surgery, holding a scalpel over living flesh and praying her hand didn't slip as she made her incision. She couldn't afford a mistake now, either. "I don't think you're broken. The piano overwhelmed me. You know me. I like to be in control. I don't feel in control around you. Ever. And then you told me you had MS, and—"

Ivy closed her eyes as if bracing for a blow.

"—and hell, Ives, I thought you were settling for me. I wasn't good enough for you before, if you remember, and I wasn't good enough for Brian, either."

Ivy's eyes opened with a flash of anger. "You know that's not true, right?"

"It doesn't matter. I wanted to hurt you. I wanted you to know how much you'd hurt me. I hate, more than anything else in my life, that I've never gotten over you."

It would be so, so dumb to love Ivy Holden. And yet.

Ivy's lips parted in surprise. "But you—"

"What I'm trying to say, badly, is I'm sorry."

"Sorry?"

"For everything. For not believing you could change. For not recognizing that I've been just as much of an ass to you as you have to me."

"I won't argue with that."

"Do not make this any harder, Holden."

A faint smile curved Ivy's lips. "You deserve someone who pushes you."

"You don't get to tell me what I deserve."

"Oh, but I want to."

"Fine. What *do* you think I deserve?"

Ivy tilted her head, the dark circles beneath her eyes adding a seriousness to their play that underscored the tenuousness of the situation. They were hiding behind the familiar, but the stakes had never been higher. "I think you deserve nice things, if you want them. I think you deserve to be happy, because you don't seem like you are, and I want that for you. I think you deserve passion. Extravagance. I think you deserve to be with someone who can make you happy and who doesn't run away from her problems—"

"What did you run away from?"

"Everything." Ivy shrugged as if this didn't hurt her, but Lillian saw the tightness around her eyes.

"Colorado?"

Ivy shifted in her seat. "I've always been good at lying to myself. When I left Kara, I didn't tell her why. I told myself it was because I was protecting her, when really I was protecting myself. I lied to you, too."

"About what?" Her heart gave a stutter of fear.

"About why I came here. That was the other thing. I knew it would never have worked out with Kara in the long run because I never got over you, either."

A relief so powerful she nearly wept swept through her.

"When I realized I might need . . . help . . . after getting my diagnosis, I knew I didn't want it from Kara. I told myself I didn't want her to give up on her dreams for me, but again, that was partially a lie. It was a way out. I took it. And I came here because I thought I didn't care about anything anymore, even you, even though I knew that was a lie, too."

"Ivy—"

"Wait. Let me finish." Ivy rubbed the web between her thumb and forefinger and stared at the table. Her next words came out in a small voice. "I'm not strong like you. I run when I'm scared, and I'm scared of everything right now. If you want to end this, please tell me, and I'll leave."

"And if I don't want to end it? What if that scares you, too, like it did before?"

Ivy raised her eyes. "Living without you is a hell of a lot scarier."

She wasn't sure how she ended up in Ivy's lap. One moment she was across the table, and the next her legs were wrapped around Ivy's waist and her hands were buried in her hair. Honey lingered on Ivy's lips. She kissed it off. She kissed, too, the hot tears that mingled with her own as her lips pressed against the corners of Ivy's mouth. Ivy's hands dug into her back. She hooked her feet around the legs of the chair and pulled herself closer, Ivy's breasts just beneath hers and the gentle curve of her skull precious in her palms.

"I never wanted to hurt you, Lil," Ivy said between breaths.

"I missed you so much." She didn't just mean over the few days of their stand-off. She'd missed her for years.

"God, Lil. You've no idea." Ivy drew Lillian's lower lip between her teeth and held it, her breathing strained as she fought back a sob. "Lillian, I love you."

Her own sob shook her. Ivy's forehead pressed into hers, steadying the tremors.

"I love you, Ivy."

Ivy groaned, part relief, part pain. She could taste the emotions on her tongue. She tasted truth, too, when Ivy said, "I always have."

Tears lit Ivy's eyes, magnifying the flecks of gold and emerald in her irises. She pulled away long enough to brush a few from her blond lashes. Moss bore that green beneath sunlit water. So did the first new leaves of spring.

Ivy would never be safe. Ivy would always push her. That was what life did, and with Ivy she felt alive.

Ivy woke in her own bed feeling refreshed for the first time in days. Warmth stirred beside her.

"Hey."

She opened her eyes to find Lillian watching her. They'd come back to her place after dinner, and before that— Memory rushed in to fill the void.

Lillian loved her.

Lillian had also made coffee, and the gesture, followed on the heels of the meal she'd cooked for her last night, stirred the small flame of hope she'd allowed once more to grow.

"I've been thinking," said Lillian as she brushed a tangle of Ivy's hair behind her ear.

Ivy relaxed into the touch. "What have you been thinking?"

"That I'd like you to be my girlfriend."

"I thought that was implied when you told me you loved me." Even now she couldn't resist teasing Lillian. At Lillian's expression, however, she smiled, and added, "yes. I would like that very much."

"We do need to talk, though."

"I know." She knew what was coming and accepted the cup of coffee Lillian handed her.

"I need you to be honest with me."

"About what?"

"Everything, but starting with your health."

Nausea gripped her stomach. She set the coffee on her bedside table. "Okay."

"How serious is this? And what can I do to help you?"

Throwing herself from a moving vehicle or into the frozen river felt easier than answering. Her tongue stuck to her mouth. She opened it anyway, preparing to force herself to speak, but there was no air in her lungs. She drew in a ragged breath, then another, and another, and still sparks danced in the corner of her vision. Distantly, she was aware of Lillian saying her name, just as she was aware of the bite of her bathroom floor tiles digging into her knees as she knelt before the toilet and vomited into the porcelain bowl.

Lillian's hand rubbed circles on her back, and her voice spoke soothing words in a language that might have been English. More bile rose. She vomited again, her stomach heaving up last night's dinner and leaving only terror behind.

And still she couldn't breathe. Lillian wiped her mouth with a tissue. Ivy let her because she was too busy shaking to do anything to stop it.

"Breathe," Lillian was saying, but she couldn't. She was suffocating on her own fear.

Pain penetrated the panic. She blinked at her arm, and at Lillian's thumb and forefinger where they pinched the bones of her wrist.

"Focus on this," Lillian said. "Focus on me."

Half-blind, she tried to nod and ended up biting her tongue. Her teeth wouldn't stop chattering. A dog whined. Lillian's eyes remained fixed on Ivy's, and gradually she managed to do as Lillian commanded. Her breathing slowed to hiccups instead of hyperventilation. Her stomach stopped trying to empty her organs into the dirty water.

"You need to tell me, Ivy."

It was the tenderness in those words, and the unflinching resolve, that made her decision. Most people would have told her she didn't need to talk about it now, or that they could come back to the topic later—but most people didn't know her the way Lillian did. They would

277

have assumed Ivy needed to be coddled, not pushed. Lillian seemed to know if backed down now, Ivy might never have the strength to say the things that needed to be said.

Between hiccups, she managed, "I'm scared."

"I am too."

"It's bad, Lil."

"Okay."

"I mean, it's not that bad yet, though there are days . . . Fuck. I hate this. I hate that I can't rely on my body. I hate that I'm weak, and broken, and that there's nothing I can do. It's going to get worse. I don't know when. A month. A year. A decade. Every time I get a flare-up I have to worry that this is the one that isn't going to go away."

She pushed away from the toilet and flushed, but she couldn't stop the words.

"I hurt. I hurt all the time. And I'm tired. I'm so fucking tired, Lil. All I ever wanted was to be a veterinarian, and sometimes I can't even hold a fucking syringe."

"You have a technician."

"What happens when I'm not strong enough to work with large animals? That's the other reason I liked Seal Cove. It's a mixed practice. But what about when I can't walk?"

"Nothing says it will progress that far. I've done the research."

"Nothing says it won't, either. Nothing says I won't end up in a diaper by age fifty, and who could love that?"

"Everyone who's ever had a partner they truly cared about."

"You don't understand. My body, fitness—it's part of me. My work is part of me. Riding. I don't know who I am without those things, and my mind—what if I start forgetting things? What if the brain fog gets so bad I can't even practice medicine from a desk? What the hell kind of life is that?"

She was shouting, and it felt good, too good, to say the words that had festered inside her for months out loud.

"I'm selfish. You deserve so much better than someone like me. I was a bitch to you, and now I'm damaged, and you—"

"Oh, shut up, Ivy." Lillian spoke sharply, and her jaw clicked shut in surprise.

"But—"

"Your problem isn't that you're sick. It's that you've let yourself believe your productivity is your only worth. You're rich. If you can't work, open a nonprofit. Start a rescue. Fund research initiatives. You still have agency. Your body, which I love and which I will continue loving even if it fails you, is not the prison you think it is. I hate that you're in pain. You have no idea how much I hate that, but that doesn't make you worthless or undeserving. Everything you just said is valid, and it's also dumb."

"It's not—"

"We're veterinarians. We solve impossible problems every day. You'll find a way to ride. You'll find a way to exercise. Maybe it won't be the same, but you also work with horses. Tomorrow you could get kicked in the head and end up in a coma. You could crash your car into a tree. You could get cancer next year, and then MS won't even matter."

"Your optimism is really making me feel better."

"I'm serious. Look." Lillian took her hands and held them in her own, as gently as if they were a pair of stunned rabbits. "I know this is terrifying. I can't understand entirely what you're going through. What I can do? I can cook. I won't ever let you give up. I'll humiliate you. I'll make you laugh. I'll do whatever it takes to keep you going. You want to spend the weekends watching movies on the couch? We'll do it. I don't like going out anyway. If you need a change in diet, I'll make it so damn delicious you'll be begging me for seconds. If you need me to tie you to your horse, I'll bring some zip ties. And who even needs to walk? Darwin's tough. We'll get you a dog sled. Do you love me?"

"Yes."

"Then you deserve me. I'll remind you of that every day, but I *will* start to get annoyed if you don't believe me."

Ivy managed a squeak of laughter.

"What do you need right now?"

"I'm fine. I—"

"Nope. Tell me what we can do to make you feel better, even if it's just for a few minutes."

"Just you."

"I'm here."

She thought of her bathtub, and, feeling very small, said, "I could also use a bubble bath."

"Okay. That's our plan, then." Lillian turned on the tap to her tub and found her stash of bath salts, bombs, and bubbles. Ivy sat on the tile floor and watched her sniff them.

"You are allowed to buy me these if you want," Lillian said as she selected a small bottle of lavender-rose bubbles.

"Noted."

"Now, stand up."

Steam from the bath clouded the mirror. All she could see of their reflections were vague shapes, and she shivered in the cold.

"You're like a purebred dog," Lillian said as Ivy stepped into the blissfully scalding water.

"How so?"

"Beautiful on the outside, so many problems on the inside."

She splashed her. "Get in here with me or I'll bite you."

Lillian undressed quickly and hissed as her toes touched the water. "Oh, it's hot."

"Don't be a baby."

The tub held them easily. At first they faced each other, knees breaking the surface of the bubbles like mountains, but then Lillian took her by the shoulders, turned her, and held her against her body. Their legs tangled beneath the foam.

"This isn't the worst."

"No. It's not," said Lillian.

"Thank you for—"

"You don't need to thank me."

"You don't know what I was going to say."

"Am I wrong, though?"

Drowsily, she shook her head. "Still. Thank you."

"You're welcome."

Ivy woke sometime later, back in her bed after a long soak, to the sound of music. She eased herself out of bed and into her bathrobe, which was a luxurious blend of softness and warmth, and followed the sensory stimuli.

A fresh cup of coffee, still hot, waited for her on her bedside. She sipped as she walked toward the bars of music, her mood rising with the notes. The door to the study was open. Inside, Lillian sat, dressed in one of Ivy's shirts and a pair of sweatpants, her fingers running up and down the scales. She leaned against the doorway, not daring to speak.

Lillian finished warming up and opened the sheaf of music. Hesitantly at first, and then with more confidence, Rachmaninoff filled the house. She felt the music through the soles of her feet and through the door frame. She felt it in her breath, and in the pale morning sunlight filtering through the study windows to fall upon the polished top of the piano, which Lillian had opened. She felt it, too, in the raw, bruised place she'd exposed to Lillian this morning. It eased the ache, each chord a salve, a balm, a promise. Lillian missed a few notes, here and there, but the music rose in tumultuous crescendo and broke and rose again as the piece moved through the bars.

"This," Lillian said as the last notes faded, "is an exquisite instrument."

"It isn't a Fazioli or a Bösendorfer," she said, putting on her best impression of her mother, "but it will do." In her own voice, she added, "You play beautifully."

Even Prudence Holden would have been impressed.

"I'm surprised I remembered so much of it, honestly."

"Practice any time you want."

Lillian turned on the bench to face her, raising an eyebrow. "I can think of a few other things we could practice."

"Well, what's the point of getting insurance if you're not willing to take a little risk?"

"Oh yeah?"

"Get on the piano, Lee."

Sweat slicked her steering wheel despite the freezing temperatures beyond the windows of her Subaru. Ivy sang along to the radio in her passenger seat, looking like a Burberry model in her sweater, scarf, and supple leather boots. Lillian pictured the introductions that were now only a few minutes away. What would June and Daiyu make of Ivy?

And what if, at the end of the evening, they decided they hated her? Would that change how she felt?

Darwin had not joined them, but Muffin and Hermione perked up in the backseat as they realized where they were headed.

"My moms spoil them," she explained as Muffin began whining in almost panicked enthusiasm. Hermione scrabbled over the middle console and into Ivy's lap so she could press her nose to the car window without getting trampled by Muffin. Today's sweater had a shark fin on the back, and Ivy toyed with it, smiling down at the little dog. If she was nervous, she didn't show it.

"Hard to blame them. You're perfect, aren't you?"

Hermione wagged her tail in vigorous agreement.

The steering wheel was damp by the time she pulled into their narrow drive. She couldn't recall her palms ever sweating like this before, and she dried them on her pants, hoping Ivy wouldn't notice. They sat in a silence punctuated only by the engine ticking as it cooled.

"This will be fine," she said.

Ivy no longer looked quite as composed, and at her words bit her lip.

"And if it isn't? If they don't like me?"

"They will." She tried to smile. It felt more like a grimace and, judging by Ivy's expression, looked like one, too.

"Well, if they don't, then at least you're spared meeting my parents."

"Do you want me to meet your parents?"

"They'll be here all summer. It will be hard to avoid. And, yes, I do want you to meet them."

"Even though I'm not a Rockefeller?"

"I dated a Rockefeller for a while. They weren't that impressed with him."

"I can't tell if you're kidding."

"I'm not."

"My moms can be . . . protective."

"Are they worse than Morgan?"

"Way worse. Nicer about it, though." Her mouth tasted coppery and dry. "It will be fine."

Ivy didn't point out that repeating a thing didn't make it true, which she appreciated.

"I'm looking forward to meeting them. Come on." Ivy opened the door and had the foresight to stand back as both Hermione and Muffin hurtled out of the car and up to the front door, scattering the chickadees at Daiyu's bird feeder.

It will be fine.

She reached for Ivy's hand, no longer caring about sweat, and together they walked up the shoveled path.

June and Daiyu presented a unified front. Ivy's hand squeezed hers, and then she dropped it and extended it to Daiyu with a "Hi, I'm Ivy. It's so nice to meet you."

Winter sunlight lit her blond hair, and the red of her scarf complimented the bright green of her eyes. June was visibly stunned, but Daiyu simply smiled and took the offered hand, introducing herself and her wife and inviting them in. June shook off the spell that Ivy's All-American appearance had cast and stepped back. Muffin and Hermione, who, for the first time in their lives had not been greeted with the reverence their presences deserved, pouted.

"Oh, get over yourselves," Lillian told them. She put a hand on the small of Ivy's back and, once boots were off and house slippers on, guided her out of the small foyer and into the living room. It looked homey and shabby. Her heart clenched as Ivy looked around.

"Sit. I'll bring out some tea," said Daiyu.

Lillian steered Ivy to the couch and sat beside her. June occupied the armchair. Her mother folded her hands in her lap, unfolded them, and then folded them again.

"You have a beautiful home," said Ivy.

"Thank you."

Silence.

The clink of cups in the kitchen seemed obscenely loud. June cleared her throat. "So, you're working with Lillian?"

"I'm mostly in large animal, but I do see a few small animal patients. Never exotics, though. That's all her."

"She's always been interested in things with scales," said Daiyu as she appeared with a tray of tea fixings. "Used to keep snakes in her toy chest. Scared me half to death."

"Really?" Ivy's smile appeared to blind June, who turned accusing eyes on Lillian, as if she should have warned her about Ivy's beauty.

"Mice, too, and we always had a bird in a shoe box."

"That was your fault," Lillian said. "You feed the entire bird neighborhood."

"She'd find injured ones, and a few babies she swore she didn't steal from the nest, though I have my doubts."

"I didn't!"

"Her voice always rises like that when she's lying. Cream or sugar?"

"Cream, please," said Ivy.

"My mom is a vet tech. It's her fault I became a veterinarian."

"Childcare was expensive," Daiyu explained. "Still is, I'm sure. My boss let me bring Lillian to the clinic because she was such a quiet baby. Probably violated several laws, but she started volunteering as soon as she was old enough."

"I cleaned kennels, mostly."

"It's an important job," said Ivy.

There was an apology in those words. Once upon a time, Ivy had mocked her for cleaning kennels. Now her eyes beseeched Lillian for forgiveness.

"And what about you? How did you get interested in veterinary medicine?"

Ivy warmed her hands on her mug and met Daiyu's eyes. "In my family, you're either a doctor or a lawyer or a hedge fund manager. My parents were disappointed initially that I wanted to work with animals instead of people. My sister is a lawyer. She actually just made partner, which is exciting, and gives my parents something to brag about to their friends."

"Veterinary medicine is just as difficult as law," said Daiyu, bristling in defense of their profession.

"I certainly think so. They're proud of me now, though, and they know I'm happy."

"Good."

Was she imagining the protective note in Daiyu's voice? And if so, had Ivy intentionally played the second-best-child card? It was a brilliant move, and she studied them both the way she might have watched two dominant dogs meeting for the first time.

"Equine medicine. You're working with Morgan, then," said June, who approved of Morgan.

"Yes. We knew each other at school, too."

"We're aware."

Daiyu shot June a warning look. "We were so happy when Morgan convinced Lillian to work at Seal Cove."

"It's a great practice."

Lillian reached for the teapot and topped off her cup for something to do with her hands.

"Where is your family?" asked June.

"My parents split their time between Florida and Rabbit Island. Moving closer to them was part of the reason I took the job here, and my sister is in Boston."

"What was the other part?"

"Mom," Lillian said, horrified—but not surprised—by June's bluntness.

Ivy turned to look at her, and she felt her face warm beneath her gaze. "I wanted to work with Lillian."

"Even though you didn't get along in school?" asked Daiyu. "We don't mean to pry, but we were surprised."

Oh, you absolutely do mean to pry, Mother.

"Lil always pushed me to be a better doctor. And . . ." Ivy paused, clearly unsure about how much to say.

"Is that a cardinal?" Lillian pointed out the living room window at the bird feeder. Daiyu's head swiveled faster than an owl's. She thanked whatever twist of fate had sent the bird at that moment.

"You work in the shipyards, right?" Ivy asked June.

"That's right."

"I love driving by there. It's amazing to me we can build things that big and they still float."

"My mom operates the cranes."

"I bet Lillian hated 'take your daughter to work' day."

"She did," said June, allowing Ivy a minuscule smile. "She's never had much of a head for heights."

285

"I rode a horse the other day."

"Did you really?" June exchanged a glance with Daiyu. "Was it a pony?"

"No. It was a very tall horse and I was very brave."

"It's true. She was," said Ivy. "Freddie is a good boy, but he's big."

"Is this your horse?" asked Daiyu.

"Yes. Here." Ivy pulled up a photo of Freddie on her phone to show Daiyu and June. The conversation strayed to animals after that, and Lillian allowed herself to relax fractionally as Ivy talked about Darwin and asked after Daiyu and June's cats, who had never forgiven Lillian for bringing dogs into their home and who spent every visit hiding in her parents' bedroom. Ivy laughed when appropriate and asked leading questions, even getting June to open up about her work. Watching Ivy, she wondered how much of this performance was genuine, or how much of it was simply a result of being raised a socialite. In time, would she learn to tell the difference?

Daiyu pulled her aside as they cleared the dinner dishes away several hours later.

"Well, she's charming."

"But are her intentions pure?" She meant it as a joke, but Daiyu considered the question with a frown.

"I like the way she looks at you. It's clear she cares. Does she make you happy?"

"Yes." *And furious and frustrated and whole.*

Daiyu nodded thoughtfully. "It will be complicated. Brian was easier in a way. This woman won't settle for just a phone call every night."

"No."

"Which is a good thing." Daiyu pulled her into a hug, and she breathed in her mother's familiar smell. "It's past time you had something that made you happy."

Epilogue

The warm May breeze whispered through the budding apple trees as Ivy walked through the pasture behind 16 Bay Road. Freddie trotted toward her, shaking his head and showing off to his pasture mate. Olive flicked an ear at him and continued grazing.

"She's a tough one," Ivy told him when he slowed to nuzzle her. "But you'll win her over."

He snorted and flicked his tail at the small cloud of blackflies following him. His spring coat gleamed, free from bruising and cuts, and Stevie had reported seeing Freddie and Olive grooming each other on more than one occasion.

"Are you happy here?"

He nudged her pocket. She yielded the concealed biscuit and waved flies away from his nose.

"Me too."

If she looked over the fence, she'd see the top of Lillian's green-house, where she was currently potting up seedlings for the large garden plot just past the pasture. Ivy had seen Olive eyeing the young lettuces sprouting there with interest.

So much had changed since the first time she'd seen this place. Her introspective train of thought had been brought on by the announcement, made earlier that day, that Morgan was moving in with Emilia permanently. She wondered if Lillian would ever make the same decision. The greenhouse tied her here, as did her love for her friends, but more than that, there was the tension that still simmered beneath the surface of their relationship. Things were improving, yes, but moving in together would create new issues of autonomy. No matter how many times Ivy pointed out she would rather spend her money than Lillian's, given its origins, the dangerous set to Lillian's chin remained.

She smiled. That stubborn independence was part of why she loved her. They'd figure it out. In the meantime, Freddie was here, as were Lillian's plants and tortoise. Splitting nights was easy enough, and she was paying Stevie and Angie generously to board and feed Freddie.

Spring had also broken the flare-up's hold on her body. She rose with only minor pain, and had, upon Lillian's urging, explained to Shawna that there were days she would need more help than others. Shawna had nodded, and they hadn't spoken of it again, but her technician had taken more initiative since that conversation. Nobody else knew. She had not decided when, or even if, she would tell her new circle of friends.

What she did know: Lillian Lee loved her, and she, Ivy Holden, loved Lillian Lee.

"And you," she said to Freddie. "I'll always love you, too."

"Hey," called a voice from the yard. She squinted against the sunlight and saw Stevie's blond hair. "Lillian says come to the greenhouse when you're done."

"Catch you later, old man."

Dusting horsehair off the front of her shirt, she set off for the greenhouse. Darwin dogged her heels and snapped at bumblebees, undeterred by his previous ill-fated encounters with his winged nemeses.

The heat inside the greenhouse immediately brought sweat to her forehead. Tendrils of hair sprang free of her bun. The sharp smell of sap and the fragrance from the tropical flowers Lillian grew year-round mingled with compost and soil. She saw Lillian at the far end bent over a potting table with her sleeves rolled up and her hair in a messy bun. Darwin sneezed.

"Hey," Lillian said, looking up at the sound. "Come here."

"What's this?"

A blue ceramic planter with intricate designs inlaid in a lighter blue glaze rested on the table. A dark red lily bloomed in the fresh soil. At its base, a profusion of familiar green leaves tumbled over the pot: ivy.

"It's us," said Lillian.

Ivy stroked the dark red petal of the lily.

"It's not a piano or anything, but—"

Heedless of the dirt on Lillian's hands, she kissed her. Lillian tried holding her hands up to keep Ivy's clothes clean. She took one and placed it firmly on her hip.

"It's so much better than a piano."

Lillian's lips curled in a smile against her own. "Liar."

"It can sit on top of the piano."

"Not enough light, and Trillium will try to eat it there."

"Then tell me where to put it, and I promise I won't kill it or let it kill our cat."

"Of course you won't. I'll be the one doing the watering." Lillian wrapped her arms around her neck and pulled away to see her eyes. "Do you really like it?"

Every show of vulnerability was a gift and a sign of the trust growing between them like the ivy on the table.

"I love it."

Lillian looked away, and Ivy nudged her gaze back up with a brush of her nose to Lillian's forehead. "It's gorgeous, Lil, and so are you."

"I got dirt all over you."

"I don't know if you noticed, but I have a very full walk-in closet, and a high-end washer and dryer. I think I'll live."

"In that case . . ." Lillian grabbed the front of her shirt in both hands and pulled her close again. Ivy closed her eyes and surrendered.

Acknowledgments

I stole liberally from my own life for this book. To that end, I must first thank my family, who, in addition to standing by me at every point in my life, gave me the ocean. Thank you, and thank you especially to my grandmother, who has made so much possible.

Privilege isn't earned. Most of us are either born with it or without it, based on factors entirely outside of our control. I am incredibly privileged. I would be remiss not to acknowledge that here in the acknowledgments section, where, if you've come this far, I have your attention for a few more moments. I am able to write and tell stories because I work hard at my craft, but also because I've had infrastructure around me for my entire life that has made it possible for me to dream and reach and achieve. I'm proud of my work. But more than that, I love stories, and I want to read more stories from voices who have not had this scaffolding. Buy queer books. Buy books from BIPOC authors. Support writing scholarship funds. Listen. Love. Vote.

My editor, Mx. Rachel Spangler, deserves many accolades. It is thanks to them that my characters express emotions instead of repressing them, and they are also always here for my snarky and periodically immature responses to their editorial comments. Many a "that's what she said" joke was made in the margins. Ann McMan of

TreeHouse Studio makes the best covers in the business. I don't know how her shelves stand up beneath the weight of all her awards. The rest of the team at Bywater Books also came together to make this book what it is. You're amazing, all of you.

Readers! You can't possibly know how much I appreciate the support and enthusiasm you've shown me as I jump around from genre to genre. Writing Romance with a capital R has been an adventure, and I couldn't have done it without you. Not just in the literal sense—though thank you for picking up this book—but the support you've shown me on social media, recommending my books to your friends, joining my Patreon, and sending me messages and emails about what these stories mean to you is such a gift, and in many ways a lifeline. Thank you. A special thank you to my Patreon Patrons, who make me laugh and smile and generally remind me why I love this crazy business.

Last here but first in my heart, Tiffany, every love story is for you. You save lives every day, and I'm so proud of all the work you've accomplished. Let the record show that any inaccuracies in veterinary medicine in these pages are entirely my fault.

The poem Ivy misquotes is Edgar Allen Poe's "Annabel Lee." Written and published in 1849, it is the last poem Poe wrote before his death that same year. Like Ivy, it frequently gets stuck in my head.

As I write, it is September in 2020. Many of us face uncertainty, grief, fear, and prejudice. I'm scared. I'm tired. I'm mourning what and who we've lost. I have no idea what the world will look like when these pages see print, but I do know this: stories are powerful. Tell yours. Tell it even if nobody seems to be listening. Tell it until we are impossible to ignore.

About the Author

Anna Burke enjoys all things nautical and generally prefers animals to people. When she isn't writing, she can usually be found walking in the woods with her dogs or drinking too much tea, which she prefers hot and strong—just like her protagonists. She is the award-winning author of *Compass Rose, Thorn, Nottingham,* and *Spindrift.*

At Bywater, we love good books by and about lesbians, just like you do. And we're committed to bringing the best of contemporary lesbian writing to an expanding community of readers. Our editorial team is dedicated to finding and developing outstanding writers who create books you won't want to put down.

For more information about Bywater Books, our authors, and our titles, please visit our website.

www.bywaterbooks.com

CPSIA information can be obtained
at www.ICGtesting.com
Printed in the USA
JSHW022316100423
40169JS00002B/2